In the
Mouth
of
The Wolf

CLARA
BRACCO

DEDICATION

This book is dedicated to my friends and family, who lovingly ~~put up with~~ supported me while I chatted their ears off about all my ideas.

AUTHOR'S NOTE

This story contains themes that might not be your cup of tea –
and that's okay!

In the Mouth of the Wolf is a reverse harem, meaning the female
character has multiple love interests. She experiences cheating
(outside the harem), the death of a family member, kidnapping, sexual
assault, and body betrayal.

CONTENTS

In the mouth of the wolf *(in bocca al lupo)* is an Italian idiom meaning "good luck," and is said to performers before going on stage.

While the origins of the phrase are unclear, one interesting theory points to the ancient myth of Romulus and Remus, orphaned twins rescued and raised by a female wolf.

According to legend, Romulus later killed his brother over an argument and went on to build the city of Rome, becoming its first king.

1
MARLOWE

"Why are you holding that bag?"

A devious smile grew slowly across my face as I grabbed a handful of mini marshmallows and dangled them over the baking dish. Looking Mike dead in the eye, I let them go, cackling when his lips flattened in annoyance.

"You're ruining it," he huffed.

Then I spread them evenly over the top and popped the whole thing in the hot oven, closing the door with a little bump from my hip. "I believe you mean I'm *improving* it," I replied with a wink. "You're welcome."

He groaned, dragging his feet towards me like a whiny toddler, grabbing me around the waist and digging his nose into the crook of my neck. "You know how I feel about these midwestern recipes. Can't we have one Thanksgiving free from all this?"

Normally I would argue against his pretentiousness, but I wasn't in the mood. I shrugged him off and set the timer. "If you didn't want to eat sweet potato casserole with marshmallows, you shouldn't have proposed to a girl from Wisconsin. We can do whatever you want for Christmas – tapas, Korean barbecue, curry… your choice. But please leave me my 'midwestern recipes' for today." My voice cracked despite my attempts to sound playful and I turned my head before he could see the tears forming in the corners of my eyes.

His expression softened and he pulled me back into his broad chest for a hug. "I'm sorry. I should have realized this year

1

would be hard. Go ahead and put marshmallows on whatever you want, I mean it. Marshmallow cranberry sauce, marshmallow stuffing… ooh, marshmallow Brussels sprouts!"

I snorted, wiping my cheeks with the back of my hand and getting back to work.

It had been only a month since my mom died from a stroke, joining my twin brother who had passed away in a car accident almost eight years ago. All I had left was a dad I hadn't seen since my fourth birthday. I was officially family-less.

Except for my fiancé, of course.

Aside from his dislike of marshmallows, Mike was the perfect guy. We had met at a networking party three years ago in Palo Alto, when I had been in the middle of my grad program.

There I was, stuffing another lamb slider in my face, when a pair of violet eyes had found me from across the room, accompanied by a devastatingly handsome smile.

Mike was a software developer working at a startup like all of the other tech bros in the room, but had managed to have a whole conversation with me where he hadn't mention cryptocurrency once. Instead, we had talked for hours about our shared love of travel and our favorite books and movies. We had left the event early to get more drinks at a nearby wine bar, and then we had ended up spending the whole weekend together, mostly in his bed.

We fell fast, we fell hard, and we had stayed that way.

I had moved into his condo in San Francisco six months later, and this summer during a trip to Mexico he had proposed.

We were planning on getting married next spring, but hadn't set a date yet because we couldn't agree on the type of wedding to have. He wanted to do something quiet and intimate, like city hall and a dinner with a select group of friends.

I wasn't opposed to the idea, but Mike came from a large family, with quite a few brothers, aunts, uncles, and cousins out in Florida where he had grown up. I was looking forward to finally meeting all of them and celebrating together. The only one I'd seen so far was his mom, and that had just been from me awkwardly waving in the background of their occasional FaceTime chats.

He insisted his family wasn't that close and didn't need to come, but Mike hadn't gotten to meet my mom before she died – she had lived in Milwaukee, where I was born and raised, and the timing had never really worked out.

While we were building a life together here in California, I didn't want him to forget his roots and regret not seeing his family more often like I did.

Thanksgiving might have been a good time to finally meet them, but with everything that had happened, we decided to celebrate at home with just the two of us this year. Travel was too expensive and too hectic anyway, so we'd opted on making way too much food by ourselves, then getting high and gorging on the leftovers for the whole weekend while rewatching the *Lord of the Rings* and *Harry Potter* movies. It certainly beat spending thousands of dollars to catch COVID on an oversold flight.

Mike poured a glass of wine and handed it to me. "Here. Why don't you go relax? All that's left are the mashed potatoes and gravy, right? I can take care of that on my own."

I gave him a kiss. "And the rolls. They just have to be heated for about five minutes."

Mike faked an exasperated sigh. "Now you've gone too far..."

The couch called my name, and I snuck a piece of cheese from the charcuterie board we'd been grazing from all afternoon. After plopping down on the oversized cushion, I was about to search for a new baking show my friend Esther had recommended when my phone rang. Normally, I ignored numbers I didn't know but I recognized the Wisconsin area code.

Curiosity got the better of me and I answered. "Hello?"

"Hello, is this Marlowe Linden?" a man asked.

"Yes, this is she." If this was a telemarketer, that was pretty low to call on Thanksgiving.

"I apologize for disturbing you during the holiday. My name is Oliver Alderwood, I'm with the Mayo Clinic Health System in Eau Claire. Are you the daughter of Mr. James Linden?"

I attempted to swallow the lump forming in my throat, setting down the glass of wine with shaky hands as the blood drained from my face. "Yes, I am."

"I'm sorry to be the bearer of bad news, Ms. Linden, but your father was brought in earlier today. It seems he suffered a stroke perhaps two or three days ago and was discovered unresponsive in his home. The doctors did everything they could, but..."

Mike popped his head into the living room, smiling and opening his mouth like he was about to say something funny until he noticed my expression.

Oliver continued a practiced speech about claiming the remains and other administrative tasks I needed to take care of as his next of kin, and I nodded along.

"I see. Thank you for calling me. I'll… I'll be there as soon as I can."

Mike rushed over, taking my pale cheeks in his hands. "Marlowe, what is it?"

I could barely register the words the man had said on the phone. I had just spent two weeks in Wisconsin handling my mom's death – her funeral, her cremation, and cleaning out her house.

My eyes shifted over to the urns of my brother and mother on one of the built-in shelves next to the TV. Was there room for one more?

"My dad died. I have to go back to Wisconsin"

"Shoes and jackets off. Remove your liquids and electronics…"

It had taken me a few minutes to register the shock of hearing the news of my dad's death, and in that time Mike had managed to book me on the next flight to northern Wisconsin, paying for the exorbitantly priced ticket without a thought.

Then he had helped me pack my suitcase and had taken me to the airport, waiting with me until I needed to head through security.

"I wish I could come with you," he said as we hugged, his face nestled deep in my neck, breathing me in. "But Jen and I have that project at work that was technically due yesterday. I can join you in a few days if you need me, okay?"

The wound in my heart that had only just started to heal after my mom's death reopened with a vengeance, and it felt like I was about to bleed out right in the middle of SFO. I had thought while cleaning out my mom's old house that I could try to get in touch with my dad at some point in the future. He hadn't come to Ezra's funeral, and I hadn't even thought to invite him to mom's, but he was all I had left. Now I would never know him, never know why he had left us.

But I couldn't submit to the pain and grief just yet – I needed to get to my destination first. I kissed Mike good-bye and got in line while my brain went into autopilot, allowing me to function just enough to make it to the gate and onto the plane.

Somehow, I managed to handle my layover in Minneapolis as well and arrived at the Chippewa Valley Regional Airport in Eau Claire, Wisconsin early the next morning. The airport was desolate, but at least one of the cafes was open.

I bought one of their seasonal drinks, then made my way to the rental car desk, pulling up the reservation Mike had also made for me. He'd even sent me a list of hotels, just in case I couldn't or didn't want to stay at my dad's place while I was here.

As I waited for the attendant to finish all my paperwork, my phone alarm beeped, reminding me to take my medicine.

Back in high school I had had the worst periods and PMS, so my mom had helped me find a special birth control that kept me feeling sane. The brand wasn't found in most pharmacies, so she had been sending it to me like clockwork every three months.

Something else I now had to figure out how to manage on my own, I realized bitterly.

But as I dug through my purse, they were nowhere to be found. In all the rush and commotion, I must have forgotten to pack them.

Shit. Now I had to deal with all this while turning into a weird, weepy, hormonal mess?

Terrific.

I got in my rental car and headed straight towards the hospital, the address punched into my GPS, planning on stopping by their pharmacy after dealing with my dad. If they didn't carry the pills, at least they could point me in the right direction. But would my insurance even cover it? Considering it was so hard to find, it must have been expensive.

I gritted my teeth as I turned the defrost setting on to clear the foggy windshield, my fingers already numb from the cold. At least the roads were dry and it hadn't snowed up here yet. I wasn't sure I remembered how to drive in less-than-ideal conditions.

Once I got on the highway, I glumly gazed out over the bleak landscape.

Being home used to refresh me, but the first thing I now noticed was how dead everything looked.

I already missed the golden hills, bright blue skies, and palm trees of California. Wisconsin had its own beauty, of course, but this time of year always seemed too melancholy. Everything was brown and lifeless, and the barren trees only accentuated the flat, endless gray horizon.

It was still pretty early when I arrived at the hospital, and the receptionist at the front desk let me know the bereavement counselor would be in soon to meet with me. I took a seat in the lobby, exhausted from the trip and numb from the cold and the loss.

My whole family was gone now. Every single one of them.

Thankfully there weren't many witnesses to my detached staring. Since it was Black Friday, I assumed most people were probably at their nearest Walmart, fighting their neighbors to the death over a discounted TV.

Those who did pass by eyed me suspiciously though, sniffing the air in my direction. I subtly checked my armpits when no one was looking, but my deodorant was doing its job. Was it that obvious I wasn't a local? Sure, I hadn't been up to this part of the state before, but I had spent most of my life in Wisconsin. I was raised on beer brats and Blue Moon ice cream.

Finally, a little after nine, a man came out of an office, calling my name. He was quite tall, with short, sandy blonde hair and brown eyes. I couldn't help but notice how well he filled out his khaki chinos and navy half-zip sweater.

My mind wandered briefly, wondering what his chest looked like underneath his top. What *I* would look like underneath his…

God, what was wrong with me? I always noticed a good-looking man, who didn't? But since I had met Mike, I hadn't really noticed so… intently. I was an engaged woman dealing with my dad's body, and here I was, practically drooling over the physique of my bereavement counselor, of all people.

"Good morning, Ms. Linden. I'm Oliver Alderwood. We spoke on the phone yesterday." I recognized his voice, of course, but today there was a richness to its timbre I hadn't noticed before. It was soothing yet powerful, like a strong massage pulling the stress from my body.

My eyes fell to the hand he held out for me to shake, and as I took it my mind flashed to other ways he could be massaging me, and then I mentally slapped myself. I needed to get a grip.

Or do you want him to get a grip on you?

I bit my cheek to keep grounded and steadied my expression as he continued talking. I didn't remember horniness being one of the stages of grief, but this man was making me feel depraved enough to add it to the list - somewhere between 'denial' and 'anger,' perhaps?

"I'll be helping you with everything you need to take care of your father. His attorney has also been contacted. He's on his way from Chicago now. I understand Mr. Linden had already set all of his funeral arrangements, so thankfully you won't have to deal with too much paperwork today."

My dad had been so put together he had an attorney? And funeral arrangements? Yet somehow couldn't even remember to send a birthday card?

The look of confusion must have been more obvious on my face than I thought. "I know this is a difficult time. Why don't we head to my office? We can speak in private there."

I shook my head, unwrapping my scarf and tossing my hair over my shoulder. "Can I see him first?"

His nostrils flared and his pupils dilated for a second before returning to normal, like I had said something wrong or offensive. Had I accidentally pissed him off? Was I being too blunt, or did I seem too cavalier? "Of course. Just follow me," he replied, his voice becoming even deeper.

The halls were quiet and empty, the sounds of my boots clacking along the vinyl flooring and the errant beep from a machine the only signs of life in the early morning hours. Even Oliver managed to walk with a preternatural silence. I chalked it up to his career. He was probably used to making his presence as unnoticeable as possible. For a man of his size, it was impressive.

We entered the room, my heart pounding as I eyed the body on the bed, sheet pulled up to his shoulders. One would think that after not seeing your dad for twenty plus years, he would seem smaller than you remembered him. Yet he still looked like a giant – although not quite as big as Ezra had been. When my twin brother had shot up to over a foot taller than me in high school, I had often joked that he stole all the height genes in the womb. At five-foot-three, I had tapped out a couple inches shorter than my mom.

I compelled myself to step closer and inspected his face. The years had been kind, and if I didn't know any better, I would have placed him at closer to forty than his real age of sixty. His hair, the same shade of strawberry blonde as mine, was still quite thick. A short, well-maintained beard covered his face, his mouth set in a thin line.

Recognition hit me like a freight train carrying memories long buried from my childhood, and a sob finally made its way through my chest. Oliver placed his arm around me. "I'm very sorry for your loss."

I normally didn't like strangers touching me, but I found him comforting and welcomed his warm yet professional embrace. Even his scent, mint and lavender, had a calming effect. I allowed myself to let go of the shock, the sadness, the fury... expressing every complicated feeling I'd ever had about my dad, right there in that room.

Oliver stood by my side without saying another word, allowing me to expel it all.

Why was I grieving for a man who hadn't even wanted to be a part of my life? I had a few happy memories from when I was little, when I had thought he was the greatest dad ever.

But great dads didn't abandon their kids.

I took in one more deep, shuddering breath, wiping my cheeks with the palms of my hands. "Thanks, I'm good now."

He nodded and led me back down to his office, where I was given a bottle of water and a box of tissues.

"Thanks, Mr. Alderwood," I said. "I'm sorry you had to come in on a holiday for this."

He shook his head. "Please, call me Oliver. And it's no problem at all. I knew of your father before he was brought in. He's done a lot of good work in our community, and it's an honor helping his daughter."

I raised an eyebrow and let out a sniffling, skeptical laugh. Somehow, I'd always pictured him as the stereotypical deadbeat dad – living in a shitty studio apartment, drinking away his paychecks and skipping out on child support. What kind of good work could he have been doing all the way up here?

"I have his belongings, if you'd like to take them. He was found at home, so he didn't have anything on him when he was brought in aside from the clothes he was wearing and his wedding band."

Wedding band? Why would he still have worn his wedding band?

Okay, the pieces were coming together now. "That explains it. Did he remarry and have a second family up here or something? Where's his other wife?"

Oliver cocked his head. "Other wife? I'm not sure what you mean. His emergency contact was his business partner, Camden Wolcott. He directed me to his attorney, who gave me your information. That was how I got in touch with you." He took a small envelope from the box and opened it, dropping the ring into my hand.

Sure enough, my mother's name was engraved on the inside.

"This doesn't make sense," I said quietly. "He walked out on us. Are you telling me they never officially divorced?"

He sighed, giving me a sympathetic look. "I wouldn't know anything about that, only that he was found alone in his home. Speaking of, you should be getting a key to the place from his attorney. I know the process of cleaning out a loved one's belongings after death can be painful, and I am happy to assist you. I am great at moving boxes."

Oliver flashed me a flirty grin. My breath hitched, and I brought my left hand to my chest as I was hit with a wave of his enticing cologne. His eyes darted towards the ring on my finger, disappointment eclipsing his friendly expression. Okay, so I might have entertained some light fantasies about the very good-looking man in front of me, but I certainly wasn't going to act on them. Had he actually considered asking me out? That must have been a major ethics violation for his position.

"Are you bonded?" he asked, pointing to my hand.

I straightened in my seat. "What? I'm engaged, if that's what you're asking."

"Why isn't your pack here, too?" His voice had become strangely clipped, like he was mad at me for not being single.

I sat back in confusion, my eyes blinking rapidly. "Pack?" What the hell was he talking about? "Not that it's any of your business, but this was kind of sudden and my fiancé, *singular*, has work. He'll come out for the funeral or if I need his help clearing my dad's house. But thank you for the offer, I guess."

His palms flattened on his desk and he took a deep breath. "Your father lived in Maiingan Hollow. You can't go there by yourself. You need a male escort to protect you. I will take you."

I clicked my tongue, put my dad's ring on the desk, and folded my hands in my lap as I centered myself before I replied. "I don't appreciate your tone or your concern, Mr. Alderwood. This is really unprofessional."

Oliver chuffed. "And I don't think you understand the dangers of an unbonded..."

"Excuse me?" I raised my hand to stop him. "What the hell does this 'bonded' and 'unbonded' bullshit mean? Is the town my dad lived in so dangerous that a woman can't even walk the streets by herself without being jumped? And why is this my problem and not something that should involve, oh I don't know, the police?"

My words hung in the air, and Oliver's expression turned from frustration to suspicion. "Do you not know…"

I refused to listen anymore. "This is really too much. I hate to be a Karen about this, but I think I need to speak to your supervisor."

At that, Oliver growled and I jumped in my seat, my heart bursting with primal fear. I snapped out of it and gave him a disgusted look. "What the hell, dude? Did you just fucking growl at me?"

Someone knocked at the door and Oliver's eyes shifted towards the sound. "What?" he snarled.

"Mr. Alderwood? This is Elias Faulkner, James Linden's attorney. Is his daughter here already?"

"Come in," Oliver said roughly. I opened my mouth in shock. How did he go from caring nice guy to aggressive asshole? And why? Just because I had the audacity to be engaged?

The attorney entered, and I almost laughed. Like Oliver, he was also very tall and well-built, his bespoke suit immaculate and perfectly tailored to his muscled physique. His skin was tanned, like he had just come back from a tropical vacation, his dirty blonde hair highlighted with streaks of gold. I hadn't been out of the Midwest that long. Surely, I would have remembered everyone looking like Greek gods. Had they put something in the water the past few years?

Elias nodded at Oliver and then extended his hand towards me. "Pleased to meet you, Ms. Linden." When I took it, the same expression that Oliver had first given me fell over his face – his nostrils flaring and his pupils dilating as he pulled me in. He shot Oliver a look.

He gestured at me from his desk and sighed. "She doesn't know."

I took my hand back and stood up. "Mr. Faulkner, did my father have you on some sort of retainer? I might need to open a case of sexual harassment against this hospital."

This time, a growl reverberated from the attorney's chest, and he stepped in front of me, his body shielding mine from Oliver's view as his eyes raked me over. "What did he do? Did he touch you?"

Oliver bared his teeth. "She doesn't know," he reiterated slowly

The attorney turned around and faced him. Some kind of silent understanding seemed to pass between the two of them, and the tension in the room started to melt. Elias sighed, rolling his shoulders and cracking his neck. "Ms. Linden, could you actually give us a moment?"

I bit my lip in frustration. Sure, they were just going to 'talk it out' and brush it all under the rug, trying to convince me I had overreacted.

Typical.

I slung my purse back over my shoulder and wrapped my scarf back around my neck.

"You know what? It's fine. My dad already has his funeral all planned out, right? It sounds like I don't even have to do anything anyway. You guys can just discuss everything and this little 'unbonded'..." I put my fingers up in air quotes. "...woman will leave it all to you. See you."

The attorney grabbed my arm. "There's still a lot to take care of here, and your father's will..."

I ripped myself from his grasp, pointing my finger in his face while my body shook with rage. "I don't want anything that man left me. Don't touch me again; don't contact me again. I'm getting on the first plane out of this backwater hellhole."

I slammed the office door behind me and stormed off into the parking garage, plopping down in my car and bursting into tears. All that testosterone in the room had me on a weird edge. What the hell was up with all that growling and posturing between the counselor and the attorney? This was all just so insulting and bizarre.

It reminded me of when I was a teenager and my boobs had come in. Like a bat signal to creeps, they had started following me around whenever I was out, telling me I smelled nice and asking for my phone number.

But back then, I had had Ezra to put them in their place.

God, I really was alone now.

After wiping my cheeks and blowing my nose, I took out my phone and called Mike.

"Hey, did you make it okay?"

His voice instantly made me feel better, and I took a deep breath to start, but he could tell just from the slight shuddering sound that something was wrong. "Shit, I should have come with you..."

I let out a pained laugh. "Yes, but not for the reasons you think." I gave him a brief rundown of what had happened at the hospital, and as I spoke, it sounded even more bizarre.

"Jesus Christ, what year is it over there?" he asked. "Do you need me to come? I can try to find a flight tonight."

I opened my mouth to respond when I heard a woman laughing in the background.

"Where are you?"

"At the office. I have that project, remember?"

"Oh, yeah." I sniffed. "Tell Jen I said hi." I had met Jen at a few of his company parties. She was always really nice to me. She kept asking if I wanted to get drinks with her and have a girls' night. After dealing with those two men, a girls' night was actually starting to sound pretty damn appealing, and I made a mental note to take her up on that offer soon.

"Of course. By the way, I brought in some leftovers, and apparently, you're right – sweet potatoes taste better with marshmallows."

"They're amazing, Marlowe! Your fiancé has no taste!" Jen yelled into the phone.

I chuckled at the confirmation. "Told you. Anyway, don't worry about coming. I'm going to try to change my flight and return today. There's no point in my being here. I'm sorry you paid so much for my ticket. This was a colossal waste of time."

"Don't worry about that," he said, reassuring me with his calming tone. "At the very least, you got some closure, right?"

"Yeah, I guess so," I sighed. "I'll let you know when I'm supposed to arrive. Do you think you can pick me up?"

"Definitely. I love you, my Lunessa."

He had started calling me that pet name in the past year, and my face warmed whenever he said it. "Love you, too."

I hung up and stared out of my windshield, through the open space between the concrete floors of the garage. Fluffy snowflakes floated lazily in the air, and my anger subsided enough that the chill was finally seeping through the woefully thin jacket I was wearing. I hadn't needed a proper winter coat in years and had forgotten how essential they were here. I shivered and turned on the car to start the heater, then opened the airline app on my phone to go about changing my ticket.

A sudden knock at the window made me scream, dropping my phone somewhere between the seat and the center console. My dad's attorney looked at me apologetically, and I grumbled as I lowered the window. "What do you want?" I snapped.

"I apologize for the way the counselor treated you and if my initial reaction to the situation offended you. You came all this way, at least let me take you out for breakfast. Then if you're game, we can head to my satellite office and discuss your father's estate."

"Estate?" I asked. "Did he leave me a bunch of useless, impractical junk that I now gotta deal with?" Wouldn't that be the cherry on this shit sundae, finding out I'd inherited his collection of obscure jazz records or antique spoons or something stupid?

"Not exactly," he replied. "There's a diner not too far from here called Betty's. Why don't you head over there? I'll meet you. Besides, I don't know if you've checked the weather, but a winter storm is coming through, and I don't think you'll have much luck flying out for the next few days."

"Crap," I groaned. Combined with the holiday weekend rush, I might be screwed until the middle of next week.

In that case, diner breakfast was sounding pretty good at the moment, too, if I was being honest. "Fine, I suppose you can buy me a meal."

Elias smiled, and my breath almost stopped. He was far too gorgeous for his own good. "It would be my absolute pleasure, Ms. Linden."

A blush crept across my cheeks, and I couldn't help myself from smiling back. Nah, this was absolutely going to be mine.

2
MARLOWE

"*Best pancakes in the world*," I read aloud, looking over the sticky, laminated menu. "Do you ever wonder how restaurants get away with those claims? Legally speaking, of course."

Elias laughed, leaning back in his seat, an adorable dimple coming to life on his left cheek. "I can't say that I have. But how do you know it's not true?"

"Hmm…" I ran my finger down the exhaustive list. "I guess I'll have to order a stack and find out. I'm sure you can expense this, right? It's for research, after all."

He lifted his hand to signal the waitress. "My favorite kind of research." His green eyes twinkled mischievously and his voice lowered. "Tell me, Ms. Linden, do you have a sweet tooth?"

The look he gave me was ravenous and disarmingly charming. As an engaged woman, it was inappropriate for me to flirt back, but he was way too cute. And the vibe I got from him seemed much more harmless than the counselor at the hospital. He felt like a safe person to joke around with. Someone I could trust.

Damn, he must have been a successful lawyer. I couldn't imagine trying to argue against this guy in court. He probably had all the judges wrapped around his finger. Good thing he was working for me at the moment.

"The sweetest," I answered, giving a small wink.

He grinned, and the scent of his cologne wafted over the table, making my mouth water more than the bacon sizzling in the kitchen. I needed to ask him what he was wearing without sounding

14

creepy so I could get a bottle for Mike for Christmas. Notes of bergamot and pepper, if my nose was correct.

"What can I getcha?" asked the waitress, leaning hard on her hip to pop out her leg.

"We'll take two cups of coffee, a short stack of your buttermilk pancakes, a short stack of your blueberry pancakes, another of your apple cinnamon…"

My jaw fell open as he continued ordering.

"Let's see, and then we'll do two orders of the carnivore platter… Wait." He paused and looked at me. "You're not on some hippy, Californian diet, are you?"

I rolled my eyes. Why did everyone from the Midwest always assume people on the west coast were all gluten-free, vegan, health nuts? "Extra sausage patties, please," I added, turning to the waitress. She blew a bubble with her gum as she jotted down the rest of our order, taking our menus and heading off.

I watched as the doors to the kitchen swung shut and whistled. "Well, I certainly will need to be on a diet after all this food. I think you ordered close to 10,000 calories."

Elias waved off my concern. "I'm sure we'll burn it off pretty quickly."

My face heated. Maybe he wasn't so innocent? He leaned forward, speaking quietly. "Reading wills is quite the workout."

"Oh." I chuckled nervously. "Right." I had to stop reading so much into things.

We got our coffees and I poured three packets of sugar and four little containers of half-and-half into my cup while Elias watched in horror. "You weren't kidding about that sweet tooth," he said. "Are you sure that even counts as coffee anymore?"

"Ha ha," I replied sarcastically. "Sorry, I don't hate myself enough to drink it black. Blegh."

The snow was coming down harder now, and while I should have been disappointed that I likely wasn't making it home anytime this weekend, part of me was enjoying the coziness of the moment. Who wouldn't want to eat their weight in pancakes sitting across from one of the hottest guys they'd ever met?

There was no reasoning to explain how I'd managed to finish half of everything Elias had ordered and not explode – sometime between the shock of yesterday and this morning, my stomach had turned into a black hole, devouring whatever was in its path. Perhaps being in the cold again had my body convinced I needed to prepare for hibernation.

Elias's satellite office wasn't too far from the diner, but the roads were getting slick and I hoped the trucks would finish salting everything by the time we were done.

The address he had entered into my phone led me to an old Victorian house that had been converted into commercial property. On the first floor, I saw signs for a notary and a small dentistry, while Elias's office was upstairs. The building was closed for the holiday and the heat turned off. I shivered as Elias fiddled with the keys.

"California has made you weak," he joked, seemingly unaffected by the low temperature.

"Nah, I've always hated the cold," I replied through my chattering teeth.

"Hm, I bet." The richness of his voice sent another shiver through my body. "Let me guess, you're the type of woman who lives most of the year under a pile of throw blankets with a mug of hot chocolate."

Something about how he had me pegged made me a little mad, but he wasn't one hundred percent right, and I haughtily corrected him, "No, I prefer Earl Grey tea, thank you. And let me guess, you spend most of your time drinking cheap beer on a cracked leather sofa, getting pissed off because the Bears are losing again?"

He let out a deep laugh. "You're almost there. I like to spend my time drinking craft beer on my immaculate, full-grain leather sofa, celebrating another Packers win."

The door finally opened and Elias led me into the tastefully decorated room.

"At least until they choke in the playoffs," he sighed bitterly.

The hardwood floors were polished to a warm gleam, and an ornately decorated Persian rug sat under a pair of damask upholstered armchairs in front of a dark mahogany desk. Built-in bookcases were filled to the brim with law texts.

Elias gestured towards a fireplace. "I have no idea if that actually works, and I don't control the thermostat for the building, unfortunately. But here." He took off his puffy, down jacket and placed it around my shoulders. "I wouldn't want you freezing to death."

Another blush crept up my cheeks, his enticing scent and lingering heat enveloping me. "Oh, thank you. Are you sure you don't need it?"

He walked around and sat in his chair, turning on his computer. "Not at all. I run pretty hot."

You sure do.

Elias gestured towards one of the armchairs. "Please, have a seat and we'll get started. Your father's business partner should be here soon. He was also named in his will."

That's right. Oliver had mentioned my dad had a business partner. But in what? "I have so many questions, because honestly, all this talk of my dad being some upright pillar of the community slash business owner slash devoted husband until the end is really confusing me."

Elias rubbed his thumb along his lip as he listened. Something about his gaze seemed calculating and predatory. Combined with his intoxicating scent and the nice coat, I was getting pretty warm, and I crossed my legs subconsciously.

His eyes darted towards the movement and his expression glazed over for a second, as though he could sense how inappropriately turned on I was.

Ugh, I wasn't normally so horny for strangers like this. He was probably exhausted. He'd just driven up here from Chicago, and I needed to stop thinking about sex.

"I don't know if I can answer all of them, but I'll certainly do my best," he replied. "Why don't we start with his business? Your father owned a large construction company with another family, the Wolcotts. They're responsible for most of the new buildings in the Chippewa Valley, and employ close to 500 people. Wolfcrest Construction is also one of the largest corporate donors in the area. You can't go to a local event or high school game without seeing their name plastered all over everything. He didn't request a large funeral, but I'm sure the service will be well attended by the community."

I didn't know whether to laugh or cry. Who the hell was my dad? All those years, not a single peep. He didn't even seem to care when his own son had died, but he could buy new uniforms for the school's football team? Could sponsor a Veteran's Day parade?

Elias watched me intently, his body still as he gauged my reaction. "This comes as a shock, I take it."

My tongue ran along the bottom of my teeth, and I looked out the window as the storm progressed. "I haven't seen him for twenty-two years. No cards, no letters, no phone calls. He's as good as a stranger to me. I suppose any news of the type of life he led would be a surprise. Although honestly, with the lack of contact, I'd always assumed he just led a sad, simple life. I gotta say, it hurts a bit to know he was so successful and put together yet couldn't be bothered to maintain a relationship with me."

He let out a deep sigh, a pained expression falling across his handsome face. It looked like he was trying to hold himself back from saying something, some secret information that would help me understand why my dad had abandoned us that would help it all make sense.

But I was probably reading too much into it. How could he know what my dad's motivations had been?

Elias let me sit with the news for a few minutes, and I tried to come to terms with it all. But for some reason, my mind kept wandering back to the meeting with Oliver.

"Why isn't it safe for me to go to his house alone?" I finally asked, breaking the silence.

Elias stiffened in his chair. "Who told you that?"

"That weirdo counselor at the hospital. He said it wasn't safe for an 'unbonded' – whatever the hell *that* means – woman to go to the town my dad lived in alone. What was he talking about?"

His brows furrowed and a look of inner turmoil presented itself on his features.

Okay, maybe it wasn't in my imagination. What was he wrestling with?

He opened his mouth to speak when heavy footsteps sounded, coming up the stairs. Elias's office door burst open, and another large man stood there fuming. He had close-cropped dark hair and a short beard, his eyes piercing blue. Underneath a brown Carhartt jacket, he wore a green flannel with a cream-colored henley shirt. His jeans were stained with paint, his work boots scuffed.

Why was everyone in this city so hot?

"What the fuck do you mean his half is going to his *daughter*?" he boomed.

And such an asshole?

The inflection on the last word raised my hackles. I assumed this must be the aforementioned business partner – and wouldn't you know it, he was a misogynistic dick with a chip on his shoulder.

Awesome.

18

Elias rose out of his chair quickly, his tone biting and volume increasing. "Camden, sit down so we can talk about…"

"I don't want to talk. I want answers!" His voice was so loud it shook the walls, and it almost made me want to shrink in my seat. He pointed towards his chest, still only looking at Elias. "This has *always* been an alpha-run business! I don't care who her daddy is. There is no way some inexperienced beta female can walk in and–"

This was getting to be too much, and I couldn't help but snicker. His furious gaze finally landed on me, then widened in surprise as his nostrils flared wildly. He looked at Elias, who nodded curtly.

I stood up and gave him my most condescending expression, flipping my hair over my shoulder. "Beta? Alpha? Is this some kind of furry thing?" The man, Camden, took an intimidating step forward, but I held out my hand and continued. "Look, I don't consent to being a part of whatever kink you have going on, and I certainly object to the use of 'female' as some derogatory insult. When Mr. Faulkner first told me I inherited half my dad's business, I was already considering selling it if possible. But now?" I scoffed, crossing my arms. "I might just keep it out of spite."

Camden's chest began to heave, and he easily cut the distance between us with his long stride. I flinched, worried he might be the kind of guy who'd actually hit a woman half his size for "threatening his masculinity," but instead he grabbed my shoulders and buried his nose into my neck, inhaling deeply.

Freeze. That was the only instinct my body wanted to follow, which annoyed me greatly. Before I found my voice and the courage to knee him in the groin, Elias ran around his desk and grabbed Camden off me. "Stop it, you idiot, she doesn't know!"

Camden roared in response, his pupils fully blown, and he shoved Elias back. Elias cocked a fist and swung towards him, but Camden dodged and barreled into his chest, slamming him against a bookcase.

I watched in horror as the two men fought, backing up until I hit the wall behind me. What the hell *was* in the water here? What had guys turning into violent cavemen at the drop of a hat? Or a sniff of the neck, apparently. And what was it all these guys insisted I didn't know?

My hand rested on my chest, and what was supposed to be a normal breath suddenly became a needy, high-pitched whine. The two men stopped dead in their tracks and rushed to my side, crowding over me with concern in their eyes.

The scents coming off them, bergamot and pepper from Elias and cardamom and cedar from Camden, invaded my lungs and made my vision hazy. My nipples tingled and my thighs clenched, while my fingers flexed with the thought of running them across their muscled chests. How could I be turned on right now? I was absolutely terrified and furious! Forget the water, there was something in the air making everyone extremely sexy, horny, and dangerously aggressive. I needed to get back to San Francisco. The sooner the better.

"Ms. Linden, I'm so sorry, I can explain…" Elias panted, his clothes disheveled.

Camden reached out to touch my face, but I pushed his hand away, pointing a finger at both of them. "I'm giving you one minute to tell me what the hell is going on before I walk out that door and call the cops."

Elias nodded, knocking Camden out of the way with his shoulder. "Yes, of course, just please sit down."

I gave Camden as wide a berth as possible and settled into one of the armchairs. Camden took the other one, his eyes never leaving me while Elias made his way back across the desk. He cleared his throat, straightening his tie and smoothing back his hair.

"Have you ever heard of shifters?" he began, clasping his hands together.

I looked between the two of them, their attention suffocating. "Shifters? You mean… like shapeshifters?"

They nodded, Camden's knuckles turning white as his fingers dug into the arms of the chair.

I sighed, getting up and taking off Elias's coat. "Well, I'll just show myself out. You are both officially insane, and… yeah. I guess that's it. Do whatever the hell you want with my father's half. Peace out." I flashed an awkward V with my fingers and headed towards the exit.

Camden rushed up and shut the door in front of me before I could leave, leaning against it as he caged in my body with his massive frame. I turned around, his face inches from mine.

"It's true," he whispered. I swallowed nervously as the space between us continued to shrink. "Shifters exist, and you are one, just like us. Just like your dad. And not only that, but you're a pretty special shifter, one we haven't seen in a long time."

His hand cupped my cheek, and he lowered his face to sniff my neck again. "Mmm, pistachio and honey," he sighed, his nose grazing my skin. "You smell so sweet, baby. Like a dream come true."

My knees went weak, and I fought the instinct to melt into his touch. "Yeah, I know. I got it from Sephora."

He chuckled, his hand moving behind my head and grabbing my hair gently, wrapping a few strands around his finger. "Nah, this is all natural." He stepped closer, until our bodies were touching, and I felt his erection through his pants.

Whatever power he had somehow managed to wield over me broke, and I finally snapped back, shoving him away. "Jesus Christ, dude. What the hell is wrong with you?"

Elias moved in his chair. "Ms. Linden, I know it sounds bizarre, but your parents, Mr. Wolcott and I... we're all wolf shifters. Over the years, we've lost our ability to connect with our inner beasts, but we still retain a significant portion of our feral DNA. Specifically, our impulses and, how can I put this? Our *social structures*."

Camden still didn't move, and I side-stepped him so I could face Elias more directly. "Social structures aren't biological."

"They are for shifters," Camden replied. He licked his lips, his eyes raking over me from head to toe.

Elias noticed and growled, causing Camden to growl back. It was all way too much.

"Knock it off!" I snapped. They whipped their heads back towards me, and Camden shuddered in what looked like delight.

"That's the cutest bark I've ever heard. Do it again, baby," he groaned, his hand reaching for his pants.

I curled my lips in disgust. "You're gross." I turned back towards Elias. "Look, this is all making a bit more sense now."

"It is?" Elias asked.

"Yep." I nodded. "My mom refused to have me and my brother live in this weird furry cult, and my dad left us so he could play werewolf in the woods with a bunch of delusional LARPers who throw around words like 'alpha' and 'beta' as if they actually mean something."

Elias's shoulders dropped and Camden took another step towards me, desire seeping through his voice. "I can show you right now that alpha means something real around here." He grabbed my wrist and forced my hand onto his bulging hard-on.

I reeled back and slapped him as hard as I could, and he let me go while laughing.

"You're a fucking pig!" I yelled, my voice shaking with rage.

Storming down the stairs, I got back into my rental car and headed to the highway at a snail's pace on the slippery roads to get to the chain hotel I'd seen on my way over. I'd get a room, barricade the door from those freaks, and book the next flight home.

None of what happened in that office had been okay, but for some reason my rage was tinged with desire, and I couldn't deny how strangely turned on I felt, which frustrated me even more. I shook my head to clear it, but my mind refused to let go of its thoughts of those two. Did they taste as good as they smelled?

I bit my lip reflexively, remembering the size of Camden's erection. The man was packing. There was no denying that. It was almost too much – would he even fit?

Goddamnit, stop it.

I turned the air conditioning on full blast and found a polka station on the radio to get my mind out of the gutter and back to the snowy road in front of me.

3
ELIAS

"You're just going to let her go?" Cam snarled.

I sighed, running my hand down my face. Did I want to let her go? No, I wanted to wrap her up and bring her down to Chicago with me immediately, hiding her in my home, where no one would ever realize the treasure I'd just found.

But unlike Cam, I wasn't a Moon-damned barbarian.

"She didn't grow up in this world. Everything we say is going to sound bat shit crazy to her. Marlowe needs to figure this out on her own."

Cam started pacing angrily. He ripped off his coat and rolled his shoulders as he growled to himself. He had always been a hot head, and today, he might have just scared off the first omega the area had seen in almost one hundred years.

I really should punch him.

"How can she not know?" he asked. "She's gotta be in her mid-twenties, right? How many heat cycles has she gone through? After the first one, wouldn't she know she wasn't human?"

I got up and walked around my desk, picking up my coat and inhaling the scent that still lingered. Marlowe scoffed at the idea of biological social structures, but the raging hard-on in my pants was proof otherwise. No alpha could resist the sweet perfume, no matter how muted, of an omega in her prime.

"She must be on hormone suppressants," I said. "It's the only plausible explanation. If she wasn't, she would have attracted every shifter in Northern California. You didn't pick up on her scent until you were just a few feet away, correct? Same with me."

If she didn't know about this world and yet was taking pills, it meant someone close to her had been lying. James hadn't talked much about his family, but unbeknownst to Marlowe, he hadn't abandoned them, at least not financially. He'd been sending her mom thousands of dollars every month for years.

It must have been a concentrated effort between the two of them to keep the truth of their children's identities a secret.

But why?

"Fuck!" he yelled, collapsing into one of the armchairs. "I want her, Elias. I want her so bad it hurts."

I scoffed, still pissed that Cam had interrupted us. I had scented her attraction to me. Sure, she had a fiancé, but engaged wasn't married. We could have been working closely for months to unravel her father's estate – I had no doubt eventually she would have given up and ended things with the human to be with me. "And you think I don't? And every other alpha who's going to get a whiff of her while she's in town?"

His hands gripped the arms, his nails running down the fabric. "If anyone lays a finger on her, I swear to the Moon…"

My mind traveled with his, and I felt my anger boil over at even the thought of another alpha trying to knot or bond her against her will before she knew what she was. Before we had a chance to make her ours.

I took a deep breath and leaned against my desk. "We can keep an eye on her while she's here, but otherwise, we can't exactly lay a finger on her, either. She's engaged to a human."

"A *human*?" he roared. "An omega that perfect needs a whole pack of alphas to satisfy and protect her. What the hell is one knotless human going to do?"

I felt his frustration deeply, but I couldn't let it overtake me and make me do something stupid. Marlowe didn't seem the type to appreciate typical alpha aggression. "Cam, you need to calm down. We have no claim over her, and she obviously doesn't want any part in our world, at least for the moment. We'll do what we can to help her with James's passing, and any legal transfers with the company, but keep your distance, and keep your knot in your pants. I mean it."

He leaned back in a huff, his legs fidgeting uncontrollably. Cam was the physical manifestation of how agitated my mental state was. That morning, getting to sit across from her in the diner, feed her, take care of her – it had all scratched an itch I'd ignored for far too long.

I'd really gotten ahead of myself on the drive to my office with plans to convert one of the spare bedrooms in my house to a nest. I had already been adding Earl Grey tea and fuzzy throw blankets to my shopping list when I pulled into the parking lot.

But Cam's idea of seduction involved shoving her hand on his cock, and he had scared her away.

I should have been ripping his head off, but I sadly related too much to the pain coursing through him. So instead, I headed towards the drink cart, blowing the dust off a bottle of whiskey – it had been months since I'd last been up here – and poured us a couple of glasses.

"I think we need this," I said, handing one to him.

"Too fucking right," he replied, downing the whole thing in one gulp.

We sat in silence, the clock on the fireplace mantel ticking away the empty seconds. She was *right* here. I could have had her with just a little more time.

"We need to let the pack know," Cam said.

I let out a pained chuckle. "What's the point? 'Hey guys, we found what might be the last omega ever and she's perfect, but she doesn't know what shifters are and Cam sexually harassed her so badly she skipped town.'"

He scrunched his face. "I didn't sexually harass her. What are you talking about?"

How could he be so dumb sometimes? "Maybe here you can walk up to a female, shove your knot in her face, and call it witty banter. But in the human world, the one *she* knows? You'd get arrested for that."

"Well, the human world sucks." His brows narrowed in disdain. "Up here, I'm practically Mr. Fucking Darcy."

I choked on my whiskey and started laughing. "How do you even know who Mr. Darcy is?"

He stared out the window. "My ex loved that movie."

That made much more sense than the first image I had conjured of Cam sitting down to read a book.

"But anyway," he continued. "My point still stands. She hasn't met the rest of us, right? What if we can get one of them to, you know, *woo* her, and help ease her into reality? Then she won't be so pissed at us anymore."

I paused. The idea had merit, I had to give it to him.

"Fine, but we only send one. She's going to be skittish and on

25

edge, and two large alphas are going to set off her alarm bells."

Camden paused, then looked up. "Professor?"

I nodded, finishing the rest of my drink. "Professor."

4
MARLOWE

"Damn it, damn it, damn it!" I yelled in a huff. I had checked into my hotel room and was tearing my bags apart looking for my birth control pills for the third time. Every pharmacy I had called said they'd never even heard of the brand, and in this weather, I wasn't about to go driving around to find it, either.

My body already felt overheated and under-stimulated, and the strange, testosterone-fueled encounters I had had with all the men in this city weren't helping matters. I wished Mike were here so I could just take out all this pent-up horniness on him.

But why was I even this horny to begin with? I was here to take care of my dead father, for god's sake. Without a doubt, the past twenty-four hours had been the weirdest of my life.

My first reaction was to call my mom, and I bit back the heartbreaking truth that she was no longer with me. More than ever, I needed her to console me, to answer all these questions I had about our life and about dad that I couldn't ask those two "shifters" back in the office.

Shifters. What the hell was that all about? Was life up here really that boring that people had to play werewolf to pass the time? Had my own dad truly been *that* demented?

Well, they could keep his inheritance as far as I was concerned. I just wanted to wash my hands of this whole godforsaken state.

As I dumped the contents of my purse on the ground again, I paused. What if that was what they wanted? If my dad owned a company that big, it must have been worth a lot of money. What if

Elias and Camden were in cahoots, trying to scare me off so I'd take some lowball offer and never come back?

Those. ASSHOLES!

This whole charade must have been some long con. Hell, Oliver might have been in on it, too! I should have known something was up the second Camden stormed into that office and acted like he was going to explode if he didn't fuck me right then and there.

And why did the idea of that make me so turned on?

I needed to masturbate badly, but I knew if I did, I would just be thinking about them. A threesome had never appealed to me before, especially since whenever Mike joked about them, he meant having one with two girls. But a ménage à trois with two guys? Specifically Camden and Elias?

I pictured myself sandwiched between them. Elias's lips on my neck while his hand kneaded my breast, pinching my nipple. Camden was rougher, needier. His hand would be on my pussy, pushing a few fingers inside me.

Camden was probably one of those guys who liked to talk dirty, whereas Elias was a gentleman. He'd tell me I was beautiful, how good I felt. But Camden would be vulgar. He'd talk about how wet I was, how much he wanted to fill me with his cock.

Would I beg him for it? Bat my hooded eyes and whimper for them to fuck me?

I startled myself when my hand worked its way into my pants, my fingers circling my clit. It felt so wrong to be getting off on the idea of fucking two men who weren't my fiancé, but I couldn't help myself any longer. Besides, it wasn't like I was actually going to cheat on him.

Luckily, I was so wound up, it didn't take long for me to come. A few more minutes of picturing Camden pounding me from behind while Elias shoved his dick in my mouth and I was moaning louder than I ever had before, and I crashed hard.

That took care of some of the ache that had been building in me since that morning, but I still felt largely unsatisfied. What I needed was a real cock buried inside me, and of course, that was completely out of the question.

Is it though? whispered a horny little voice in the back of my mind

Ugh, why was I like this? I didn't know which felt worse, coming to the thought of someone else, or not feeling as guilty about it as I probably should have.

I love Mike, I love Mike, I love Mike…

That was my mantra as I took a shower. When I finally emerged, having washed away the shame and grime of what had happened that day, I turned the thermostat up as high as it would go to drive out the cold that had seeped into my bones, and then settled in for a long overdue nap.

I hadn't slept much on the flight the previous night, and when I woke up it was dark. Completely disoriented, I checked my phone. It was already seven, and my stomach rumbled despite eating so much that morning.

Was that really just this morning? It seemed like days ago.

Stretching, I walked over to the window and peeked out of the curtains. A thick blanket of snow covered the world and plows flashed yellow lights as they went about the Sisyphean task of trying to clear the roads.

Yeah, there was no way I'd be driving anywhere for the time being.

Luckily the hotel had a restaurant attached to the lobby, so I got dressed and went downstairs, determined to make the best out of what might be my only option for the next couple of days.

My worries disappeared as I heard festive norteño music, and the smell of chili, grilled meats, and cheese filled my nose. Yes, I could definitely eat nothing but Mexican for the foreseeable future.

It was a small place – inside only held a long, wrap-around bar, with tables and booths set around the edges of the room. Neon beer signs and painted tropical birds made of tin adorned the pastel pink walls.

When I walked in, about half the men sharply turned their heads from the Badgers game on the large TV, their eyes narrowing as I approached the hostess. The atmosphere turned thick, and getting my meal to-go now seemed like the best option.

I ordered my burrito at the hostess stand and then sat in the waiting area by the exit, ready to high tail it to my room as soon as it was ready. Whenever I lifted my eyes, I captured the stares of large men, all giving me the same kind of look I'd seen on Camden, Elias, and Oliver's faces. The hair on the back of my neck stood up, and I gulped as someone headed towards me. I looked down at my phone, trying to ignore him.

Please walk by, please walk by, please walk by…

"Well, what's a pretty thing like yourself doing all alone on a night like this?"

My eyes went up... and up, and up. The guy must have been at least six-foot five. His head was shaved, and chest hair stuck up out of the collar of his t-shirt. He was thick, the kind of guy who could snap a woman my size like a twig.

Ignoring him seemed like a bad idea. Especially after everything I'd experienced so far that day, I thought the guys around here didn't seem the type to shy away from physical assault.

"Same as anyone else, just getting some dinner and waiting out the storm," I replied flatly, turning my attention back to the Reddit thread I'd been pretending to read.

He chuckled. "Yeah, I bet you are. My room's real cozy. Why don't you wait up there with me?"

"No, thank you. I'm engaged." I flashed my ring.

The man lowered himself until his face was level with mine, bracing his hands against the wall on either side of me and trapping me between his arms. He took a deep breath, closing his eyes and sighing. "What kind of fiancé would let his unbonded omega out by herself in shifter territory?"

My heart stopped. Was everyone in this city in on this stupid role-play? "I appreciate your concern, but I'll be safely tucked away in my room once I get my meal, so no need to worry."

His scent assaulted my senses, and I started to cough. Tobacco and licorice, about as unappealing as it got. Who would pick that kind of cologne? But as I breathed it in, my will power began to shrink, as though I might actually do whatever this man told me to.

A deep growl resonated in his chest, and I sat up straight, ready to obey. "You're going to come upstairs with me and ride out this storm while riding on my knot. Got it?"

My mouth opened to say yes, wondering what the hell a knot was, but a firm hand grabbed him on the shoulder and pulled him away.

"She's under the protection of Pack Wolcott. You need to back off."

My savior was two or three inches over six feet, with jet black hair that curled slightly at the ends. His brown, upturned eyes glared at the other man beneath round glasses, his plump lips flattened. My gaze ran down his well-defined jawline to his broad shoulders. Despite his leaner physique and dressier outfit – a light blue dress shirt, sleeves rolled to the elbow, and khaki chinos – the corded muscles that ran down his forearms hinted at a man who knew how to use his body. My mouth drooled as I pictured those arms around me.

The other man rolled his shoulders forward and cracked his knuckles, staring down at him. "And why should I give a shit about Pack Wolcott?"

Scoffing, my savior leaned over and whispered something, so quietly I couldn't hear. But I watched as the big man's face paled. He turned to me, giving a rushed apology, and then walked out.

"Jesus, what did you say to him?" I asked, the stupor finally receding.

"Nothing polite enough to repeat in front of a lady," he replied. The scent of sea salt and jasmine danced around me, and I found myself dazed and horny all over again. Crap, this wasn't any better.

He reached out a hand to shake mine. "My name is Archer Lim. I knew your father."

"Well, that makes one of us," I joked. I touched his palm and felt a tingle shoot through my arm. From the look on his face, it seemed he had felt it too. "So, uh, what can I help you with?" I asked.

He bit his lip, looking around the room, then lowered his eyes. "Elias and Camden sent me. They're worried about you."

Hearing their names again made my heart skip a beat. Was I angry at them? Turned on? I didn't even know.

I'd go with angry for now.

"Oh, are they? Feel free to tell them to eat a bag of dicks." Archer's eyebrows raised in amusement, and I continued. "I'm not going to be scared into a low-ball offer for my dad's half of his company. As soon as this weather lets up, I'm on the first flight back to San Francisco and I'm going to find my *own* lawyer to sort out this mess. Tell Camden to buckle in because I'm not letting any of this go without a fight."

He let out a low chuckle, then pulled me up from my seat. "Elias said you were funny. Come on, we have a lot to talk about, and I think you all may have gotten off on the wrong foot."

The hostess came out with a Styrofoam box. "Marlowe? I have your order."

I took it and gave Archer a sarcastic salute. "Thanks for the rescue, but I don't think forcing my hand on someone's crotch really qualifies as 'getting off on the wrong foot.'"

Archer winced. "Yikes. Can't argue with you there. More like 'attempting to get off on the wrong hand,' then."

Now it was my turn to laugh. Archer tilted his head, gesturing

31

slightly to the open booth next to him. He was still large enough to be intimidating, but he didn't emanate aggression and violence quite like Camden or the other man who had come up to me tonight. He seemed calmer, more protective. More akin to Elias, whose aura hadn't been too bad at first either.

I sighed and apologized to the hostess, asking if I could eat my takeout there instead. She shrugged apathetically and went back to her phone.

"Okay, fine," I said, "but just know that I still don't trust a single one of you."

He nodded, holding my food while I scooted onto the seat. "A wise decision."

5
ARCHER

She was everything Camden had crudely yet emphatically described –
beautiful, enticing, intelligent, and funny. Her long, wavy, strawberry
blonde hair framed her heart-shaped face perfectly, and I wanted
nothing more than to kiss each of the freckles that dusted her blushed
cheeks.

Her round, hazel eyes darted around the room nervously, and
I hated that her first introduction to her people had left her drowning
in alpha pheromones. It was oppressive even for me, so I couldn't
imagine how she was dealing with all of this. She hadn't been exposed
to this world before and had no practice in handling shifter males.

I shuddered to think what would have happened to her if I
had arrived just a few minutes later – the first omega in the Chippewa
Valley in a century, bonded to that loser against her will.

She might not have wanted it, but until she *was* bonded, she
needed protection. And if I wanted it to be me and my pack mates,
then I had to keep my anger and desire in check before I scared her off
like Camden almost had.

I'd be trading words and possibly fists with that idiot later,
because this angel in front of me could possibly be ours, if we worked
carefully. Sure, she was engaged, but her fiancé was a human and, if
Elias was correct, being around this many alphas could trigger her first
heat after a lifetime of hormone suppressants. She would quickly
realize that marriage with a human couldn't satisfy her, nor could a
human husband protect her on his own.

I allowed myself a moment or two to picture what Marlowe

33

would look like naked, and then dismissed the images. I couldn't be like the alphas of long ago, taking advantage of a female in the throes of a heat. I was better than that.

My pack was better than that.

Well, everyone but maybe Camden was better than that.

Sometimes I regretted that I'd let him talk us all into bonding right before we graduated high school, and I was now forever tied to that moron just because fifteen years ago, the four of us had played football and liked getting drunk together on the weekends.

Although I supposed we'd all actually turned out alright.

Elias had gone to law school and opened his own firm in Chicago, serving shifter clients all over the upper Midwest.

Camden had taken over Wolfcrest Construction with James Linden after his own father had died two years ago. Although now that James had passed away, he might be running it with Marlowe. If we could convince her not to write us all off, that is.

Nolan was the youngest mayor in Maiingan Hollow's history. His progressive policies were helping to revitalize our local economy, and it still shocked me every time I came back to visit and saw our once dilapidated downtown, now a bustling hub of commerce and community.

And then there was me. After getting my Ph.D. from Northwestern in Biomedical Sciences, I had taken a tenured position at the University of Wisconsin - Eau Claire. Half the staff there were shifters or humans who knew about our world, and it was nice to not have to hide myself all the time.

It also gave me the chance to do my own research on our people. In addition to omegas, the ability to shift into our wolf form had disappeared over the last century, and recently we'd seen an uptick in a fatal disease we called Shifter Repression Syndrome. The genes responsible for transformation were still present in our bodies and were partially active, causing physical distress whenever we tried and failed to change. As a result, the energy and biological systems once used for shifting were being constantly triggered, and since they couldn't complete the process, it led to a gradual shut down of our vital organs and bodily functions, ultimately ending in death.

I had been utterly useless as I watched my own father wither away from the disease five years ago, and I suspected it might be what had taken James Linden as well.

But tonight, I was out of my lab, and my job was to "woo" the beautiful omega sitting in front of me. The beautiful, engaged omega.

The beautiful, engaged omega who didn't know what she was, why she was special, or that our world existed.

No pressure at all.

She devoured the burrito in front of her and eyed the fish tacos I had ordered longingly.

"Do you want one?" I asked.

She blushed, clearly struggling internally with the hunger building inside her. As her perfume deepened, I began to worry that Elias might be right about the hormone suppressants. Her first heat could start here and she'd have no idea what was happening. Would we have the willpower to help her through it without falling into a rut? It was already hard enough just sharing a meal with her.

The scientist in me was curious to observe the changes in her biologically and behaviorally during a heat, something only omegas experienced. But the alpha in me wanted to fuck her until she collapsed on my knot in orgasmic delirium.

Thank the Moon for this table covering the very obvious erection in my pants right now.

Perhaps I could ask my sister, a beta who lived in Maiingan Hollow with her husband and kids, to help find a female-led safe space for her. Those types of places had existed many years ago when omegas were still a part of our communities. But with how rare she was, once her scent or the word of her got out, every alpha in the state would come looking. She wouldn't be safe even with an army of females guarding her.

"Are you sure you aren't going to eat it?" she asked shyly.

I smiled, sliding her the rest of my plate. "I had a big lunch. Don't worry about me," I said. A low vibration rumbled through my chest, the alpha in me pleased that I had provided for this little omega. I was surprised she could hear anything over the sound of the TV blasting the college game, but her head tilted and she eyed me warily.

"What's that sound?"

Decision time. Do I deny she'd heard anything, keeping up with her delusion that she was a normal human and shifters didn't exist? Or do I take a risk, slowly getting her used to the idea that we were most definitely a different species altogether.

"Me," I replied, deciding to ease her in. "I'm purring."

She burst out laughing, covering her mouth before any food came flying out. I gave her my water as she started choking.

Some people would consider laughing so hard you spit out your dinner to be undignified, but all I saw was an adorable female I wanted to scoop up in my arms and spend all night with, finding different ways to make her smile like that over and over.

"I'm sorry," she said, residual giggles escaping from her chest as she blotted the corners of her eyes. "Did you say you were purring? Like a cat?"

I placed my elbows on the table and folded my hands in front of my face, watching as her eyes focused on my forearms. What was it with females and forearms? Not that I would dare complain. If she liked them, I'd let her look at them as long as she wanted.

"You could say like a cat, if that helps you make sense of it. But purring is a behavior found in alphas. It's a sound we make when we're content, or when we want to comfort someone."

She set the taco down and wiped her hands on a napkin. "I'll bite - let's say this whole 'shifter' thing is real. Why were you purring?"

I reached over, wiping a drop of salsa off her lip. "I am content. You were hungry and I fed you. Providing for you makes me happy."

Her tongue dipped to where my finger had just been. Her nervousness enhanced her scent, and I closed my eyes as waves of pistachio and honey washed over me. What I wouldn't give to lick that sweet perfume off her delicate skin.

"Why would providing for me make you happy?"

I smiled. "Because you're an omega, and I instinctively want to take care of you."

She straightened up, and I worried I might have said too much. Marlowe was engaged – did she really need another alpha coming onto her?

Instead of running away, she grabbed a chip and shoved it into her mouth, her mind working as she chewed. "What does that mean? I still don't understand."

I nearly purred again. She was curious, and I loved that she was asking questions. "Shifters are born in one of three biological classes. Alphas, who are typically male, make up about twenty percent of the population. We tend to be physically large and have a unique anatomical trait that makes it difficult for us to live outside of shifter communities. Betas represent the majority of us at seventy-five percent and are male and female. Visually, they are almost indistinguishable from humans these days but still retain some of our wilder instincts. Omegas like yourself are usually female, smaller in stature, and only come in at about five percent."

I kept an eye on the other patrons at the restaurant. Out of the eight or so guests, two were alphas, three were betas, and the rest were humans. Shifters had settled pretty seamlessly into the Chippewa Valley a hundred and fifty years or so ago. The dense, isolated forests and cold temperatures suited our hot-blooded animal forms.

Even though we no longer ran through the wild, we still appreciated the weather. At least alphas and betas did. Omegas, physically, were much smaller, and would depend upon their packs to keep them warm during the long, dark, winter nights.

"Okay," she said, "Aside from their rarity, why are omegas so…"

Her hands moved as she struggled to find the word.

"Coveted?" I suggested.

She nodded. "Sure, let's say that. So, in this make-believe world of shifters, what makes omegas coveted?"

"Shifters have a natural inclination towards pack-forming, and the males are also aggressive to a fault. Having a pack ensures a system that can rein in deviant behavior that endangers our society. But historically, the heart of the pack, especially for alphas, was the omega – the one who balances the pack with her calm demeanor."

She rolled her eyes. "So, omegas are just demure little sex toys that men can fuck their aggression out with before they go crazy and shoot up an office building?"

I coughed, a blush now creeping on my cheeks. "That's one way to put it, I guess. We're biologically wired to desire each other. From scent to sound, my body reacts to yours more than it does with beta females or human women. Imagine you've spent your whole life eating salads, and then suddenly someone places a steak in front of you. That's kind of what it's like for an alpha when they come near an omega."

Marlowe gave me a calculating gaze. I hadn't chased her off yet, which seemed to be a good sign. "But if there are so few omegas, does that mean most shifters just spend their lives eating salad?"

I needed to choose my words carefully. Our old customs were so different from the human ones she was raised in. So different from what shifters were even doing now. "Omegas typically choose a whole pack to bond and mate with."

She went quiet, and I watched her intently as she absorbed all of the information. "You mean, one woman with several men? Aren't there any problems with that? Jealousies, favoritism, that sort of thing?"

"Sometimes," I admitted. "Although my pack and I have no

experience with an omega, so I can't give you any firsthand accounts. But generally speaking, we understand that should our pack be blessed with one, we will need to share. And there are several times a year when males are… thankful that they have packmates who can help."

She had finished all of the chips and the rest of my tacos, and now started to pick at the errant shreds of lettuce that remained on the plate. "Are you still hungry?" I asked.

"No," she sighed, shaking her head. "I just feel like I could really use a drink."

I gave her a knowing nod. "I understand. Even if you don't quite believe me yet, this day must have been very stressful for you. Have you given yourself time and space to grieve the death of your father?"

While she gathered her thoughts, I flagged down the waitress and ordered two frozen margaritas. Her eyes widened. "How did you know that's what I wanted?"

I purred. "It was a lucky guess."

We remained in comfortable silence until they arrived. She finally found the words after a few sips of her drink. "My dad was as good as dead the day he walked out on us. Grief isn't quite the right word for what I'm feeling right now."

I wanted desperately to heal her ache, help her uncover the reasons why she had been raised in secret as a human. To help her process these complicated feelings and bring her peace. But I kept my distance for now. I would need to wait until she made it clear she was open to my advances.

"Anyway, what were you saying before, about alphas needing help sometimes with an omega?"

"Ah, yes, about that…"

The bell above the door rang, and I cursed under my breath as Camden stomped in. He shook the snow off his coat, his eyes scanning the room. They widened and a smile grew on his face as he headed over.

Marlowe noticed my gaze and turned around to see what had taken my attention. "That mother fucker…" she whispered.

I growled. "My thoughts exactly."

"Marlowe, Professor! Fancy seeing you here!"

6

CAMDEN

I smelled them as soon as I walked in the door.

Archer was my pack mate; I could pick up his scent a mile away. I knew it almost as well as my own. But Marlowe's pistachio and honey perfume was even stronger than it had been that morning, and her arousal was like a punch to the gut. I wanted Archer to win her over, and with his pretty face and calm personality, I knew he was our best shot. But it wasn't *me* bringing out that response in her, and the feeling was more upsetting than I realize it would be.

The pack and I had never dated the same female before – betas weren't made for that, and despite our best efforts to preserve our shifter ways, the disappearance of omegas and our dwindling numbers inevitably meant human culture was going to creep in. We were raised on the virtues of monogamy, and I had long resigned myself to the idea that I'd be settling down with a beta someday.

Not that betas were bad. I had dated a lot of beta females, and some of them I might have even considered marrying.

But thank the Moon I had never pulled that trigger, because now that this sweet omega had walked into my life, I'd never be able to settle for anything less than her. And that meant learning to share.

The look Archer gave me was positively murderous.

Good. He'd had enough alone time with her tonight.

I'd asked Elias to look up as much information on her as he could after she left his office. She'd gotten a master's degree from Stanford, so she must be smart. Maybe that was why she seemed to get along with Elias and Archer so well.

But brains didn't always mean paychecks. I might have looked like the scruffiest out of our pack, but I was actually the wealthiest. Wolfcrest Construction had been started by her dad and mine, and I had been the one in charge of the whole thing for the past few years.

Archer could run a lab, Elias could run a courtroom, and Nolan could run a city council meeting, but me? I ran a multi-million-dollar company. Maybe I couldn't debate politics or literature, but I certainly wasn't dumb.

I needed to start over with her, show her I wasn't a mindless grunt. That I could provide for her, build her a big house with a custom-designed nest, whatever she wanted. Whatever she needed. I'd be her willing slave if she'd let me.

But the look she gave me when she finally found the target of Archer's glare told me I had a lot of work to do.

"Marlowe, Professor! Fancy seeing you here!"

I sat down next to Marlowe and hid the disappointment on my face when she scooted as far away from me as she could. However, the way she was trying to subtly sniff the air, and the wave of her perfume that followed meant she liked the scent I was giving.

Good.

"Camden," Archer said through gritted teeth. "I thought we agreed that you needed to give Marlowe some space."

I ignored him and called to the waitress for a menu. While she made her way over, I looked at the table. "Frozen margaritas? Damn, sounds good."

I ordered three more, along with a carne asada plate and some nachos.

"So," I started. "How much of the lesson have I missed, Professor?"

He let out a low growl and I puffed out my chest in amusement. Riling him up was too easy.

"Why do you call him 'professor'?" Marlowe asked.

She had addressed me, and her tone wasn't dripping with acid. I took a deep breath. This could go well; I just needed to cool it.

"Because he is one. Archer works at UW Eau Claire."

Her eyes lit up, and she turned back to Archer. I quelled the beast inside me that wanted to wrestle for her attention. *Sharing is caring.*

"You are? That's so cool. Which department?"

Archer gave me a smug smile and then looked back at our omega. "Biology," he answered.

She laughed, and the sound sent a wave of pleasure down my

spine. Damn, I wanted to make her laugh like that for me.

"I should have guessed with the way you were talking about shifters. It was a very biological approach. You know, if they were actually real."

Archer cocked an eyebrow and leaned forward. "We are very much real, Marlowe." His voice was so deep and sultry it was almost turning *me* on. "Have you noticed since you arrived this morning how much stronger your sense of smell has become? How you've picked up on scents that seem to attract and entice you from certain males? How you've been eliciting strange reactions from the males around you?"

Marlowe glanced between the two of us nervously, taking a sip of her drink. Her sweet perfume coated the air and Archer and I both shuddered.

"Baby," I whispered. "We can tell how turned on you are, and it's killing us."

She looked at Archer with shock on her face, waiting for him to disagree or tell me off but instead he nodded. "Has your appetite increased? Do you feel flushed? Aroused?"

Marlowe's jaw dropped open and she quickly crossed her legs. What I wouldn't give to feel the way they wrapped around my head...

"Do you take any special pills, Marlowe?" he asked quietly.

"Just birth control," she whimpered. "But I forgot them at home."

Archer and I looked at each other and both swore. "She could go into heat by the morning. We need to get her out of here," he said.

"On it." I took out my phone and headed towards the hall near the bathrooms, where it was a little more private. I flagged down the waitress on the way and told her I wanted my order to go while the phone rang.

"Hey Cam, what's up?"

"We're headed to my cabin. Meet us there."

"Are you kidding me? In this weather? Dude, I finally finished coordinating all the snowplows and road closures. I'm in my sweats, I'm ready to call it a night, and I don't really feel like risking my life just so you can get plastered and snowed in."

I took a deep breath, trying to keep my volume low and out of earshot from any opportunistic alphas who could hear me from the bar. "Linden's daughter is here and she's about to go into heat. She needs a safe place and safe alphas."

"Heat? Wait, she's..."

"Yeah."

He paused, letting the news sink in. "Holy shit, are you sure?"

"Yes!" I said louder. "But she's not ready. This isn't... this isn't that kind of heat, and she doesn't need that kind of help."

I heard a rustling of fabric as he got dressed, switching to speaker phone. "Look, I'm not going to be mad just because I can't get my knot wet, but what do you mean she isn't ready? How old is she? Because if she's like eighteen, I don't really feel comfortable..."

"Gross, she's twenty-six, you pervert."

I heard him scoff, his voice muffled as he responded, "Wait, how does that make *me* the pervert?"

"Anyway," I continued, "it's a long story. We can tell you when we get up there."

Yeah, I was a little disappointed I couldn't get my knot wet either, but I was mostly worried. Marlowe didn't even know what she was, and she'd likely been on hormone suppressants her whole life. Or at least since puberty. She had no idea what was coming for her, and honestly, I was afraid of how we would all react, too. It had been hard enough keeping my hands off her this morning when she hated my guts, but in the middle of her first heat, when she was begging for someone to fuck her? I didn't think even Archer was prim enough to withstand that.

But we had to try. And even if we failed, at least it was us and us alone. If any other pack got a sniff of her here, it could be a bloodbath.

"Alright, I'm leaving now. I don't know how long it's going to take though. I sincerely doubt anyone's cleared the backroads."

"Just get there when you can. Archer thinks we still have til morning, at the earliest."

His front door slammed shut and I heard his car beep. "In that case I'll swing by the store. It should still be open. We're going to need supplies, right?"

Shit, we would, wouldn't we? I had some non-perishables up there, but I didn't think Marlowe would appreciate eating canned beans for a week straight.

"Cookies," I mumbled.

"What?"

Elias had told me about their conversation over breakfast. "She... she likes sweet stuff, get lots of cookies and crap."

Nolan chuckled. "Damn, spoken like a real alpha taking care of his omega. She's already got you wrapped around her finger, doesn't she?"

I huffed. "You're not going to sound so high and mighty once you meet her. Elias nearly killed me this morning."

I would've done the same thing if I'd been in his shoes, but I'd never seen that kind of aggression in Elias's eyes before. Even in high school, when we played football and were nothing but raging bags of hormones, he'd always been Mr. Cool Guy. Seeing him go off the rails and get so messed up over a female was all the proof I needed of the power omegas held over us.

"What the hell, you've all met her already? Why am I the last to even know?" he asked.

"She only arrived this morning, and she's been in Eau Claire this whole time. So like I said, it's a long story and we need to get going ourselves."

"Fine, fine. I'll see you up there with a whole bakery's worth of sugar."

I grinned. I *was* worried, but I also looked forward to the smile on Marlowe's face when she saw how much we wanted to spoil her.

7
MIKE

❖ ⌒⌒ ❖

Grace ground her cunt against my face while Jen rolled her hips along my cock. My balls tightened as Grace moaned, tensing her body while holding onto the headboard, her climax rushing towards her.

"Fuck, yes, Mike, don't stop!"

I nicked her clit with my tooth and lapped up the drops of blood, her thunderous screams spurring me on. Once she finished coming, I pushed her off and then pulled Jen down onto my chest, holding her still as I thrusted up into her furiously.

Her moans were delightful, and I kept up my steady assault. Grace crawled behind her, licking her fingers then pressing them up against Jen's ass.

"Yes, yes, yes!" Jen screamed.

"Yeah, you like that?" I asked, forcing another whimper from her throat.

Hm, it wasn't quite the same pitch as Marlowe, but she was trying. I'd shown the two of them the videos I'd secretly recorded of me and Mar so they could improve their performances.

They also didn't taste as sweet, nor did their cunts wrap around me as nicely.

But that's why Marlowe was my Lunessa.

She was the queen, the one I loved the most, and the rest of the women were brought into my servaglio to fill in the gaps where the Lunessa fell short, or when she needed a break.

Luckily for me, Marlowe's appetite was almost as voracious as mine, so I only needed my servaglio when she wasn't home and for the few acts she wasn't keen on doing.

I'd never given Jen a passing glance at work until about a year ago when I'd brought Marlowe to a company party. She had been drunk, and while Marlowe had been in the bathroom, Jen had told me how attracted she was to the both of us and would have loved to be our unicorn.

Marlowe wasn't ready for that yet, but I certainly had been.

I started fucking her during lunch breaks, and during an eventful business trip to Shanghai, I had revealed what I was and what our relationship would look like if she wanted to continue. Jen was a rare woman - bisexual without a jealous bone in her body. She desired Marlowe as much as she desired me, so she was the perfect second.

Grace had caught my eye about three months earlier, working as the hostess at Marlowe's favorite restaurant. Like Jen, she had seemed interested in the both of us. I had slipped her my number after dinner, and she had stopped by my condo one evening when Marlowe had been out with her friends. Unlike my Lunessa, Grace adored ass play, so after some careful coaching, I welcomed her into my servaglio as my third.

Jen's panting grew more frantic, and Grace's face disappeared between her ample cheeks. I picked up the pace, fucking her with everything I had. She'd take every inch of my cock and every drop of my cum and then thank me for it.

"Yes! Oh fuck, yes, Mike!" she sighed, her orgasm rippling through her. I pushed Grace away and turned Jen around to her back, pushing her knees up to her chest so I could find my own release. From this angle I could hit her even deeper, and I stopped at the grimace of pain that showed on her face.

"Does that hurt?"

She nodded, and a dark grin took over my expression. "Good."

I fucked her even harder until I exploded inside, thrusting my cock as far as it could go. A bead of sweat dropped from my chin onto her cheek, and she wiped it off, licking her finger.

"Now, what do you say?" I smirked.

Jen gave me a blissful smile. "Thank you, master."

Perfect. I grabbed her hair again and leaned down, slamming my mouth onto hers. Our tongues wrapped around each other's hungrily, and then I moved my lips down her neck. The hard pulse of her vein called to me, and my canines grew in hunger.

"Please," she begged.

My teeth sank into her neck and she moaned, another orgasm rippling through her. Her blood was bitter and somewhat earthy, like a good IPA. Once I closed her wound, I beckoned Grace over, taking her wrist and sniffing it, watching as her mouth parted and her eyes glazed over, waiting for my bite and her own venture into oblivion. With one tooth, I drew a line, licking up the dark drops as her knees buckled, threatening to collapse.

My vigor and energy returned, but I was still feeling unsated. They'd never be enough on their own, I needed my Lunessa.

I'd snuck little sips from her here and there when I could, when she was either too sleepy, drunk, or high to notice, but I hadn't fully drawn from her yet. Once she was locked down, once she was mine forever, I'd start bringing her more fully into my world. She wasn't ready to know what she and I were yet, and she certainly wasn't ready to meet the rest of my servaglio.

Our servaglio.

I had known she was a shifter from the moment I'd seen her at that networking party. Our kinds had never really gotten along, and if my father knew what she was, he'd refuse to have anything to do with me anymore. In fact, I had planned to avoid her entirely that first night. But then her scent had made its way across the room, my cock hardening and teeth growing in response.

Once I had gotten closer, I had realized she smelled so enticing because she was a rare omega, and had been completely oblivious to the fact. It was then I knew I had to have her. Not only because it meant one less jewel for those filthy mutts, but because she was also every bit as delicious as the stories claimed. I might not have been an alpha or had a knot, but her sweet perfume and ravenous libido, even with suppressants, were like no other.

I had avoided meeting her mother – given she had been the one supplying Marlowe with her "birth control pills," she would have known what I was immediately, but I was thankful for her help in keeping my Lunessa hidden from her people. So I could enjoy her all by myself.

Did the vampyrs of old know the pleasures of having an omega in their servaglios? Surely, I couldn't have been the first one to have figured it out.

I supposed in the past it had been difficult obtaining one, though. Omegas had been guarded as a precious resource fiercely by shifters and typically bonded to a whole pack once they reached the age of maturity. Their sex drives were so ravenous they needed several males just to satisfy them.

Whereas vampyrs like myself were the opposite. We usually required at least five women in our servaglio to tend to our outsized libidos. With Mar's appetite I could make do with as little as three, but I knew it wasn't in her nature to share a male with other women.

Just like it wasn't in mine to share with other males.

Hearing of her experiences with those men, undoubtedly alpha males from the sound of it, in Wisconsin worried me. I'd reluctantly let her go into shifter territory to deal with her dad's death. I really should have gone with her, not just because it was hard to go even a day without fucking her, but because I was worried someone might figure out what she was.

But she had her pills, and was already figuring out a way home, so she should be fine. Plus, it also meant I had some free time to service Jen and Grace. I neglected them more than was appropriate since Marlowe was enough, but I could see it on their eager faces just how much they missed me.

Jen in particular was tired of waiting and desperately wanted me to finally bring my Lunessa into the fold. Not just since it would mean no more sneaking around and hiding for us – she was also dying to fuck her, even though I had warned her that Mar didn't seem too interested in women.

"She'll love us, you know," Jen said as she cleaned herself up. "I'm a professional pussy eater. And if she tastes as sweet as she smells…" She picked up one of Mar's dirty shirts from the laundry hamper and inhaled deeply.

Watching my servaglio get turned on by each other made me harder than anything. I came up behind her, grinding my cock against the small of her back while I kneaded her breasts. I imagined the three of them with me, my ultimate fantasy. "Even sweeter," I sighed.

Grace huffed. "I don't know why you're so obsessed with her, Jen. Yeah, she's cute, but it sounds like she's a total pillow princess."

A hiss escaped my lips as I turned around, my vision blurring around the edges. "What did you say?"

She swallowed nervously, trying to laugh her comment off. "Oh, just… you know, she just seems like she's too good to…"

I grabbed her by the throat and slammed her into the wall. "Too good for what?"

The absolute nerve of this woman, to insinuate anything about Marlowe. My love.

Jen grabbed my shoulder, trying to pull me off. "She didn't

mean it, Mike. Grace is just a little jealous. Who wouldn't want to be your Lunessa?"

Her pleading failed to sway me. Jealousy in a servaglio was a poison. I'd watched it destroy my brother's life, when his Lunessa was murdered in her sleep by his number two. He had destroyed all six remaining women, needing to start from scratch, and had never been the same again.

Grace desperately pulled at my hands, and I brought my lips to her ear. "You are not half the woman my Lunessa is. You are replaceable, and she is my goddess. If I hear one more unkind word towards her come out of your mouth, I will bleed you dry and throw your emaciated corpse into the bay. Do you understand?"

She nodded, her face turning purple.

I finally released her, and she crumpled on the floor, gasping for breath.

What made her insult even more infuriating was how untrue it was. Out of my checklist of sexual requirements, Marlowe met nearly every one.

Enthusiastic? Check.

Good at oral? Check.

Always willing? Check.

Into role-play? Check, I'd recently discovered. My cock hardened at the memory of the slutty maid's costume she'd bought for our anniversary. Yes, it was cliché, but she had never broken character. I couldn't wait to explore more with her.

Jen wrapped her arms around my neck and tried to take my attention away from Grace, getting my focus back on her. This was why she was a good number two, she was born to play peacemaker. "Have you showered since the last time you and Marlowe fucked? Maybe I can still taste her on you."

I chuckled. "You can certainly try." I grabbed her hair and helped push her down to her knees. Her tongue eagerly lapped the head of my dick, and I smiled in adoration as her lips opened and took me in. Was there any greater joy than watching a woman devour your cock?

I relaxed as she sucked the anger out of me, pulling me further into her mouth. I was about to close my eyes and think about my Lunessa when a corner of white plastic caught my eye, sticking out from underneath the dresser. It looked familiar.

The blood drained out of my face and I yanked Jen off me. "Ow – Mike, what's wrong?"

"Shut up!" I yelled, getting down on my hands and knees to

grab the small container. I inspected it carefully. "Is this…"

Jen shrugged. "Looks like birth control pills. Marlowe's out of town though, right? Just use condoms for a week or so when she gets back, you'll be fine."

"No," I spat. "It's not fine, you fucking idiot. These are the pills that keep her hidden from other shifters." I waved them in her face and then threw them across the room. "Without them she's a walking bucket of chum, and every alpha in the state is about to go into a feeding frenzy."

I needed to get her.

Now.

8
MARLOWE

Archer and Camden stood on either side of me as we headed to my room in the elevator. I didn't want to believe shifters were real, but Archer had described my symptoms so accurately it was scary. I knew something had felt off about me ever since I had arrived here.

I *was* becoming more sensitive to smells, I *was* ravenously hungry, and I *was* insanely horny. If I didn't know any better, I'd think I might be pregnant. But I took my birth control religiously.

Well, until this morning that is.

The birth control pills, that had to be it. I vaguely remembered feeling strange like this when I was near the end of high school, when my mom had first gotten them for me.

I was just suffering from not taking the pills, that was all. That had to be it. If I could just find a pharmacy...

But Archer and Camden had insisted we needed to leave. "If you think that man who approached you before I arrived was bad, you have no idea what's going to happen if we don't get you out of this hotel before your heat starts."

"Heat? Come on, you can't be serious." Yeah, I was strangely turned on, but who wouldn't be with the attention of a couple of hot guys? Calling it a "heat" was too much. I wasn't an animal; it was just side effects from the hormone withdrawal.

Right?

Camden pressed the emergency stop on the elevator and I lurched into him. "I know you still don't think our world is real, but just... trust me for a second," he said, his voice hypnotically husky as he took my hand. "I shouldn't have done this at Elias's office, but it might be the only way to prove it to you."

Archer growled behind me and Camden snapped at him. "Sometimes we need physical proof, and you should know that as a fucking scientist."

He raised his hands in defeat and Camden's eyes dropped back to mine. "I'm sorry." He unbuckled his pants and shoved my hand onto his dick. I tried to pull it away but he held my wrist tightly. "Does that feel human to you?" he said carefully, closing his eyes as he swallowed.

"This is assault! Let me go!" I struggled against him, waiting for Archer to step in but he just sighed behind me.

"I'm sorry, Marlowe. Perhaps you should touch him."

Wrong. This was so wrong, for so many reasons. But they weren't going to let me go until I gave Camden a hand job in this elevator apparently. Why was I such an idiot? I was leading two men I didn't know back to my hotel room. Men who had made it clear they were into me.

Seriously, what did I think was going to happen?

I held back the tears that had sprung to the corners of my eyes and relaxed my fingers, allowing him to rub them against the base of his cock. I just needed to get this over with, get out of this space with them and try to call 911 or get someone's attention.

Only something about it *was* different – the bottom of his shaft was almost swollen to two times his girth. I looked up at Camden in shock, his eyes still closed. He breathed heavily and licked his lips.

"It's called a knot, baby. All alpha males have them. And your body is designed to take them."

I whimpered at the thought of it, and suddenly a gush of liquid came pouring out of me and into my underwear. My body felt feverish, and my hand tightened around Camden's dick. My mind cleared of all thoughts except one.

Sex.

I needed sex now, and I wanted it with these two.

A high-pitched whine escaped my lips, and I pushed myself against Camden, desperately trying to touch his skin.

He released my hand and held still, his body tense while Archer grabbed my arms and pulled them behind me.

"Please," I begged. "I can't explain it, but if someone doesn't fuck me right now…"

I had tunnel vision, and it went straight to Camden's crotch. I

51

just wanted to feel him inside me, as though it was all I'd ever wanted, all I'd ever needed. My body was an empty vessel, waiting to be filled.

"Shh…" Archer purred. The vibration soothed me, and I relaxed into him. "You're going into heat, Marlowe."

No. No, no, no. Heat for humans wasn't real. This didn't make any sense. More liquid dripped out of me and I whined again.

"Fuck, Archer," Camden groaned, his pants still undone. He gripped the side rails of the elevator, his knuckles turning white. "I don't know if I can do this."

Archer continued purring. "Get yourself together. She needs us. Can you think of anyone else you'd trust to take care of her right now?"

My mind was a wanton mess as I tried to concentrate on the words Archer was saying. Care… who… what? But when I felt his hardened cock behind me, I blanked, and the all-encompassing need for sex took over.

"Archer," I whimpered. "I need you…"

A shudder went through his body, and he started purring again. "I've got you, don't worry. We're going to help you and make sure you get through this without violating your trust."

"I don't care!" I cried. Trust? Trust for what? I wanted to know what that knot felt like, I wanted to feel it from both of them. "Violate me all you want. I need you inside me!"

Camden banged his head against the wall and Archer moaned, his grip on my arms tightening. Then he shook his head. "No, Marlowe. Not like this."

The next few hours were a blur. I vaguely recalled sitting on Archer's lap in my room while he held me and purred, watching Camden struggle to gather and pack my things. In my desperation to find my pills earlier, I'd made quite the mess, and it was taking him a while to get everything back in my bags. Especially since every few minutes, he'd double over as though he were in pain, clutching his cock through his pants.

Next thing I knew we were in a truck, Camden cursing as he drove through the snow. Archer continued to hold me as he purred nonstop, which kept some of the stronger urges at bay. But I had soaked through my pants, forcing them to open the windows for fresh air.

"You don't smell bad," Archer insisted, running his hand down my hair. "Quite the opposite, in fact."

Somewhere along the way we had picked up Elias, and Archer handed me over to him in the back of the cab, while he took deep pulls of the fresh, cold air, his body shaking from the effort.

"Hey there, California," Elias purred. In all the frenzy, I'd almost forgotten how gorgeous he was, and traced the outlines of his jaw with my fingers while I sat on his lap.

"Are you going to fuck me?" I asked. I took one of his hands and guided it down my pants.

He jerked it away quickly, and I watched his Adam's apple bob in his throat. "I want to, more than anything, but you'll hate me if I do. Why don't you tell me about your fiancé instead?"

Mike? Why should I think about him? I didn't want to think about the dick that was too far away, I wanted to ride the dicks that were right here! And they had *knots*!

Elias purred again, and I took a deep breath, trying to focus. "Mike... we met in Palo Alto. He's in tech. He works at a start-up."

Camden snorted from the driver's seat. "Figures..." he muttered.

Elias ignored him. "What does he look like?"

Why was it so hard to conjure up his image? Every time I tried to think of the love of my life, one of the three men in the truck popped up instead. I reached back further, recalling the way he looked on the day he had proposed.

"He's tall, with black hair and pale skin. His eyes... they're beautiful."

I remembered him now. He was gorgeous, too, and amazing in bed. Another stream of liquid came out of me and Elias tensed, moaning softly.

"Dude!" Camden yelled. "Why are you trying to get her turned on? I'm going to crash."

Elias closed his eyes, his breathing shallow. "Sorry, I thought... it was an experiment. It failed. I know better now."

I should have been embarrassed by how wet I was, it looked like I had peed my pants. But for some reason all it did was turn me on more. I quickly maneuvered myself around Elias so I was straddling him. I wrapped my arms around his neck and started grinding myself against his hardened cock, and he pursed his lips.

"Guys, I don't think I'm going to make it," he said, his voice strained.

I wasn't either – because if I didn't get fucked soon, I was pretty sure I was going to die.

All the windows in the truck lowered completely and I cried out from the sudden blast of cold air. Elias pulled me in tightly so I couldn't move and began purring loudly.

My grinding stopped, and I relaxed into his embrace.

"Sweet Moon, thank you," he whispered.

The smell of bergamot reminded me of Earl Grey tea, and I let out a satisfied sigh as I closed my eyes.

9

NOLAN

"That'll be $456.79."

I tapped my card against the chip reader and grinned at the cashier. I hadn't stopped grinning since I'd gotten the call from Cam.

She eyed the groceries amused. "Stocking up?"

"Yeah, you never know in a storm like this," I chuckled. I started packing everything carefully, making sure to put the meat in different bags than the Oreos and Sour Patch Kids.

After loading everything in the trunk, I set out for Cam's cabin. On a good day, it took two hours to get there from Maiingan Hollow, but in a storm like this? I'd be lucky to make it by dawn.

I cracked open one of the energy drinks I'd just bought and turned the volume on the stereo way up, blasting my road trip playlist.

An *omega*. I was still reeling from the news. Linden's daughter was an omega – unbonded from the sound of it, and going through her first heat. And we were the lucky alphas to help her out.

Well, not in the way I wanted to. My cock was already hard and I willed it to calm down.

I didn't even know what she looked like yet, for Moon's sake. Or if she was cool, or even wanted any of us. And we certainly weren't going to take advantage of her just for the experience.

But if we came out the other end of this and she did decide to bond with our pack... It had seemed like an impossible dream to even consider that we'd have an omega of our own someday. Maiingan Hollow was a special enclave just for shifters, and from what I'd gathered talking to the village heads of similar communities, omegas had disappeared everywhere. Just like our ability to shift into our inner wolves, it was a vital part of our biology and identity that we'd lost in the past century.

We could survive without shifting and without omegas, but those two experiences were supposedly the greatest joys in an alpha's life. I felt like I'd been cheated out of my true purpose, no matter how fulfilling my job as mayor was. My bed was empty and at night, my chest ached, a deep longing punctuating every moment I was alone.

But that could soon change. If my pack did this right, we could have our very own omega.

My house was old and had been built by the alpha who had first founded our town. The nest room had been converted to a storage closet ever since I'd moved in, and I couldn't wait to finally use it for its intended purpose.

But in my rush to leave, I didn't even think to clear it out at all. We could set up a temporary nest in my room until we redecorated, since that room was the warmest. I didn't mind sleeping in one of the guest bedrooms or even the couch until then.

I laughed, surprised at how far ahead of myself I was getting. Camden had the biggest house, with room not just for a nest but the whole pack. It made way more sense for us all to move into his place.

Maybe this would finally bring Elias back home, too. There was no way he'd be able to handle living in Chicago if he had an omega back up here.

I upped the speed on my windshield wipers and groaned to myself. The roads were worse than I had thought, and I fought back my instinct to rush. If I went too fast and spun out, I'd get there even later.

Slow and steady – pretty much the opposite mantra of an alpha shifter, but it would have to be mine tonight if I wanted to meet her.

I sang along to "Back in Black" by AC/DC, wondering what kind of music she liked. I'd love to make a playlist for her, something we could listen to together.

Visibility was piss poor, but I knew these roads like the back of my hand. I chugged the rest of my energy drink, rolled down my window, and howled into the snowy abyss.

10
ARCHER

Marlowe was still asleep when we pulled up outside of Camden's cabin nestled deep in the north woods.

We were all on edge, especially Camden after driving the whole distance himself. I had offered several times to take over, but he had refused to let anyone else drive his "baby." I had thought he was referring to his truck at first, but he pet Marlowe reverently, kissing her on the forehead as we made our way inside.

Reading about the effects of an omega's heat was one thing, but experiencing them was something else entirely. My cock was in pain, my erection having lasted hours. The rest of the pack was just as bad off as I was, and we grumbled about needing to take long showers, making sure not to wake Marlowe.

Elias carried her into one of the bedrooms, laying her down gently. We watched as she winced, her arms searching for the heat of an alpha now absent from her touch.

"Go take care of yourself," I whispered to him. "I can handle omega duty for the next few hours."

"We should watch her in pairs."

Elias and I turned around to Camden, who stood with his arms crossed as he gazed at her. His focus snapped back to us while we waited for an explanation. "At least I'm honest enough to admit I can't be trusted alone in here, something you two haven't yet. We need to be ready to pull each other off her if we feel the urge to rut."

"Who would have thought Cam would be the voice of reason tonight?" Elias smirked, his hand absentmindedly grabbing his crotch.

57

Camden snorted and rolled his eyes. "Whatever. Go blow your load in the shower. Just make sure you clean it up, though. I don't want to be scraping cum off the walls all week."

Elias raised his eyebrow. "Aye aye, captain. Thanks for the permission to jack off."

Marlowe stirred and Elias grimaced, closing the door silently behind him while he left to find some relief.

I took off my shoes and crawled into the bed next to her. She sought me out immediately, her hands grabbing my arms and pulling me close. I settled her into my chest, purring her and myself into a blissful sleep.

"Which one of you bitches is going to help me with all these groceries?" Nolan yelled out cheerfully.

It must have been around four or five in the morning, and before any of us could warn him, Marlowe's eyes shot open and she sniffed the air. She must have been pleased with Nolan's scent because she soon released a wave of her own. I cringed at the sound of bags dropping, his heavy footsteps running down the hall as Camden crouched, ready to pounce. He burst into the room, his face glazed over with lust.

Marlowe raised herself up on her elbows, biting her lip and whining sweetly. Camden tackled Nolan to the ground before he could jump on top of her. Nolan was fighting and kicking like a wildcat while Camden dragged him out.

"I told you, no knotting!" he yelled.

Nolan roared, too far gone to articulate a response.

Not that he needed to say anything. We all knew exactly how he was feeling.

Elias got up from where he had passed out and raced down to help subdue our pack mate.

Meanwhile Marlowe had turned into her own version of feral in my arms. Despite her lack of strength, she was much harder to subdue than the raging alpha in the living room. My cock felt like it was going to explode, her pheromones driving me crazy. Her thighs were still covered in slick, and I felt the need to rut start to come forward. My vision blurred, focusing only on the omega pinned beneath me, and I growled.

"Guys... I need your help here!"

Camden came rushing back in, putting his arms around my waist and yanking me off the mewling omega.

"Please!" she begged. "Why won't you fuck me? I need you!"

Nolan roared again, and I heard the sound of bodies falling and furniture scraping across the floor.

What a disaster. Why did any of us think we could handle this?

"My bag!" Elias yelled from the other room, where he was fighting off Nolan. "I have something that might help!"

I ripped myself away and dashed towards the second bedroom, dumping out Elias's duffle in a heap on the floor. Mixed in with his clothes something fell with a *thunk*, and I dug out the silicone object.

A vibrator? I breathed a sigh of relief. "Elias, you're a genius!"

I ran back to her bedroom, where Camden was attempting to settle her back down to the point that a purr could calm her. Instead, I took off her wet jeans.

"Dude, what the fuck?" Camden asked. "We said…"

"I know what we said!" I yelled back. The scent of her slick filled the air, and I slipped her panties off next.

I took a moment to compose myself, as Camden closed his eyes and tried his best to disassociate from the situation.

She was completely drenched, and my mouth suddenly felt parched. All I wanted was to wrap her creamy thighs around my head and lick her clean.

I slapped myself in the face.

Focus!

Clicking the vibrator on, I brought it down to her clit, slowly circling around her perfect bud. She sighed sweetly, grinding her hips against the toy.

"Wha…" Camden had stopped pretending he was somewhere else and now watched in awe. "I… does this count? As not…"

"Shhh…" I replied. "Maybe it's a gray area if we're holding it, but we're not going to survive if she doesn't get any relief."

He swallowed the lump in his throat and slid down the bed, his attention focused on the vibrator now pumping slowly in and out of her perfect pussy.

Marlowe arched her back, panting heavily. "Yes," she moaned. "More, I need more!"

I grabbed her hand and guided it towards the toy. "Do you want to try?"

She bit her lip, writhing in pleasure as she took her hand back, gripping the sheets below her and shaking her head.

"I need your spoken confirmation, Marlowe," I said, my voice low and controlled. "Who do you want holding the vibrator – me or you?"

"You," she whined. "Archer, I want you."

My breath hitched, and I didn't think it was possible, but her words got me even harder.

I slid it in further, careful not to brush her skin with my fingers. I watched as she closed her eyes, her lids fluttering and lips parting when I brushed the toy past her G-spot.

Her hips bucked, and her panting grew more frantic. From the base of the vibrator, I could feel her pussy clench, and she moaned as an orgasm rippled through her body. Then she collapsed, a deep sleep claiming her almost immediately.

Camden blinked a few times, then dug through the closet behind him, soon bringing out a blanket. He covered her bare bottom half.

"I need… a shower."

He stumbled out of the room like a zombie, and Elias held Nolan by the scruff of his neck, entering in after him.

"I'm so sorry," Nolan whispered. "I had no idea…"

"It's okay. I don't think any of us really did. You're just the unlucky bastard who got hit with a full wave of it. The three of us have been with her during the build up, so we were only marginally more prepared." I gestured towards Elias. "Good thinking with the vibrator. Did you know it was invented by a shifter?"

He raised an eyebrow. "Is that right?"

"Human history says a doctor invented it to cure female hysteria, but that was an easy cover for the truth. What female is more in hysterical need of release than an omega in heat?"

11
MIKE

I slammed my fist down on the counter, causing the gate agent to flinch. "What do you mean it's full?" I yelled.

She cleared her throat, avoiding my gaze to look at the screen while her fingers flew across the keyboard.

"I'm sorry, sir, but with the holiday weekend and the storms, there's simply no way to get you on the next flight."

I pinched the bridge of my nose in frustration, releasing a throaty groan. I'd flown to Dallas, then to Denver, where I was supposed to get a flight to Minneapolis and then another to Chippewa Valley Regional Airport, but those had both now been cancelled.

"Get me to Chicago or Milwaukee, then" I replied. "I'll drive from there."

After another few minutes of rapid-fire keystrokes, she looked down in terrified defeat. "The earliest I can get you there is Tuesday," she reported in a timid voice.

I bit down the urge to reach over the counter and wring her worthless neck, taking a deep breath instead and employing a more "compelling" approach.

"*Hannah*," I purred, looking at her name tag. Her eyes fluttered warily towards mine, and I kept her locked in my stare. "*Hannah, sweetheart, you'd do anything to help me, wouldn't you?*"

Her mouth opened slightly and she nodded.

"*Good, perfect. Now, I need you to get me as close to Eau Claire as you possibly can, as soon as you possibly can. You'll even bump someone off a flight for me, won't you?*"

"Yes," she replied breathily. "I'll do anything to help you."

Her dilated eyes returned to her screen, and within a minute she was printing a boarding pass for a flight to Chicago that was departing in forty minutes.

"Thank you, Hannah. You're such a good girl."

She nodded, and now that my anger was subsiding, I noticed the nice shape under her uniform. That red scarf around her neck was quite convenient, too.

"Hannah, you're going to take your break, and meet me in the family restroom by the Newsstand in five minutes. Do you understand?"

"Yes."

I snatched my boarding pass and walked off, delighting in the groans of frustration that grew as Hannah set a placard on the desk informing the line she'd be back in fifteen minutes.

Just a quick snack, and then I'd be on my way to my Lunessa.

12
ELIAS

We'd arrived at the cabin in the early hours on Saturday, and Archer confirmed on Monday evening that Marlowe had likely gotten over the worst of it.

"I give it one, maybe two more days. Tops," he mumbled, shuffling into the kitchen and pouring himself a cup of coffee. The nights blended into the days, and time had ceased having meaning. The only thing that mattered was whether she was awake or not.

When she was up, her heat consumed her. Full body spasms and panting until Archer took out the vibrator and helped her come.

He insisted on being the only one to use it, which angered us all at first. Especially me, since I had been the only one with the foresight to bring it. But his argument was sound – "I'm pretty sure I'm the one she trusts the most out of the pack, and when she snaps out of this, she won't feel as used as she would have if we'd all just taken turns. We need to make this feel as clinical as possible."

When she'd finally pass out from exhaustion, she'd sleep fitfully, tossing and turning unless she was in one of our arms, purring her into a state of calm and serenity. For that, we did take turns, and I'd never felt more at peace. Even if I was in a constant state of priapism, being in her presence was like nothing I'd ever felt before. Suddenly, I had purpose, reason, goals. I'd expand my firm, get a bigger place, build her a proper nest, eat healthier, learn how to bake… all my plans for the future laid themselves out seamlessly, as though I'd just been waiting for the right catalyst to put my life together.

I was a ship unmoored, finally finding my harbor. And her

name was Marlowe.

Unfortunately, I also had work. I took another bite of my cereal as I cleaned out my inbox. I had a few important cases that really couldn't be put off, but everything else, I put on the back burner or passed onto my partners or associates. James Linden had been one of our biggest clients, so it was easy to fudge the truth and say I was still up here dealing with his estate. They might have been less grumbly if I mentioned we'd found an omega, but it didn't feel right announcing Marlowe's existence before she would even accept it, or could become bonded to a pack for her protection.

And we would do whatever it took to make sure she chose us.

It was Nolan's turn to sleep next to her, and now that I was caught up somewhat on work, I had some free time to research the human who was standing in our way.

The rational part of my brain knew it was wrong to try to break them up, that Marlowe loved him, and he was in all likelihood a nice guy. Hell, if it was possible to let a human join a shifter pack, I might allow it just so it meant our omega could become ours.

But humans weren't the sharing type, regardless of their newfound "discovery" of polyamorous relationships. Besides, that wasn't what an alpha and omega pack really was, anyway. We loved one female, one omega, and she loved her alphas back. That was it.

His Facebook and Instagram profiles were set to private, and both profile pictures were just stupid landscapes. My lip curled in disgust. If I was engaged to a creature as lovely as Marlowe, she'd be the subject of all my photos. Not some stupid beach.

He *was* the kind of douchey guy to have a robust LinkedIn account, though. Professional headshot, lots of posts patting himself on the back for how hard he was "grinding," endless jargon and buzzwords, and plenty of name dropping.

Ugh, these kinds of guys were the worst. And Marlowe liked him?

Nope, no way. I wasn't going to get jealous about this. You didn't win hearts by bad mouthing the competition, you did so by proving how great you were all on your own.

I left the site and went to Amazon, ordering boxes of her favorite tea, sweatpants emblazoned with the word "California," and the fluffiest blankets I could find. When this was over, we'd take her back to Maiingan Hollow – to Cam's house, since his was the biggest. She could stay there as long as she liked while she sorted out what being an omega shifter meant now and what she wanted to do about her inheritance.

A soft whine floated through the air, breaking the silence. My cock instantly hardened, and Archer sighed contentedly. "Well, back to work, I guess," he said with a smile.

"Yeah, don't look so glum about it, asshole," I muttered, getting up to put my empty bowl in the dishwasher.

He whistled a jaunty tune and headed back to Marlowe's room, closing the door behind him. I quietly followed, and leaned against it with my ear, hanging on every word.

"Archer, please…"

"I'm right here, don't worry. It's almost over."

I placed my forehead and palm on the door, biting my lip and stroking my dick through my pants as the buzzing started and she began to moan. Fuck, I couldn't wait until I was the one causing her to make those sounds.

I finally resigned myself to another lonely date with my hand in the shower, and headed towards the bathroom once more.

13
MARLOWE

I woke up in a room I didn't recognize, in clothes that weren't mine, next to a man who wasn't my fiancé.

Camden stirred with me, stretching and yawning by my side. "Mornin', baby. Do you need me to get Archer?"

"Wha…?" I was flooded with fragmented memories of the past few days. Flashes of me out of my mind with horniness, begging for cock. I cringed from embarrassment but also fear – had any of these men actually fucked me?

I remembered Archer had taken the edge off with a sex toy, but I didn't think anyone had actually touched me, aside from cuddling. Mike and I had had some wild, weekend-long sex marathons before, and I had usually felt quite sore afterwards.

Aside from dirty and hungry, I seemed to be fine down there.

But whatever had happened wasn't okay, and I certainly wouldn't have been fine if Mike had done that to another woman, I knew that.

"Oh god…" I whimpered, covering my face with my hands. "What have I done?"

Camden sat up, his eyes sad and filled with concern. "Hey, hey, Marlowe, this isn't your fault. You didn't do anything wrong. We tried to tell you about the heat…"

"Heat?" I yelled, scrambling away from him. "You guys must have drugged me. What happened – that's not natural!"

I stumbled out of the bed, my legs weak, and rushed out the door and down a hall. I came into a large living room and open kitchen in an A-frame building. A winter wonderland outside tall windows took my breath away, and I saw Archer and Elias sitting on a plush couch working on laptops, while a third man I didn't know watched TV.

They all stood as they realized it was me, and Archer cleared his throat cautiously. "Marlowe, how are you feeling?"

My heart raced, and I wrapped my arms around my chest. I wore a large t-shirt bearing the logo for Wolfcrest Construction and nothing else. Several days' worth of sweat covered my skin, my hair was disgustingly greasy, and my mouth was dry.

"How long?" I asked quietly.

Elias took a tentative step forward, while the third man rubbed the back of his neck.

"How. Long?" I asked again, punctuating each word.

"About four and a half days," Archer responded. "It's Wednesday morning."

A shuddering breath slammed through me and my knees buckled. Elias caught me before I could fall, but I screamed and pushed him away, backing up into the wall. I slid down it until I landed on the floor

"What the hell did you guys do to me? Heats aren't real. You must have slipped something into my drink!"

Camden came up to my side, sitting down next to me. "You really think there's a drug that can do all that? Think about it, babe."

Since when was he some voice of reason?

I sniffed, then closed my eyes and went through the date-rape drugs I'd studied. As far as I knew, none of them really made someone that deliriously horny.

Maybe they'd given me MDMA? But that only lasted a few hours, and the few times I'd tried it, it had mostly just made me touchy-feely.

Besides, if a drug that turned people into wanton messes for half a week straight existed, I definitely would have heard about it through my job at a woman's advocacy nonprofit.

The man I didn't know sighed and walked into the kitchen. "I'm making breakfast. Who wants some?"

My stomach rumbled like I hadn't eaten in days. If what I had pieced together from my flashes of memory were correct, then that was likely the case.

He grinned, pointing a spatula at me. "Pancakes?"

I nodded slightly, and he slapped a dish towel over his shoulder as he grabbed a bowl and whisk, turning on a Bluetooth

67

speaker.

Smooth reggae beats filled the room and Camden stood up, offering me his hands. "Here, let me show you where the bathroom is. I bet you wanna take a shower, right?"

My bottom lip trembled and I nodded again, letting him help me. I left Archer and Elias in the living room and followed Camden down the wood-paneled hall. "This is my cabin," he explained. "The pack and I come up here every once in a while to drink, let off some steam, and be idiots."

How idiotic? Like kidnap-a-drugged-woman-and-rape-her idiotic?

I wanted to be furious, but once the initial fear, anger, and confusion over my situation faded, my gut began to whisper to me that these guys hadn't tried to take advantage of me in my frenzied state. Not one memory of someone's cock inside me, or a hand on my breasts, or a mouth on my skin. The vibrator, yes, but I also remembered begging to be fucked, and Archer cooly and calmly asking for my consent each time to help me get off with a toy instead.

I attempted to calm down, taking note of the pictures of the four of them over the years that hung on the walls. "How did you meet?" I asked.

Camden opened a closet and took out a towel, handing it to me with a proud smile on his face. "We played football together in high school."

I hugged the towel to my chest and stopped at a photo of the four of them in their uniforms, looking like they probably won a four-way tie for prom king. Meanwhile, when I was in high school, I'd been busy doing stuff like organizing a school walk-out over dress code policies that discriminated against female students.

"Elias was the quarterback, Nolan and I were linebackers, and Archer was a wide receiver."

I raised my eyebrow. "You say that like it means something."

He pursed his lips in mock anger and messed up my hair even further than it already was. "Yeah, yeah, insert joke here about peaking in high school, whatever. I bet you were valedictorian or something really nerdy."

I pushed the bridge of pretend glasses up my nose. "Um, actually, I was the salutatorian…"

"Ugh," he groaned. "Of course. You got salutatorian written all over you."

I laughed. A real, genuine laugh. I didn't know why I wasn't feeling more traumatized. And why I found it so easy to joke around with Camden.

Or why I still found him so sexy.

For now, at least, I could trust them. I *had* to trust them, if I was ever going to make it back to civilization.

"Oh crap," I realized. "I haven't talked to Mike in days. He's gotta be out of his mind. Do you have cell service up here?"

A low growl reverberated out of his chest, but he shook it out. "No, but I have Wi-Fi. I think your phone's dead, but I'm sure one of the pack will let you use their computers if you want to email him. Now that your heat is over, we're going to head to my place in Maiingan Hollow so you can figure out your next move. Whether that's heading straight back to San Fran, or working with Elias and me to figure out what to do about your dad's half of the company, or whatever."

"Okay, first of all…" I held up one finger. "… don't call it San Fran, and two…" I held up another. "… I thought you didn't want to share the company with a, what did you call me, 'beta female?'"

He grabbed my fingers and sighed. "Look, I may have *overreacted* a touch when I found out your dad's half was going to his daughter who I'd never met and assumed didn't know jack shit about construction, rather than to me, like he'd hinted at over the years."

I swallowed the lump in my throat, my fingers still in his hand. "My dad promised you the whole company?"

"Argh," he grunted, rubbing his head in frustration. "More or less. I knew he had kids, but he never talked about you, and he treated me like his son most of the time. Especially after my old man died. It's complicated."

Complicated indeed. Had my dad been super old school and "manly," wanting someone like Camden as a son versus Ezra or an omega daughter?

But Ezra had been super masculine and would have easily been friends with this group. He had played a ton of sports in high school and had been bigger than all these guys. Besides, my dad had left when we were four, before he could have even known what Ezra and I were like.

And then why would he have ultimately given me, his daughter, his half of the company anyway?

None of this was making sense.

I looked back at the photo of the four boys, now men, now an "alpha pack," and asked quietly. "So do you still want it?"

He took a step closer, his jaw set tight as his eyes inspected every inch of my face. "If not having it means you'll be in my life, I'd much rather you keep it. Even if I'm just CC-ing you on emails you'll never reply to, even if you're just Zooming into board meetings once or twice a year, it's worth it."

My heart raced, and he leaned down, nestling his nose in the crook of my neck as he inhaled deeply.

"Why?" I asked, my voice a hoarse whisper. "You barely even know me."

His finger lightly ran down my arm, and I bit back a gasp, squeezing the towel tighter.

"I don't think you're ready for that answer yet. Not until you can accept what you are."

He pulled back and our eyes locked, his baby blues slowly losing the battle to his dilating pupils. His gaze fell towards my lips, and my lashes fluttered as his face grew closer.

"Cam!" a voice barked from the kitchen. "Let her take a shower, for Moon's sake."

He exhaled deeply, giving me a quick kiss on my forehead. "Use whatever you want in there, babe."

Then he slapped me on the ass and walked back towards the living room.

Dammit, that was close. *Too* close. And with Camden, of all people. If it had been a drug or a weird hormone imbalance from the birth control pills that had caused my four-day horny black-out, there were likely still traces lingering in my system and I would need to be careful.

I stepped under the rainfall showerhead and smiled when I noticed the brand-new pink bottles of floral shampoo and conditioner.

After thoroughly cleansing my hair and skin, I stepped out and wrapped the towel around my body, realizing I had no idea where my stuff was. When I opened the bathroom door, I found someone had left my suitcase in the hall for me while I'd been showering. I dug out some sweatpants and my favorite Stanford sweatshirt, and then padded barefoot into the kitchen.

The smell of bacon and butter drew me in, and Elias, Archer, and Camden were all sitting at the table, happily scarfing everything down.

"There's a chair over here for you," said the man I didn't know. He carried over the frying pan, adding more pancakes to the stack on the central platter. "I'm Nolan, by the way. Nolan Wilk. We uh, didn't get a chance to talk much, but I came here just a little after you all arrived."

Like the others he was tall, at least three or four inches over six feet. His dark brown hair was cut stylishly, with bangs falling adorably into his equally dark brown eyes. I admired the way his large, muscular frame moved around the kitchen with grace and ease. He leaned closer as he added some strips of bacon to my plate, and his scent of bourbon and vanilla triggered a memory of him cuddled up next to me, purring while he ran his fingers through my hair and told me how he wanted to take care of me.

My stomach was a jumble of knots, and I mumbled my thank you as I shoved a bite of pancake into my mouth.

Camden laughed. "That's four for four!"

Elias elbowed him in the chest, and I looked up from my plate. "What are you talking about?"

"Nothing," everyone but Camden said in unison.

I swallowed my food. "I really hate being left in the dark, and I also hate jokes being made at my expense. Just say it."

Archer shot Camden a dirty look and then turned his attention towards me. "We're not making fun of you. Camden is referring to your arousal from scenting Nolan. He means you're attracted to all of us."

And just like that, whatever moment I'd had with Camden was ruined. I put my fork down and dabbed my mouth with my napkin. "Archer, can I use your computer? I need to email my fiancé."

14

NOLAN

A few hours after breakfast, we were ready to head back to civilization. I knew I was going to return to some angry council members for leaving town in the middle of the storm, and I wasn't looking forward to hearing them bitch and moan about having to pick up the slack.

I'd been working my ass off for years to bring Maiingan Hollow into the twenty-first century. With some helpful government contracts, Camden had turned Wolfcrest Construction into one of the biggest employers in the Chippewa Valley, and young families were actually moving *in* instead of *out,* looking for greener pastures in Madison or the Twin Cities. I was reinvesting that money straight back into the community, proof of which could be seen in our schools, our clinic, our infrastructure... Maiingan Hollow was a good place to live.

But did I ever get any thanks? Nope, just nonstop, ungrateful complaints about shit I didn't even have any control over.

Sorry your neighbor's cat keeps shitting in your vegetable garden, Mrs. Silvano, but I can't really do anything about it.

A whiff of pistachio and honey settled my nerves, and I glanced at the beautiful omega sitting in the passenger seat beside me. Apparently, Cam's comment had really gotten under her skin, and she had asked if she could ride with me instead of him and the rest of the pack back to town. I couldn't wait to get to know her better and had had to hide how excited I was for the hours we'd be alone together.

Besides, it was only fair, since I hadn't gotten a chance to talk to her outside of her heat.

She scrolled through my playlists, a small smile on her face.

"Are you going to be my DJ?" I asked. I was dying to know what kind of music she liked.

"Maybe," she hummed. "You listen to a surprising amount of divorced dad rock."

"What?" I wanted to grab my phone back and refute her claim, but I couldn't take my eyes off the road for too long. It was still quite slippery despite the storm ending on Sunday.

"Nickleback?" she asked with a sneer of disgust.

"Hey," I started. "It's not cool to hate Nickleback anymore. Didn't you get the memo? I mean, I dare you to listen to 'How You Remind Me' and not start belting."

Her laugh chimed like a bell, and my chest tightened at the sound of it, knowing I was the cause. "Okay, you're on. If I can resist, you owe me an ice cream sundae."

"And if you can't, you have to split that ice cream sundae with me. You ready?"

Twenty minutes later and we were both still singing like our lives depended on it. We'd moved on from early 2000s rock to my 70s list and had started jamming out to Elton John and ABBA.

Was she off key a bit? Yeah, and it was adorable. But it was the determination and effort she gave each performance that filled an empty part of my heart, one I'd neglected for so long I'd forgotten it even existed.

She was more than just an omega, and my burgeoning feelings for her weren't just based in biology. Marlowe was my perfect match, the kind of female I wanted to make pancakes for, to go on road trips with, to share a life with. Hearing her voice calmed my soul, and I couldn't help dreaming about coming home to her after a long day of work, curling up on the couch and taking turns giving each other massages.

How were we going to convince her to bond with us when Cam kept screwing it up with his big, stupid mouth?

15

MARLOWE

"Do you mind if I stop by my office?" Nolan asked. "I need to pick up a few things and just check in with my staff real quick."

"Sure, no problem."

A wooden, hand painted sign welcomed us to Maiingan Hollow.

Population 12,941. Home of the Warriors.

"Warriors? You mean you aren't the home of the shifters or the wolves?"

Nolan laughed. "A little too on the nose, don't you think? Besides, while this community may be for people like us, we still have to interact with the human world. We need to blend in and assimilate if we don't want to be hunted into extinction."

"Assuming this is all real, of course."

The corner of his mouth lifted in a smirk. "Of course."

I still wasn't ready to admit I believed shifters existed and that I was one of them. Despite everything I'd experienced since arriving, my brain didn't want to release its hold of the world I knew and dive head first into the possibility that there were other species of people. People that, until now, I thought only existed in fairy tales and horror films.

We pulled into a parking lot, and Nolan turned off the engine. "I'll only be a few minutes. It's probably for the best if you stay here."

I knew we were close to Camden's house, but we'd been in the car for hours and I had been looking forward to getting some fresh air and stretching my legs. "Why, embarrassed to be seen with me?"

Nolan reached over and grabbed my chin, turning my face towards his. "If you were my omega I'd be howling it to the whole Moon-damned town. But seeing as you're not, and you're unbonded, it's really not a good idea to advertise your presence quite yet."

His brown eyes were pleading, his smiling face now serious and unwavering.

"No one's told me what 'unbonded' means yet," I replied.

He cocked his head to the side. "Really? Big oversight on the guys' part. Bonding is the act that connects a shifter to a pack. It's unbreakable, the sign of ultimate commitment. Alpha packs are wired to desire an omega, and if you don't have one, one can be forced on you. Imagine some random man burst into your home and forced you to marry him and his friends, and there was no stopping it or ever escaping."

My heart raced, and a lump formed in my throat. That did sound awful.

"But you guys didn't do that to me?"

His hand moved to cup my cheek, his thumb gently rubbing circles on my skin. "Shifters are still people, sugar. Some of us may be dirtbags, but that doesn't apply to everyone. We would only bond with an omega who wanted to be with us."

The windows began to fog, obscuring us from passersby. Nolan's bourbon and vanilla scent surrounded me, and I took a deep breath, finding comfort in the smell. "Is it possible for an omega to bond with a pack…" I struggled to find the words.

"Platonically?" Nolan responded.

I nodded.

He sighed, pulling away and back into his seat. "Maybe. But I wouldn't want that, and I don't think the guys would either."

The silence between us was thick and oppressive. "Can't handle the friend zone, eh?" I joked, my voice cracking.

I liked Nolan. I liked Elias and Archer, too. Hell, even Camden had his moments. They were all so handsome it almost hurt to look at them, and there was no denying the chemistry I felt when we were together. And while I had always been a strong fan of monogamy, part of me felt comfortable with the idea of us all being in a relationship, strangely enough.

But I was engaged to a man I loved, a very human man who I didn't think would appreciate me coming home with four new boyfriends. Or packmates. Or whatever they'd be called.

"It's not like that. I'd love to have you as a friend. But when an alpha bonds with an omega, he changes. He no longer desires another female. You'd be sentencing us all to a life of unrequited love."

That definitely didn't sound fair.

"But," he continued, "if you're really ready to accept this life, I can help you find a pack. Betas form packs too, and while they are also drawn to omegas, the pull isn't as strong. Especially if you're in a pack with only females. They could offer you protection from predatory alphas."

A beta female pack. A sisterhood. That actually didn't sound too bad. "And they would be fine with me living so far away?"

"We're not really meant to be apart for long. Even our pack struggles with Elias being in Chicago most of the time. There's a shifter town like Maiingan Hollow in Northern California, though, near the Oregon border. I can get in touch with their council and see if there are beta females closer to San Francisco who'd be interested."

Tears welled in the corners of my eyes. Why did that make me so happy? I still didn't even believe in all this. "You'd do that for me?"

Nolan looked down, closing his eyes and releasing a deep breath. "Cards on the table? I want you, sugar. My pack wants you. We're willing to do whatever it takes to convince you to bond with us and be ours. But I know that's not really an option, and I would rather see you safe with a pack that can respect your choices than throw you out to the wolves."

He exited the car before I could respond, leaving me to drown in his admission. The ring on my finger felt heavy and my chest tightened. I did love Mike. He wasn't any less good looking than this "pack of alphas" I'd somehow fallen into up here. Mike was smart, caring, and funny. He treated me like a queen, and he didn't deserve this doubt now growing inside me.

I took out my phone, and gasped when I saw the dozens of missed calls, voicemails, and texts. I'd sent him an email before we left the cabin, but hadn't bothered to check for a response on the road since my phone was charging and I didn't have any cell service.

Mike: Everything alright?
Mike: I found your birth control pills, do you need help getting a
new pack out there?
Mike: Hey, just checking in, I haven't heard from you.
Mike: Marlowe, you're starting to worry me.
Mike: Seriously, you need to call me back ASAP.
Mike: I'm on my way to Eau Claire.
Mike: Shit, the weather is diverting flights, I'm going to Chicago
instead. I'll rent a car from there.

Mike: Just landed in Chicago, where are you?
Mike: I called the local hospitals and the police stations, they
   don't have you.
Mike: Getting gas in Madison, I'll be in Eau Claire in a couple
   hours.
Mike: I checked into the DoubleTree. Please, call me.

My blood ran cold. Mike had been here since Sunday, worried
sick about me, all while I'd been holed up in a cabin four hours away,
getting fucked by a vibrator. I knew the guys wanted me to go to
Camden's house, but I needed to get to Eau Claire and come up with
some excuse as to why I'd been MIA for so long.

Would he buy that the storms had knocked out the power
here? No, not for that long.

Could I say my dad's house had no service? No, I had sent him
an email that morning. It had been brief, just a quick note to say I was
alive, but hadn't included any details.

Crap, this wasn't good. I wanted to call him, but I was too
afraid to speak to him until I could come up with a plausible
explanation for my radio silence. One that didn't involve shifters, heats,
or alpha packs.

I got out of the car in a panic, running into the building to find
Nolan. On instinct, I knew his scent and touch would help calm me
down, and I followed the signs towards the mayor's office. As I
rounded the last corner, I stopped dead in my tracks. Nolan stood in
the hallway, computer bag in hand, while some woman in a skirt
laughed and tapped his arm in a playful punch.

I couldn't think anymore. All I saw was red, and the breath I
expelled rumbled in my chest. Nolan and the woman both turned
towards me, mouths agape.

"Marlowe? Is everything okay?"

"He's *mine*," I snarled. Anger and jealousy possessed me, and
I ran forward to tackle the bitch, ready to rip out her throat for daring
to touch him.

Nolan stepped in my path, grabbing my wrist as I raised it in
a swipe. He pulled me into his chest, his other hand wrapping around
the small of my back and purring in my ear. "Calm down, sugar. She's
my cousin."

The adrenaline abandoned me, and I pushed myself away from
him, backing up into the wall. What the hell had come over me? I'd
never attacked anyone in my life, especially over a boy. Especially over
a boy that I wasn't even dating. I was engaged to Mike! I had come in

here to figure out how to salvage my relationship with him, not get into a cat fight with a stranger!

The woman gasped in surprise, her hand on her chest. "An omega? Nolan, where did she come from?"

Nolan walked slowly towards me, not taking his eyes off mine even while he spoke to her. "I'll call you later. It's a long story. All you need to know is that Marlowe is James Linden's daughter, and she's here for the funeral and to deal with his estate."

I dug my fingers through my hair, pulling the strands in frustration. "I'm so sorry, I'm so…"

"Shhh," he said quietly. Once he was within arm's length, he pulled me back into his embrace. "I'm not mad, and Megan's going to be fine. We're shifters. We're used to a little aggression every now and then. It's actually really flattering, to be honest."

I wept, letting his scent bring me back into a clear head space. "You don't understand. I called you mine. You can't *be* mine. I have someone, someone who loves me, someone who's losing his mind in a hotel room in Eau Claire right now because he hasn't been able to reach me for five days."

Nolan tucked my head under his chin. "I see. Let's head to Cam's, we'll figure out what to do from there. I'm assuming you need a ride and an alibi, correct?"

I pressed my face further into his chest, inhaling deeply as I nodded.

"Megan, can you reschedule my meetings for the rest of the week?"

"You got it. And uh, nice to meet you, Marlowe. Welcome to Maiingan Hollow."

16
ARCHER

Elias and I rode back into town with Camden, on Marlowe's request. And honestly, I was a little relieved. I didn't want to speak with her until she had a chance to process what had happened during her heat.

All the other guys had done was sleep next to her, but I'd done much more than that. Even if it was for her own good, and even if I never touched her beyond what I could do to help in the moment, she could easily see it as a major violation. And I wouldn't blame her if she did.

The truck pulled up to Camden's home, and I was reminded that he wasn't always a total dumbass, at least when it came to construction. He'd helped design and build the house himself when he was only twenty-one, taking charge under the eye of his father and James.

The wood and stone exterior blended into the surrounding landscape, with massive windows that reflected the drifts of snow that had accumulated in his front yard.

Camden opened the heavy oak door, leading us straight into a large, open space. The double-high atrium soared above us and was bathed in natural light, making it seem somehow both cozy and grand. He turned on his fireplace and collapsed in a heap on a large U-shaped leather couch, leaning his head back and releasing a sigh. Elias brought in some Amazon boxes that had been left on the doorstep and began opening them.

"We should probably wash these first, right?" he asked, holding up several large, furry blankets. "Cam, where's the laundry room?"

"Downstairs," he grunted.

I sat down a few feet away from him, taking out my phone to check my email. I'd lied and told my department I had the flu, canceling my classes for the week. It was bad timing, what with finals right around the corner. But we weren't covering any more new material so they were only missing review, which they could do on their own.

A text came in from Nolan.

> **Nolan:** Leaving my office now. Don't make a big deal out of it when we arrive, but she threw an omega fit when she saw me with Megan, and said I was hers.

"Holy shit…" I whispered.

"Hm?" Camden grunted.

"She claimed Nolan."

Camden bolted forward. "What did you say?"

I showed him the text, and he stood up and howled.

Elias came back into the room, his body tense and alert. "What is it, what happened?"

"She wants us!" Camden cried. He shoved my phone in Elias's face and howled again. "I fucking knew it. She's going to dump the fiancé and bond with us!"

I put my hands out to slow him down. "Okay, let's not get ahead of ourselves, here. Marlowe reacted on instinct. It doesn't mean she's changed her mind."

She'd been off the hormone suppressants for nearly a week, and while her biology might be realigning, she had still been brought up in the human world. In the argument of nature versus nurture, expecting her to break up with a man she'd loved for years just because her inner beast wanted another she barely knew was a hard sell.

Elias read over the text several times. "I mean, it's not *bad* news. But Cam, if there's anything that can screw this up, it's you. Do not breathe a word of this to her, got it?"

Giggles bubbled between his lips as he pretended to shut his mouth and lock it, but the look of pure delight was still written all over his face, and he jumped around the living room, stopping in front of me to thrust in my face while he hummed to himself.

I scoffed and pushed him away. "Get it out of your system now. She can't know we know."

We needed to be here for her, but every time we – and by we I meant Camden – came on too strong, her guilt over her fiancé would kick in.

But perhaps this was good for another reason. How much longer could she deny the existence of shifters when she was reacting this way to perceived threats? Humans didn't typically go nuts at the sight of their partners standing near someone who could be their sexual competition. And the humans who did tended to have a shifter somewhere in their line.

The sound of car doors closing had Camden looking like he was about to burst. "Camden!" I barked. "Go take a cold shower, you're going to ruin this."

He growled, but when Elias nodded his agreement, he swore under his breath and stomped upstairs.

Nolan opened the door and Marlowe stuck her head in tentatively, looking around and subtly sniffing the air for danger. I was sure she didn't even realize she was doing it, which made it all the cuter. Finally deciding it would be safe, she stepped through and took off her shoes. "Wow, this is a nice house."

Elias chuckled. "Cam would be real happy to hear you say that."

She rolled her eyes as she made her way to the fireplace, warming her hands while we did our best to maintain plenty of distance. "Well in that case, it's a dump."

Nolan cleared his throat nervously, giving me and Elias pointed looks. "Marlowe's fiancé is in Eau Claire. She needs a ride down there and a plausible excuse as to why she hasn't talked to him since Friday."

Disappointment coated the air. Of course he would fly out here if he hadn't heard from Marlowe. I'd expect no less from a devoted partner. I hated him for having her, but I could at least respect how much he cared. Even if he was just a human, he would do what he could to protect her.

"I see," Elias responded, trying hard not to sound too downtrodden. "I can take you. And for an excuse, why don't you just say you've been grieving more than you expected and had just turned your phone off? It's simple, and you don't need a web of easily provable lies to prop it up."

She shivered slightly. "Thanks, that sounds good. I just need to call him, and then can we head over? I know you probably don't want to be in a car again so soon…"

Nolan handed his car keys to Elias, who started putting on his coat. "Not at all, it's not that far. Besides, I have some work to do in my office. Two birds, one stone and all that."

"There's a spare bedroom down the hall, why don't you call Mike in there?" I offered.

Marlowe breathed in deeply, steeling herself for what was likely going to be a very difficult conversation, her gait slow and full of dread.

Once the door clicked shut, Nolan whistled, getting our attention. "She was ready to tear out Megan's throat," he said in an excited whisper. "She growled – *growled*! Her first omega tantrum, it was glorious. I never thought I'd be lucky enough to have an omega ready to throw down for me before. And she's not even in our pack yet!"

"*Yet* being the operative word here," I reminded him. "Elias, you can't bring this up with her. She needs to figure this out on her own. Coming to terms with her identity means she will likely realize her incompatibility with the human fiancé. But if we try to force it, she might deny us further out of fear or even spite."

The water upstairs turned off, and Camden came out of the bathroom wrapped in a towel. "I can smell her," he bellowed from the balcony. "Where is she?"

Nolan groaned. "Dude, get some clothes on. She's talking to her fiancé. He freaked out when he couldn't get in touch with her and flew up to Eau Claire a few days ago."

Camden gripped the railing tightly, his knuckles turning white. "That human piece of shit is *here*?"

"That human piece of shit is my fiancé, thank you very much, and I just lied to him for the first time in our relationship. So who's the real piece of shit now?"

Marlowe's face was streaked with tears, her hands shaking as she made her way back to the living room. Nolan approached her first, rubbing her arms. "How did it go? Is he okay?"

I held back rushing in to comfort her as well, my hands balling into fists at my sides. An omega in distress kicked every beastly impulse into overdrive, but I doubted she would appreciate me rubbing my scent all over her.

She bit her lip, her eyes glassy. "I've never heard him so upset before. Elias, can we go now?"

His shoulders slumped. "Of course, California."

17
MARLOWE

My heart raced as we pulled up to the front of the hotel. "You can just drop me off here."

Elias put the car in park and reached over, grabbing my hand. His bergamot and pepper scent washed over me, followed by a fresh wave of my own guilt. Another man's smell shouldn't simultaneously calm me and turn me on like this. When had I become such a horny, unfaithful monster?

"Are you sure you don't want me to stay and wait?" he asked.

I really did, for some reason. But I didn't think Mike would appreciate having my dad's very attractive lawyer acting like a chaperone.

"No, it's probably for the best you don't."

He gave my hand a final squeeze before letting go. "I understand. You have my number in case you need anything, right? I'll just be right down the road."

I took a deep breath, steeling myself to leave. "I… I don't even know what to say." Even after I convinced Mike I was alive and apologized enough to make up for the torture I'd put him through, I still needed to interact with Elias and Camden regarding my dad's inheritance. Knowing these feelings existed between us was going to make it impossible.

"You don't need to say anything. Take your time, and we'll deal with your father's will when you're ready. Even if you need to return home first for a while. We're not going anywhere."

I couldn't explain why, but I was having trouble getting out of the car. "Nolan offered to set me up with a pack of beta females in California," I blurted in an attempt to continue our conversation.

His eyes lit with amusement. "Did he, now? But why would you need a pack of beta females if shifters don't exist? What did you call us, 'delusional LARPers' or something to that effect?"

I let out a small laugh. "Yeah, something like that. Hypothetically speaking, if shifters did exist and I was an omega, I'm still unbonded. And if I want to walk freely without an escort for the rest of my life, I need to find a pack, right?"

He rubbed his chin with his thumb, watching me carefully. "Yes, you would. But I actually know a very nice pack right here that happens to have an omega position available, if you're interested. And I think we might be able to offer you a bit more protection than beta females."

I studied his face, the way his blonde hair curled ever so slightly at the ends and fell into his green eyes. He sported a scruffy beard from days of not shaving, and his lips looked kissably soft.

My breath hitched and his nostrils flared.

"I want to marry Mike," I said. Was it to convince myself or Elias? "And I don't think he'd be okay with the type of relationship an omega would have with a pack of alphas. And I can't sentence you all to a life of permanent blue balls, either."

Elias sighed, looking out the window. "Marriages fail all the time, California. But pack bonds are for life."

His scent saturated the air, heating my core. Shit, was I actually wet? I still had to meet Mike. This wasn't good. Why was my body still reacting this way?

He turned around quickly, his pupils dilating as he looked at me. "Archer didn't want me to bring it up, but I have to," he said. "You're attracted to us. I can smell the arousal on you. And you want to claim us. You turned feral today at the sight of another woman just touching Nolan. You can't deny it when the evidence is overwhelmingly in our favor. I know you love your fiancé, and I'll respect whatever decision you make. But really think it over. Don't just choose out of obligation or convention."

I clenched my thighs together. "I've been on pills that have suppressed my shifter hormones since I was a teenager. At least, that's what Archer thinks. If I go back on them, these urges will go away, and I'll stop…"

"Stop what, being who and what you are? Is that really how you want to live your life?" I felt my heart leap up my throat as he continued, his chest heaving. "It suited you well enough when you thought you were just a human, but now that you know you're not, how can you refuse this integral part of your identity? You'll be living a lie, constantly in fear that one day the meds will stop working and you'll have to explain to your husband why you need him to fuck you for four days straight as you descend into a heat. Why strange men are beating down your door screaming about knotting you when your scented slick attracts every shifter in the city."

I placed my hands over my ears and dropped my head. His words cut like glass, leaving me bleeding in my seat. Maybe he was right, maybe he wasn't, but I wouldn't know until I saw Mike. Would I feel relieved? Disappointed? I was torn in a million directions and each one would mean leaving someone in pain behind me.

"I have to go," I whimpered. I opened the door quickly before Elias could stop me, leaving my bag in the trunk. I would get it later. I just needed Mike.

I sprinted inside and pushed the call button for the elevator, double checking the room number he'd texted me, and knocked on the door once I arrived. He opened it in a flash, his face wracked with worry. He picked me up by my thighs and cradled me into his chest as I wrapped my arms and legs around him. Then he closed the door and walked me over to the bed.

"I was so scared. Don't ever do that to me again," he said, his voice shaking.

I sobbed into the crook of his neck, wordlessly nodding. He didn't have a natural musk like the alphas, but he smelled like home. How could I ever have even considered leaving him?

He laid me down on the bed, his hands holding my cheeks. His violet eyes carefully inspected my skin while his fingers ran up and down my neck like he was searching for an injury. "Has anyone touched you? Hurt you?"

My face flushed. "No," I replied, even though it felt like a lie. "I'm fine. It's just been really hard dealing with all my dad's shit."

He closed his eyes, breathing hard as his hand crept around my throat, gripping it softly. "I was afraid I'd lost you. I would tear the world apart for you, my Lunessa. Without you, I am nothing."

His mouth crashed into mine, angry and relieved and claiming. We separated only briefly to take off our tops, and the familiar sight of his chiseled chest released my slick, as the alphas had called it. Mike's eyes darkened and he panted. "Your pills – you haven't been taking them."

How did he even know, and why was he reacting like a shifter? Was I really so potent even humans could tell when I was turned on? "Sorry, I…"

"Shh…" he placed a finger on my lips. "It's fine, just let me fuck you. I need to be inside you before I can think clearly again."

"Shouldn't we use a condom?" The haze of lust wasn't so thick I'd forgotten that at least.

He unbuckled his belt, pulling his pants down and releasing his hardened cock. "I'll pull out."

Before I could object, he'd tugged my leggings off, using them to tie my hands above me. Once we were both completely naked, he sat on top, straddling my waist. "You're *mine*, Marlowe."

I'd never seen Mike like this before. He'd always taken a more dominant role in the bedroom, however this was ferocious. Frenzied, even. I was a little scared but also excited, wondering what exactly he was going to do to me.

He grabbed my throat again, tighter than he had before. "*Mine.*"

"Y-yes, Mike."

His mouth lowered to my neck, kissing and biting gently down my chest until he reached my breasts. He took my nipple between his teeth, pressing down until I yelped in pain. His cock twitched at the sound of it, and he groaned as he lowered himself further to my sex, wrenching my legs apart.

His eyes bored into mine, and the first lick sent me straight into oblivion, my back arching in pleasure.

"You taste so sweet. You have no idea."

His tongue lapped me greedily, circling my clit and delving into my pussy. I moaned, struggling against the ties that kept my hands together. I wanted to run my fingers through his thick, soft hair, but that was off the table tonight it seemed. He wanted to be in control, likely from feeling so *not* in control since I'd left. I would let him do whatever he needed to and would enjoy every second of his delicious torment.

My breath quickened as my orgasm neared, a high-pitched whine escaping my lips. I was so close, just…

Suddenly, Mike leapt over, grabbing my chin and forcing his tongue into my mouth. I vocalized my disappointment, but enjoyed the kiss, leaning into him until he pulled back roughly. "You think it's going to be that easy? No, you won't come until I allow you to."

He crawled up further until his cock was in front of my face.

He leaned against the wall behind the bed with one arm for support, the other gripping the base of his shaft. His corded muscles twitched in the faded light. "Open."

I did as commanded, and he began easing himself inside my mouth. Slowly at first, watching in awe as my lips enveloped him, hissing from the feeling of my tongue running along his skin.

He started thrusting faster, ignoring my grunts as his girthy length triggered my gag reflex and sent tears to my eyes.

"Take it, Lunessa. Your body was built for this. For me. You're going to take my cock wherever and whenever I want to fuck you. Do you understand?"

He pushed himself up until his balls slapped my chin, then grabbed my hair roughly. "I asked you a question."

I nodded, another stream of slick running down from me as he continued. I'd never known this kind of treatment could be such a turn on, but being the object of his desire was thrilling. I couldn't believe I'd almost let a passing limerence, or four, come between us.

He didn't stop punishing my mouth with his cock, going faster and faster until he groaned, thick ropes of cum exploding down my throat. "That's a good girl," he cooed. "Swallow it all. That's your reward."

I batted my eyelashes and nodded, doing as he instructed, licking my lips as he pulled himself out, his cock still pulsing.

"Fuck, you're so perfect." He kissed me again and backed away, his hand kneading my breast and pinching my nipple sharply. It slid down my abdomen back to my clit, rubbing it gently. "You're so wet for me. You missed me, didn't you?"

"Yes," I moaned, writhing from his touch.

"Did anybody else touch this pussy while I was away?"

Why did it feel like he knew something strange had happened to me? He'd never been so jealous or insecure before. If we went to a bar or party and someone tried to hit on me, his reaction was usually to laugh because he was so confident that I would never leave him.

"No," I breathed. It wasn't technically a lie. Archer hadn't touched me directly, at least.

His fingers slid inside me, circling my walls and pushing against my G-spot. I bucked my hips, desperate for more.

"Good, because who does this pussy belong to?" He whispered, his breath caressing my ear, his tongue running up the outer shell.

"You!" I cried. "Please Mike, fuck me!"

He chuckled, shoving his fingers in deeper. "Begging for more of my cock already? That's why you're special, Lunessa. You're insatiable. And luckily for you, so am I."

Then he flipped me over, my hands twisting in the leggings, and pulled my ass up into the air. He positioned himself behind me, clicking his tongue as he ran his hand down my back. A sharp crack on my ass cheek elicited a muffled scream as I buried my face in a pillow, and he soothed the pain by rubbing the skin with his palm.

Mike had jokingly spanked me in the bedroom before, but never like this. I clenched in anticipation of the next slap, yelping when it came swiftly after.

His fingers pushed inside me again, and he took my slick and applied it where he'd struck me. "This turns you on, doesn't it? Getting punished for your bad behavior. You're normally such a good girl and I don't have to resort to such lessons, but perhaps it's time for you to misbehave a little more often. Within reason, of course."

He slapped me again and the slick ran down my leg in a steady stream. "Mike, please…" I begged. I knew this wasn't my heat – I still had all my faculties, but for how horny I was, it might as well have been. My pussy was achingly empty, and I arched my back further.

"You're so desperate for my cock, aren't you?" He rubbed the head against my entrance, and I tried to push back into him. He tsked and slapped me one more time.

"I'll decide when you're ready, Lunessa. I am your master, and you will obey me. Tell me you know this now."

I turned my head, gripping the leggings desperately that bound me. "Yes!"

His hands wrapped around my hips and his cock speared into me with such force my head almost hit the headboard. His thrusts were angry, hard, and fast, but exactly what my swollen, wet pussy needed. I whined in pleasure, his fingers digging into my skin so hard I thought they might leave bruises.

He lost himself to the sex, no longer speaking as he fucked me thoroughly. My climax hastened, and my inner walls clenched around him as the euphoria built. My finally orgasm tore through me, and I panted my release with soft, desperate cries.

Finally, he slowed for a moment until he thrust one more time, coming inside.

"Wait!" I breathed. "Mike…"

He grunted, pulling himself out once his dick stopped pulsating inside me, flipping me over again and crawling over my body.

"I told you, you're *mine*. That means when I want to come inside you, I will." He then headed to the bathroom, closing the door behind him and going straight into the shower.

I laid there, stunned, tears pricking the corners of my eyes. Mike had never come inside me when I asked him not to. And he'd never just abandoned me like this after sex. I had enjoyed the roughness of him, but only because I thought it would be followed by cuddles.

This was simply punishment. Cold and cruel.

I finally wriggled my wrists free from the knot of leggings, and sat up, reaching for my phone so I could look up the closest pharmacy to get the morning after pill.

When I touched the screen, I realized I'd grabbed his by mistake, but the text that popped up made me pause.

Jen: We miss you, get back your Lunessa so we can be whole.

Why was Jen using that word? What did she even mean by "we?" There was a video in the next text from her, and I opened his phone to see what it was.

Jen and some woman I didn't know were fucking. Begging for Mike to return.

On our bed.

Bile crept up my throat as I scrolled through their text history. How could he do this to me? Nude photos, videos of them having sex, of Mike and I having sex, and him and other women, punctuated with messages about wanting to fuck them and me, too.

They went back months. He'd been fucking his coworker and so many others, and they knew about me. Wanted me to *join* them.

My whole world turned upside down, the blood draining from my face. This wasn't just cheating. There were so many layers to this betrayal, I couldn't count them all.

I held back the vomit as I got dressed, pulling on my stretched-out leggings and throwing a sweater on top. I didn't even bother with shoes, I just needed to get out of there.

I grabbed my phone and ran out of the room, tears blurring my vision as my trembling fingers tried in vain to type my passcode. I had to call Elias. I wanted him to hold me and take me back to Maiingan Hollow. My gut, my heart, knew I would be safe with my guys.

My *pack*.

I heard the door slam open and Mike rush down the hall,

calling my name as the elevator doors closed in his face.

"Marlowe, it's not what you think!"

I held myself, heaving and sobbing until I reached the lobby. I stumbled out, looking for a place to hide and wait until Elias could get me, and my breath stopped when I saw him pacing by the windows. He looked up as I approached, growling at my disheveled and distraught appearance. Quickly making up the distance between us, he pulled me into his chest, his scent creating a perfect bubble of comfort around me while I cried.

"I had a weird feeling. I couldn't leave. What happened? Did he hurt you?"

Before I had a chance to speak, the elevator dinged and Mike ran out, calling my name.

There were a handful of people around, some parting for him while others looked at him in disbelief and disgust.

He found me in Elias's arms and hissed. "Let go of her!"

I felt the power surge out of Elias's muscles as he yanked me behind him, snarling. "Bloodsucker…" he seethed.

"Mutt," Mike spat back.

Chaos erupted, as half the staff began to crouch into battle readiness, the other half running in terror. Mike cracked his neck and bared his teeth, his canines elongating and sharpening.

My face paled. Bloodsucker? Mutt? Did they know each other? "Elias," I whispered. "What…"

"Vampyr trash," he bellowed. "She doesn't belong with you. She's one of us."

Vampyr? Like… vampire? What the fuck was going on?

Mike's eyes scanned the room, watching as the shifters tightened around him. "I'm not here to fight. I'm here to take my fiancé home. We live as humans, and we don't bother anybody. Come, Marlowe." He gestured for my hand.

Grabbing Elias's shoulder for support I yelled back at him. "I'm not going anywhere with you. You've been cheating on me!"

The rage that emanated off Elias was palpable, and the other shifters growled in response, circling closer and closer. Unbonded or not, it seemed shifters stuck together as one in the face of outside threats. And Mike, my shitty, cheating fiancé, was a threat.

"If you'd let me explain, Lunessa…"

"Lunessa?" Elias asked incredulously. "You mean to force her into a servaglio? An *omega*?"

Mike hissed again, "Don't pretend like you know anything

about them. My servaglio and I worship her."

Lunessa. I'd always thought it was just a cute pet name, but all this time, it had a much deeper meaning. And I wasn't sure I wanted to discover what that was.

I ripped the ring from my finger and threw it at him. "We're done, Mike. I don't want anything to do with you, or Jen, or whoever else you've been fucking. Just go home!"

He winced at the sound of the ring bouncing off the floor, then picked it up and sighed. His face softened as he looked into my eyes. *"Lunessa, my love, you don't mean that. Come, let's talk about this back in the room."*

His words washed over me like a warm, gentle breeze. All the anger and fear left my body, and I felt happy. At peace. I dropped my hand from Elias's shoulder.

Of course I didn't mean it, Mike was my fiancé. I loved him. He would have a very reasonable explanation about this whole thing.

I took a step back towards him when a dominating bark brought me back to my senses. "Marlowe, *stop!*"

My tunnel vision cleared, my wrath returning. "What the hell…"

"You think you can compel your way out of this?" Elias asked, facing Mike. "I should rip you limb from limb, but for Marlowe's sake, I will give you ten minutes to gather your things and leave. You will never bother her again, do you hear me?"

"I'm not leaving here without her!" Mike yelled back. He ran towards Elias, fangs bared, as Elias started towards him.

"No!" I screamed. My heart was beating so hard I thought it might burst through my chest. Pain shot through my limbs, and I collapsed on the floor, my body contorting and my bones breaking, bending, reshaping. I felt my face grow outwards, and hair cover my skin as my clothes ripped apart at the seams.

My tail twitched, and I raised myself on four shaky paws. A whine escaped my snout, the people around staring at me in awe.

"Marlowe…" sighed a male. He smelled familiar, smelled safe. But the male behind him reeked of death and danger.

I whimpered, then ran straight out the door, and into the snowy woods beyond.

18
ELIAS

I still couldn't believe my eyes. Marlowe, my beautiful omega, had shifted into a wolf in the lobby of the DoubleTree Hotel in Eau Claire.

Her omega designation was rare enough already, but shifters had long thought the ability to transform had disappeared, like losing a vestigial limb.

Yet there she was, and she was glorious. I felt pressure welling up inside me, throwing itself against some unknown blockage that was stopping me from shifting with her. All I wanted was to lick her nose and run wild through the woods in playful chase.

"Marlowe…" I said quietly, trying not to frighten her.

Her honey-colored coat rippled over her small, lupine body. Hazel eyes met mine, and she sniffed and whined in my direction, taking a step towards me. But her focus swung to the bloodsucker, and her tail tucked between her legs.

She made a small sound and barreled through the door, disappearing into the dark and snow.

The vampyr started to chase her but I tackled him from the side, slamming him into the reception desk. His head smacked satisfyingly against the hard wood, and his body relaxed.

"Go, alpha. Find your omega. We'll take care of him."

I looked back at the beta shifters who had stepped in, ready to fight against our mortal enemy as he threatened one of our kind.

Nodding my thanks, I took off into the woods after her.

Night fell early during the winter months in Wisconsin, and while I might not have had the ability to fully shift, I still carried enough wolfish traits to follow her trail through the darkness. I called Archer while I trudged through the snow, trying to stay on top of her scent.

"Is everything okay?"

"No!" I replied, panting heavily. "The fiancé… he's a vampyr, and…"

Thick growls interrupted my sentence, and someone snarled in the background. Most likely Cam.

"We're on our way," Archer said quickly.

"That's not it! Marlowe shifted. Completely. Her wolf took off. We have to find her."

None of the pack could respond, the news stunning them into silence. Archer finally spoke, his voice thick. "There are human farmers in the area that would shoot a wolf on sight."

My heart leapt into my throat. "Then you better hurry down here."

After hanging up I stopped and howled, hoping she might reply. The woods were quiet, save for the far-off sound of traffic from I-94.

"Fuck," I cursed.

Marlowe was one in a million. She was beautiful, smart, funny, but could also be the key to helping our whole species regain our connection to our inner beasts. Archer must be salivating as much at the prospect of bonding to her as he was about studying her.

But mostly, I just wanted to protect her, and that longing charged through our pack's bond. There was no telling how far she could run or where she would be when she shifted back. She'd be naked and alone in the middle of the woods, facing below-freezing temperatures. Dazed, confused, with the memories of Mike's true identity and his betrayal still coursing through her.

I growled at the thought of it. All this time, she'd been unwittingly choosing a fucking bloodsucker over us.

Vampyrs and shifters had known of each other for centuries, but we never really interacted much, choosing our own paths to keep under the humans' radar.

But then the Great War happened.

No one knew what had sparked it, but one day around a hundred years ago, battles had broken out between our two peoples all around the world, some lasting for months. When it ended, we fell into an uneasy truce and avoided each other whenever possible.

Luckily that was pretty easy considering we tended to settle in very different climates - shifters in the north and vamps in the south.

Human lore got one big thing wrong about vampyrs – they didn't hide from sunlight; they reveled in it. Shifters ran hot, desiring the cold of the north and of long winters to keep from overheating. Vampyrs were similar to reptiles, however. Their blood ran cold, and they needed the sun to live comfortably.

Their societies also differed from ours with how we formed groups. Shifters had packs. An alpha pack with an omega was often seen as the ideal, but packs that mixed alphas and betas, or were comprised of only betas, also existed and formed families and households.

Vampyrs, on the other hand, could only sire male children, and as such, had developed a practice of creating groups called "servaglios," wherein they would recruit several human females to serve as their concubines. The Lunessa was considered the main female, his wife for all intents and purposes.

Omegas would wither away in a servaglio. They needed several males to tend to them during their heats. A male who couldn't devote himself fully to an omega would leave her in pain, physically and emotionally.

And what would a vampyr even want with a shifter anyway? Could an omega and a vampyr even conceive?

The idea enraged me. Marlowe had smelled and looked like sex when she found me. Knowing a vampyr had tasted her, filled her, held her and loved on her…

I shoved back those thoughts. I would take those frustrations out on him if I ever saw him again. But not my Marlowe, not my sunny California. She didn't even know what *she* truly was. How would she have known her fiancé wasn't human, either?

Her neck had been bite free, at least. That was one thing vampyrs and shifters had in common – we formed bonds through bites. But while shifters bonded only to form a pack, vampyrs could bond with countless humans to turn them into their submissive thralls. It made it easier for them to feed.

Vampyrs lacked some sort of protein in their blood that they needed to survive and supplemented it through feeding from others. Feeding didn't kill their victims, but a vampyr could succumb to bloodlust and drain a human dry if they weren't stopped.

Thankfully their saliva's venom didn't last in the bloodstream too long, so affected humans could be free of their curse as long as they weren't bitten regularly. But lovers in a servaglio would be bonded to often, eventually becoming permanent slaves.

A bitter wind whipped across my face and I welcomed its sting. I took a deep breath, hoping I was downwind of my little wolf, but the air was devoid of her sweet scent.

Shouts sounded from behind me, and light reflected off my eyes as I turned towards the approaching males.

"A fucking vamp?" snarled Cam. "Please tell me you ripped him to shreds for daring to touch her."

"I left a few betas in charge of his fate. I couldn't waste a second."

Nolan grabbed my shoulder. "Revenge can come later. You did the right thing. Let's get going, our girl needs us."

I nodded. "More than you know."

19
THE TAWNY WOLF

The cold was refreshing as I bounded through the woods. Every smell enraptured me. Every sound and movement drew my attention. I didn't bother hiding my presence, and prey scattered around me.

I wasn't on the hunt, and it wasn't hunger that drove me forward. Fear had started me on this path, but now it was bliss. Excitement. Freedom.

Any whiff of humans had me running the other way. I'd had enough of their kind. Where was mine? I howled a call, looking for my pack, but no one responded.

I had a pack, didn't I? A deep loneliness and longing swept through my bones, and my next howl was desperate.

Where are you?

I wandered further. A nearby stream was almost frozen over, but a quick paw on the thin ice had opened a spot. The water was clear, soothing the burning thirst inside me. Clouds obscured the moon, and I howled again at its absence. I followed the stream north. It seemed as good a direction as any.

Perhaps my pack was that way.

My limbs grew tired as the sky eventually lightened into day. I needed a safe space to rest. Where had I rested the night before? I couldn't remember.

I knew I should be avoiding humans, but an enclosed, red cavern seeped warmth into the dawn air. I pushed my way through the opening. Large prey animals voiced their concern at my intrusion, but I paid them no mind. A dark corner, covered in straw, offered a good a place as any. I laid down my weary body, placing my head on my paws. Humans were loud, their scent potent. I would easily wake before any approached.

Satisfied I had chosen a good spot, I closed my eyes.

"Easy, girl..."

I growled at the intruder. How foolish I'd been. Without a pack I couldn't allow myself to sleep deeply so close to humans.

His hands were empty, at least. I knew trouble with humans started whenever they carried something. I crouched, ready to lunge forward and grab him by the throat.

"*Sit.*"

My body sat on its own accord, following the dominating command of the alpha in front of me. How could he speak my language? I whined, finding the pressure to obey suffocating.

"*Return.*"

I sucked in a breath, and my body began to twist. My skin was stripped of its fur, the cold hitting me like a punch to the gut.

My senses dulled as my snout shrank, and I fell back asleep inside the human who shared my soul.

20

MARLOWE

Panic rose in my gut. I was naked on the cold, dirty floor of a barn, while an older man, dressed in flannel and thick snow pants, stared at me in awe. The dominating scent of black truffle and grass enveloped me, and I shivered in disgust.

"Well, what do we have here?" he chuckled. I tucked my legs into my body and wrapped my arms around them, trying to cover as much of myself as possible.

"Can I please use your phone?" I asked meekly. I didn't know any of the guys' numbers by heart, but I could at least call information and ask for the number to Wolfcrest Construction or Maiingan City Hall. Both should lead me somewhere.

"Sure thing, sweetheart. Why don't I take you into the house?" He grabbed a scratchy-looking blanket and wrapped it around my shoulders, then placed a spare pair of rubber boots in front of me to slip on. "It's a good thing I found you," he said. "Was that your first shift?"

I nodded dumbly. "Yes, I need to get in touch with my pack."

"Your pack?" His eyes scanned my body slowly. "I don't see any bond marks."

With a burgeoning beer gut, thinning hair, and leathery skin from a lifetime of working outside, this guy looked old enough to be my dad.

The way he looked at me was anything but fatherly, though – he was an alpha, and I needed to be careful.

"We're bonding soon, just working out the arrangements.

They, um, wanted to finish my nest first."

I had no clue what that even meant, but I remembered flashes of the guys mentioning them when I'd been in my heat. I needed to at least fake like I knew what I was talking about.

"Of course." He nodded slowly. "Gotta impress you, right?"

We walked up the slippery, worn wooden steps onto the porch. "If you have a cell phone, I can just call from out here…" I said.

He pulled me inside. "Nonsense, you're going to freeze to death, little thing that you are. I'm sure you'd love something hot to drink, right?"

The house was warm, and the smell of the coffee soon drowned out his alpha odor. "Sit right here, I'll get ya a cup. How do you take it?"

"Um, black is fine," I said nervously, looking around for a landline. An old guy like this in the countryside would definitely have one. I finally spotted it on a side table in the living room. "If you don't mind, I'd really like to call my pack now, they must be worried sick."

He handed me the drink and sat down next to me at the old linoleum table. "I bet they are. If you were my omega, I'm sure I'd be tearing the county apart looking for ya."

I retreated further into my chair, looking into my chipped Milwaukee Brewers mug as I felt his gaze linger. "So, can I?"

"What's the rush? I've never had the chance to see an omega in all her glory before, at least let me enjoy the company while I got it." His voice turned rough, and I shuddered at its bite.

He sighed, reaching over to clumsily pluck a piece of straw from my hair. "And you shifted too, that's incredible. The last one who could shift in my family was my grandfather, I think. I felt the drive, but nothing ever came of it. How'd you do it?"

I took a sip of the burnt, bitter coffee. Of course, it would be better with lots of cream and sugar, but I just needed something warm in my belly. I kept my eye on the phone. "I really don't know. I wasn't even trying, it just happened."

"Hm," he grunted. "I wonder if you'd pass the power on to any pups."

The little heat that had accumulated in my body rose to my cheeks, and he chuckled. "Aren't you the cutest thing, blushing at the thought of it? Me, on the other hand… let's just say the idea of filling you with pups is giving my body a very different reaction. What do you say? That pack's wasting their time with you, sweetheart. I could have you bonded to mine by the night, birthing your first by the summer."

I coughed, trying to disguise the visceral reaction of puking at the idea of doing anything with this man. "Please, I already have a pack…"

"You don't if you aren't bonded yet. It's finders-keepers at this point, and now that I've found ya, I think I'll keep ya."

I threw my coffee in his face and bolted for the door. He screamed in a rage, slamming his body into mine just as I'd reached the handle.

"I was gonna be so nice," he snarled. "Take real good care of you." He picked me up with ease and threw me over his shoulder.

I kicked and screamed, willing my wolf with all my power to come back, but she was exhausted, sleeping off the all-night run.

He headed up the stairs, pushing us through a door into a bedroom. Then he grabbed two belts from on top of his dresser and threw me on the bed. While sitting on my chest, he secured my wrists to the metal headboard.

"But if you wanna act like a bitch, I'm gonna treat you like one."

"Please," I begged. "Let me go, I don't want to bond with you. I have a pack!"

He spat on the ground and then grabbed me by the throat. "You'll be begging to bond with us once your heat comes. Until then, you're going to learn how to act like a good omega."

He closed the door, turning a key and locking me in. I growled my frustration and pulled my hands as hard as I could, but they wouldn't budge.

I heard him chuckle as he headed back down the stairs, then the sound of his voice on the phone.

"John, you're never going to believe what I found…"

I had writhed and wriggled myself into a tired so deep I couldn't fight it any longer and fell asleep soon after my capture.

I was woken up with a slap, yelping in pain and surprise to find three men now standing around the bed, their pupils blown and mouths salivating. Next to my captor was a bald man, his face covered in a thick beard. He was large, his muscles threatening to bust through his work shirt.

The third man also appeared to be in his fifties, tall and gangly with a greasy comb-over. He sat down next to me, hands hovering over my naked body. The blanket had long been taken away from me.

"Paul, you weren't exaggerating. She's a beaut," he said. His fingers lightly grazed my collarbone, and he leaned into my neck and inhaled deeply. "I've never smelled anything so sweet in my life."

"Let me go!" I screamed. "This isn't right. I have a pack!"

"*Shut your mouth!*"

The alpha's command robbed me of my voice, but I was able to still release a pathetic sounding whimper.

The three men simultaneously groaned, grabbing their crotches. "Fuck, my dick hasn't been this hard in years," said the third one.

Paul, my captor, grinned. "It's fate, I tell ya. All these years, saving myself for an omega, and one finally just shows up on my doorstep. Naked as the day she was born."

The thin man's hand traced down my chest, slowly circling my breasts. His touch made me sick. "When's her heat coming? I've always wanted to experience a true omega heat."

I pulled at the restraints again. When my wolf woke up, he was first. "I'm going to rip your fucking throats out."

Paul's hand rose to strike me, but the larger man growled, pushing him against the wall. "Don't you touch her like that. Don't you know anything?"

Paul sneered. "Bitch needs to learn her place."

The thin man next to me sighed. "She's an omega. All cute little bark and no bite. You really that threatened right now? She's naked and tied to your bed. What's she going to do?" He turned his attention towards me. "Don't worry about him, we'll get him in line. What do you like to eat? I'll get you whatever you want."

I weighed my options. The large one was protective and didn't like the way Paul was treating me. The thin guy didn't like it either, but he certainly wasn't against touching me without my consent.

They didn't seem smart enough to knowingly play a good cop/bad cop routine, which meant I needed to use their group dynamic to build a wedge.

I sniffled, turning to look at the thin guy. "What's your name?"

He smiled, his teeth yellow and crooked. "I'm Greg. What's yours?"

"Marlowe," I said softly, batting my eyelashes. "Could I just have a coffee? With cream and sugar?"

His hand brushed the hair out of my face while he looked longingly into my eyes. "Anything for you."

Paul grumbled. "She told me she took it black."

Greg snapped back. "That's because she doesn't trust you, dumbass! Marlowe," he purred, looking back at me. "John will stay up here and keep you company while Paul and I get your coffee. You sure you don't need anything else?"

I shook my head and smiled. "No, thank you."

Paul shuffled out angrily and Greg followed, leaving John and me alone. His hands were balled into fists at his sides, and he eyed the door before he came around and took Greg's place on the bed. "I'm real sorry about this. You gotta understand though, we've never had an omega before. We thought you'd gone extinct or something."

He chuckled softly and then his face became serious. "We can't lose our one chance to be happy. But we'll make you happy, too. And don't worry about Paul. I won't let him touch you like that again."

His sweaty, meaty hands gently grazed my cheek, and I leaned into his touch. A shudder ran through his body, and he composed himself as he withdrew.

"John," I whispered. "Can't I at least wear something? I'm so cold, and Paul didn't even let me..."

"Oh shit, yeah, of course." He leapt off the bed so quickly the mattress bounced, and he stuck his head out the door. "Paul! You got anything she can wear?"

Paul's frustrated voice called from the kitchen. "Shit, I don't know. Shouldn't we just keep her naked? You know, until she's bonded?"

John turned towards me and I let out a whine. He bit his lip and yelled louder this time. "She needs clothes, NOW!"

He came back to my side. "We'll get you something to wear for today, but I can pick up something nice from the store later. I bet you like dresses, right?"

I fought back the urge to roll my eyes. Dresses were fine and fun to wear sometimes, but I lived in jeans. Instead, I giggled. "How'd you know?"

He blushed, rubbing his hand along his head. "Just a guess. Omegas like pretty things, so..."

I was almost expecting him to start asking me about the rabbits when Paul and Greg returned. "One coffee with cream and sugar."

Greg set it on the nightstand and then helped me sit up as best I could with my hands still tied with the belts. John cleared his throat. "Maybe we should let her get dressed first? And we can undo her hands while we're here, can't we?"

Paul crossed his arms. "She stays restrained whenever possible. I forgot to tell you, she can fully shift."

Greg and John looked at me and laughed. "Well, you're just full of surprises," Greg said. "I guess those threats to rip out our throats had some oomph to them after all."

"She still deserves clothes," John grumbled.

Paul sighed and went into his closet. "I think I have a box of Suzanne's old things in here…"

A few minutes later, he'd managed to find me a large old house dress that smelled like mothballs, but it was certainly better than nothing. They only released one hand at a time to help me put it on, and then Greg pulled me up slightly so I was sitting up.

"Here, your coffee's getting cold." He held it up to my lips and tipped it slightly to allow me a sip, and I took it gingerly.

Paul's anger simmered in the air. "Where was all that sweetness when you nearly burned my face off this morning, huh?"

I took delight in the red, puffy skin on his cheeks, but pretended to cower, and a growl reverberated through John's chest. "Watch the way you speak to her!"

Paul threw his hands up in the air and stormed out of the room.

Greg and John shared a knowing look and then followed him.

I looked out the window into the gray sky, sending a plea for my pack to find me.

"I'm sorry," I whispered. "I'm ready now."

21
CAMDEN

"I got something over here!" I yelled. Large paw prints gathered at a spot near the stream and then continued northward. We'd wandered throughout the night, the sky now turning to blue as dawn approached.

She had to be tiring soon. Archer had versed us on his research into full shifts during the drive over. Marlowe was alone, with no pack and no home to return to. She'd likely wander aimlessly until she exhausted herself, seeking shelter to rest and possibly revert back to her human form.

There was nothing but farms out here, and wolves typically gave people a wide berth. Would she find safety in time? A few hours without clothing in these conditions could kill her.

I didn't wait for the others to follow as I trailed the prints up. She was heading back to Maiingan Hollow, whether she realized it or not. Was she trying to find us?

We weren't bonded yet, but I ached for her all the same. I was also furious she'd been tricked by a vampyr, that he'd thought he could take one of ours into his servaglio. And I was shocked by her shift, but it was a race against the clock and I refused to entertain any worst case scenarios.

Nolan caught up with me, the second most physically fit out of the four of us. Elias and Archer were strong, but they had desk jobs and didn't get outside as much as me or Nolan. Nolan was a very active and hands-on mayor and spent most of his time pitching in wherever he could. And then there was me, of course. My muscles weren't for show, and most of the new construction in Chippewa Valley was proof of that.

"Here." Nolan handed me a beef jerky stick, and I nodded my thanks. I wasn't hungry in the slightest, but for Marlowe's sake I would eat. Food meant energy, and I needed every ounce of it if I was going to find her.

My eyes narrowed in on a tuft of light brown fur hanging off a low tree branch. I gingerly grabbed it, rubbing it in my fingers and releasing her sweet scent. I sighed, tucking it into one of the pockets on my vest. "This is her, alright."

Never in my life had I hated the fact that I couldn't shift more than I had when we'd gotten that call from Elias. That gift had left our people years before I was born, the last full shifter dying while I was still in diapers. How could you miss something you never knew?

I supposed you could say the same thing about omegas. I never thought I'd ever meet one, let alone bond with one.

And then Marlowe walked into our lives. For a fleeting moment, I saw a happy future. One with love and family.

And then she had promptly shifted and ran out of it.

I wasn't going to let her go without a fight.

"We'll find her, Cam," Nolan reassured me. Although he was probably saying it as much for his own peace of mind as he was for mine. "She loves your house. You could convert one of the bedrooms into a good nest for her."

"She can have the whole basement, for all I care. Whatever she wants."

My basement was the mancave to beat all mancaves. Fully carpeted, large screen TV, wet bar, pool table – the works. It had taken me years to get it right. But I'd rather it go to her than spend another second down there without her by my side.

"You think she'll still let you watch the games, though?"

I let out a weak laugh. "Hell, I'd watch them on my phone, with headphones, as long as she's sitting next to me."

Our feet crunched in the snow, the paw prints unwavering in their trek. "Crap, what if living in San Fran's made her a 49ers fan?" I asked.

"Moon forbid," he chuckled.

I think I might forgive her for that, though.

Adrenaline pushed us forward, and if anyone was feeling tired, no one looked it or dared say it. By early afternoon, the prints had led us to an old barn. Poor thing must have been drawn to the warmth of it. We snuck inside, and her scent ended on a pile of straw.

"She was here," Archer whispered. "There's no blood, thankfully. She must be inside that house."

I took out my phone. "Has she tried to call any of you guys?"

They checked and then shook their heads. "I doubt she has our numbers memorized," Elias responded.

The barn reeked of alpha stink and I growled. "Someone has her. She would have found a way to get in contact by now otherwise."

Nolan rolled his shoulder. "Let's go get her back, then."

22
MARLOWE

The gross old farmer pack finally reentered the room. Paul had a vicious sneer on his face, while the other two appeared penitent, refusing to look me in the eye.

This didn't bode well.

"We've decided," Greg said. "You owe Paul an apology."

Was that it? Just an apology?

Not that he was owed one, anyway. The guy had kidnapped me – how dare I try to escape?

I forced my features into an expression of contrition and faked my best teary pout. "I'm really sorr—"

"Not with words, omega."

I felt the blood drain from my face as Paul started unbuttoning his shirt. "I'm gonna knot you, and then you're going to thank me for my hospitality. It was my barn you chose to sleep in, after all. It's the least you can do."

Panic burst in my chest and I pulled on the restraints. No, this couldn't be happening, I had to convince the others to stop him.

"But I'm not in heat…" I whimpered desperately.

Paul laughed, pulling his pants down next. "Don't matter, we can just consider it practice."

I looked at the rest of the pack for help. Greg was touching himself through his pants, his eyes burning with desire.

He was Team Paul, then.

But John looked appropriately ashamed. I needed to fully bring him over to my side.

"John, please…"

Paul grabbed my chin. "Don't look at him. He can fuck you later. I found you, so I get to go first."

He lowered himself on top of me, and I burst into full sobs, my wolf still maddeningly quiet. "John! I don't want this, I'm not ready! Please do something!"

He gulped. "Paul, maybe…"

"Shut up!" Paul barked back. His weight was heavy on top of me, and I struggled uselessly beneath him. "Just gotta get you warmed up, I guess." His mouth crushed into mine and I gagged from his rancid scent, whipping my head back and forth, trying to catch John's eye.

He finally stepped in, grabbing Paul's bicep. "I only agreed to this if you wouldn't hurt her."

Wow, what a gentleman. It was only rape if he was rough, apparently.

Paul fought back, trying to wrench his arm away. "She needs to learn her place. I make the rules – not her." He grabbed my hair in a tight fist, causing me to cry out in pain.

The sound drove John into further action. He snarled and ripped Paul off me. "I told you to be gentle!"

Paul caught his footing and stood beside the bed, shoving John back towards the door. "Knock it off, she's mine!"

They started grappling with each other, their fight spilling into the hallway. I tried in vain to pull myself free. If I yanked hard enough, could I break or dislocate my wrists?

Meanwhile Greg sighed, his vision clearing while he sat down next to me on the bed. "Why can't you just be nice to Paul?" he asked. "It'd make everything so much easier."

Paul had to be the ringleader, there was no other explanation as to why the other two kowtowed to him so much. It was time to really kick this mutiny into overdrive.

My lips trembled and I batted my eyelashes, speaking in a hushed voice. "He scares me. That's why I shifted and ran away from my other pack. I need to feel safe. The way I do around you."

His hand flexed by his side as his alpha instincts fought for control – I just needed to push him over the edge.

"You'll protect me, won't you?"

John and Paul's fight had moved onto the first floor, the sound of their bodies crashing into furniture echoing up the stairs. The room shook as one of them slammed into a wall below us.

"Won't you, Greg?"

His pupils dilated and he shuddered, a raspy purr crawling its way out of his throat. "Of course, Marlowe. I'd do anything for you."

I was about to ask him to free my hands when the tumbling and cursing went eerily silent. Greg's eyes didn't move from mine as he called out, "You guys good now?"

Footsteps thundered up the stairs, and a familiar figure rushed into the room, tackling Greg into the wall. I cried out at the sight of Camden, covered in blood and pummeling the old, dirty alpha with his bare fists. The violence would normally have made me sick, but today it was my salvation, and tears of joy sprang from my eyes with each sickening crunch and squelch.

Archer entered in next, his shoulders slumping as he approached my side. "Marlowe, are you okay?"

His eyes scanned my body and I nodded, my voice cracked with relief as I wiggled my arms. "Yes, can you help me with these?"

He carefully removed the restraints, massaging my hands to get the blood recirculating.

"You really came for me?" I whispered.

Elias and Nolan entered next, sheathing hunting blades around their waists.

"Always," Archer replied, closing his eyes and breathing in deeply. "You may not be pack, but…"

"I want to be," I interrupted. Camden's fists stilled, and they all looked at me, hanging desperately on my every word.

"And not just because of this. My wolf, she… she helped me realize. I was trying to find you last night. She knew before I did, and I'm ready to admit it now. I'm a shifter, I'm an omega, and I want to be in your pack."

The guys looked at me in shock, and suddenly my breath quickened. What if they'd changed their minds after finding out about Mike? Or maybe they thought what had happened here had tainted me somehow?

"If you'll still have me…" I added quietly.

Camden stood from where Greg lay motionless, his chest heaving. Then he reached over and grabbed my face, resting his forehead against mine as he released a strangled, rumbling sigh. I melted into his scent, cardamom and cedar soothing my aches and relaxing my tensed muscles.

"That's the dumbest fucking thing you've ever said, babe. There is absolutely nothing you could do or that could happen that would make me stop wanting you. And trust me, I speak for the whole pack."

I looked up as the other three grinned, nodding in agreement.

Archer scooped me up, and Nolan leaned down to kiss me on top of my head.

"Welcome to Pack Wolcott, sugar. Let's get you home."

23

MARLOWE

Nolan and Elias stayed behind to clean up the mess. The three alphas who had held me were dead, but we were on a farm full of animals and I didn't feel comfortable abandoning them all.

Since they had all traveled there on foot, Camden took Paul's truck to drive me and Archer back to his place.

We squeezed into the cab of the old Ford F150, with me sandwiched between them. "Adding grand theft auto to the list of charges now, are we?" I joked, as I took sight of the blood on my cheeks in the rearview mirror. Perhaps I should have been more traumatized, but humor was my go-to coping mechanism and it was doing a bang-up job so far.

Camden placed his arm behind me as he turned his head and backed up out of the driveway. I bit my lip as I watched his hand effortlessly turn the wheel, heat blossoming in my core.

His eyes flickered to me for a second before they went back to the road, a grin slowly growing on his face. "Well, Archer was going to take this back after we got you safely tucked away at home, but I kinda like it now. Do you think the cops will notice?"

Archer snorted but didn't reply, instead addressing me. "I want to let you know, Marlowe, that the only thing we want from you right now is for you to recover and heal. There are no expectations, we just want to take care of you. You still haven't dealt with your father's estate, and I'm sure untangling your life from your ex will be a difficult process as well."

I took a deep breath and nodded. "So, Mike's a vampire?" I

111

asked. "But he never, you know, drank my blood."

Camden grumbled under his breath, and Archer took my hand and gave it a reassuring squeeze. "*Vampyr*, yes. And I don't know why he never drank from you. They do need blood to survive, he must have been getting it from other sources. Maybe he was afraid that shifter blood wouldn't be sufficient."

Was that why he was cheating on me so much, because he needed to feed from humans? Not that it was an excuse.

"Tell me more about vampyrs. I need to understand exactly what Mike is."

Archer gave me a small smile, and began a short lecture on vampyr biology and culture, what Lunessas and servaglios were, and the truce that had followed an old war between our two kinds.

Shifters, vampyrs... this world was stranger than I had thought, and I still had so many questions. "Are there any other mythical creatures I should be on the lookout for? Centaurs, leprechauns, mermaids perhaps?"

Archer laughed. "No, just us, as far as I know."

"Mermaids would be hot, though," Camden added.

A growl erupted from my chest before I could stop myself and Camden shivered in delight. "Aw, are you jealous?"

Oh god, was I? I had to admit that I had been feeling a bit more feral in the past few days, but I definitely didn't like the idea of being so insecure.

Maybe that was because things weren't official yet.

"What about the bonding?" I asked.

Archer and Camden looked at each other, and then Archer cleared his throat. "There's no rush on that either."

I shrank into my seat. "Because you guys want time to figure out if you really want me?"

Camden clicked his tongue in frustration. "Babe, now *that* is the stupidest fucking thing I've ever heard. I'll pull over right now and bite you if you want."

"I – wait, bite?" I asked.

Camden nipped at me playfully and I yelped.

"Thank you, Camden, for that wonderful demonstration," Archer said, rolling his eyes. He returned his focus towards me, brushing a piece of my hair from my forehead. "There's still a lot for you to learn about shifters, and I want to make sure you understand everything before going forward. Bonding is done through bite. For regular pack mates, it's a meaningful, soul-changing experience. For alphas and omegas, though? It's more…"

His hand gestured in the air as he tried to find the word.

"Erotic," Camden chimed in.

I drew a sharp breath and Archer sighed. "Yes, thank you. So you see, while we're all very, um, *willing*, to bond with you, we want you to focus on recovering."

Camden chuckled. "Oh, I am more than willing. I am literally aching to sink my…"

"Camden!" Archer snapped.

I placed a hand on my throat, my chest tightening. Arousal pulsed through my veins, but my mind still defaulted to its factory setting – *engaged to Mike* – dampening my desire with shame and guilt. I needed to start learning how to submit to my attraction, and not let it feel like a betrayal.

Camden cleared his throat and placed a hand on my knee, squeezing it gently. "But yeah, I can wait until you're ready."

We pulled up to his house, and after he and I exited, Archer slid over into the driver's seat. "I'll see you in a bit. Try to prioritize your healing, okay?"

He headed back to Paul's house, and Camden whistled as the vehicle disappeared back up the road. "That really is a cool truck. Anyway…" He turned toward me and scooped me up into a bridal carry.

I laughed, my legs kicking in the air. "I can walk, you know!"

"I don't care, I just want to hold you."

He brought me inside and up the stairs, finally placing me down inside a spacious bathroom, the heated tile floors feeling heavenly on my filthy, bare feet.

"I'll be right back with a towel and some clothes."

I avoided my reflection in the mirror, not wanting confirmation on what a hot mess I must have looked like.

As soon as Camden left, I peeled off the dress and jumped into the shower, sliding the frosted glass door closed. The hot water seeped straight to my bones, my worries circling down the drain with the dirt and dried blood that sluiced off my skin.

I raised my hands in front of my face, turning them over and remembering what they looked like as paws, while flashes of my trek through the forest ran through my mind.

Holy shit… I can turn into a wolf.

I closed my eyes and tried to feel her out where she rested inside of me. It was like I could see her – curled up and passed out, still exhausted from our first shift.

Camden knocked, and my wolf's tail began to wag slightly, one eye opening in curious interest, before falling back asleep. I came back into myself when he entered. "Your stuff's on the counter."

I opened the shower door a crack and peeked my head out. His knuckles were cut and bruised from the attack, and my eyes wandered up his toned arms to his handsome face. His blue eyes were tired, but warm and inviting. A wave of his cardamom and cedar scent hit me like a freight train, and suddenly it wasn't just water running down my legs.

"Do you want to join me?" I asked, slightly impressed by my own boldness.

Camden's mouth opened in surprise, but it quickly closed and turned into a huge grin. "Fuck yeah, I do."

He tugged his henley off, and I bit my lip at the sight of his sculpted chest, my fingers dying to run through the light dusting of hair that covered his pecs and then trailed down towards…

Oh my god, his huge cock. I hadn't properly gotten a chance to look at it in all its glory yet, but my mouth salivated at the sight of it – long, thick, with a bulbous knot at the base. That was supposed to fit inside me?

Camden stepped straight into me, backing me into the wall as his eyes met mine. "Do you want some help washing your hair?"

I nodded mutely, and he grabbed a nearby bottle, squirting a generous amount into his large, calloused palms. He motioned for me to turn around and I obeyed, moaning in pleasure at the feeling of his strong fingers digging into my scalp.

"Watch out with those noises, babe," he chuckled, his erection jutting against the small of my back. "I'm trying to be a gentleman, here."

I looked over my shoulder, glancing down briefly at the offending member and then back to his face. "You have my permission to stop trying."

He visibly shivered, one arm wrapping around my waist while the other worked all the suds from my hair. His lips lowered to my ear, teeth nipping along the outer shell.

"Are you sure?"

I turned and curled my arms around his neck, pulling him flush against me; my wet, naked breasts sliding against his skin. His mouth found mine, capturing it in a kiss, while his hands ran down my sides until they curved around my ass, squeezing gently.

His cock throbbed against my stomach, and he ground it into me as his kiss traveled along my jaw and down my throat. "You're perfect, Marlowe," he whispered, his voice low and husky. "A fucking dream come true."

Slick trickled down my thigh again and I whimpered. "Camden, I want to feel your knot. Please…"

I knew he was trying to be gentle and respectful, but I didn't want a slow, meticulous session of love making. I needed a hard, fast fuck. I needed to see what that knot could do. I'd needed to know ever since I'd touched him in the hotel elevator.

All doubts about my non-human biology had disappeared, and I released my pent-up desire for the crass and very hot alpha now naked and rubbing his hard body against me.

A growl of want and desire rumbled through him, and I whined in response, desperate for friction to relieve the building ache between my thighs.

Camden bit his lips, pushing me against the wall. "I want to lick your sweet pussy, feel you come on my tongue…"

"No!" I said firmly. I grabbed his cock, lowering towards my entrance. His hand gripped one of my thighs, holding it in place while I wrapped my leg around his waist. "Right now, I just need you inside me."

He smiled on a sharp intake of breath. "Can't argue with my omega, now can I?"

He took my other leg and held me up, his cock nudging its way inside, but stopped before he thrust more deeply. "You tell me if it's too much, okay?"

I whined again, trying to push myself onto him. "Just fuck me, Camden."

His tongue invaded my mouth at the same moment his cock pierced me, and I gasped around him in delirious pleasure. His thickness filled me completely, his knot like a fleshy cock ring that hit deliciously against my clit. Each thrust was a tsunami of euphoria, and I lost myself in his hooded eyes, watching his expression as every push brought us closer to mutual release.

"Yes," I cried. "Just like that, don't stop!"

I felt the muscles in his glutes clench beneath my calves, his hands tightening around my thighs as he kept up his punishing pace. "You feel so good, baby, like you were made for me."

The sound of our wet skin slapping against each other and our panting breaths elicited a wanton moan, his knot stimulating my clit while his dick hit my G-spot from the inside. My orgasm hurtled towards me, and I pulled him in closer with my legs as my walls clenched around him.

He felt so good, so right. Like all the sex I'd ever had before was just practice for this, the main event.

I screamed my release, not caring if anyone could even hear me, and then gasped as Camden's knot pushed fully inside me, locking into place as he came. The pain from the stretch subsided and my orgasm extended further, as my body convulsed around him. I'd never experienced such sexual bliss in my life. Stars framed my vision as pure pleasure like I've never known consumed me.

"Camden," I sighed. I pulled myself in tighter to his embrace, digging my face into the crook of his neck, inhaling the scent even the shower couldn't wash away. "Oh, Cam."

He grunted, still coming inside me, the excess now escaping and leaking out of my entrance.

Words finally returned to him. "Babe," he said, his voice raspy. "Marlowe. My Marlowe, my omega. I'm yours."

We stood under the heat of the running water, shaking and panting heavily. I'd never felt so sated in my whole life. With his knot still firmly stuck inside me, he carefully stepped out onto the bathmat, and took me to his bedroom, water dripping on the floor the whole way.

He gingerly sat down on the edge of the mattress, laying down on his back and pulling me down on his chest while we caught our breaths.

"So… this is knotting," I chuckled. "Are we just stuck like this forever now? Not that I'm complaining."

He purred, his hands running down my back. "I don't know, I've never knotted before. I think it's supposed to deflate after ten or fifteen minutes."

"Mmm," I replied, nestling into his chest. "Mandatory post-coital cuddles. I like it."

His hands ran up and down my back, sending shivers across my body. "Well, it's supposed to help make sure you get pregnant."

Pregnant? Oh my god, I wasn't on birth control. And Mike had come in me, too. That's right, I had been searching for pharmacies when…

Just as I started freaking out, he began purring, holding me down tightly. "Shhh, you can only get pregnant when you're in heat. You're fine."

The confirmation I wasn't currently ovulating and the vibration from his purr calmed me. "How often does that happen? My heat, I mean."

I rested my cheek against his chest, reaching up to gently scratch his beard. He pushed into my touch and sighed contentedly. "I'll double check with Archer. But it's only a couple of times a year, I think."

Thank goodness for that. My eyelids became droopy, sleep calling to me until I snapped back fully to consciousness at the sound of the front door opening.

"Hey, we're back!" yelled Nolan. "You guys upstairs?"

My face flushed and my heart raced again. I pushed myself off him onto my arms. "Shit…"

"Shit?" he repeated questioningly. "What's wrong? Are you embarrassed they'll know we fucked?"

"Yes? No? I don't know. This whole dynamic is really new to me." I closed my eyes as the sound of their footsteps and voices came closer.

Cam pulled me back down in a big hug. "They're not going to be anything other than happy that you're happy, and maybe a little jealous. But that doesn't mean you gotta nurse their feelings and knot them all tonight to make things even, got it? We're taking this at your pace."

My pussy clenched around him again and he bit back a moan. "Babe, we're going to be locked a lot longer if you keep doing that."

Elias pushed the door open. "Hey, you left the shower…" His sharp intake of breath and the scent of bergamot and pepper that practically exploded off him informed me of his reaction to the sight of Cam and me on the bed.

I turned my head towards him and watched as he stared in fascination. "Damn, California. Do you have any idea how hot you look taking in his knot like that?"

Archer and Nolan entered behind him, both releasing their own waves of scented arousal.

"Oh god," I muttered, burying my face into Cam's chest. This group relationship was going to take some getting used to.

Cam's hands ran over my back and down the curves of my ass possessively. "You guys are making her nervous. Wanna give us some privacy?"

Archer got out of his daze first, grabbing a blanket from the foot of the bed and placing it on top of me. "I'll, um, get cleaned up

117

and order some pizzas."

"Can you get one Hawaiian, please?" I asked, my voice muffled.

Nolan snorted. "Hawaiian? Shit, we may have to rethink this. I don't know if I can be bonded to someone who likes pineapple on pizza."

Cam growled viciously when I flinched and Nolan took a step back. "I'm kidding! Calm down, alpha. Hawaiian it is."

Archer grabbed the other two and pulled them out of the room, closing the door behind him.

"I. Am. Mortified." I whined once I'd heard them retreat back downstairs. I felt like we were teenagers who just got caught with their braces stuck together.

Cam sighed. "You should be. Pineapple on pizza? That's practically a hate crime."

"Hey!" I cried. I reached over and bit his nipple. His body tensed, and I felt his cock harden inside me. His knot expanded, brushing up against my G-spot and I came again.

My orgasm triggered another one in him, and he roared as he released inside me, thrusting up from below. He collapsed into the bed, twitching as his cock pulsed inside me.

"Well," he said breathily. "I think we might need to restart the clock." I loosed a deep, contented sigh and settled into his chest. He kissed me softly on the top of my head. "Not that I'm complaining,

24
NOLAN

The pizza was cold on the counter by the time Camden and Marlowe made their way to the kitchen. Normally I could eat a whole large pie by myself, but the sound of them coming, over and over, dulled my appetite.

My cock ached at the sexually sated sight of her, her scent mixed thoroughly with Cam's.

He wasted no time becoming the affectionate alpha, but he had always been the most tactile out of all of us. She stood at the kitchen island, grabbing a slice of the untouched Hawaiian while he wrapped his arms around her from behind, kissing and nibbling at her neck.

I willed the green-eyed dragon away, focusing instead on the way she had tried to attack Megan for touching me. I didn't need to be jealous because I knew she wanted me, too. It was just a matter of time before it was the two of us knotted for hours, sharing orgasm after orgasm, my seed leaking down her leg...

"So," Elias started, breaking me out of my reverie, "I know this is probably the last thing you want to talk about..."

Marlowe tilted her head, inspecting him nervously as she set her slice back down. "What is it?"

"Your father's funeral."

Her face fell, and Cam snapped. "Dammit, Elias, is this really the time? After everything that's happened today?"

Elias sighed. "If I could wait any longer, I would. But it's already been a week. He wants to be cremated – shifter custom," he added, addressing Marlowe. "First his casket will be placed at the temple. There will be a brief ceremony, but the viewing will last for three days to give the whole town a chance to pay their respects. Afterwards, he'll be sent to the crematorium, and then that's it. You can have a reception if you want, but I don't think anyone is expecting it."

Marlowe nodded uncomfortably. "Yeah… Wait, temple? Was my dad Jewish?"

There was so much she didn't know.

"We have our own religion," I answered. "I think the closest frame of reference would be Paganism, but it's a little more complicated than that."

She arched an eyebrow. "Okay, I have a ton of questions, but I guess they can wait. So, when is the ceremony, then?"

"Sunday," Elias replied. "I can take you shopping if you need something to wear."

"No, I brought a black dress, just in case. I bought it for my mom's funeral." She stared at the slice of pizza in her hands, her voice soft. "I didn't think I'd be needing it again so soon."

Cam pulled her in for a hug, tucking her into his chest as he rested his chin on the top of her head. "You don't have to worry about anything, we'll handle the logistics and stuff."

The room fell silent. Uncomfortably so.

I cleared my throat. "Anyone want to watch a movie?"

Cam was still fully Velcroed around Marlowe, and she turned around in his arms to face us. "Sure, what did you have in mind?"

I smiled. "I was more curious what kind of movies you like, sugar."

Her face turned an adorable shade of pink. "Oh, um, I'm not really picky."

"Marlowe," Elias teased. "Come on, you can tell us."

Her hazel eyes darted between us, and then she lowered them and mumbled something.

"What was that?" I asked.

"I said I don't watch a lot of movies. I like K-dramas."

Archer burst out laughing. "Seriously?"

Marlowe huffed, crossing her arms. "Yes, seriously. My friend Esther from grad school introduced me to them."

He walked around the island and leaned into her face, grabbing her chin as his voice lowered an octave and he said something in Korean. For all we knew he could have been reciting the instructions for programming a TV remote, but it sounded very smooth.

She swallowed nervously, her arousal coating the air. "That was really hot."

"K-drama it is then," Elias said, adjusting his pants.

Ten minutes later, we were settling into another large couch in the basement, bringing the pizzas and some drinks with us. Elias wrapped her up in one of the blankets he'd bought for her, and she scooted in between Archer and myself, excitedly searching through Cam's Netflix account.

She finally settled on a show called *Be My One*, shushing us when the opening credits faded.

"Aw shit, I gotta read?" Cam grumbled as the first line of dialogue and subtitles started.

She released the sweetest little growl I'd ever heard, and he chuckled in response. "Sorry, babe."

It didn't take too long before he was out cold, and by the way Elias's eyes were drooping, he'd soon be next.

Archer was just as engulfed in the show as Marlowe, though, and they whispered little comments to each other.

I was having more fun watching her.

But after three episodes, I still didn't know what was going on, and her head had fallen on Archer's shoulder, her chest rising and falling with the soft rhythm of sleep.

Archer paused the show, whispering quietly. "Why don't you take her? I still have some work to catch up on."

I gulped, excited at the prospect of cuddling my omega all by myself for the night. "You sure? You don't want to join us?"

He turned and gave her a quick kiss on the top of her head. "I do, but I also don't want to overwhelm her with an onslaught of attention. She needs time to adjust to being the center of four alphas' lives."

I wasn't going to wait for him to change his mind. I picked her up and carried her up to the second floor, right into the room Camden had said could be mine.

I laid her in the bed, and then took off my t-shirt and pants, slipping in beside her. She sighed and rolled into me, nuzzling my chest and inhaling deeply. "Mmm, Nolan?"

"Yes sugar, I'm right here."

"You smell really good."

I swelled with pride, and my cock swelled with desire. *Down, boy.*

"You smell pretty good yourself."

She yawned, her body wriggling as she scooched even closer. "Pistachio and honey?"

I laughed, wrapping my arms around her. "Yes, nutty and sweet."

Her breathy sigh tickled my skin, and then her leg wrapped around my hip, bringing her sex flush against my erection. Her arousal grew and spurred her on, and she sleepily rubbed herself against me.

I bit my lip, trying to keep my inner beast from just flipping her over and rutting her right here.

She had to be sore, though – she was just knotted for the first time today. Was she already down for round two?

Her delicate fingers wandered up my chest and rested on my cheek, and she tilted her head upward for a kiss.

Her lips were soft and tender, and I felt her pert nipples harden beneath her t-shirt. Her tongue parted the seam of my mouth to play with mine, and I felt like I could burst at any moment.

She was so perfect, so beautiful, and so tempting.

"Are you sure? Aren't you tired?"

Her hand shot down my boxer briefs and grabbed my cock. Okay, she was sure.

I turned her on her back and rolled on top of her, grinding into her crotch as she moaned her approval, her hands roaming my body while we kissed.

Fuck, I was going to come in my underwear if I wasn't careful. I wanted to slow down, but I was starved for her love. Her perfume was intoxicating, her touch demanding.

I sat up and removed her shirt, then lowered myself to her neck and started kissing and licking every inch of skin bared before me.

My tongue traveled down to her breasts, large and soft. They could have been any size and they would have been amazing, but they fit my hands perfectly and my cock twitched at the thought of pushing them together and fucking the tight space in between.

Not tonight. We had lots of time to get creative in the bedroom.

Her back arched as I lapped her dusky pink nipples. I covered them with my mouth, gently scraping the skin with my teeth and then sucking them, flicking them with my tongue while they were held captive. Her breathy pants and frantic grinding told me she liked everything I was doing.

We really were made for each other.

I made my way further south, pulling off her sweatpants and

underwear. She was sopping wet with slick and leftovers from her earlier session with Cam.

"He filled you up good, didn't he?" I licked the juices from her pussy and she whined in pleasure, her hands reaching for my hair. Her nails scraped gently along my scalp as I continued lapping, burying my face in her sweet sex as I impaled her with my tongue.

"Nolan," she panted. "That feels amazing."

The sound of my name from her lips was angelic, and I took her clit gently between my teeth as my fingers pumped inside her, running along her inner walls.

She hissed at the slight sting, and I released her nub and alternated between licking and sucking her into oblivion.

I could die right here. This was how I wanted to go to bed every night and wake up every morning.

Marlowe bucked her hips in response, and I worked her harder, feeling her climax approach.

"That's it," I said. "Come on my face, sugar."

Her body tensed and then released, sweet slick pouring out of her gloriously swollen pussy. I licked it up greedily, loving the way her taste mixed with Cam's. She was ours now, and this was proof of it.

As her body relaxed and turned into jelly, I took off my boxer briefs, releasing my very needy cock. "Are you ready?" I asked.

She nodded wordlessly, her legs spreading as she waited for me to fill her.

I wish I could have taken a picture of her in this moment, she was so sexy. So ready to let me have her. How did I ever get to be so lucky?

I thrust inside and gasped. Her channel was simultaneously tight yet pliant, the wet, warm walls stretching to accommodate my girth. My mouth crashed into hers, taking her bottom lip between my teeth as I set a hard, steady pace. Her arms wrapped around my torso, fingernails digging into my skin as she held on.

My orgasm was coming fast, but I didn't want it to end yet. I pulled out and then flipped her on her stomach, leaving her flat as I pushed between her folds, fucking her from behind.

Her muffled moans and pants were my undoing, and she came again, her pussy choking my dick. On instinct and with one final push, my knot secured me into place inside her, and I unleashed a torrent of cum with my release. My vision darkened for a moment; the feeling so intense I was afraid I might pass out from the pleasure now overtaking every cell in my body.

This was the power of the omega, a creature so perfectly built for sex it brought alphas to their knees. I collapsed on top of her, relishing the way the curve of her back and ass met my chest, but rolled over to my side to avoid crushing her for too long.

I spooned her as my cock continued to spasm inside her, feeling her body writhe and twitch with each aftershock of our orgasms.

A purr overcame me, wrapping her up as tightly as I could.

I never wanted to let go.

"I'm so glad you chose us," I said quietly, running my hand up her side. It felt like my life was finally complete.

"I'm so glad you chose me, too," she replied.

Chose her? She wasn't a choice – she was a gift from the Moon herself.

I wanted to tell her that but she'd already started to fall asleep, so I simply held her instead, committing every detail of the night and her face to memory.

The door opened slightly and Archer stuck his head in, smiling as he looked us over. "Well, perhaps I should have joined you."

"Mmm, next time. Tonight, I selfishly want her all to myself."

He sighed, rubbing his hand down his face. "I don't blame you."

Marlowe stirred in my arms, her eyelashes fluttering as she awoke. "Archer?" she whispered. "Is that you?

"Yes, it's me."

She opened her eyes fully and raised herself up on her elbow. "I selfishly want you here, too."

Archer looked at me for confirmation and I shrugged. "What sugar wants, sugar gets."

He tried unsuccessfully to hide the grin on his face as he entered and closed the door behind him, stripping quickly down to his underwear. He slipped in on the other side, facing Marlowe.

"I want to see what your pussy looks like taking my pack mate's knot," he said, his voice low and commanding.

She clenched around me, turned on by Archer's dominance, and timidly raised her leg.

Archer lowered his face right next to where we were joined, running his fingers along her stretched skin. She moaned quietly, and I began kneading her breasts and kissing along her neck.

"Fascinating," he whispered. He suddenly stuck out his tongue and licked the length from my balls to her clit, sending a wave of pleasure between the two of us. My knot re-inflated, and her breath caught in her chest, another orgasm building inside her.

"That's it." Archer smiled, spurring us on. He licked her clit again and then stuck his fingers in her mouth as she opened it to moan. She closed around them, sucking as they pumped. Below, he kept a steady, oral assault on her sensitive bud.

Every sensation she felt rippled through me, an erotic chain reaction that left me ready to explode again. When I came once more, Marlowe screamed around Archer's fingers, but he didn't stop.

A garbled "please" escaped her puffy lips, but Archer was relentless.

"Such a good girl. You can take another, can't you?"

Marlowe nodded, a tear forming in the corner of her eye as Archer devoured her clit again. My balls twitched, ready to shoot another load. I couldn't believe I had anything left in there.

Her moans and pants crescendoed into a loud cry, and I roared, releasing even more of my seed.

Archer's gaze bored into me while I came, and his grin was nothing short of devious. He was enjoying the hell out of torturously pleasuring Marlowe in order to make me orgasm, too.

He lowered himself again and licked up the cum that had leaked out around her entrance, sucking until he had gathered it all in his mouth. Then he came back up and kissed her, using his tongue to push it all in. She took it all and swallowed.

Holy fuck.

The pack and I had never shared a female before, and to be honest, I was a little apprehensive about fucking Marlowe with company.

But Archer was diving headfirst, and it was kind of hot.

"Good girl." He patted her on the cheek as he praised her.

I groaned as the words set off another chain reaction of orgasms between Marlowe and me, and Archer sat back, admiring his handiwork.

"Please," she moaned. "It's too much…"

He tutted as he laid back down, taking her face in his hands. "Yes, that's enough for tonight. Go to sleep, *yeobo*."

She surrendered to exhaustion, and I followed soon after.

25
MIKE

I adjusted my cufflinks as I made my way down the marble hallway. I had fought my way free from those beta shifters at the hotel easily enough, and then driven straight to New Orleans without stopping.

Marlowe's departure from my servaglio had caused a deep wound. Not just to my ego, but also physically. Once a vampyr has chosen a Lunessa, a need for her love and devotion becomes like a drug. The strength of the servaglio depended entirely on the strength of the bond between the master vampyr and his Lunessa.

If she knew how much her rejection was killing me, she would come back. There was no way she could write off the years we'd been together for something as inconsequential as concubines, because Jen and Grace meant nothing to me. They were warm bodies meant to take care of my needs when my Lunessa was unavailable. I had originally chosen them due to their willingness to not only take a seat below Marlowe, but also their desire to worship her as much as I did.

If Jen and Grace didn't please her, I'd get rid of them in a heartbeat.

Hell, for Marlowe's love, I had decided I was willing to forgo a proper servaglio altogether.

But I had no chance of winning her back alone now that a pack of alpha shifters had set their sights on her. My blood curdled at the thought of them bonding with her already, filling her with their knots…

I needed help.

Vampyrs were normally solitary creatures. We didn't form

communities with each other like shifters. We had our servaglios, and then kept out of each other's ways.

Unless one of us was wronged. A slight against one vampyr was a slight against us all.

I stopped in front of the large wooden doors, clasping my hands behind my back. I nodded a curt greeting to the vampyr guards, waiting for the summons.

Minutes ticked by, when a voice finally boomed. "Enter."

The guards opened the doors and I walked into the dimly lit chambers, dropping to one knee and averting my gaze. "I, Michele Sanguinetti of the San Francisco order, give my thanks to the Vampyric Council for agreeing to hear my plea."

"Rise," sighed a bored vampyr. I stood again, my eyes scrolling along the curved table placed on a large dais. The five elders sat before me, shadows dancing across their pale faces from the dim candlelight that illuminated the room.

The high elder's Lunessa approached me, a beautiful woman with dark, smooth skin and hair tightly curled in a halo around her cherubic face.

She held a chalice and knife, and I offered her a smile as I grabbed the blade, running it along my palm. I hissed at the sting, forcing my hand into a fist so she could collect the drops of my blood in the cup. Once she determined I had given enough, she took the knife back and offered the chalice to the elder at the far right, who took a sip and passed it down.

I took out the handkerchief I had prepared, wrapping it around the cut while the elders tasted my intentions.

"Speak," commanded the high elder, apparently satisfied with my offering.

I bowed my head in supplication. "It is with a heavy heart that I come to you today, seeking vampyric assistance to retrieve my Lunessa. She was taken three days ago, her love swayed against me by shifters who coveted her."

"You mean she dumped you."

I bristled at the accusation, keeping my head low so they wouldn't see the grimace on my face. "As you know, grooming a Lunessa takes time. She hadn't learned the ways of our people yet, and, in her shock, sought comfort from those who would do anything to hurt us in order to punish me."

One of the elders tapped his chin in thought with a thin, bony finger. "I find it difficult to believe that a woman would prefer a shifter over a vampyr. Are you... insufficient? Lacking, in someway?"

I took a deep breath, ignoring the cruel snickers from the other elders. I had known this question was coming. "My Lunessa is also a shifter."

A chorus of hisses erupted, and the high elder spat on the ground in disgust. "You dared contaminate our bloodline with a mutt, and now have the audacity to ask us to help you do so? Leave. This is over."

They started to get up, but I blurted out, "Have you ever tasted an omega?"

"Omega?" One of the elders turned back towards me, raising an eyebrow. "Omegas are extinct. What are you talking about?"

From another pocket I took out a bag with the underwear she'd left before she'd run off. They were coated in her slick, the scent potent enough to fill the room with her pheromones.

The elders inhaled deeply when I opened it, their pupils dilating and teeth growing. "What is this magic?" one elder whispered, his hand reaching towards his groin.

I closed the bag, tucking it back into my pocket before the memory of our last meeting drove me to tears. "It's not magic. Omegas are biologically made to draw lust from males. She is beautiful, her body taut yet yielding, and her libido matches my own. I made the mistake of adding to my servaglio before she was ready, but the true error was believing I should even have one. A vampyr needs several women to sate his desire, and an omega requires a pack of virile alpha males to do the same. Together, we only need each other. We are the perfect pairing."

The high elder called to his Lunessa, requiring her to tend to the erection Marlowe's scent had given him. She dipped below the table on her knees, and he sighed as she made quick work with her mouth.

"Be that as it may," he grunted. "You would sully the heritage of your own sons with such a Lunessa."

"Sullly, or improve?"

The table broke into another round of hisses, and I held my hands up and bowed again. I knew it was a tough sell, but I couldn't let it deter me. "I'm not saying every vampyr should mate with a shifter, but what if my sons inherited alpha strength, and imperviousness to the cold? Help me retrieve her, let me breed with her, and if you find my offspring wanting, I'll cull them myself."

Of course, that would never happen. I wanted a family with Marlowe more than anything, and recurring dreams of us surrounded by little auburn-haired boys with freckled faces taunted me every night. But the lie was worth the risk.

The high elder groaned when he came, patting his Lunessa on the cheek as she retreated back to the shadowed recesses of the chamber. "You're asking a lot. We risk restarting a war between our species should we attack a pack, who by all rights have a greater claim over the omega than you."

"She is MINE!" I snarled. Stunned by my own disrespect, I dropped to my knees. "Please. The loss of a Lunessa is one of the greatest pains a vampyr will know. And the taking of one is a crime against our people. By the Vampyric Code, Article 2, Section 3, you are honor-bound to accept my request of a unit of no less than twenty warriors to retrieve her."

The high elder turned to his left and right, gauging the reactions of the four others. The elder to his left shrugged. "He's right."

The elder at the far right looked at his nails. "I'm fine either way."

The other two pursed their lips. "Article 12, Section 19?" one offered.

A slow grin grew over the high elder's face.

Article 12, Section 19? I racked my brain, trying to remember what rule he was referring to.

"I see you're confused, Mr. Sanguinetti," the high elder drawled. "If you want to force our hand using the Vampyric Code, then allow us to do the same. 'As recompense for the retrieval and safe return of a lost Lunessa, the vampyr shall forfeit his claim to her for one night, yielding her chamber to his brethren in his stead.'"

I swallowed back the bile that rose in my throat, and my hands balled into fists, shaking at my sides. It was either a night with the elders, or a lifetime with the shifters.

"You cannot expect to extol the wonderful pleasures of copulating with shifter omegas and not allow your elders a taste."

Lewd chuckles and smacking lips echoed in the stone chamber. I closed my eyes and spoke through gritted teeth. "I agree."

"Excellent. Elder Roth will gather our strongest warriors. They will be ready to march upon the shifters in approximately one week. We will contact you then."

One week? She could be fully bonded to them any day now, which meant only their death could release their hold. But with twenty vampyrs, it could be done.

"Thank you. I will await your call."

26
ELIAS

"Shred or keep?"

I looked up from the box of documents I was working on to inspect the paper Marlowe now held in front of me. She had announced that morning that she really just wanted to keep her mind busy to try to process everything that had happened and had decided that starting the painstaking process of going through her dad's house was just the project she needed.

Archer had tried to argue that what she really needed was a therapist, but I had shushed him and offered to help her go through the office.

Not just because it would give me some alone time with her, which I craved after discovering I was the only one who hadn't even kissed her yet, but also because I understood how she felt. When my parents had died, the only thing that had helped me deal with the grief was delving headfirst into my work.

"Shred."

We'd been at it for hours, and a large garbage bag full of shredded paper sat next to the desk.

I rubbed my eyes, allowing them to unfocus and look around the room to relieve the slight strain from all the reading I'd been doing, and I frowned at the hidden safe built into the wall across from me.

James had left a lot of detailed instructions in his will, but there had been no mention of that.

We had found it entirely by accident when Marlowe noticed a crooked painting. As she had tried to straighten it, she had heard a weird scraping sound and looked behind to see what had been catching the canvas.

Whatever was in there, James had intended to take it to his grave.

She went back to her own pile while biting her lower lip in thought. By now, she'd been able to figure out which sorts of records weren't worth holding onto, but she still double checked with me every once in a while.

Were she one of my paralegals, I might have been annoyed. But I knew why she was really asking – she was just as aware of the fact that we hadn't fooled around yet as I was and wanted to cut the silent tension in the room.

And I could never be angry at my omega for desiring my attention.

I stood up to stretch and released a huge yawn. "Okay, California, I think we need a break. Are you hungry?"

She laughed. "Why are you guys so obsessed with feeding me?"

I walked around the desk and grabbed the arms of her chair, leaning down into her face. "It's an alpha thing. We love to provide. Is there something else I can do for you, then?"

She shuddered, and I let a smirk through at the pride of turning my omega on. To my surprise, she threw the papers on the floor and grabbed my face, pulling herself up to kiss me.

I grunted my shock at her boldness, then pulled away. With one swipe, I cleared the desk, then picked her up and set her on the edge, my lips meeting hers in desperate, ravenous need.

Everything about her tasted sweet. I peppered kisses down her neck, inhaling her heavenly scent. Her legs wrapped around my waist, and my hands rubbed up her thighs and under her skirt. I groaned as I found her sex completely bare, her slick now coating the front of my pants as my crotch prodded against her.

"You naughty little thing," I chuckled, nipping her ear. "Were you planning this?"

She reached up, her teeth catching my bottom lip, and her hands answered for her as they made quick work of my belt. "Knot," she breathed, releasing my dick. "Now."

She was going to be the death of me. Or at least the death of my career. How could I ever look at a desk the same way again? I grabbed the hair on the back of her head and pulled, forcing her face to tilt up towards mine. "Look at that – our sweet little omega has become so greedy." I rubbed the head of my cock around her clit and watched as her expression melted into one of pure pleasure.

She whined, pushing her hips forward to try to slide onto me, but I tsked and backed up. "Wicked, wanton little thing. If you want my knot, you're going to have to work for it."

The growl that escaped her lips was so hot I nearly gave into her demands. "You certainly won't get it that way," I chided.

Her hands grabbed at my chest, unbuttoning my shirt and savoring my skin underneath. She leaned forward, licking my nipple and drawing it into her mouth.

I groaned my approval, then backed up again. "You're on the right track."

She grinned her understanding, sliding off the desk and onto her knees. I watched in awe as her pink, soft lips enveloped my cock, her tongue expertly sliding around my head, and then up and down the shaft as she brought me in further.

I lost myself to the exquisite wet warmth of her.

"That's it, you'll earn my knot quickly if you keep this up."

She hummed her appreciation at my praise, the vibrations sending a wave of pleasure up my spine. I ran my fingers through her thick, strawberry blonde hair, watching the way her eyelids fluttered at the feeling of my fingers lightly digging into her scalp. My omega liked head rubs. Very good to know.

I resisted the urge to thrust into her mouth, wanting to know how much of me she could handle, and what she was comfortable with. She struggled with my entire length, hitting her gag reflex in her effort to swallow more of me.

My hand rested on her cheek, wiping away a tear that had pooled in the corner of her eye as she strained to fit me in. "My sweet little omega, don't hurt yourself."

She shook her head, releasing me for a moment. "You taste so good, Elias. I want more." Then she swallowed me again, my knot growing in anticipation.

Fuck, how did I get so lucky? I couldn't take it a second longer, and I pulled out, grabbing her arms and lifting her up, then flipping her onto her stomach on the desk. I entered quickly and without warning, my knees weakening at the feeling of her pussy clenching around me. I met no resistance, her walls drenched in slick, and she grabbed the edge of the other side of the desk, panting beautifully with each thrust.

I probably should have felt a twinge of shame for rutting my deceased client's daughter on his desk, but all I felt was pure bliss, the kind of enlightenment that could only be had between an alpha and his omega.

She was mine. My purpose, my love, my everything. The center of my universe, my light in the dark. I would devote myself to her happiness every day until my dying breath.

"Elias," she moaned. "Harder, please!"

I'd been holding back slightly, careful of how small she was compared to me. But I should have known better – her body was made to take a thick alpha cock. And a thick alpha cock she would have.

I held her hips and pounded into her with everything I had, the desk scraping against the floor with each thrust. Her walls tightened around me, and my knot was the biggest I'd ever seen it, throbbing in anticipation. With her release came mine, and I pushed my knot with one final shove forward, locking myself inside her. I roared as my cock exploded, leaning onto the desk with one hand to steady myself as I continued to empty my seed. I didn't even know it was possible to create that much cum, but our orgasms triggered greater and greater pleasure in each other and my cock continued to throb.

Once I was sure my balls had to be empty, I grabbed her around her stomach, picking her up and off the desk as best I could and collapsing into the chair, letting her fall back into my chest.

"I feel like I've never properly had sex before now," I chuckled, catching my breath. "Like everything in my life was just a practice run for this."

"I know what you mean," she replied, reaching back to run her fingers through my hair. "How could I ever have a normal cock again after this?"

A growl rippled through me. It wasn't fair to be jealous or angry at someone for their exes. Moon knows I had plenty of my own. But vampyrs were another story, and the thought of the two of them having been together for years filled me with rage. How dare a bloodsucker try to take what was ours?

"You never will."

"Mm, no, I definitely will not."

Her neck sat tantalizingly close, and my anger from watching the vampyr try to take her from me the other night took over. Perhaps I should have allowed Cam to go first – he was technically our leader, even though he'd never exerted his authority over us before and we didn't operate as a pack that way. But my desire to possess and protect the sweet little omega on my knot propelled me forward. I brushed the hair from her creamy skin and struck hard into the crook of her shoulder.

Her body lurched and she yelped in surprise, but I held her steady in my arms and between my teeth, letting the power of the bond course through us.

When the pain made way for pleasure, I released her, lapping up her sweet blood and closing the wound.

Another orgasm tore through her, and mine soon followed. I kept a tight grip, one hand splayed across her abdomen and the other grabbing one of her breasts, while she held onto the arms of the chair, riding out our shared release.

"Elias, did you just…?"

"Yes," I answered, my voice heavy and low. "You're mine forever now, Marlowe."

A smile crept over her face as she sighed, leaning the back of her head against my shoulder. "Good."

27

MARLOWE

They say smell was the sense most strongly connected to memory, and my dad's lingering scent of sage and vetiver hit me hard, dredging up long forgotten childhood scenes. I remembered what it felt like to sit on his lap while he read to me, the scratchiness of his whiskered chin when he kissed my scraped knees.

Trips to the park, sledding in the winter. Hugs after tantrums and secret cookies when my mom wasn't looking.

The night he never came home. My mom crying in their bedroom.

I had hoped he'd left some clues to his disappearance. What had been so important he had to leave, so important he'd never see his family again?

But so far, we were coming up empty.

Elias had confirmed that while most of his friends and acquaintances knew he'd been married since he still wore a ring, not as many people had known about me and my brother, and he had apparently never talked about us.

But he had been such a valuable and successful member of the community with his business and outreach that no one had really questioned it.

We were almost finished going through all his paper files. Thankfully, my dad had been enough of a luddite to insist on hard copies of everything, because I wasn't sure we'd ever be able to get into his computer.

The safe was also a mystery. I hoped he'd been forgetful

enough that he'd written the code on a scrap of paper and shoved it in a desk drawer, but we unfortunately hadn't had such luck.

A folder in one of his cabinets labeled "Oakmoss Fellowship" caught my eye, and my body went stiff.

Elias noticed my reaction, quickly coming to my side. "What is it?"

"The Oakmoss Fellowship… that's the one I received. It paid for my undergrad and graduate tuition."

My hands shook as I opened the file. My applications were the only papers inside. Tears sprang to my eyes as my fingers ran down the pages, reading my answer to the essay question about the biggest obstacle I'd overcome in my life.

I'd written about losing him.

"Did you know about this?" I whispered, my voice cracking.

He shook his head slowly, placing a reassuring hand on my shoulder. "I remember helping him set this up, but that's where my involvement ended. I never knew it was for you."

I gulped, clutching the file as I closed my eyes. "I only knew about the fellowship because of a random email I received. I just applied on a whim. I even encouraged Ezra to apply, but he wanted to take a gap year and travel before going to college. He died before…"

Elias wrapped me up in his thick arms, bringing me to his chest. He didn't say anything, just offered silent comfort while I processed my discovery.

"I really thought he'd just been a deadbeat, skipping out on child support." I sniffed.

"Hmm," Elias responded.

I backed up and looked at his face. He had the same expression from back at his office when we first met.

"Spill it," I said. "You know something."

He pursed his lips and looked to the side for a moment, his eyes softening when he finally looked back at me. "Do you know how your mom paid for everything?"

I swallowed, thinking back to my childhood. We had lived in a modest three-bedroom home, with enough money for essentials and a little extra. As a little kid, I hadn't thought it was strange that my mom didn't work because so many of my friends' moms also stayed at home, until I had realized that was because they had dads.

When I had asked her about it, she said that we lived off a small inheritance she had received from her parents, long since dead.

Still, if he had been so wealthy, if his company had been so successful, why the disparate lifestyles? Why the secret fellowships?

None of it was adding up.

I looked back towards the safe, an idea popping in my head. I wiped my cheeks and crossed the room. "I wonder…" I whispered to myself.

I entered six numbers, and the door clicked open.

Elias came up behind me. "You figured it out? What was the code?"

"Mine and Ezra's birthdate."

He sighed. "Should have been our first guess."

"No," I replied, carefully swinging the door open. "Honestly, before this moment, it would have been my last."

Inside was filled with photos of me and my twin brother – school pictures, birthdays, Halloweens, and Christmases. Vacations in Door County, trips to the zoo and Six Flags. All tucked into envelopes addressed to my dad in my mom's handwriting, with no return address.

Further tucked in was a small bag. I yanked it out, unzipping it quickly and taking the contents out one at a time, handing them to Elias to hold. Three thick bundles of cash – one US dollars, one euros, and one pounds. Next came four passports. The first one was for my dad, but it said he was from Texas and listed his name as Murray Peterson. The following three were for me, my brother, and my mother – our faces photoshopped, our names all changed.

"What the hell is this?" I gasped.

I could feel Elias's shock and confusion clearly through our newly created bond. "Honestly, I have no idea. I didn't help him with any of this."

He took the bag and all its contents and set them on a nearby side table, then held my hands in his. My mind raced with questions and emotions and memories, and a deep purr from Elias anchored me back. "Marlowe," he said. "I didn't know your father that well – mostly through Cam growing up, and then when I started my firm he became one of my first clients, keeping me on retainer to help with his personal affairs and the company every now and then. That was it."

I looked around the room, trying to get a picture of the male my father was, but I was coming up blank.

"What was he like?" I asked quietly.

He raised a hand to my cheek. "Cam could answer that question better than me."

"No," I shook my head. "I want to hear your experiences, too."

His eyes looked up as he gathered his thoughts. "He was quiet, but warm and kind. The kind of male who didn't seem like a yeller. He just exuded strength and dominance. He was quick to help, quick to try to figure out solutions to any problem you came to him with. And he really wanted to uplift the shifters of this town. Even though he was alone, I think he really enjoyed being a part of the community. Having it around him."

"But not his family," I whispered.

Elias drew me in for another hug. "I'm sure you don't want to hear this, but I don't think he left you all from any lack of love. Fathers don't create fake non-profits to fund their children's college tuitions or fill secret safes with years' worth of their pictures and an emergency go-bag to whisk them out of the country because they don't care. They do it because they're scared."

I digested his words, finding them at odds with the image I'd built of my dad for the past twenty-two years of my life. The deadbeat who couldn't even be bothered to come to his own son's funeral.

But had his distance really been motivated by something else? "What does a shifter have to be scared of?" I asked, my voice shaking.

His forehead touched mine. "I can't think of anything powerful enough to rip a male away from his pups. Protecting our families, our packs... it's our prime motivator."

"Could... could he tell I was an omega, maybe? Or that I could shift..."

Elias interrupted gently. "Possibly, but designations aren't revealed until we reach puberty. At four, you'd have been just like all other female pups. Perhaps a little punier, though," he added with a wink before continuing. "And a shifter's first full transformation usually happens closer to maturity."

That was one hypothesis I could rule out, then. "Does my dad have any other family? Close friends?"

"Family, not that I know of. Friends, maybe. Cam would know best, with your two families having owned a business together."

It was all too much. I needed to talk to my pack, come up with a list of people my dad knew and any potential threats in the area. "We should probably head back. I think I've had enough life-shattering moments for today."

I reached out through the tenuous connections I felt now that we were bonded, but they were fraught with simmering anger.

"They're mad, aren't they?"

Elias chuckled. "They'll get over it."

28

ARCHER

We felt it immediately.

The true power of a pack bond, the one that linked shifters telepathically, had disappeared along with our ability to fully shift. But we could still sense each other. And the feeling of a fifth soul, the bonding of a new member in our pack, rippled through us like a wave of electric shocks.

We'd been standing around the kitchen island, discussing the logistics of Marlowe's move from San Francisco to Maiingan Hollow when it happened, the impact buckling our knees.

Camden recovered the fastest.

"That son of a bitch!" he yelled, slamming his fist on the granite countertop. "He had no right!"

He raced towards the door, but Nolan chased after him and tackled him to the ground before he could slip his boots on.

"Wait a minute, you idiot!" he seethed, trying to pin Camden on his back. "If you bust in there, guns blazing, you're going to make her think they did something wrong."

Camden struggled to push Nolan off him. "*He* did something wrong. As pack leader I get dibs when it comes to bonding new members, especially an omega! Archer, back me up!"

I sighed, pinching the bridge of my nose. "I understand how you feel, but Nolan's right. You're going to ruin what is likely a really special moment for her. And while I would have preferred waiting a bit until she was more comfortable with pack life, if she's fine with this, we should be, too."

Camden growled, kneeing Nolan in the groin and shoving him away. "Fuck you and your logic. Elias disrespected my position, and as pack leader, I need to put him back in his place."

Position. I rolled my eyes. Every pack needed a leader, and some packs adhered to that kind of hierarchy more than others. Strength wise, we were more or less at the same level, although I had to admit that Camden had the most fighting skills and could use those to beat any of us in a fight if it came to it.

But that wasn't why he was our leader. Camden had been chosen for two simple reasons – one, because it was his idea. And two - the Wolcotts were one of the most powerful families in our community. Wolfcrest Construction employed a lot of the town, including my own father when he and my mom had first moved here from Korea. Socially speaking, it made the most sense for us to be under him.

Until now, he'd never really mentioned it unless he was joking. He might have had no problem acting like a cocky bastard when it came to impressing females, but truthfully, he was a pretty humble guy. Put the four of us in a line, and no one would guess he was our pack's leader or that his net worth was in the millions.

It was actually amusing to see him so spitting mad about pack rank right now.

"Well, whatever you do, make sure Marlowe doesn't see. She's going to think you don't want her," Nolan groaned, recovering from Camden's cheap shot.

Camden roared his frustration, getting up, stomping over to the couch, and flopping down. "She knows I want her. More than anything."

"Then show it," Nolan offered. "Next time you have the chance, bond her yourself. Archer and I will even refrain until you've done it, right?"

He gave me a look, and I raised my eyebrow. I hadn't planned how to exchange a bond with her yet, thinking I'd probably just play it by ear. Now that I was being asked, I ran through the various positions we could find ourselves in when I finally sunk my teeth into her soft skin, but coughed and cleared my throat before my cock got too excited.

"Right, we'll wait for you."

Camden played with the zipper on his hoodie and grumbled. "You fucking better."

For being our supposed leader, he really was such a child

sometimes.

He sulked a bit longer, until Elias and Marlowe finally returned a few hours later. Camden did his best to put on a happy face... well, a neutral face, but Marlowe made a beeline for him once her shoes were off, giving him a big hug.

"You're upset. I can feel it, now."

Elias mouthed a silent, sorry-not-sorry apology, and made a quick escape upstairs. I would question him on the details of the bonding later, but for now, I wanted to watch our omega in action.

Omegas were meant to be the glue that held packs together, that neutralized our aggression. Today was her first test, and I was riveted already.

Camden slumped his shoulders, wrapping his arms back around her and kissing her on the head. "I'm not mad you're bonded, baby. I'm mad because Elias beat me to the punch."

She tilted her head up, batting her eyelashes. "But you got to knot me first, right?"

He started a growl but it petered out pretty quickly, and his hand dropped to grab her ass. "Damn right, I did."

With a yelp and a giggle, she kissed him on the cheek and then we all heaved a sigh of collective relief as calm cleared the hostile atmosphere.

We'd met her only about a week ago, and she already knew how to soothe Camden. Would Marlowe employ the same techniques if another alpha of our pack needed talking down? While doe eyes and hugs were perfect for our 'intrepid leader,' that certainly wasn't the most effective way to reach me when I was angry.

I was curious to find out if omega skills were intrinsic or learned.

She cleared her throat. "Hey, so Elias and I found some interesting stuff at my dad's, and I really want to talk to you all about it."

"Oh?" Nolan asked. "Like what? Some skeletons in the Linden family closet?"

Her face paled slightly, and Camden bared his teeth back at Nolan.

"Wait, for real?" he asked.

She reached out towards Camden, bringing his arm around her waist. His face lit up, clearly thrilled that our omega found comfort in his touch.

"Yeah, I want to talk about it with Elias here too, but I have a feeling he's hiding from you all for the moment."

We exchanged a knowing glance. "Can't imagine why…" I murmured.

Nolan checked his watch. "I'm sure we'll get this resolved by dinner. We can talk then."

She nodded her thanks, and I switched the subject to something I'd wanted to ask her earlier.

Ever since she'd fully shifted, the scientist in me had been dying to run some tests. We hadn't really addressed it much, due to what had happened, but now that she was bonded, her wolf should have had a better sense of home and safety.

"Marlowe, would you be interested in coming with me to my lab tomorrow? I have a little work to catch up on, but I also wanted to take the opportunity to get some blood samples from you. If that's okay, of course."

Her eyes lit up. "Yeah, sure. I'd love to learn more about what you do, and I'm curious to learn why I can shift into a wolf when most of you can't."

"None of us can," Nolan corrected. "The last full shifter died an old man over thirty years ago."

"Damn, so I'm the only omega and the only full shifter? What are the chances?"

"Astronomical," I replied. "I hate to turn you into a guinea pig, but if you're open to testing, it could lead to the answers we've been looking for."

Marlowe nodded, chewing her lip while her eyes fixated on some spot across the room, the true scope and gravity of her uniqueness settling in. "No, yeah, I get it. I'm happy to help, however I can."

Camden pointed a finger at me. "Just don't go turning her into a pin cushion or anything."

I gave him a mock salute. "Yes, alpha."

He flipped me off and then turned Marlowe around, leading her to the basement. "So, we watched your K-drama yesterday, which means today we're going to watch one of my favorite movies. Do you know *Die Hard*?"

Marlowe scoffed, flipping her hair. "Excuse me, do you think I lived under a rock before I came here? Of course I know the greatest Christmas movie ever made."

Camden pretended to stumble and clutched his heart. "Babe… where have you been all my life?" He threw her over his shoulder amid a flurry of shrieks and laughter.

"Not a Christmas movie," Nolan half-heartedly called from his spot at the island, eyes now glued to his laptop screen.

"Quit being such a Gruber!" Marlowe yelled back.

Camden howled as he barreled down the stairs.

I chuckled to myself, feeling at peace with how our omega not only fit seamlessly into our pack, but how she had brought us back together. Eau Claire wasn't that far away, but I had bought a house there a few years ago and rarely found any reason to come back to Maiingan Hollow anymore – aside from seeing my sister and her pups. And Elias stopped coming regularly after his parents died.

He now peeked over the balcony, calling to us from the upstairs walkway. "Cam still pissed?"

I growled in response. "We're all pissed. That was reckless."

He sighed, running his hand sheepishly through his hair. "I know, I'm sorry. It's not like I planned it or anything. I had my knot in her, totally blissed out, when suddenly all I could think of was her piece-of-shit, blood-sucking–"

"We get it," Nolan interrupted. "The bond certainly protects her now, and we all wanted it anyway. Best to just move forward, especially since we still need to deal with the vamp in some capacity when we help Marlowe get her stuff from California. Also, I don't want to alarm anyone, but if she truly was his Lunessa, he might not be willing to let her go that easily. We need to be prepared in case he returns."

Elias cracked his knuckles and rolled his shoulders. "I'd like to see him try. What's one vampyr going to do against four alpha shifters?"

"Well, Elias Faulkner *Esquire*, perhaps this is more your purview than mine, but I've been researching vampyr laws and there is some precedent for the ex to get assistance from his council to retrieve her." Nolan slammed his laptop shut and crossed his arms. "I have an omega *and* a town to think about, you know."

Elias leapt over the railing, landing on the first floor with a large thud. He rushed Nolan and grabbed him by the collar. "And what is *that* supposed to mean?"

"Everything good?"

We all turned towards the basement stairs where Marlowe now stood. "There's just a lot of tension I can feel right now."

Elias released Nolan's shirt, then stormed passed us and headed back up stairs. Marlowe came over first to Nolan. "Hey, why don't you grab some snacks and watch the movie with us? I'd love to point out all the ways you're wrong."

He snorted. "Okay sugar, except for the fact that Bruce Willis himself said…"

She stuck her fingers in her ears. "La la la, can't hear you! See you down there in a minute. Don't forget the Red Vines!"

The frustration radiating off Nolan dissipated as we watched her skip towards the staircase, making her way to Elias next. He chuckled to himself, grabbing the movie candy from the pantry and going downstairs to wait for her return.

I desperately wanted to observe how Marlowe dealt with Elias, but it was already clear she knew exactly what she was doing.

Nolan loved to feel needed, so she gave him a job. Elias required a few moments to himself when he was upset, which was why she didn't go to him first.

A round of laughter from Elias's room and the easing of the bond told me she'd succeeded there, too.

"Well done, Marlowe," I whispered to myself. I threw a bag of popcorn in the microwave. Life was definitely about to get much more entertaining.

29
MARLOWE

"Just because it takes place during Christmas, doesn't mean it's a Christmas movie," Nolan said as he closed the front door, carrying the freshly delivered Chinese food over to the kitchen island. Why we always ate there and not at the perfectly functioning dining table, I would never know.

"Christmas music," I said, listing my arguments on my fingers for emphasis. "Decorations. Family. Love…"

"Genre," he replied. "No Santa Claus. Too violent…"

"Oh, for Moon's sake," Elias grumbled. "My General Tso's chicken is getting cold."

Once we all settled in, and I made fun of Camden for not being able to use chopsticks, Elias and I went over everything we had found in my dad's office.

Archer looked the most thoughtful. "How much do you know about your parents?"

"In what way?" I asked.

He set his chopsticks down on his plate and wiped his mouth, then steepled his hands in front of his chin in contemplation. "Where are they from? How did they meet?"

"I…" Wait, what did I know about my parents? I had asked my mom before about our family history, for both school projects and my own curiosity. Why did those memories and conversations feel foggy now? "I can't remember."

Archer leaned forward, his curious expression intensifying. "Let's focus on your mom first, since you knew her the best. Where

145

was she born?"

"Wisconsin," I replied quickly. "She was definitely born here. I... I think?"

"Did you come across her birth certificate at any time?"

My mom's death had been much more emotional for me, and my high school friend had offered to help me pack up her house. Thankfully it hadn't taken long, since my mom was a minimalist. But I didn't recall coming across any vital records aside from mine and Ezra's in her paperwork.

"No, I don't think so."

"What's her maiden name and date of birth? I can ask one of my paralegals to start looking," Elias offered.

"Her name is Thistle. Thistle..." It felt like my brain was stalling. "This is really weird; it's like it's at the tip of my tongue but as soon as I start to say it, it disappears."

Camden dumped more of the beef and broccoli on his plate, completely unfazed. "Maybe she was from one of those shifter communes," he suggested, shoveling a forkful of rice in his mouth.

Archer tilted his head, considering. "That's... actually a good possibility."

"Shifter communes?" I asked.

"They're like the fundamentalist version of shifters," Nolan explained. "They live off the grid in rigid, conservative hierarchies, away from humans and modernized shifters like us. We don't know too much about them because they don't trust outsiders enough to let us visit, but over the years there have been escapees. Unfortunately, they don't speak much about what goes on there except to ask for a place to hide."

That would explain a lot about my mom. She always seemed so flustered by technology and sometimes spoke like she was from another century.

"Are omegas and shifting abilities gone from there, too?"

Archer shrugged. "No one knows. We don't communicate with them. But if your mom ran away from one, it would make sense for her to not have a full name or proof of birth and also be terrified of being discovered and dragged back. Especially once she had you and your brother."

I shivered. I'd just escaped those gross old alphas on the farm – the idea of being taken away to join a pack even more dominating than them was nightmare inducing.

"Hey," Elias said. "You don't have anything to worry about.

You're bonded to us now. No one is taking you away."

Reassurance shot straight through the bond from Elias into my heart, spreading warmth and protection.

I wondered what my mom would think of me now. She had gone to great lengths to hide me from shifters, and yet here I was, bonded to a pack of alphas.

"But what about my dad? Could he have come from one of those communes, too? Cam, how did our dads meet?"

He put down his fork and grinned. "It's the funniest story. They met at an arm wrestling contest at some bar outside of Osseo. Your dad won, and then my dad got pissed, and they started fighting. After they beat each other up enough, they bought each other drinks and then started talking. My dad was trying to build his own house, and your dad said he had some experience and offered to help. So then..."

A small pang of jealousy started slowly stabbing me in the chest as he continued. I imagined Cam had a ton of stories about my dad like this. Hell, he'd even admitted to me that my dad had treated him like his own kid.

But I would never get the chance to know him like that.

Elias reached over and grabbed my hand, sensing my pain. "Thanks, Cam. Marlowe, I'm sure I asked for your dad's records when drawing up his will. I might have copies back in Chicago."

Nolan nodded in agreement. "Maybe you'll find more as you continue going through his house, too."

We'd already gone through most of his office at his home, but there were other places he could have possibly kept more information. "Yeah, maybe. Cam, did my dad have an office at the company's headquarters?"

"Yup. He wasn't using it much once I kinda took over for him and my old man, but we never touched it."

"Great, can you take me there sometime next week?" I asked.

"No problem, babe. You should probably meet the higher-ups anyway."

Nolan's lo-fi dinner soundtrack filled the air with calm melodies and beats, and I felt almost overwhelmed with love and support. It had been just over a week ago that I was living in a two-bedroom condo in San Francisco, engaged to someone I thought was the love of my life. Now I was back in Wisconsin, bonded to four guys who called themselves alpha males unironically, in a five thousand square foot house.

But it already felt like home.

30
ARCHER

We walked through a nearly empty campus. It was Saturday, and with finals coming up, most students were holed up in their dorms, the library, or the local cafes to study.

I had to admit, it looked pretty bleak, and I felt a little self-conscious while I cleared my throat. "It's no Stanford, but I get to work with and teach a lot of shifters, and…"

"What do you mean?" Marlowe asked, looking at me curiously. Against the white snow, overcast sky, and nondescript buildings, Marlowe's strawberry blonde hair and hazel eyes were a bright contrast that nearly took my breath away. A ray of sunshine, a lone flower. Her pink, pouty lips looked kissably soft, but I fought the urge to take her in my arms.

"Sorry, did I have resting bitch face or something? I was just lost in the nostalgia of it all. Don't you wish you could go back to your undergrad days sometimes?" she sighed wistfully.

I chided myself for letting my insecurity get the best of me. I knew by now Marlowe wasn't a snob. Why did I think she'd judge me for working at a small state school?

"Sometimes," I admitted. "Life sure was a lot less complicated back then."

But I also hadn't had an omega, either.

I unlocked the door to the biology building, leading her to my office on the third floor. Normally I preferred the lively sounds of students on their way to class with the semester in full swing, but today the silent, dark hallways provided the privacy I required for testing. Not

148

to mention my desire to keep Marlowe away from prying eyes and noses.

"Just put your stuff on the chair, and then we can get started in the lab." I placed my computer bag on the desk and took off my coat, turning around to the sound of my door closing and locking.

Marlowe leaned against it, biting her lip and looking nervous. "Professor, you wanted to see me?"

I arched an eyebrow, wondering what she meant. But then my cock hardened, figuring out what was going on faster than my brain had. Her heavy perfume coated the air, and I fought the urge to smile, setting my expression into a disappointed frown instead. "Yes, please take a seat, Ms. Linden. I'm afraid it's quite serious."

I'd never entertained a student-professor fantasy before, despite having been the object of a few innocent crushes over the years. But if Marlowe wanted to play, I was game.

She shuffled into the chair, knees together. Averting her gaze, her cheeks blushed. "It's about my test, isn't it?"

I rolled my sleeves up, placing my arms in front of me on my desk and clasping my hands. "It is. You got every question wrong. It was worth fifty percent of your grade, so I'm afraid you're going to fail my class."

She held back tears, releasing a shuddering breath.

What a talented little actress. I wondered how far she was interested in taking this.

"Please, Professor Lim. If I don't pass, I'm going to lose my scholarship. I can't pay the tuition on my own, so I'll get kicked out of school! Could I take the test again? Or is there any... extra credit I could do?"

She unbuttoned the top of her shirt, her fingers tracing down her cleavage and revealing a black lacy bra.

I tsked. "Ms. Linden, do you think a little peep show is enough to raise your grade by fifty points?"

She pulled down her bra, now exposing one pink, hardened nipple. "How many points is a breast worth?"

I sat back in my chair, crossing my arms. "I suppose I could give you five points per breast. As long as I get to touch them."

She took off her shirt and bra completely, walking topless around my desk. After pushing my knees apart, she leaned against it, fluttering her eyelashes coquettishly. "Please, Professor."

My cock twitched in my pants, aching to be free. But I wanted to take my time, as I was already having too much fun. I held her heavy breasts in my hands, inspecting them closely. My thumbs brushed lightly against her nipples, and she giggled. "Your hands are so warm and big. But I bet your tongue would feel nice, too."

I chuckled deeply. "Have you been thinking about my tongue?"

"Everyday in class, Professor. I like to sit in the back, so I can touch myself while I imagine your tongue all over me."

I pushed her down on her back slightly as I stood, lowering my mouth over the beautiful, creamy mounds, drawing her nipples into delicate peaks. She moaned as I licked and sucked, dragging my teeth over her soft skin.

"Ten points, Ms. Linden. Forty more to go." I sat back in my chair, watching as her bottom lip trembled. "I'll give you fifteen more points if you show me exactly how you like to touch yourself while you think about me."

Her hands shook as she slid her jeans down her hips, stepping out of them to reveal a black, lacy thong to match the bra. She slid her hand down her stomach, all the way to her sex, pushing the underwear aside to rub her clit. I bit my thumb, rubbing my other hand over my erection as she slipped her fingers inside her pussy, whimpering while she slid them in and out. "I like to imagine your cock is fucking me, Professor. Just like this."

She spread her legs wider, inserting three of her fingers inside herself now, and I bit back a groan, remembering exactly how sweet she had tasted with Nolan's knot deep inside her. Her commitment to the role was commendable, because I was about to lose my mind.

Breathy moans turned into frantic pants, and I watched as she made herself come to the thought of me, her eyes closed and lips parted in pure bliss, back arched as the pleasure released in her tense muscles.

I grabbed her hand as she pulled her fingers out of herself, licking them clean.

"Professor!" she gasped.

"I have a confession of my own," I said, letting go of her. The tether of control was fraying, and all pretense of calm was falling by the wayside. I could feel my need for her growing into an unhinged intensity, unlike anything I'd ever felt before. "I know you touch yourself in my class. And when I'm at home, I touch myself while I think about you."

She blushed. "Would I get any points if you showed me?"

I unbuckled my belt and unbuttoned my pants, bringing my cock out and stroking it in my hand. "No. But I'll give you five points if you'll let me come on your tits."

She kneeled in front of me, grinning wildly. "Oh, thank you, Professor! You're so generous! I would have let you come on my face for two."

Fuck, the cheek on this female. I grabbed her chin. "Watch your tone, young lady, or I'll deduct all you've earned and then some. What will you possibly do for your grade, then?"

She rubbed her hands along my thighs, looking up in thought. I started masturbating in earnest, watching the way her breasts bounced with each jerk.

"Would you be interested in fucking me from behind while I blow one of your friends?"

She asked the question so innocently I nearly laughed. That particular image had been one of my main fantasies during her heat when I took care of myself in the shower. But hearing the words coming out of her mouth, knowing she had also thought about it, quickened my orgasm, and I felt it building much faster than usual.

"Mm, don't make promises you don't intend to keep, Ms. Linden."

She presented her chest as my release neared, gripping onto my legs for support. "Oh, I fully intend to keep it. I've seen you in town, Professor. I've watched you and your pack. Maybe all four of you would like to take turns?"

I growled as thick ropes of cum exploded onto her chest, sticking to her perfect skin. Her perfume, now mingled with my scent, invaded my senses and kept my cock from becoming flaccid. She swiped her finger and scooped up a drop, licking it off.

"You taste delicious. Would you like to see?" She smeared my cum around her skin, taking some into her mouth. Then she leaned up and kissed me, pushing it through my lips with her tongue.

This omega was my undoing. My cock once more fully hardened, I was done with games, and I pulled her onto my lap, kissing her furiously. Her slick covered my pants, and my semen smeared all over my shirt. Thank the Moon I kept a change of clothes here for when I went to the gym.

She raised herself onto her knees and positioned the head of my dick at her entrance. She grabbed it underneath her, rubbing it along her clit like her own personal toy, throwing her head back and moaning. "How many points for knotting me, Professor?"

I grabbed her waist and pulled her down hard, bucking at the feeling of how perfectly her pussy gripped my cock. She gyrated her hips over my knot, whimpering with need.

Beautiful. My moon, my stars, my world. Her long, wavy hair fell in cascades down her smooth back, her pistachio and honey scent filling the room.

More. There was no such thing as enough with my omega. I would always be in need of her. I picked her up and stood, laying her on top of my desk and leaning over her, watching her face as she succumbed to the pleasure I gave her. She wrapped her legs around my waist to pull me closer and I obeyed. Whatever she wanted, it was hers.

Her walls tightened and as she found her release, I pushed my knot fully inside her, my vision blurring from the ecstasy. The literature on knotting could not do this feeling justice. Like no sex I'd had before, like no drug I'd ever tried – it was a state of pure euphoria. My orgasm did not stop, and I emptied myself inside her over and over.

"A million," I mumbled, finally regaining a modicum of authority over my faculties.

"What was that?" she asked breathily.

"You get a million points for letting me knot you."

I wrapped my arms around her back and lifted her off the desk, sitting back in my chair. Her sweet smell would linger enticingly in my office for weeks. It was a good thing winter break was starting soon. I didn't think I could get any work done, nor let any of my shifter students in here, for a very long time.

And I would definitely never look at my desk the same.

"That's great, because I have you for Anatomy next semester, and I think I'm going to be coming to your office hours every day for help."

31

MARLOWE

I rolled up my sleeve and winced.

Archer tsked. "This is just the rubbing alcohol. You need to relax."

I dug my nails into my palm as he prepared to draw my blood. "Are you sure you're qualified to do this?"

"When did I say I was qualified?" he chuckled darkly.

"Wait, wha— Ow, you son of a bitch!"

Blood filled the tube sticking out of the crook of my elbow and I grimaced, turning my face to the side. "That was mean," I hissed through gritted teeth.

"Mean, but necessary. The longer you think about it, the more likely you are to faint. Is it needles or blood you don't like?"

He tugged on the end of the rubber band on my bicep, extracting the needle and pressing a cotton ball over the pin prick hole. "Hold this."

"Needles I think," I replied. "I mean, nobody likes needles, right?"

He labeled the small vials and then stuck a piece of medical tape over the cotton ball to keep it in place. "If you say so. I've never minded too much myself. But I'll keep the draws to a minimum, then."

The thought of getting pricked again made my face pale, but I knew how important this research was to my scientific alpha. "I'm happy to help if I can. Have you thought about getting samples when I'm in my wolf form?"

His eyes twinkled, and I should have known he'd already run

through all the tests he wanted to conduct. "Yes, but first we have to see if we can even get you to shift again."

He put away the vials of my blood, and I bit my lip at the sight of him working in his lab coat. Sexy professor, sexy doctor... My pulse raced with the promise of all the games we could play.

Unfortunately, not only could shifters scent arousal, but the bond I had with my pack meant even my private thoughts and feelings weren't so private anymore. Archer gave me a knowing look as he walked back over. "Ms. Linden, is there something you'd like to share with the class?" he asked, his voice low and sultry.

I crossed my legs tightly and then my arms. "That depends, will it get me out of running?"

He nipped me playfully on the nose. "I'm afraid not."

Our next stop would be the Exercise Science Department, so he could conduct a treadmill test. He wanted to see if stress was the key to my ability to shift, which meant I needed to run while he measured my heart rate and blood pressure. And, possibly, induce a shift.

It didn't seem safe to do so on a college campus, but Archer assured me the building would be empty. Apparently, the dean of that department was also a shifter, and had locked it down that afternoon as a favor.

"Besides, it's not going to take too long," he said. "Surely, you can endure fifteen minutes of cardio?"

Surely not. A co-worker had once convinced me to sign up for a 5K charity run with her, and the only thing that had propelled me over the finish line had been the thought of killing her.

I gave Archer my saddest whine and he groaned, his face contorting as he fought the urge to give in. "Come on, that's not fair. I don't use my alpha bark on you."

A snort erupted from my chest. "Alpha bark? What the hell is that?"

He shot me a very evil grin, running his tongue along the bottom of his teeth. His hands in his pockets, he leaned over, taking a moment before he finally spoke in a commanding tone. "*Up.*"

My body moved of its own volition, hopping out of my chair and standing at attention.

"*Ten jumping jacks.*"

Once more I obeyed, and my mouth dropped open in shock at the total and complete control he could wield over me. "How are you doing this?"

He leaned against a table, crossing his arms and looking way too pleased with himself. "Sheer force of dominance. Your omega whine induces a similar effect, especially over your bonded alphas."

Archer then walked over and stood in front of me, taking my chin so he could look down into my eyes. "But I only use it on bad girls."

A shiver ran down my spine. "I don't think that's the motivation to behave that you think it is."

He tilted his head, inspecting me carefully. "Oh? It doesn't frighten you to know I could force you to do nearly anything I wanted?"

I licked my lips, imagining Archer or my other pack mates commanding me in the bedroom. It didn't frighten me because I trusted them not to take advantage. "Quite the opposite."

His pupils dilated and he inhaled sharply. "Very good to know." He released my chin and cleared his throat. "But you still have to run."

"Well?" I asked after the cool down, still trying to catch my breath.

"Aside from you looking amazing in shorts and a sports bra," he replied as he removed the censors from my skin. "And being an absolutely pathetic runner, I can't really say. I'll have to analyze the data more closely later and compare it to other shifters."

"I won't have to do this again, will I?"

Archer shook his head in disbelief. "I might make you do this again just because you so desperately need the exercise."

I groaned. "I might not be able to run but I am not out of shape. I walk all the time! And I'll have you know that when Mike and I went to Europe last year, I was averaging well over twenty thousand steps a day without complaint."

His name slipped out of me easily, my mouth running faster than my mind's desire to never talk about him again. But we'd been together for so long, and despite how our relationship ended, I had been happy with him. So as much as I wanted to paint all our memories with a sour brush, I couldn't. At least not yet.

My pack, however, was a different story. I picked up on the quiet growl from Archer and quickly changed the subject. "Any chance we can get some lunch on the way home? I'm starving."

Archer gave me a small smile. "Of course. Why don't I take

you to the Moonlight Diner in Maiingan Hollow? You haven't gotten to explore the town much yet, right?"

"Oh my god, yes, that would be great." The only part of Maiingan Hollow I'd seen had been City Hall, so getting to experience more of the town that might become my home was exciting.

He gave me a quick kiss on the forehead. "Go ahead and get changed, I'll meet you outside in fifteen minutes. I just have to clean and return this equipment."

The Moonlight Diner was so quaint I could die. The waitresses wore outfits straight out of the 50s, and a jukebox in the corner played a steady stream of Elvis, Chuck Berry, and the Everly Brothers. We made our way across the white and black checkerboard floor to a booth, and after sliding across the red vinyl seat, I opened the menu and looked it over with glee.

"Do you want to split the fried cheese curds with me?" I asked.

Archer's eyes twinkled with amusement and he adjusted his glasses. "You can take the girl out of Wisconsin…"

"…but you can't take the Wisconsin out of the girl, yeah yeah. Do you want some or not?"

"Always."

The rest of the menu looked just as enticing, and I was ready to order everything when the waitress came over and smiled. "Hey, Arch, long time no see. How's Ivy doing?"

Ivy? Who the hell was *Ivy?* I could feel the rage building inside me, and I closed my eyes and began to breathe deeply.

Archer noticed my agitation and responded quickly. "My sister? She's quite well, thank you. I'm excited to meet my new nephew."

My cheeks heated with shame. After I'd nearly clawed Nolan's cousin's eyes out, the guys had assured me my irrational feelings of jealousy were normal, but I still hated that even the idea of them knowing other females made me react so viscerally. And like Megan, Ivy was family, for god's sake.

"Another nephew! That's what, four pups now? Tell Shane to give her a break already."

Archer smiled. "Will do."

"And hey…" Her voice lowered. She placed a hand on the table and leaned towards him, her back facing me. "Can you tell Cam to give me a call? We were supposed to see each other last weekend, but he totally ghosted me."

Okay, this was too much. Cam was *mine*.

My hands balled into fists, and before I could leap out of my seat Archer whipped his head back to me. "Marlowe, *stop*."

I let out a small yelp, the bark freezing me in my spot. The waitress finally turned around and looked over at me. "Is this… your girlfriend?" she asked, her eyes narrowing while she tried to suss out our dynamic.

Archer cleared his throat. "Marlowe, this is Rachel, a friend from high school. Rachel, this is Marlowe, our pack's omega."

Cue the record scratch.

Rachel's mouth dropped open and the tables closest to us turned around to see, murmurs of "did he say omega?" coming from their lips.

The town would have found out sooner or later, but the unplanned public outing, combined with the raging desire to rip Rachel's throat out for thinking she could take one of my alphas had me feeling far too exposed and volatile. This wasn't exactly how I had wanted to introduce myself.

Finally, the rational, empathetic, *human* side of me regained control, and I noticed the deep hurt falling over Rachel's face. She and Cam had planned a date, and then he had dropped her for me without so much as a good-bye text. He and I were having words when I got home.

"Omega?" The word was a pained whisper. "But I thought…"

She didn't finish the sentence, and her words hung heavy in the air, her heartbreak palpable. I felt the feminine urge to reach out and comfort a fellow female hurt by a dumb guy, but I was probably the last person she'd want anything from. It was my fault Cam had dumped her, after all.

Archer gave her the space to process the news, waiting patiently until she looked back at him. "When did you all meet?"

"Last Friday," he replied, his voice calm. "Marlowe is James Linden's daughter. She met Camden and Elias to go over his will."

"I see." A few more moments went by before she shook out her shoulders and plastered a sad smile on her face. "Well, it's not like I thought we were going to get married or anything. Anyway, what can I getcha?"

Archer ordered for us so I wouldn't have to talk to Rachel, and I sent him a silent thank you.

"Okay, coming right up. And hey, Marlowe?"

I looked up sheepishly.

"I'm sorry if I upset you."

"Me?" I replied. Rachel seemed like such a nice person, and my anger over Cam's treatment of her and my own reaction began to simmer. She didn't deserve any of that, from him or me. "Oh, you didn't do anything wrong. Cam certainly didn't tell me he was seeing someone, either. If I'd known…"

She ripped the order ticket off the pad and laughed. "Alphas are idiots."

I grinned, darting my eyes towards Archer and then back up to hers. "Exactly."

Rachel left, and once she entered the kitchen, I dropped my head on the table, moaning in embarrassment. "Oh my god, that was so awkward. Please don't tell me you have a string of old girlfriends you've left in the lurch that I have to be worried about, too?"

Archer sighed, rubbing the back of his neck with his hand. "No, not me. But Nolan and Camden were two of Maiingan Hollow's more prolific bachelors. You're going to run into some exes, of course, but also some bitter females that will be mad you've taken both of them off the market. Word's going to get out soon now that Rachel knows, since she's friends with everybody."

Ugh, could this get any worse? I folded my arms and rested my head in them, blowing an errant hair out of my face. "This is why I like big cities; small town dynamics are so fucked."

Archer gave me a knowing shrug. "Well, Elias would agree with you on that. Which reminds me, we need to have a pack meeting soon."

"Pack meeting?" I snorted. "What, are we going to sit around in khaki uniforms and recite the Wolcott oath?"

Archer reached over and pinched my nose. "Very funny. But yes, we need to discuss how we're going to operate moving forward. Do you really want to move to Maiingan Hollow, into Camden's home? Do you want to continue working? Typically packs with an omega live together, but that doesn't have to be our arrangement if settling in a small town won't work for you. We'll all suffer if you're unhappy."

I sat up and looked out the window. The past week had been an absolute whirlwind, and I'd been avoiding thinking about the logistics of making this new life my reality. Coordinating with Mike to get my stuff, moving across the country, quitting my job…

My job. I liked what I did, and I felt a sense of pride and

fulfillment in work and getting paid. Could I find something like that out here? Or would being a "house omega" be just as rewarding? I didn't even need to ask the pack to support me, because with my dad's inheritance, I likely wouldn't have to work again if I didn't want to.

And would I even like living here? I *did* prefer big cities. Not just for the relative anonymity, but also the amenities and opportunities. I liked theater, I liked art, I liked innovation. Did I need a self-driving car to take me home from a night at the bar? No, but it was still awesome to live in a place where that was normal.

I also liked living in California. Ocean, mountains, and plenty of sunshine. Farmer's markets 365 days a year. I could get weed *and* boba delivered to my front door at the same time through an app.

Archer watched me carefully, reading my every thought as though they were written on my face. "The Twin Cities aren't so far," he said gently. "We could help you settle there and then visit on the weekends."

My gut churned at the thought of it. I couldn't imagine just seeing my pack two days a week. I'd only known them for eight days, four of which I couldn't even remember, but they'd already become the most important people in my life. I couldn't even sleep unless I'd hugged and kissed each of them good night.

"Or," he continued, "Elias offered to bring you to Chicago. We'd still try to make weekend visits work, but at least you'd be with one of us all the time."

Archer sure had a lot of suggestions. I raised an eyebrow. "You guys have been talking about this without me?"

He shrugged. "It's been weighing on us. As much as we're enjoying this honeymoon period, we all have responsibilities that have been put off, and we need to return to the real world soon. But we don't want to do that without a plan because your happiness and safety are now our top priority."

I bit the inside of my cheek to keep from crying. "All I know is, living away from any of you will be impossible."

Archer had reached over to grab my hand when Rachel exited the kitchen, balancing our order on a large tray. "I don't even like considering it, either."

"Okay," Rachel chirped as she approached us. "Two double bacon burgers, cheese curds, and two root beer floats. Enjoy!"

I smiled my thanks and as soon as she was gone, I switched my plate with Archer's.

He tilted his head in confusion and I whispered, "I'm not saying she spit in my burger. But I know that if I had just found out I was serving the female who stole my boyfriend, I might spit in her burger."

"Oh, so I get the spit burger then?"

I pouted. "But I thought you were into that kind of thing?"

He rolled his eyes and took a quick bite. "Brat," he mumbled.

I popped a cheese curd in my mouth and winked. "Thank you, alpha."

32

MARLOWE

I barely had my shoes off before Cam ran into the room, picking me up into his arms and burying his face into my neck. "Mm, I missed you so much, babe."

My heart craved the attention, but I was still upset. "I know someone who missed you, too," I sighed. "Her name's Rachel. Ring a bell?"

Cam stilled, slowly setting me back down on my feet. He shot a look at Archer, who walked by, patting him on the shoulder for luck before heading upstairs and leaving him to face me on his own. Nolan looked up from where he was working at the kitchen island. He closed his computer and smiled, bringing his hands up behind his head, ready to enjoy the show.

Cam panicked, and I secretly enjoyed watching him squirm. "She means nothing, I swear it. I haven't even thought about her since I met you."

I crossed my arms, tapping my foot. "Yeah, that's entirely the problem! You didn't think to shoot the poor female a text and let her know it was over? So she wouldn't have to find out by meeting your omega while she was at work?"

Nolan whistled in amusement, and Cam shot him a dirty look before turning back to me. "I would have told her eventually, I just…"

"Has she tried to text or call you since last weekend?"

"Uh…"

The guilty look on his face enraged me. "You stood her up and then ignored her? That's a horrible way to treat people, and you

161

know it."

He hung his head. "Yeah…"

"You're going to call her," I demanded, pointing a finger in his chest. "*Call* her, not text, and properly apologize. You're not going to try to justify yourself. If she gets mad, you're not going to get defensive. You're going to acknowledge her feelings and admit you were wrong. Got it?"

His shoulders slumped and he looked down to the floor. "Got it."

"Good." I gave him a pat on the cheek. "And finally, you're going to buy me a giant box of chocolates to apologize for the awkward situation you put me in."

He nodded and then slinked off down the hall into his office, closing the door behind him.

"Damn, sugar!" Nolan said. "You almost killed my cousin for standing next to me, but after meeting Cam's ex you sympathized with her? Does that mean you like me more?"

"Ha ha," I replied, getting a can of sparkling water out of the fridge. "Maybe I've just evolved. Did you ever think about that?"

Nolan stared at me for a moment and then grinned. "Archer barked at you, didn't he?"

My stomach clenched and I choked on my sip. "Shut up!"

"Ooh, does our little omega like being ordered around?"

The slick dripping into my underwear answered his question, and he patted his knee. "*Sit.*"

My legs propelled me forward all on their own, and Nolan pulled me up onto his lap. "This is very good to know," he purred into my ear. "I think we can have a lot of fun later."

I felt his cock harden beneath me and I nodded wordlessly, my breathing becoming shallow. "I don't like anal."

Nolan burst out a laugh. "I'm sorry, what?"

"Anal. I've tried it, and I don't like it. Just letting you know what my boundaries are."

He stopped laughing and wrapped his arms around my stomach tightly. "Thank you for telling me. I'd never make you do something you didn't want to." He opened his laptop back up and clicked on a tab in his internet browser. "I found this recipe online. I was thinking of making it tonight. Does it sound good?"

I gave it a quick look. "Lasagna? Yeah, sure."

"Not you, too." He grunted in frustration, scrolling down to the ingredients list. "Look, it's lasagna al forno. It's more authentic. It uses bechamel sauce instead of ricotta cheese."

"Si, certo, sembra deliziosa."

Nolan spun me around in his lap. "You speak Italian?"

I shrugged. "Maybe I spent my junior year studying abroad in Milan."

"Mmm, say something else."

"Ti voglio bene," I whispered in his ear.

"Oooh, donde está la biblioteca?" he responded, running his hand up my leg.

"Damn, nothing impresses a girl like high school-level Spanish."

His nose ran along the outer shell of my ear. "Obviously. So, do you want to go shopping with me?"

I wanted to do something else with him more, but shopping also sounded fun. I slid off his lap and headed back to the door. "I'm not going to run into any of your jilted lovers, am I?"

"No," he replied, closing his laptop. "I properly dispose of my lovers when I'm done with them, like a gentleman."

I slipped my shoes back on. "Nice to know chivalry isn't dead."

I was not prepared for how well everyone knew Nolan.

He was the mayor, and I should have anticipated that. But he was stopped by half the people we walked by, and looked so happy introducing me as his omega.

I smiled through my introverted pain and put up with the small talk and weird stares. It was clear people had a lot of questions, but thankfully kept them to themselves.

He whistled while pushing the cart down the aisle, asking me to hold his shopping list. "What do we need next?" he asked.

"Um... one pound of ground beef and one of ground pork."

We made our way to the butcher's counter, grabbing our ticket from the take-a-number dispenser. There were seven people ahead of us, and the woman whose turn it was couldn't seem to make up her mind. Nolan gave me a knowing look as the waiting crowd shuffled in mild annoyance.

"Hey, Signorina, do you think you could head to the liquor store next door and pick up some bottles of wine?" He handed me his card. "This might take a while."

"Sure thing. So, like, a nice Riesling, then?"

He looked at me dumbfounded. "I… what…"

"Oh my god, I'm kidding! Don't worry, I'll pick the most expensive reds they have." I gave him a kiss on the cheek and walked away, ignoring his continued sputtering.

Most of the wine in the attached store was from California, and I recognized one of the brands from a weekend Mike and I had spent in Napa.

Well, not picking that one, then.

I tried to push him out of my mind while I looked for a Chianti or something similar.

I chuckled to myself as I skipped over the Pinot Grigio, happy that Nolan had passed my little wine test. A sweet, white, German wine with lasagna? Inconceivable.

The bell over the door rang as it opened and I heard a couple of females enter, laughing with each other. A light, clean scent preceded them.

Betas, I surmised. Archer had helped me learn how to distinguish between different shifter designations through smell. Alphas, and omegas, apparently, had the strongest scents, while betas tended to be more subtle.

They came down the aisle I was in and their voices dropped to whispers.

"That's her."

My face heated, and I put the four of the closest bottles of Merlot I could find in my basket and walked past them to the register. I just wanted to leave.

"Omega whore," one of them spat.

I whirled around. "Excuse me, what did you say?" I might have been shy, but I could still stick up for myself. At least a little.

"You heard us. One alpha isn't enough for you, you need a whole pack?"

My heart stuck in my chest. I'd been warned just a few hours ago that some of the females in town might be a bit jealous, but I hadn't thought they'd be mean enough to say it to my face.

I also couldn't help but be surprised. The guys had made it seem like one omega with a whole pack was normal. Expected, even.

"But that's how it's done…"

One of them stepped closer, leaning down into my face. "You know, we betas were doing just fine when omegas went extinct. Alphas stopped treating us like consolation prizes. Now your kind is back, and

164

you've gone and bonded to the four hottest alphas in Maiingan Hollow? Greedy slut."

My bottom lip trembled, and I ran to the register, willing the tears at bay.

"Omega, eh?" the cashier asked, taking a deep breath. "Damn, you smell divine."

I couldn't take it any longer. I left the wine on the counter and ran back to the grocery store, finding Nolan talking to some man while he was still waiting. He smiled as I approached but scrunched his eyebrows when he noticed my empty hands. "Don't tell me there wasn't anything decent in there…"

I shook my head and held out my palm. "Can you give me your keys? I just want to wait in the car."

His eyes ran up and down my body and he grabbed my shoulders. "What's wrong, did someone try to touch you?"

"No, I just… I don't want to talk about it here."

The growl that rumbled in Nolan's chest was so loud, the whole butcher section cowered, backing away from us. "Marlowe, tell me."

"Please," I begged. "We can talk about it at home."

His eyes were still on me, darkening by the second. "Stu, do you mind watching my cart for a minute?"

The man he'd been talking to swallowed nervously. "Yeah, no problem, bud."

Nolan took my hand, pulling me outside forcefully and back into the liquor store. "Nolan, please, don't…"

He scanned the aisles until he found the two betas in the back, the only other customers. He growled again, and they both stood at attention. The guilty looks on their faces when they noticed us spoke volumes. "What did you do to her?" he snarled.

They shrank into their shoulders and averted their eyes but remained silent. "*Speak*," he commanded.

"Nolan!" I yelled before they could respond. "I don't want to do this."

His growl sent another wave of dominance through the small store, shaking the bottles. "They hurt you, Marlowe. I can't allow that to happen."

"*This* is hurting me," I whimpered. "You're making this worse."

He released a deep breath, but pointed at the two females. "If either of you so much as look at my omega again, I will…"

165

"Nolan!"

He roared in frustration and pulled me back outside. "You have to let me protect you!"

Nolan was enraged, his reaction more than I could handle. "This isn't protecting *me*," I replied. "You're just protecting your ego!"

The look in his eyes was murderous, and for the first time, one of my alphas was actually scaring me. My heart raced, and I backed up slowly, a sad, submissive whine escaping my throat.

The sound brought him back to his senses and he shook his head in disbelief, the rage in his face melting into regret. "Sugar, I'm so sorry if I scared you... Please don't look at me like that."

Oh god, what had I gotten myself into? I'd just signed myself up for a lifetime with four males I barely knew. I felt protected when they killed those alphas who'd kidnapped me, but would they really kill two females just for being catty? Catty but, also, *probably*, justified?

"Can I please just wait in the car while you finish shopping?" I cried.

He stepped forward, wrapping his arms around me. "I would never hurt you. You're my everything."

"Please..."

Nolan placed his forehead against mine and put his hands on my cheeks. "Tell me you know I wouldn't hurt you."

"I know," I lied. Because how could I? I worked in women's advocacy; I'd helped dozens of domestic violence survivors escape their abusers. I knew the warning signs, the patterns, the progression. Alphas were walking bags of aggression and testosterone – violence was in their nature. Could being their bonded omega really spare or protect me? And what about the other females in this town?

Nolan sighed, finally giving me his keys. "I'll be done soon." With a kiss on the cheek, he walked back into the store and I found his car in the parking lot, letting myself into the passenger seat.

I curled up into a ball and finally released the sobs that had been building inside me. I was now 0-2 on having a normal interaction in this town. Could I really make a life here? With this pack? In a weird, horny, traumatized state, I'd bound myself to near strangers. Strangers who could kill grown males with their bare hands.

Strangers who'd made it clear they weren't ever letting me go.

A knock at the window brought me out of my misery, and I screamed.

"Marlowe, it's just me. Are you okay?"

I wiped the fog off the glass and saw Elias, near desperate with

166

worry. "I felt your pain through the bond. What happened?"

I wiped my cheeks and opened the door. "First of all, you need to stop sneaking up on me when I'm in a parked car. Second, it's nothing. We can talk about it later. How did you get here?"

"Drove. And it's not nothing, Nolan seems upset, too. Did you guys fight about something? I know he can be a pedantic asshole sometimes."

I closed my eyes, replaying our argument in my head. "Kind of."

He growled, breathing deeply through his nose. "Well, the pack will deal with him later. You're coming with me. You don't need to be here anymore."

"But what about—"

"I'll text him, don't worry. Come on."

I left the keys in the cup holder and followed Elias to his car. "I don't want to say it's perfect timing, but I actually finished making something for you that might make you feel better."

"What is it?" I sniffed.

He patted my knee. "You'll see."

33
MARLOWE

Archer and Camden were pacing the floor when we arrived, talking over each other until Elias held up his hands. "She doesn't want to talk about it yet. Let's give her some space."

Cam pushed past him and hugged me anyway. "Your apology chocolates are in your nest."

"My nest?" I felt my wolf stir under my skin, the first time since I'd shifted that night at the hotel. She was... happy. Excited.

"Dammit, Cam. I was just about to surprise her." Elias huffed.

Cam turned around, a snarl overtaking his lips. "You took her initial bonding from me; I'm just making things square."

Bonding.

I was bonded to this pack now. Forever, by the way it had been described to me, which meant there was no escape. Even if they all turned out to be violent psychos. Had this been a giant mistake?

Elias clutched his chest and winced in pain, looking towards me in horror. "You regret the bond?"

Archer stood up to Elias and grabbed him by the shirt. "This is why I wanted to wait. The bond is new enough that she can still reject it. Do you have *any* idea what that would do to us?"

"Guys," my voice was barely a whisper. The tension, the fighting, the anger... I felt every negative emotion running through the pack and wrapped my arms around my stomach. "I can't take this. Everything hurts."

Cam picked me up, wrapping my legs around his waist while he held my chest against his, purring deeply. "I know. We fucked up today, huh? We got just the place for you to feel better."

He brought me upstairs to a room I hadn't been inside yet, setting me down in front of the door. It opened with a gentle push. "Surprise!"

I couldn't explain why, but the space instantly calmed me. Everything about it was soft and cozy – big, fluffy blankets and pillows were piled everywhere, and small fairy lights were strung along the wall. An air diffuser in the corner released a steady cloud of lavender-scented mist near a large potted plant, and a white noise machine played soothing nature sounds. Even the carpet was covered in plush rugs.

As promised, a box of chocolates waited for me on a nightstand, next to a giant bed covered by a light, gauzy canopy.

"This is a nest?" I asked, running my fingers along a blanket draped over an overstuffed, boucle-upholstered armchair.

"This is *your* nest. Omegas sometimes need a breather from dealing with their alphas, so it's tradition to build a little sanctuary filled with their favorite stuff where they can get away from us. Most of the credit goes to Elias, he probably has the best taste. At least that's what he told us. Of course, I don't want you to hate it, but if you do, I'd be happy to rub it in his face."

The console table under the mounted TV included a little token from each of the alphas – a Packers bobblehead from Cam, a Bluetooth speaker for music from Nolan, a coffee mug emblazoned with the California state flag from Elias, and a book on the history of shifters from Archer.

My breath caught in my chest, and Cam's face fell. "Shit, you do hate it?"

I shook my head. "No, I absolutely love it." I might rearrange some things, but other than that, it really did feel like my own personal refuge from the storm of aggression and frustration I felt raging through the pack bonds.

He released a sigh of relief, bending down to kiss me. I stopped his lips with my finger. "Now get out."

Cam grinned. "Yes, ma'am."

I waited until the door closed until I let myself collapse on the bed. Everything was so soft – I just wanted to wrap myself up like a burrito, eat the chocolates, and watch the terrible new Christmas romance that had just been released on Netflix in peace.

But the book that Archer had selected was calling to me. I went up to grab it off the table and brought it back over to my bed, hoping to find some solace and perhaps a little insight into a world I

169

was struggling to find my footing in.

The text was dry, but the contents were fascinating. Unlike humans, who could trace their origins to a specific place, large groups of shifters seemed to spring up randomly at different places and points in time. Cultures all around the world had different myths about us, so it was somewhat easy for historians to pinpoint when certain populations came into existence. The Navajo had skinwalkers, the Celtics had the Fianna, India had the Rashasa, Japan had kitsune, and so forth.

Some scientists and historians wondered whether shifters were simply humans with mutated DNA – after all, we looked nearly identical and could have children together – and that perhaps some perfect storm of weather or disease or natural disaster could trigger an entire population to change in the same way.

Once I got to how shifters escaped the Black Plague, my eyes began to gloss over a bit. I set the book aside and decided to give my brain a break with that awful movie.

34
CAMDEN

"Well?" Elias asked as I came back down the stairs.

"Operation Eyrie was a success." I closed my eyes, reaching through Elias to check in with Marlowe. The bond was smooth and peaceful. "Can't you feel how much better she is already?"

Elias's jaw ticked in annoyance. "Yeah, but you kind of stole my thunder, and I wanted to…"

I arched my eyebrow and he huffed, giving up. "Okay, fine. I owed you one."

I nodded and jumped over the back of the couch to sit, the weight on my chest lifting as I flopped down. "Now we just gotta beat the shit outta Nolan."

My hands curled into fists at my side. What the hell had he done to her? Gotten into some weird fight about how tomatoes were technically a fruit or something stupid like that? I knew how much he loved being right about dumb shit.

"Look," Archer started. "No matter what happened, we need to remain calm and not stress Marlowe out any further. Did you not feel her regret over the bond? If she rejects it…"

My chest still ached from the sharp pain of her remorse.

Archer, in typical Archer fashion, had put together a "handbook for alpha-omega bonds" based on his research for us. Shifters were social animals – we learned by watching others' behaviors. Since there hadn't been an alpha-omega bond here in nearly a century, we didn't have any examples to go by. We were going off instinct and outdated anecdotes mostly, so Archer wanted to be thorough.

I'd skimmed through most of it – it was a little dense to get through, but I had read the warnings about bond rejection.

Omegas had a built-in cooling-off period and could reject bonds if they tried hard enough. In the past, some alphas had found a loophole by just barking at their omegas until the bond was settled, never giving them a chance to be alone enough in their thoughts to initiate the break.

But we weren't those types of alphas.

If an omega was able to successfully dissolve the bond, it was said that the alphas would never be the same. They'd go through life feeling like a part of them was always missing and wouldn't be able to form a bond with anyone else. It was like losing your soul.

Marlowe was already my everything. The first thing I thought about in the morning and the last thing I thought about at night. Even a taste of her bond rejection had been one of the worst things I'd ever felt.

I touched base with her again, and she seemed better for now. Tranquil, even. I wanted to keep it that way.

"Okay, fine," I grumbled. "We'll beat the shit out of him figuratively, then."

About ten minutes later, Nolan finally pulled up, bringing the groceries inside.

I kept my mind focused on Marlowe and her need for non-violence as he entered, tail between his legs. "What the fuck happened?" I yelled.

Calmly.

He sighed and put the bags down on the floor, running his fingers through his hair. "I don't know. Really. I asked her to go to the liquor store and pick out the wine, but she came back empty-handed and on the verge of tears. She wouldn't tell me anything, so I took her over there and found two guilty-looking, bitchy beta females. I saw red. I knew they'd done something, but Marlowe kept begging me to leave it alone. She and I argued and… I think she thought I was going to hit her."

Archer leapt over the distance between them and pummeled him into the ground.

Elias and I looked at each other, our eyes wide open in surprise. So much for Mr. We-Can't-Beat-Each-Other-Up.

Nolan didn't even put up a fight. He accepted every punch until Elias and I finally pulled Archer off him. "How could you?" he

172

seethed. "She regrets the bond because of you!"

I nodded at Elias and he took Archer out of the room to cool down. I sighed and walked over, helping Nolan back up. Blood dripped from his nose and his eyes were starting to swell shut. "Well, it's a good thing Marlowe needs some space because if she saw you right now, she'd likely freak out all over again."

Nolan walked over to the kitchen and grabbed a bag of peas out of the freezer, bringing it to his cheek while looking at me suspiciously. "How are you the calm one in all of this?"

I chuckled darkly. "Oh, beneath this placid surface, I'm a hurricane of fury, believe me. But Marlowe's tucked away in her new nest and seems to be feeling better, and my desire to keep it that way is greater than my need to kill you. At least for now."

He snorted. "Well, that's comforting."

I took a deep breath, bracing myself for what would come next. For a difficult decision I might have to make, depending on the answer. "I have to know. You said Marlowe thought you were going to hurt her. Were you?"

His eyes widened in horror. "Never," he answered emphatically. "Cam, how can you even ask that?"

I cracked my neck. "You know I had to. I love you like a brother, but if you're a threat to Marlowe…"

He shook his head in shame. "I get it, but the same drive to protect her runs in me, too. Just the idea of it… I can't even imagine. It's unthinkable."

He slumped down on one of the stools around the island, gingerly checking the skin around his eyes. "She said something that got to me, and I was mad. Really mad. But all she saw in that moment was an angry alpha who'd just threatened two females, and I think she thought I was going to…"

He couldn't even say the words, his shame was a heavy stink.

I rubbed my hand down my face. "What did she say to you?"

"Does it matter?"

"Yeah, kind of. I want to know if she was right or not."

He switched the bag to his other cheek. "She kept telling me to drop it about whatever those two betas had done, but I couldn't. When she finally dragged me out, she said what I did wasn't about her. It was about my ego."

My eyes closed as I tried to think about it from her point of view. She wasn't used to physical displays of dominance. For an omega who had until last week believed she was a human and who had lived in a world with only humans, that kind of male aggression would likely be terrifying, especially towards another female. Nolan could have listened to her and let it go, but once it was publicly out there, he'd be perceived as weak for not protecting her. Even if the offenders were female. He had needed to make an example of them to make sure the community didn't think it was okay to treat her poorly.

"I really want to know what they said to her," he added.

We held the silence between us for a minute. "Not gonna lie, if it'd been me at the store today, I would have done the same thing," I finally replied.

"Yeah?"

"Probably worse."

"Yeah," he chuckled. "Probably."

"So, who does she hate the least at the moment that can try to coax it out of her?"

Nolan sighed, putting down the peas and heading back towards the groceries by the front door. "I don't want her to feel ganged up on, but I think this is something we need to talk about as a whole pack."

Maybe he was right. "Well, why don't you get started on your stupid lasagna, then? She might open up over dinner."

I left him to it and then went downstairs to watch something, but I felt on edge and couldn't get comfortable or concentrate. After an hour or so, I went upstairs to listen outside of Marlowe's door to make sure she wasn't crying.

"Cam? Is that you?"

Shit. Her hearing had gotten a lot better since she had shifted. "Yeah, sorry, just checking in. I'll leave you alone."

I took a step to move when she replied quietly. "Can you cuddle with me?"

Score.

I walked in and found her on the bed, wrapped up, looking like a swaddled pup in a blanket while watching some movie. "Join my cocoon?"

"Hell yeah, let's metamorphosize, baby."

A small smile grew on her face, and she gestured to her table, where a half-empty box sat. "The chocolates are acceptable, by the way."

After rearranging the blankets, I crawled up behind her on the bed, pulling her into me and losing myself in her sweet smell. Marlowe was a drug, and I was hopelessly addicted. "What are you watching?" I asked.

"*A Christmas Through Time.*"

Her ass fit deliciously against my crotch, and my cock hardened. "Sorry about him. Can't do much about it."

"That's fine," she answered listlessly. "Just be quiet, I'm into this."

I did as instructed, not wanting to get kicked out. Being invited into the nest was a big deal.

But the movie was already halfway through, and the story was confusing me. "Wait, I thought they were broken up."

She grumbled under her breath and paused the film. "They *will be* broken up in the future. The movie is about a guy who is living through every Christmas of his life – past, present, and future – until he learns the true meaning of the holiday and proposes to his girlfriend who he's been stringing along."

"Oh, so it's a stupid version of *A Christmas Carol?*"

She raised her eyebrows suspiciously. "You've read Dickens?"

"Who? I'm talking about the movie with the Muppets."

Marlowe sighed deeply and allowed herself a laugh. "Your English teacher must have *loved* you."

"Jokes on you, I was Mrs. Silvano's favorite." I waited a beat before asking, "Sooo, you like this kinda stuff?"

She turned the movie back on. "I know it's silly, but yes. My mom and I loved watching crappy holiday romances together. It's my first Christmas without her."

"Ah shit, babe, I'm sorry."

She grabbed my hand and placed it on her stomach, settling into me further. "Thanks. This year's going to be different and hard for a lot of reasons."

I could relate. The first year after I'd lost my dad, I was a mess.

"Let me know if you have any other holiday traditions, I'm more than happy to participate."

She squeezed my hand in thanks, and I shut my mouth for good.

I still didn't really follow, but of course the main character realized he was being a dumbass and saved his relationship and the holiday all in one big romantic gesture at the end.

When the credits started to roll, she paused the TV and turned around to face me. I waited for her to say something, but she remained quiet, her eyes studying mine.

Her expression was thoughtful. Wary. She reached for my

cheek, her fingers lightly grazing my beard, and I relaxed and purred in response. The tension evaporated from her small frame.

"Today really sucked, but this is nice."

I gave her a quick peck on the nose. "I think so, too."

Her hand wandered down towards my chest, biting her lip and giggling. "This is really nice, too."

The sweet scent of her arousal filled my nostrils, and my cock obeyed its siren call. "Not as nice as these," I replied, lowering my head between her breasts and inhaling deeply.

Her laughs gave way to moans, and light touches turned into desperate grabs. Our clothes fell to the floor and we entwined our naked limbs, crashing against each other like waves against the shore.

Everything about her was soft – her skin, lips, hair… Her body was the yin to my yang, and we fit together in perfect harmony.

My mouth traveled down the column of her neck, tasting and savoring every inch of her perfection. "Cam," she sighed, her head tilting back as her eyelids fluttered shut. She said my name like it was a prayer, but didn't she know she was the goddess here?

Our first time together had been hot and heavy, but today, I wanted to properly worship my little omega and show her how good I could take care of her.

"You're so perfect," I breathed. My lips traveled further, encircling her pink nipple. I drew the peak out with my tongue, licking and sucking until she squirmed beneath me. Then I moved onto the next one.

After her other nipple received the same treatment, I headed further south. Her legs parted for me without hesitation, and I nestled myself between them, running my hands up her delicious thighs while teasing her clit with light licks. One of her hands went above to grab onto the headboard, while the other landed on my head, her fingernails scratching my scalp with just the right amount of pressure.

My tongue dived straight into her pussy and she gasped, her back arching as I ran it back up to her clit, circling with greater pressure. She tasted even sweeter than she smelled, her honeyed slick coating my beard as I lapped her into a frenzy. Every one of her pleasured whimpers caused my cock to twitch with the need to be inside her, but I wanted to feel her come on my face first.

I drew her clit gently between my teeth, flicking it with my tongue while her orgasm built. My fingers slid into her wet pussy, brushing up against her G-spot and pushing her over the edge. Her fingernails dug in deeper as she cried out, her muscles shaking as her breathy panting began to slow.

My cock was done waiting, and I flipped her on her side, spooning her from the back while I pulled her thigh up in the air. I pushed myself in slowly from behind, watching her face as she adjusted around me.

It felt like she was made for me, and it took no time at all before I could push all the way to my knot, thrusting slowly and deliberately, feeling every soft inch of her while she felt every hard inch of me.

Marlowe reached behind and grabbed my hip to steady herself, meeting me with her hazel eyes and her own grinding. I let go of her leg and began rubbing her clit again and she threw her head back into my chest. Her next climax came fast, and mine followed soon after at the feeling of her clenching around me.

One final push and my knot locked inside her, and our orgasms continued. I emptied myself, the pressure on my knot so great I thought I might pass out from pure pleasure.

Here, in my omega's nest, with her in my arms and my knot in her, I was in heaven. How could life ever get more perfect than in this moment?

I held her in tightly to my chest, my lips finding my way to her neck again. The faint, silvered scarring from Elias's bonding taunted me, but I couldn't bite right now. I had to wait for her to want it. If we pushed it too hard, especially with the doubts she'd had today, we could force her into a rejection. I couldn't risk it.

Instead, I licked the spot, sending a wave of ecstasy through her body that got sent right back to me – not just through the bond, but also through her clenching around my cock again. I moaned through my next release, squeezing her breasts as I came.

Our breathing eventually steadied, and I lightly brushed her skin with my fingers, enjoying every peak and valley the side of her provided while we waited for my knot to deflate.

"You know," she started, her voice quiet. "I imagined you'd be the type to spew the filthiest stuff when we had sex."

My knot inflated slightly. "You thought about us fucking?"

That was hot.

Her cheeks turned adorably pink. "It was the first day we met, after I called you a pig and checked into my hotel. I guess the heat explains why I was so inexplicably horny, and I tried to… relieve myself. All I could think about was you and Elias."

I bit my lip, riding out the next chain of orgasms, my knot and cock hardening at the very idea of our little omega pleasuring herself to a fantasy of me. When we finally returned to Earth, I nipped her ear and lowered my voice as I whispered, "And you thought I'd say all kinds of nasty shit, huh? Like what?"

"I don't know," she whined, turning her embarrassed face into the mattress. "I can't remember exactly. I just thought you'd be the type of guy who'd say 'fuck' and 'cunt' and 'slut' and stuff like that."

My hand drifted down her abdomen. "Do you want me to?"

She shook her head. "No, I think you're perfect."

I groaned, surrendering myself to the next wave. I couldn't believe I'd never gotten to experience this before. Betas weren't built for knots, but omegas… It was the orgasmic aftershocks, extending our pleasure for twenty to thirty minutes after sex, that made me finally understand what "knotting" really meant. Growing up, it had almost been like an urban legend. Archer had even once speculated, years ago, that if omegas disappeared, alphas or knots might be next.

Well, thank the Moon that hadn't happened yet.

"Babe, you can't say stuff like that, it's going to go straight to my head."

She wiggled her ass and laughed. "Mm, which one?"

It took almost forty minutes for my knot to finally deflate.

35

MIKE

"Amore!" Grace called as she and Jen descended the escalator to the baggage claim.

I rolled my eyes. Why did I ever think she would be a good addition to my servaglio? I let my cock decide too much for me sometimes. It really should have taken more than a well-placed brush of tits against my shoulder to be given such an honorable position.

At least I wouldn't have to deal with her for too much longer. I had invited her and Jen down to New Orleans to wait with me while the Council gathered their warriors. One last hurrah before I broke things off.

They didn't need to know that part yet, though. I had bought them tickets under the guise of needing comfort due to the loss of my Lunessa.

Which was true – I'd find comfort in their wet pussies, tight asses, deep throats, and then cut the cord.

I wouldn't miss Grace too much, but Jen really would have been the perfect second. She might have been willing for a few afternoon quickies in the company bathroom when this was over, but once I retrieved Marlowe, I would keep the promise I intended to make – I would have no servaglio aside from her. She would be enough for me.

"How you holding up?" Jen asked, giving me a hug while I watched Grace struggle to lift her impractically large suitcase from the baggage carousel. I should probably be helping her, but ever since she had insulted Marlowe, I didn't really hold any fondness for her anymore.

The thought of draining her brought a small blossom of a smile to my lips.

Vampyrs typically preferred to take as little blood from humans as possible. For one, there was usually no need to kill – the amount required through feeding was hardly fatal. For another, there was no point if you had a servaglio. They were a renewable, willing source of sustenance.

And besides, dead bodies left too many questions, and if discovered, a mob of angry humans could too easily destroy one of us.

But I'd also heard that the amount of blood imbibed when draining a human could induce the most exquisite orgasms for weeks. Orgasms I could share with my Lunessa.

Yes, this was sounding more appealing by the minute. In fact, it was almost poetic – Grace's final act would help prove how wrong she was about Marlowe's bedroom proclivities.

"As well as I can be, given the circumstances," I replied.

"Circumstances being your ex-Lunessa's currently getting railed by a bunch of jacked werewolves?" Grace added, blowing a piece of hair out of her face after finally joining us.

I clenched my jaw and closed my eyes. *I can't kill her in an airport full of humans, I can't kill her in an airport full of humans…*

"Dammit, Grace, what the hell is wrong with you?" Jen responded on my behalf.

Grace sighed, unwittingly signing her own death warrant. I doubted I could last the whole week if she kept this up.

"Come, I have a suite at the Hotel Monteleon. Why don't you two freshen up there and rest? We're expected at Sang Noir tonight."

Jen's eyes lit up in anticipation. Sang Noir was a vampyr club, one of only four in the country – the other three being in LA, Miami, and Atlanta.

Thanks to New Orleans' association with fictional vampyr tales, desperate women came to the city in droves looking for beautiful males to role-play their blood sucking fantasies with. For actual vampyrs, it made for the perfect hunting ground, and my kind had flocked here for the steady stream of willing women ready to be bit, fucked, and forgotten.

It was a fitting place to bid adieu to my servaglio.

I winked at Jen, running my tongue over my sharpening canine suggestively, but the invitation made me nervous. One of the elders from the Council had reached out after our meeting, asking if we could speak more on my relationship with Marlowe. He had said he was rethinking his support of this whole campaign, and I needed to convince him otherwise.

Grace didn't stop talking the whole way back to the hotel, and I was starting to consider getting her a separate room. How she had such little self-awareness was baffling to me. I returned none of her affections, shot down all of her sightseeing plans, and ignored her questions more times than I could count.

Yet she blathered on, completely undeterred.

She disappeared into the bathroom as soon as we arrived and Jen cleared her throat, speaking quietly. "It's okay, Mike. She's getting on my nerves, too. She told me on the flight that she thinks she can replace Marlowe, and that's her goal while she's here."

I whipped my head around to face her and seethed. "She said *what?*"

"She really doesn't have a clue. Look, I know it's not my place to have any kind of say over your servaglio, but..."

I placed my phone on a side table and walked up behind her, pulling her into my chest and grabbing her throat. She relaxed into me while my grip tightened, her immediate submission hardening my cock. "Jen, as my second, you are always entitled to have an opinion on anyone below you. Speak your mind."

She released a breathy moan, arching her back and pushing her round, curvy ass against my dick, rocking back and forth. "You can do better than Grace. She doesn't deserve you. She doesn't understand you or what you have with Marlowe. She'll always be jealous she's not your Lunessa."

"Mm, and you're not?" I asked, my teeth grazing the thin skin of her neck.

"Never," she sighed. "I'm only jealous of you for getting to fuck her."

My hand wandered down under the band of her leggings, finding her dripping wet. She gave a sweet little gasp as I slipped a finger into her cunt, running it along her inner walls while she squirmed and writhed in front of me.

"Such a good girl, Jen. The perfect second. Would you like a reward for your behavior?"

"Yes," she groaned, tilting her head further to the side.

I added a second finger, whispering in her ear, "What would you like?"

She reached a hand up and grabbed my hair. "Whatever you

want to give me."

My cock throbbed in response. "Good answer."

My teeth sank into her neck as I pushed against her G-spot. Her orgasm tore through her as she panted and whimpered, her knees buckling from the pleasure. Blood dripped onto the carpet, the coppery tang filling my mouth.

After drinking my fill, I licked the wound on her skin closed and led her closer to the bed, pushing her down on her stomach and pulling her leggings and underwear down and off. Her ass rose beautifully in the air, slowly circling in anticipation.

My belt unbuckled and my zipper undone, I pulled out my cock and prodded the head against her entrance, then lowered it slightly to tease her clit again. "You'll come again for me, won't you?"

"Always," she replied, her voice husky in post-bite bliss.

I nudged my cock in an inch, enjoying the way she pushed against me, desperate for more, and happily obliged.

Jen was no omega, but for a human she was almost perfect. That was part of the reason I wanted to bring her to the club with me tonight. I was hoping to find a new master for her. Even if I couldn't keep her, I'd trained her well enough that some other vampyr could reap the rewards.

Every thrust brought me slightly more inside her tight cunt, and she moaned in response. "Harder! Fuck me until it hurts!"

Who could argue with that? I grabbed her hips and thrust all the way to the hilt, my balls slapping violently against her wet skin.

Her gasp and grimace told me I'd succeeded in bringing her the pain she craved. I was about to pull out and go again when the bathroom door opened.

"Hey, you're getting started without me?"

My dick softened a touch at the grating sound of her voice, but before I could respond Jen turned to look at her and yelled. "Shut the fuck up Grace, this isn't for you!"

Grace's face turned red and she mumbled something under her breath, retreating to lick her wounds.

"Mike," Jen whimpered, her fingers gripping the bedspread. "Please, don't stop."

I fucked her until she cried.

Jen's outburst had effectively shamed Grace until we were finished.

After showering, I let Grace know very clearly that I was in no mood for her mindless chit chat and reminded her that, as the lowest ranking member of my servaglio, she was expected to be humble, demure, and above all – silent.

Her apology was quiet, but when she reached for my crotch, I twisted her wrist until it almost snapped. How did she still not understand?

"You'll get my cock when you've earned it. Do *not* embarrass me tonight."

I had told them to pack for a night out, and at least I could trust the both of them on that. Grace wore a skintight, black dress with cutouts along her stomach and a high slit in the skirt. A large bracelet attempted to hide the bruises from our earlier conversation.

Jen had chosen a navy halter jumpsuit made of velvet, with silver pumps and large hoop earrings.

And they both matched my simple black suit and maroon shirt. I had skipped the tie, leaving the top button opened. Hiding your neck was a sign of weakness among vampyrs, and I needed to display my strength that evening.

"You know what's expected of you," I reminded them from the front seat of the Uber. "Elder Sable wants to know about Marlowe, so we're mostly going to talk about her. As my servaglio, you need to be in agreement with anything I say. Any hint of discord reflects poorly on me and my ability to choose women appropriately. That could mean the revocation of the Council's warriors."

I turned around and faced Grace directly, scowling. "Can I trust you to keep your mouth shut and face neutral?"

"Yes, master," she whispered, her eyes focusing on the purse on her lap.

"If you ruin this for me, Grace, I swear to the Moon, I will kill you. Slowly and painfully."

The Uber driver side-eyed us nervously, and I shifted in my seat to face him. "*We're just joking.*"

His eyes darkened. "Yes, you were just joking."

The car dropped us off in front of an empty alley in the French Quarter, and we followed the ivy-covered brick walls until we arrived at a small, nondescript red door. I knocked, and a pair of violet eyes glared at us from the peephole.

"Password?"

I bared my fangs in response, the peephole sliding shut as the heavy locks were lifted and the door opened.

"Enjoy your evening."

I nodded at the doorman and headed down the long hallway, following the din of voices and jazz music, the smell of iron-rich blood and aged bourbon heavy in the air. At the end were a set of heavy curtains, and I pushed them aside, holding them open behind me for Jen and Grace.

We were greeted by a human hostess wearing a mesh mini dress and nothing underneath, her neck covered in puncture wounds and her expression vacant.

"Name?" she asked slowly, wavering slightly on her stilettos.

"Sanguinetti."

Her eyes went in and out of focus as she scrolled down her list. "Oh, here you are, at Elder Sable's table." She looked up, a slow smile spreading across her pale face. "You're a sexy one, aren't you? Care for an amuse bouche?" She offered her neck to me, but I simply kissed her skin, my fingers trailing lightly over her nipple sticking straight through one of the holes of her dress.

"Some other time," I replied.

She shrugged. "I'll be here all night if you change your mind. This way." She gestured with a finger, beckoning us to follow.

I tried not to look too much like it was my first time there, but my gaze wandered around the space as the hostess led us further back into the club.

The atmosphere was thick with lust and hunger, the scent of arousal coating the inside of my nose as I breathed in. Dim, amber lights flickered in shadowed corners like fireflies.

The ceilings, high and arched, were draped in dark silk, while sleek leather couches and ornate chairs were filled with my kind and their servaglios. Vampyrs conversed while women simply draped themselves in the periphery, offering pleasure in whatever manner their masters wanted.

Jen's excitement was palpable, and I could feel her desire to engage in the activities building. Grace was mostly nervous, and I hoped it was over her fear of angering me further.

We were led to a recessed booth, the table small to allow for plenty of room in front of the upholstered, rounded seating. Elder Sable was the youngest of the Council, around fifty years old or so. His brown hair was still thick, slightly graying at the temples, and his violet eyes crinkled. He was making good use of the space already, nodding towards me as the woman on her knees in front of him bobbed over his crotch.

"I would stand, but…" He groaned, taking a sip of his drink and running his fingers through the woman's hair.

I chuckled. "Yes, clearly. Elder Sable—"

"Call me Will."

"Will, this is the rest of my servaglio, Jen and Grace." They bowed their heads slightly.

The blonde woman on his dick popped up, her lipstick smeared. "Hey, girls! I'm Madison."

Will grabbed her chin and forcefully held it. "Who said you could stop?"

She rolled her eyes and giggled, licking from his balls straight up his shaft to his head, before plunging him in her mouth again.

"Gotta keep a tight leash on the younger ones, their generation wouldn't know respect if it slapped them across the ass." He spoke roughly, grabbing her hair for emphasis. She moaned and he thrust up inside her, forcing her to gag.

"Yes," I replied, giving Grace a pointed look. She recoiled, shrinking into her shoulders. "They certainly forget their place sometimes."

Will gestured across from him. "Sit, sit. Take your cock out and relax."

Jen slid in first and then I followed, wrapping an arm around her while I pointed towards my crotch and whistled at Grace. She got on her knees and went to work, while I flagged down a waitress. "Two whiskeys, neat."

Vampyrs weren't social by nature, and with San Francisco's smaller population, I didn't meet with my kind very often. Truth be told, I preferred the company of humans. And Marlowe, of course.

But I couldn't say I'd never been curious about clubs like these before, and I was happy to finally experience one.

Clearing my throat, I started with pleasantries.

"I hear your Lunessa is expecting. You must be excited," I said, shoving Grace's head down hard until she coughed.

"Yes, but as you know, vampyr births are tricky. I lost my first Lunessa to childbirth around fifteen years ago. This one's been on bedrest and sex is off the table. My servaglio is trying to make up for her, but I still find myself coming here most nights. I can't wait 'til the vampling is out, I miss her."

Two women in the booth across from us fingered each other, and Jen squirmed while she watched, clenching her thighs together.

Will noticed her reaction, intrigue coloring his features. "You

185

want to join the fun, don't you?"

She looked at me for permission to reply and I nodded. "Desperately," she whispered.

He inhaled sharply. "Tell you what, chérie – why don't you take off that contraption and get yourself warmed up. I should have a free spot on my lap in a few minutes. I'd love to discuss business with a face full of your bouncing tits."

Jen's smile reached her eyes, and she swiftly untied the straps to the halter top, shimmying out of her jumpsuit. With one hand pinching her nipple, the other went straight for her cunt, slowly rubbing her clit while watching the women across from us. They now noticed her, too, their eyes glued to Jen's spread legs as they came closer to their releases.

Will turned his attention back to me. "I take it this is their first time?"

I nodded and then shrugged. "Mine, too, actually. The closest club to where we live is in Los Angeles, and I don't go down there very often."

"La Luna Roja!" he sighed wistfully, rubbing Madison's head and tangling her hair through his fingers. "That's a shame. Every vampyr needs to visit at least once in his life. Perhaps when you and your Lunessa are reunited, you can bring her there."

Exhibitionism wasn't one of my kinks, but getting to fuck her in a room full of my brethren would be a dream come true. I adored showing her off.

As long as she was back on her hormone suppressants, of course. Her unblocked scent could cause a riot.

Madison's head bobbed with greater urgency, and Will stopped her, holding her still as he came, grunting loudly. He patted her on the head as he pulled out. "Go get yourself a drink, find another cock, whatever you want."

She kissed him on the cheek. "Thank you, Daddy." With that, she sauntered towards the bar, and Will turned his attention to Jen. Her fingers were fully inside herself as she kneaded her breast.

"Look at you," he remarked, his flaccid dick already hardening. He gave it a few strokes until it stood tall once more. "Ride me."

Jen obeyed, removing her fingers from her dripping wet pussy and sliding over to where Will sat, sinking herself on him with a moan. With one hand on her ass, Will grabbed his drink with the other, sipping slowly as Jen began to roll her hips across his lap. His eyelids fluttered and he swallowed with a hard sigh.

Will then brought his mouth down to Jen's nipple, biting into her as she threw her head back and drowned in pleasure. As much as I enjoyed Jen, it was in this moment I knew for certain that she was not Lunessa material, at least not for me. I felt no possession over her, and watching her melt into a puddle while fucking another vampyr elicited no feelings other than pride. Pride in having found her and for successfully bringing her into this world.

After a few deep pulls, Will released Jen's nipple and sat back up, licking the blood off his lips. "There really is something to these California girls. I can practically taste the sunshine."

"You should try them after a trip to Napa." I winked, finally feeling my own release building.

"I can only imagine," he moaned. He picked Jen up by her ass and then slammed her back over his cock. "Fuck, if this is your second, your Lunessa must be a goddess."

I shoved my cock into Grace's mouth forcefully, making my next points clear. "You have no idea. The tightest cunt, the highest libido, all wrapped up in a perfect, taut little body."

She was also intelligent, empathetic, and funny. And the way her eyes would light up whenever she found me in a crowd always made my heart skip a beat, making me feel like I was the love of her life.

Because I had been, and she was mine. I had been so close to getting everything I'd ever wanted. But like Icarus, I'd flown too close to the sun and was now dealing with the consequences.

But this was not the time to talk about my Lunessa's personality or the depth of my feelings. Maudlin declarations of love were the last thing this Elder likely wanted to hear.

Thoughts of Marlowe brought me closer to my orgasm. I thrust into Grace's throat and shuddered, spilling my seed down her throat. As I pulled out, cum dribbled down her chin and I whispered, "Go find someone else to fuck, and stay out of the way."

She nodded, wiping her face with the back of her hand. As soon as she stepped out of the booth two vampyrs dragged her into another one, and I ignored her muffled cries.

Will arched an eyebrow and I waved my hand in dismissal. "I am thinking of replacing her. She might be a better match for someone here."

Jen reached behind her, grabbing the edge of the table for balance as she ground harder against the Elder. His hands slid up and down her waist, and then he lunged forward and bit her other nipple.

Her orgasm triggered his, and they came together.

I waited patiently, sipping my drink until he was satisfied. He slapped Jen's ass and grunted for her to move. "Clean yourself up, chérie, and hurry back. I'm not done with you yet."

She licked the outer shell of his ear and got up. We both watched as she swung her hips down the hallway towards the bathroom, her head held high and blood dripping down her breasts.

Will whistled low, shaking his head in amusement. "If you're ever thinking of letting *that* one go, I have plenty of space," he said, flagging down the waitress for another drink and a wet towel.

"You like her?" I asked. This could be the in I needed.

"Sure. Is she good with others?" he asked.

I waited for the waitress to deliver his order, and he wiped off his cock and handed the towel back.

"Amazing. She loves pussy as much as cock, and she doesn't have a jealous bone in her body."

He laughed, but his expression was dubious. "And you want to get rid of her, too? What's the catch?"

I swirled the ice in my glass, reminding myself who this was all for. "My Lunessa. I think the shock of our lifestyle scared her off. Omegas… they are our shifter equivalent in a way. Their appetites are voracious. They need several partners to fulfill them and are not open to sharing. The prospect of my divided attention made her angry."

"Then find a new Lunessa," he replied flatly, his eyes narrowing. "I am failing to understand why an omega would be a good match for a vampyr."

I swallowed, taking a risk with my next words. "Because she is, quite honestly, more than enough for me. I got greedy with Jen and Grace, filling my biological imperative to create my servaglio. It's taken almost losing her to realize I don't need them."

Will scoffed and crossed his ankle over his knee, leaning back into his seat. "This is why our strength is depleting, our powers disappearing. You young vampyrs have assimilated into human culture to the detriment of our species. Monogamy will never sate us. Our desires are too great for one female."

"Vampyrs are weakening?" I asked. This was news to me.

"We used to fly, Michele. Did you know that?"

Fly? The look on my face must have confirmed something to the Elder, and he continued. "I suppose some of the loss of information is due to our kind's lack of oral tradition and tendency towards isolation. It's so easy to forget between the generations. I can assume, then, that your father or grandfather never told you, did they?"

I shook my head in disbelief. "No, never."

"We used to be stronger, more virile… So many lost their lives in the Great War with the shifters. Those beasts cut us down to devastating numbers before a truce was found. Is breaking the treaty worth it for one omega Lunessa who, by all accounts, left you of her own free will?"

My hands curled to fists at my sides as I recalled the way that hulking blonde mutt had held her in the hotel. She only left me because of him and the others in his pack.

Between just the two of us, things had been perfect. I knew she would realize that soon. She might have even realized it now, but with four alphas foaming at the mouth to bond with her and claim her as their own, she'd never be able to escape them without help.

Jen returned, ready to go again, but Will pointed to a vampyr sitting at the bar, his eyes raking across my second's generous curves. "His name is Charles, and he would love to eat your pussy right now. Won't you let him?"

Charles beckoned her closer, licking his lips. "You don't have to tell me twice," Jen laughed. She blew us a kiss and skipped over, and I watched as she took the stool next to him, still completely naked and completely unashamed. He dropped to his knees and began devouring her, her eyes rolling back into her head as she leaned back against the bar.

My attention snapped back to Will as he spoke. "See? That is what we should be pursuing. Not a house in the suburbs with a white picket fence. Young vampyrs have grown soft, caring more about a woman's feelings than their own needs."

I didn't answer. I could see his point of view and might have agreed with him before I had met Marlowe. But that party in Palo Alto had changed everything I thought I knew about myself, about this world. It was as though her very soul had imprinted on mine the moment our eyes met and I had caught the briefest hint of her pistachio and honey scent.

"A true Lunessa would welcome a servaglio," he continued, "and the break it affords her to recover from her master. Then she can please him completely refreshed."

"That's just it," I countered. "She's never needed to recover. I only see my servaglio when I physically cannot be with my Lunessa."

"Obviously," he snorted. "Look at your second. She is starved for attention."

My shoulders fell, turning around to see how Jen was doing. Another vampyr was now feeding from her neck, while a bar tender was pouring a shot into her open mouth.

And the sight of it did nothing for me.

This kind of lifestyle had been appealing when I was younger and single. But now? I would rather spend every evening at home, cuddled up next to Marlowe on the couch while watching her silly K-dramas.

The Elder wouldn't understand that, though. No, the only way he'd understand was by fucking her.

"Jen is yours," I said. "Once I depart for Wisconsin to retrieve my Lunessa, I will cede ownership to you."

Will watched her, slowly stroking his cock. "And in return?"

"I only ask that you honor the agreement, and help me bring my Lunessa home," I responded, clasping my hands together on the table.

His eyes shifted towards mine, narrowing. "Including my night with her?"

Unlike Jen, the thought of Marlowe sleeping with the Elder in front of me filled me with rage. But what else could I do? "Yes. As much as a vampyr loathes to share his Lunessa, if it means she is returned to me, and if it helps you see why she is so unique, then it will be more than worth it."

"So be it." He threw back his drink. "You will bring Jen to the Council and exchange her for your warriors when we call you. I'll even add an additional ten, to be safe. I'm very curious to see if this omega is as good as you claim."

I placed my palms on the table and bowed until my head touched the surface. "So be it."

Grace's high-pitched panting broke through the air. "And what about that one?" he asked.

I shook my head. "Her temperament is wanting. I was actually thinking about draining her."

A smirk grew on his face. "I love a good draining. Why not bring her too, and we'll make a feast out of her with the rest of the Elders?"

I smiled, relief relaxing my tense muscles. Tonight had gone even better than I had hoped. The promise of warriors would be upheld, and I had found a new home for Jen and a solution for Grace. "So be it."

36
MARLOWE

Just as Cam and I finished showering, Nolan yelled that dinner was ready. The delicious aroma of cheese and a rich Bolognese sauce had already reached my nest, and my mouth was watering as I raced down the stairs.

I stopped dead in my tracks when I saw Nolan's face – his eyes were black, and his lip was cut.

"Cam!" I cried, turning around in anger. "What did you do?"

He looked indignant, holding up his hands. "Hey, I didn't do it! I'm perfect, remember?"

"It was me."

I whipped around at the sound of Archer's voice, finding him not looking quite as contrite as I would have liked while he set plates around the kitchen island. Elias had his back towards me, opening the wine, and Nolan was finishing mixing the salad.

Like nothing had happened.

"Seriously? And you all are fine with this?" I asked.

Cam put his hand on my shoulder and sighed. "We're alphas, babe. We try to use words, we really do, but at the end of the day, we're still not human. Our tempers run hot, and we sometimes resort to fists to settle differences between us."

I shoved him off, losing my appetite. "Yeah, and does that include betas? Females? Omegas? If I piss you off, are you going to punch me, too?"

"Never," Nolan replied emphatically, coming to my side. "Marlowe, we would *never* hurt you. *I* would never hurt you."

It was easy to say that now when our emotions had cooled, but outside the liquor store, I had seen a look in Nolan's eyes that shook me to my core. Even if he did think he was incapable of ever laying a hand on me physical, emotionally I was still suffering from his actions. "But you did. That's what I was trying to tell you. Do you want to know what those women said?"

Their expectant eyes all fell on me.

"They called me a whore."

Snarls erupted from the pack. "Enough!" I yelled. They quieted at my command, hands balled into fists at their sides.

Proving my point, I sadly realized. "Since omegas disappeared, shifters have adopted more human practices like monogamy, right?"

Archer nodded. "That is correct."

I took a deep breath. "Okay, so put yourselves in a beta female's shoes, then. The resurgence of omegas would be a threat to their dating pool, their relationships, even their safety. They called me a whore because I'm bonded to four alphas, one of whom dropped his beta girlfriend like a sack of potatoes after just a whiff of me."

"Hey," Cam retorted. "She wasn't my girlfriend, we'd only been on a few dates."

I gave him a pointed look. "What if she had been, though? Or what if you two had been married, and then you met me? Let's say the rest of the pack was single and bonded to me. Would you be able to resist me? Would I be able to resist you? Could you handle just sitting out of my heat?"

I watched as my words hit them, as the realization sunk in. Cam rubbed the back of his neck. "Well, shit…"

"Yeah, exactly. I'm an unwitting Jolene in a town full of Dollys. So Nolan, when you stormed into that liquor store, guns blazing, all you did was justify their fears. That even the affable, friendly mayor could become so obsessed over an omega he'd threaten to kill two females just for being a little bitchy. I was upset because I could understand where they were coming from, and because I had foolishly thought that once I was bonded, I could live here and be treated like a normal person."

"You can, and you will be," Nolan responded. "It'll take some getting used to, for all of us, the town included. But you'll find your stride. You'll make friends…"

"Friends?" I scoffed. "How can I have any friends if they're worried their partners are going to fall in lust with me the moment I walk by them?"

The room fell silent. My chest heaved in anger, and then Cam looked up and shrugged. "Lesbians?"

Archer groaned and Elias and Nolan just shook their heads in disappointment.

His brows furrowed, and he huffed. "No, hear me out. Female omegas are only magnets to males, right? Lesbian alphas and betas aren't going to be drawn to her the same way. They won't be jealous. Nolan, have Megan take Marlowe to Shifting Sapphic next weekend."

My mouth hung open in shock. I didn't know whether Cam was an idiot, a genius, offensive, progressive, a combination thereof, or something else entirely.

"Megan isn't gay," Nolan said flatly, pinching the bridge of his nose.

Cam rolled his eyes. "Yeah, I know, but Marlowe shouldn't go to a bar alone, and we're not allowed inside. A female family member is safest, and Ivy's off the table because she's like, thirteen months pregnant or some shit."

"There isn't enough research on the effects of omega pheromones on homosexual shifters," Archer replied. "You know as well as I do that exclusive same-sex relationships were deeply frowned upon in shifter culture until recently. For all we know, Marlowe could elicit the same reaction from a gay alpha female as she does from a straight alpha male."

I picked up my plate and served myself a slice of lasagna and some salad, then grabbed a whole bottle of wine. "Alright, I'll just go eat in my nest alone while the big, strong alphas discuss my future, then punch each other. Good night."

They let me go without a fight.

At least they let me go the best they could. Every ten minutes or so, I could hear one of them pause at my door, listening to make sure I wasn't too upset.

To be honest, I was too numb to feel much of anything. I needed time to process everything that had happened, but it felt like every time I started to feel better, some fresh new hell would reveal itself to me.

The heavy meal and wine combined with my seventh rewatch of *The Office* lulled me into a comfortable daze, and soon enough, I fell asleep. Alone.

My wolf stirred.

I hadn't felt her since the last time I had shifted, but now she was awake – restless and nervous. There was something driving me into setting her free that evening, and I couldn't resist the call any longer. I shed my clothes and left my room.

The house was quiet and dark, my pack having retired for the night. I needed to be careful as I tiptoed down the hallway and stairs. My shifter senses had sharpened tremendously in the past week, so I knew how well we could hear even the tiniest creak from the floorboards.

I made my way to the back door, sliding it open and biting my tongue to keep from gasping as a blast of frigid air hit my nude body, covering my skin in goosebumps. It was snowing again, and I could feel the whine from my wolf, desperate to roll around in the soft, pillowy drifts that had accumulated in Cam's backyard.

When I had shifted before, it had just happened. There had been no stopping or controlling it, so I wasn't entirely sure if I was doing any of this right. I closed my eyes, imagining a gate in my mind. I slowly unlocked the latch and opened it, letting her through.

37

THE TAWNY WOLF

The crisp wind blowing through the small opening beckoned me, but the sudden smell of an approaching male from behind sent a growl through me, and I turned around.

A human – the one I had seen before, the one who smelled good – had found me.

"Easy, California, I'm not going to hurt you," he cooed. "I just wanted to see what was going on. You're not going to run away again, are you?"

I chuffed. The human part of me called this home, and her body was too weak to survive without my fur. I would return when it was time to relinquish my control.

"Good, just checking. Are you going far?"

I turned back to the darkness, taking a step out into the night. I just wanted to be outside. I leapt into the snow, shaking and snapping at the falling snowflakes. I was made for the cold; I was made for the trees and the streams.

The human male stood in the doorway, the temperature not bothering him like it did my human. He simply watched, and I decided to let him for now. Something stirred in him, something I almost recognized...

My human was angry at him, I could feel, but she trusted him. So I would too.

He was her pack. Where was mine? I knew they must be around somewhere. I paused my game and howled, begging them to join me. I wanted to chase and be chased.

The human stepped outside slowly, and I trotted over. Company was company, I supposed. At least until my pack arrived.

"Beautiful," he whispered.

I nipped his arm gently. *Obviously.*

His hands ran through my coat, and I pushed myself into him for more. The touch felt nice.

"You like that, girl? Yeah, I know you like the head scritches."

His weird paws scratched behind my ears and I closed my eyes. Humans were definitely good for something if they could do that. He stopped, but I wanted more. I jumped and pushed him over with my paws, landing on top of him so he'd be trapped, forcing him to continue until I decided he was over.

"Whoa there!" he laughed. "Okay, okay, I get it." I licked his face in thanks, and he laughed again.

Just then another scent hit my nose, and I stilled. It was a wolf. Like me.

Pack?

I tilted my head towards the source, watching a darkened silhouette emerge from the forest.

I got off the human and took a few steps towards him. It was definitely a male. His scent reminded me of something, but I had no memory of it.

He came closer, inspecting us carefully.

Pack? I asked again.

Pack, he confirmed. *Come.*

I made to follow him when the human behind me snarled. I turned around and watched as his body contorted into a shape like mine. His skin coverings shredded as his body grew, elongating.

With a growl, his shift was complete.

He leapt in front of me, baring his teeth at the other. *Not pack*, he warned. *Liar.*

Liar? Why would wolves lie?

This new wolf, he was my human's pack. Now he was my pack, too, I could feel it. So I knew he was right about the other one.

Leave, my pack mate demanded to the intruder. He snarled, positioning himself in front of me.

The other wolf stared at us for a moment more, then finally turned around and walked the other way.

Pack? I asked the human-now-wolf.

He came over and nuzzled my neck, his scent solidifying our bond. *Yes.*

I whined in excitement. My pack was here! I snapped at him gently, then turned around and crouched, my tail wagging. *Play*?

He bounced on his front legs. *Play*.

Then he chased me into the woods, and we didn't return until the sun rose.

38
NOLAN

"What the…"

The door to the back patio was wide open, a small snow drift accumulating inside. Several large pawprints dirtied the hardwood floor and further onto the carpet. I followed the path into the kitchen, where I found the fridge also open, half its contents spilled on the floor next to Marlowe and Elias. They were both naked and filthy.

"My lasagna," I moaned. I had made a ton of it, looking forward to the leftovers for my next few lunches, but the pan was empty and their faces were covered in red tomato sauce.

Elias bolted up, his eyes wide. "Holy shit…"

"What the hell happened?" I demanded.

He grinned, completely unaware of how ridiculous he looked. "I shifted."

My heart leapt all the way into my throat. "What do you mean, you shifted?"

Elias burst out a laugh, running his hand through his hair in disbelief. "Last night, Marlowe shifted again and then… so did I."

"Impossible," I whispered. I turned back around and inspected the pawprints again. Sure enough, there were two sets, two different sizes. Marlowe finally stirred and I faced them again. "How?"

"I don't know," Elias replied. "I heard Marlowe come downstairs last night and I followed her, just in time to see her shift and go outside. I watched her, pet her a bit, and then another wolf showed up. I can't explain it, I just knew – that wolf was a shifter. An alpha male we couldn't trust. Something inside me snapped, and I

198

shifted to protect Marlowe."

Unbelievable. It was too much to wrap my mind around. I wanted to go get some coffee but there wasn't a clear path to the counter after Marlowe and Elias had destroyed the kitchen in a fit of wolf munchies.

Marlowe groaned as she sat up, clutching her midsection. "Oh my god, my stomach. I ate too much."

I wanted to be mad and tell her it served her right, but it wasn't like she had been in control.

Cam finally emerged from his room. Like me, he only saw the mess by the back door first. "Dammit, the housecleaner isn't coming 'til Tuesday. I'm not waiting til then. Someone needs to clean this up right no—What the fuck?"

He froze next to me at the sight of the kitchen.

"They shifted," I explained, as Marlowe seemed too sick to talk and Elias was still slightly freaking out.

"*They*? As in, both of them?"

I nodded and then directed him towards the prints. "See? Two sets."

His mouth dropped in shock, but then he quickly recovered. "Well, shit."

"Yeah."

Archer finally joined us, and I walked him through the situation.

His eyes lit in excitement. "This… this is amazing. I have a guess, but I don't want to get ahead of myself. I need to get a blood sample from Elias and head to my lab right away.

"Slow down there, Professor," Cam replied. "No one is going anywhere until this…" He gestured towards all the mess. "…is all taken care of. I'd ask these two to do it but…"

Marlowe finally stood up, one hand over her mouth as she bolted for the bathroom. We all winced at the sound of her puking her guts out.

There went my lasagna.

Elias's eyes started to clear, and he began to take stock of the damage he and Marlowe had done to the groceries and the floor. "Um, wow, getting flashbacks of what happened here. We might want to start wolf-proofing if this becomes a regular thing."

Cam stomped off to the closet where he kept the cleaning supplies, mumbling under his breath about how it wasn't fair that Elias had shifted but he hadn't.

I offered Elias a hand and helped him up. "Take a shower and then you can work on the carpet stains."

"Right, yeah…"

Marlowe continued retching while Cam shoved bottles of kitchen cleaner into my hands and a mop into Archer's. "And I'm not doing shit. I'm the one who pays Linda."

Instead, he pulled the collar of his t-shirt up over his nose and knocked on the bathroom door. "Babe? I'm coming in."

I rolled my eyes and then my sleeves, getting to work. A curse slipped its way under my breath when I saw they'd eaten all the lunch meat, too. That was almost $200 worth of food they'd gone through. And after the incident at the supermarket yesterday, I wasn't really looking forward to going back again so soon.

I kept my mind busy thinking about how Marlowe and Elias could shift while I cleaned. It was already strange enough that Marlowe had the ability. Was it tied to her being an omega? Or perhaps she'd inherited the ability from her mom? Maybe the shifters from the communes hadn't lost it like we had.

But then how could Elias shift? He was the one who had seen her shift twice. Maybe watching the transformation triggered his latent genes to finally react? Was it the threat to Marlowe by the other shifter?

And who even was that shifter?

"So, what are you thinking, Arch?" I called out.

"I'm not going to say yet. I don't want to pressure Marlowe or get our hopes up."

Ugh, I was dying to know. "Can't even drop a hint?"

"Nope," he replied quickly. "Too risky."

Dammit.

I glanced up at the calendar and groaned. "Today's her dad's funeral. Do you think she and Elias are going to be okay?"

Marlowe appeared from the bathroom wearing Camden's shirt, and he led her back up the stairs. "You fuckers almost finished yet?" he snapped.

"Dude, this wasn't even us," I yelled back, but he ignored me.

"…eggs, ham, turkey, apples…"

Elias had finished showering, taking his sweet ass time and getting out of the majority of the clean-up. I had moved on to making a new shopping list to replace everything the two of them had eaten when he re-entered the kitchen

"At the very least you can go get the new groceries, right?" I asked him.

"Huh? Oh yeah, sure." He poured himself a cup of coffee on autopilot, sitting down at the island and staring off into space.

I clicked my tongue against my teeth. It wasn't fair to be jealous, but at least I could be annoyed. "That good?"

"When you slept with Marlowe, did you also feel a sense of completion? Like you'd finally done something wonderful your body had been made for, and you couldn't imagine going back to a life before it happened?"

Walking into Cam's cabin that first night and just smelling her sweetness had been enough to trigger a latent, biological switch that had lain dormant in my soul. A switch that, once turned on, couldn't be turned off again. A switch that drove me to fulfill a greater purpose.

Knotting was just a confirmation of that feeling.

"Yes," I replied softly, thinking of my fight with Marlowe. I hoped I hadn't done irrevocable damage to our relationship.

"Yeah, shifting's like that."

Marlowe had to be the key to shifting, but Archer was right. Until we knew how or why or if it was something she could even awaken in all of us, we needed to give her space.

I still had to talk to her, though, the sooner the better. Nothing had been resolved last night, and now that I was thinking more clearly, I should be able to articulate my side a little better. Not that I wanted to be right, or even believed I was right. Not one hundred percent, anyway. I just wanted her to see my point of view, and understand that, while my reaction might have seemed extreme for someone who had grown up in human culture, for shifters, it was normal. Expected even.

That didn't mean I couldn't change, though. Especially if that was what she needed.

39
MARLOWE

Nolan knocked on my door around noon. "I take it you don't want anything for lunch?"

I groaned. Even after throwing up everything I'd eaten in my wolf form, I still felt like my stomach was full. How was that even possible?

"I don't think I want anything for the next week," I replied. I stared at my phone, looking at the text my friend from grad school had sent that morning.

> Esther: Haven't heard from you in a while, how are things?

I wasn't even sure how to respond. Would it be better to cut off all my old human connections? How could I explain my life here now?

"You still there?" I asked.

Nolan opened the door about halfway, careful not to cross the threshold. "Can I come in?"

"Yeah, I need your advice on something."

I could tell he was excited to be asked for help, but he was trying to play it so cool it was almost cute. He sat on the edge of my bed. "What's up?"

Turning off the TV, I showed him my phone. "How do I explain my life to my human friends?"

He ran his tongue along the bottom of his teeth while he thought. "You broke up with your fiancé because he was cheating on

IN THE MOUTH OF THE WOLF

you. That's easy enough. You came to Wisconsin to deal with your father's sudden death and his estate. That's also fine. You need to spend some time out here to figure out what to do with your inheritance – nothing shifter-y about that."

"Okay, but you know what I mean…" I gestured towards him.

The corner of his mouth lifted. "Does this mean you're no longer second-guessing the bond?"

I took my phone back and rolled away from him, staring at the wall to think without getting distracted by Nolan's stupidly handsome face. After last night, I didn't think my wolf would allow me to leave the pack since she had accepted Elias as her own. If I ever tried, she'd likely force a shift and head straight back to him. And if the others ever learned to shift, too, I suspected she would feel the same way about them.

And I wanted to be here, it wasn't like I was resigning myself to these guys. I wasn't ready to call it love yet, but it was pretty damn close.

However, things needed to change if this was going to work. While the guys were sure that the old ways shifters operated by were socially acceptable, from the interactions I'd had in town so far, it was clear not everyone felt the same way. We still needed a lot more pack meetings to iron out exactly how things would proceed from now on.

"Perhaps," I replied. "But going back to my question – how do I even explain you all?"

"You don't," he answered quickly, as though he was already prepared for the question. "In order to blend into human communities in the past, omegas would often choose one of their pack mates as a public husband. For legal purposes, for social purposes… whatever kind of situation required an omega to have one partner like a human."

Oh yeah, he'd been thinking about this. "Hm, so let's hear it."

"Hear what?"

"Your argument as to why it should be you."

He grinned. "Well, I don't have my PowerPoint slides on me at the moment, but I think I can present my case without them." He exaggeratedly cleared his throat, thumping his chest a few times for good measure, then began. "Your public husband should be the one whose company is the hardest to explain without a ring. Elias is your father's lawyer and Cam is your business partner. If you go out to a meal with them, it's not a date; it's a meeting. So that leaves me and Archer."

I clasped my hands together, tapping my fingers. "Go on."

"As my omega, you'll likely attend public events with me. Your picture could end up in the paper, describing you as my partner. If you were supposedly married to Archer, that would raise some eyebrows, wouldn't it?"

"Or," I countered, "I have my master's in public policy. Wouldn't it make sense for me to work in local government, even as a volunteer? I could just as easily be described as a colleague."

He looked at me dubiously. "A colleague I'm touching all night? Sugar, there's no way I can keep my hands off you for that long."

I beckoned for Nolan to lay down next to me, and he happily slid under my mountain of blankets. "Then how do I explain going out with Archer?" I asked.

"Your dad died young, from some disease Archer is researching. You can pretend he's a genetic counselor or something."

I picked up his hand and placed my palm against his, marveling at the difference in size. "Archer is remarkably restrained in public. He could probably keep up professional appearances better than you could."

"See? I knew you'd agree. So, when should we get married? I've always been partial to a spring wedding, but I could be convinced to wait until the fall, if that's what you'd prefer."

I laughed, wincing from the way it jostled my stomach. "Hold on there, cowboy. I'm still pissed about yesterday."

He swallowed, turning on his side to look at me. "I won't apologize for wanting to defend you."

I knew he wouldn't, but that didn't mean it was okay. "Then match the defense with the offense. If someone tries to hurt me physically, by all means, tear them apart. But verbally? If you feel the need to step in, bust out your roasting game, because this will not work if you Hulk out every time a female lashes out when she's jealous or threatened."

"It's instinct, though," Nolan sighed. "You tried to attack Megan and Rachel yourself, remember?"

Oh crap, he had a point with that.

"Yeah, but I didn't try to justify my reaction. I don't want to be that kind of person, and I'm trying to be better. Can't you?"

He paused, considering. "What if a male tries to hit on you? Can I still punch him?"

"Depends if he's serious or not." I shrugged.

"And how will I be able to tell that?"

I turned on my side to face him, our noses close to touching.

"Just check with me. If I nod, go for it."

A relieved grin spread across his face. "Deal."

My stomach gurgled ominously. "Terrific. Now, if you would be so kind, would you escort me to the bathroom? I believe I have another appointment with the toilet."

"Well, better keep it short. The funeral is in two hours."

40
MARLOWE

I donned my funeral dress. It was made of a heavier knit, styled with a crew neck and long sleeves, falling to just below my knees. Perfect for late fall and early winter, so I sent a sad, sarcastic thanks to my parents for having the foresight to die in the same season.

Despite Nolan's suggestion that he become my public husband, I rode with Cam and Elias to the temple, since we three were the closest to my father.

The outside of the building was rather simple and reminded me of the late-modernist churches I'd go to with my friends and their families as a kid whenever I slept over at their houses on Saturday nights.

"I thought you said shifters were Pagans?"

"We're similar, but not the same," Elias replied. "But we also have to keep up appearances in case humans pass through. You know how it is in rural America – if we didn't have something that looked like a Christian church, humans would be suspicious."

I thought back to that awkward moment in kindergarten when my teacher had been assigning roles for our Christmas pageant and I had asked who Jesus was. Everyone had looked at me like I had two heads.

"Yeah, I know."

Cam opened the door to the building, and the gentle hum of the HVAC system and the echo of hushed voices greeted me, the air calm and fragrant from incense.

Unlike the intricate detailing and majesty of a cathedral, the space felt sleek and cool. The floor was polished stone, reflecting the modest, dark pews and the white flower arrangements placed alongside them.

At first glance, the large, empty wall at the front appeared to hold an abstract crucifix. But as we got closer, the stark, angular lines and proportions felt off. My eyes widened in shock when I noticed the center figure – an elongated, distorted crescent moon.

There were other details as well that spoke to the temple's true deity – crescent moons and other celestial symbols were strategically placed inside all the artwork and carvings on the altar.

My gaze then fell to the open casket, and my heart raced. I grabbed Cam and Elias's hands to steady myself, my heels clicking down the aisle as I approached.

My dad looked peaceful, and I took in every feature, every line, every color of his face and willed it to memory. It would be the last time I ever saw him.

He looked so much like Ezra it hurt.

But he wasn't my twin brother, he was James Linden. Our dad. A male who had left, but perhaps not of his own volition. Who had watched from afar, manipulating my life in the background so he could still be in it, in some form or another.

I smelled them before I heard them and soon, Nolan and Archer had joined us, surrounding me with their love and support.

Perhaps my family was gone, but I wasn't alone.

41

ARCHER

Marlowe was still a little reticent about "coming out" as our omega, but had agreed to let Camden bring it up during his eulogy.

He talked mostly about how lucky he was to have learned how to be an alpha, not just from his own dad, but Marlowe's as well, and gave two anecdotes to illustrate his point – one funny, one poignant.

I was impressed by how relaxed he seemed in front of the crowd. He didn't have the best vocabulary, but he was relatable and clearly had everyone's rapt attention. If Nolan wasn't careful, Camden might have a chance against him in an election.

"Finally, I want to thank James for one last gift – introducing me to his daughter, Marlowe."

A few hushed murmurs had Marlowe sinking slightly in her seat, her face blushing. My poor little omega hated the spotlight.

"I'm certainly not the type to cling to old ways just because that's what's always been done. If some old method or tradition doesn't work for you, find a new one. It's something James and my dad taught me when I first started working at Wolfcrest Construction, but it carries over into my life, too."

He paused, his eyes carefully scanning the room. "But not all traditions are bad, either. Most of you all probably heard already because a shifter can't shit in the woods without half the town knowing about it by sundown…" *Pause for laughter and dramatic effect.* "…but Marlowe is an omega."

Nolan wrapped his arm around her shoulders as she cringed, the outbreak of whispers growing louder.

"And she's bonded to my pack."

The crowd reacted even more strongly, and Marlowe winced at each question we overheard.

"The whole pack?"

"She's bonded to four alphas?"

"Who does that anymore?"

"I thought that was a myth!"

Camden tapped his finger on the pulpit for a few seconds to let everyone get the initial shock out of their system. "Okay, that's enough, just shut up now." Once everyone returned to silence he continued. "Maybe after a hundred years, we've gotten used to single pair bonding, and that works for some shifters. And when it does, it's beautiful and great. But for me, my pack, and our omega? We're a unit, and it's what we want."

Nolan's grip on Marlowe tightened. Elias, who sat on her other side, placed a protective hand on her knee.

"And I didn't mean to use her dad's funeral as an opportunity to get on a soap box, but he went to great lengths to protect her from her identity. She grew up thinking she was a human until she landed here last week. But she hasn't received the warmest welcome here and that pisses me off. We're better than that. Because what do we do when the Moon fades from sight?"

"We will wait," the crowd replied in unison, "for she always returns."

"Yeah, she finally did. And her dad just fucking died, so quit being assholes."

I was sure if the microphone hadn't been attached to the podium, he would've liked to drop it. It certainly was an effective closing statement, if a bit dramatic for my tastes.

He stomped back down to the front row, gave Marlowe a big kiss, and then sat down.

A few people clapped, unsure of what to make of Camden's speech, while others just coughed nervously.

The Priestess ended the ceremony by trying to tie some of what Camden had said about tradition to how we needed to remember our roots and learn to balance the old with the new.

Afterwards, a line of people grew to get a chance to meet Marlowe and offer their condolences, and while she was clearly uncomfortable from all the attention, the interactions felt genuine and kind. Welcoming, even. A few had even heard of the incident at the liquor store and apologized on behalf of the town's females.

209

I hated to admit it, but I was impressed. With his speech, Camden had managed to warn everyone against hurting Marlowe without any of the violence she despised.

Perhaps he was a better pack leader than we gave him credit for.

Everyone but me returned home when the whole thing was finally over. I instead headed back to my lab. I was too excited to start my work.

I took the samples from Marlowe and Elias, as well as some others to test as a control and ran them through the centrifuge. It would only take about fifteen minutes, but it felt closer to an hour as I paced circles around the lab.

Hunches and guesses. My mind was spinning faster than the vials, and I couldn't even slow it down enough to form proper hypotheses. I knew what I was looking for.

Kind of.

It was possibly crazy, but I could feel it. I was on the verge of something huge, a breakthrough for our species.

A buzzer signaled the end of the centrifugation and I raced over, my hands practically shaking as I took the samples out. First was mine – at a glance it was normal. The red blood cells were at the bottom, a thin buffy coat in the middle, and then the translucent plasma.

Next, I grabbed Marlowe's. It was nearly identical aside from a fourth layer on top. It was pearly and iridescent, appearing as dense as mercury yet moving as lightly as oil.

I took a deep breath, finally examining Elias's.

It was smaller, but sitting like a hat on top of his plasma was a layer of this fourth substance, the same color and density as was in Marlowe's.

Bingo.

I isolated the substance and began preparing it for protein analysis with the mass spectrometer. I wouldn't get the results for another day. Once I'd prepared the samples, I took another drop and placed it under the microscope.

What I saw took my breath away. I could hardly describe what I was seeing, it was as though someone had managed to liquify moonlight. The drop glowed with its own incandescent light, pure and ethereal. Tilting the slide caused the substance to move in a way that defied the laws of gravity, floating like jellyfish underwater instead of a liquid on a flat plane.

"Luminis…" I whispered.

That was what I would call it.

The results wouldn't be available until tomorrow, and it was getting late. I took the remaining Luminis and put it in another vial to show the pack when I got home. I couldn't wait to share my discovery with Marlowe.

The roads were blissfully empty, although that wasn't surprising for a Sunday night. I turned on a random playlist Nolan shared with me a couple years ago, mostly music from the 60s. He certainly loved his classics.

A smile grew on my face, thinking of Marlowe when "California Dreamin'" by The Mamas & The Papas started. I sang along quietly, drumming my fingers on the steering wheel when a pair of glowing eyes got my attention. A wolf, dark as night, stood in the middle of the road. My heart pounded as I hit the brakes hard to avoid it, but the icy roads caused me to go into a spin and I careened into a ditch, everything going black.

My head and chest were killing me, and blood dripped down my face. I opened my eyes and tried to take stock of the accident. My ribs were cracked, and I likely had a concussion. My vision was doubling, and I shut my eyes tight.

I needed to call an ambulance.

I took a deep breath, steeling myself as I reached to where I thought my phone might be in the center console. Pain rippled through my torso, and I clenched my teeth as I blindly felt my way, following the auxiliary cord it had been attached to.

I noticed the movement outside in my periphery.

That's right. The wolf.

What the hell was a wolf doing here?

It ran up to my window, and then, in a quick contortion of hairy limbs, rose into a large male, fully nude. He gripped the handle to the door and ripped it clean off, then lowered his face until it was level with mine.

I couldn't focus on what he looked like, my vision blurry and my mind too fuzzy. All I could pick up was his alpha scent – almond and cherry.

"I'm coming for her," he said. "Your pack can do nothing to stop it."

I blinked, willing my consciousness to stay with me. "Why?"

"You do not need to know, it will not save you. It will not keep her from him."

Adrenaline and anger from the threat against Marlowe sharpened my senses, and I growled, leaning my head back and trying to get a better look at the shifter's face. I could make out long hair, blonde, a beard, and pale skin covered in tattoos. "'Him?' Who's 'him?' She belongs with us."

"No," he replied. "She has always belonged to him. It's only a matter of time until they can be together."

He transformed back into a wolf, running off into the night.

I passed out once more.

42

MARLOWE

Elias was sent to the grocery store to make up for us eating everything Nolan had bought while under wolf influence, so it was just Cam, Nolan, and me who headed into the basement to watch the Packers game.

Despite no one in my family ever being that big of a pro-football fan, I knew better than to try to get between a cheesehead and his team, and dutifully sat down between my two alphas as they glued their eyes to the screen and discussed plays and statistics.

I meanwhile finally found the courage to text Esther back.

> Me: My life has pretty much done a 180 since Thanksgiving. My dad died, and I'm in Wisconsin indefinitely while I deal with his half of a company he owned. Oh, and get this - turns out Mike's been cheating on me with a lot of women. So... not engaged anymore!

I'd barely heard the sent notification when she was FaceTimeing me. I got up off the couch and slinked to a corner of the room to answer.

"Hey Es—"

"I'm sorry, what? You need to go over everything in detail because that whole message just gave me the text equivalent of whiplash. Start at the beginning. Your dad died? I didn't know you had a dad. Well, I mean, in your life, that is."

"Yeah, super long story," I sighed. I went over in detail everything I could, finally ending on Mike's betrayal and my decision to stay here while I worked out what to do with my newfound wealth. "I'll be back in SF sometime soon. I still need to get all my stuff from Mike's condo. I'll let you know when I'm in town, we really need to get drinks."

Cam and Nolan's loud yells at the TV drew Esther's attention. "Wait, where are you? And who was that?"

I took a deep breath, nervous to start combining my new and old lives. I walked back to the couch and turned the camera around. "The guy on the left is Cam. He's my dad's business partner, and he's letting me stay with him while I'm getting on my feet. And the guy on the right is Nolan, Cam's friend."

A commercial break started and Cam grinned, reaching over and snatching the phone from me. "Hey, who's this?" he asked, Nolan scooting over to get into frame.

"Hi, Marlowe's friend!" Nolan called.

"Um, hey," she replied. "I'm Esther. Nice to meet you."

"Esther!" Nolan said. "You're the one from grad school, right?"

She laughed nervously, tucking a piece of hair behind her ear. "Yeah, that's me."

"Grad school, huh? Esther, tell me…" Cam shot me a shit-eating grin and then looked back at the phone. "Has she always had a thing for professors, or is that just a recent—"

"Oh my god!" I yelled, grabbing my phone back. "What is this, high school?" I huffed and went upstairs. "Sorry about that."

Esther gave me a knowing look. "Girl…"

I closed the door to the stairs and sat on the couch in the living room. "What?"

"Are you kidding me? What is going on in Wisconsin? 'Cause damn."

I blushed. "Yeah, I kinda had the same thought."

"And they both totally like you. I can tell! That's a real Sophie's choice right there."

If she only knew.

"I just found out the guy I've been with for three years and was going to marry has been fucking other women the whole time. I'm not really thinking about that."

I hated lying to her, but it was better this way for now.

"Right, sorry. I can't believe that. I always got the impression he worshiped the ground you walked on. In, like, a creepy way."

He really had been the perfect boyfriend and fiancé, and with

214

how often we were together, I didn't even know how he had the time to be sleeping with so many women.

"I think he was just a master manipulator, love bombing me constantly to keep me distracted."

Esther frowned. "I wish you weren't so far away right now. I want to give you a hug."

"Me, too. It's been too long! Tell me about your new job. You started a few weeks ago, right?"

Her face lit up. "Yes! My new boss is amazing. What a difference it makes not working for a total narcissist…"

We talked for another thirty minutes, until she finally had to go. "I'm meeting Gabriel for dinner soon, but keep me posted on how everything's going! And if you need a proxy to handle untangling your stuff with Mike here, let me know. I'd love an excuse to yell at him. Possibly hit him."

I laughed. "I would pay so much money to watch you kick his ass."

"How much we talking about here? Because word on the street is you're flush with cash…"

I paused, looking up in thought. "How about dinner at the House of Prime Rib?"

She pursed her lips and then nodded. "Acceptable. Okay, see you later! Let me know which guy you choose!"

Esther hung up before my face could give it all away.

"Why didn't you tell her it's me?"

"Christ on a cracker!" I yelled, jumping a foot in the air. "Dammit, Nolan, how the hell did you sneak up on me? I need to put bells on you guys…"

He stood behind me and shrugged. "It's a gift. So, why didn't you tell her you're choosing me?"

"I'm not sure I've officially signed off on that plan yet," I huffed. "Sneaking up behind me is going to dock you a few points."

"Points?" he asked. "Oh, so this is a competition now?" His eyes lit up and he leaned on his arms against the back of the couch, bringing his face closer to mine. "I'm very good at winning."

A wave of bourbon and vanilla washed over me and my nipples hardened. "Aren't you watching the game?" I asked, my pulse quickening.

His pupils dilated and he ran his nose along the outer shell of my ear. "I have something far more beautiful I'd rather be doing."

Nolan let out a low growl and then nipped at my ear lobe. I

became wet with slick, my need for him gnawing away at my core. "Nolan," I whimpered, leaning back into the couch.

His lips gently caressed my neck while his hands came over my shoulders and grabbed my breasts, kneading them over my t-shirt. I watched our reflection in the window, spreading my legs as I grabbed his upper arms. His eyes raised slightly, and he smiled, noticing how I was looking at us.

"Look at how sexy you are, sugar. Do you have any idea how hard it is keeping my hands off you?"

One of them traveled down further, slipping under my sweatpants and underwear. "Fuck, you're so wet. Is that all for me?"

I moaned as his middle finger rubbed my clit, circling and pressing while staring at my face in our reflection.

"All for you," I replied, rolling my hips to meet his slow, deliberate movements. His finger then pushed inside me, his palm rubbing hard and bringing me to climax. The first one when I was this turned on always came quickly, and my nails dug into his hardened biceps as it built, panting heavily until he gave me my release.

"That's it," Nolan purred. "You're so pretty when you come for me. Can you show me again?"

I nodded wordlessly, my voice stuck in my throat. My whole body felt like jelly and I couldn't move, so I gave into the ecstasy and surrendered myself to his arms. He picked me up and took me upstairs, ignoring Cam's frustrated screams coming from the basement.

"What the fuck is wrong with you? How did you miss him? He was right there!"

We went into my nest and Nolan gently laid me down on my bed, turning the lights down low and connecting his phone to my Bluetooth speaker. The slow, sensual beats of an R&B song floated across the room, and Nolan took off his clothes, taking his time and keeping his eyes on me. I drank him in, admiring the shadows that formed beneath every muscle on his sculpted chest, following the trail of dark hair that led straight down where the V of his abdomen pointed. His large cock was straight and hard, the knot already inflated. He moved towards me next, removing my clothes with the same, languid pace, setting the mood – not for rushed, desperate fucking, but deliberate, passionate sex.

Once we were both nude, he lowered himself on top of me, kissing me from my forehead down, appreciating every inch of skin he came across with reverence. I relished how special he made me feel, how prized.

As he got closer to my pussy I became even wetter with anticipation, but he skipped over it, heading down further to my thighs, my knees, and my calves. When he got to my feet, he sat up, bringing one up to massage it. His strong hands applied the perfect amount of pressure, and my eyes rolled back in my head from pure bliss.

"That feels amazing," I moaned.

When he finished with the first foot, he left it resting on his shoulder before he moved to the next one, expertly wrenching out my stress and tension until I felt like a happy puddle of goo. After he brought my other foot over his shoulder, he made his way back up, kissing the inside of my legs until he reached my pussy again.

Now his tongue began to work in greater earnest. It pierced me, lapping me up and tasting me as though he were starving. "You're so sweet, sugar. When I die, I want to be right here between your legs."

"Don't die yet," I laughed. "I'm so close."

He chuckled in return and focused his mouth on my clit, his fingers now working inside me. My orgasm built again, and I ran my hands through his thick brown hair. "Nolan," I sighed. What else could I say? My body told him exactly how good he could make me feel.

I climaxed again, my back arching as I panted and whimpered, pure bliss running through my veins. Once I came back down, I felt limp, and Nolan made his way back up towards my face, kissing along the path again. His lips met mine, and I tasted my slick on his tongue.

"Are you ready for me?" he whispered, rubbing his erection against my stomach.

I reached down and stroked him, swiping the drop of pre-cum from his head with my thumb, bringing it back up to my mouth and licking it off. "Always," I answered, my voice breathy.

The look in his eyes was electric, and I spread my legs wider as he settled into me.

His cock nudged at my entrance, and he pushed slowly, pausing every few seconds to allow my body to adjust to him. He continued forward until he'd entered me, full to his knotted hilt.

Nolan grunted, grabbing my hands and raising them above my head. He intertwined our fingers and pulled out, just as slowly as when he'd entered. Then his hips began to move in expert motions, rolling and thrusting to the beat of the music, hitting every spot inside me deliciously.

This wasn't even sex. It felt like we had transcended into something more, something divine and sacred, our bodies working for a purpose greater than just an orgasm.

"Marlowe," he whispered, my name an invocation on his lips, never faltering as each thrust of his cock slid into me with perfect precision.

His knot rubbed against my clit, and while I wasn't ready for this to end, we both felt our releases building, the rapture reaching its zenith.

The words spilled out of me before I even knew I was saying them. "Nolan, I love you."

His head snapped up and his eyes met mine, and I faltered for a second, thinking I'd made a mistake. But his thrusting became frenzied, and as I came he pushed his knot inside me, locking us together while his orgasm filled me. "Marlowe," he moaned. "I love you, I love you, I love you."

A tear escaped down my cheek, and I released his hands so I could wrap my arms around his back and bring him down on top of me, feeling our orgasms through each other. He kissed along my jaw and then down my neck. With a sudden growl, he bared his teeth, and then sunk them into my shoulder.

I inhaled deeply with the initial pain, but it was replaced by pleasure and I came around his cock again, triggering another release.

My connection to him was immediate, and I felt all his emotions — his love, his devotion, his happiness... everything. I mirrored them back, wanting him to know how absolutely wonderful he was.

Nolan licked at the bite and then kissed me again. "I don't care if it wasn't my turn. I didn't want to live another second without you being completely mine, in every way possible. I love you so much."

I released a shuddering breath. "I love you, too."

43

CAMDEN

"Fucking hopeless," I moaned, sinking back further into the couch. 42-13 to the Seahawks?

Elias was back from picking up the groceries and had come downstairs to watch the end of the game with me, but his mind was elsewhere.

"You good?" I asked, finishing my beer.

"Hm? Yeah, sorry. It's just so strange, feeling my wolf inside me now."

I bit back my jealousy. He'd bonded with Marlowe first and now he could fully shift? I knew Archer was being cagey about his testing, but even an idiot like me could see the connection between the two.

Elias was my pack mate and one of my best friends. I was happy for him, of course. I wasn't a complete monster.

But it should have been me.

"I bet," I replied. "By the way, I bought some security cameras for outside the house. This whole business with the other full shifter has me on edge, and I'm not feeling too good about someone lurking around and trying to lure Marlowe away."

Elias growled. "Good idea. I'm starting to worry," he began, picking at the label on his bottle. "Let's say Marlowe's parents were runaways from a shifter commune. What if those communes never lost their ability to fully shift or breed omegas? What if, now that Marlowe's off the suppressants and is living here, they've discovered who and what she is, and want to take her back?"

I might not have had a realized wolf inside me like Elias, but my beastly instincts roared at the idea of anyone thinking they could take Marlowe away from us. Whatever she and Nolan were doing upstairs, I could feel the trickles of their happiness and the love building between them. She wasn't just an omega; she was our heart, the center of our universe. And if that motherfucker set one more paw on my property, I had two silver shells in the chamber of my shotgun with his name on 'em.

"That's never going to happen," I responded coldly.

A jolt hit me, running through my veins like lightning. The hit wasn't as powerful as before, but I knew it immediately.

"That ASSHOLE!" I got up to run upstairs and tear Nolan a new one but Elias leapt up quicker and blocked my path.

"I know I don't have a leg to stand on here, but Marlowe doesn't deserve you bursting into her nest and ruining her moment. Besides, we both know they're knotted. Are you really going to beat him up when she's attached to him?"

My chest heaved. "I gotta do something, I got too much anger in me right now." Everything I'd been suppressing for the last few days because I knew how much Marlowe hated aggression was boiling over. Her stupid vamp ex, those gross old alphas who had tried to take her, Elias bonding her first, the way I had messed up with Rachel, the incident at the liquor store, that other shifter showing up in the middle of the night and trying to take her... And now, Nolan had just bonded her against my orders while I sat here alone, watching a shitty game of football.

Elias pushed me. "You need to fight? Let's go, come at me."

I rolled my shoulders and cracked my neck as I lowered myself into a crouch. "You asked for it."

44
NOLAN

Heaven.

That was the only possible explanation I had for where Marlowe and I had gone tonight. I had to fight the urge to pinch myself and prove I was still alive.

I rolled us on our sides, my knot slowly deflating as we stared into each other's eyes.

How was it possible to feel this much love for someone after only knowing them for a week? I was thirty-three years old, not some silly teen. It should have felt foolish to say the "L" word so fast, especially since I knew she felt that way with three other males.

But I was blissfully free of any jealousy or embarrassment. Instead, it was as though the emotions she felt for my pack mates only enhanced what we had. That we would build on it and make it even greater as our connections deepened.

We were made for this. We were made for each other.

A sudden crash from downstairs brought us back into reality, and Marlowe's brows furrowed in concern. "Cam's really mad."

Yeah, he was. I couldn't really blame him, I had fully intended to wait to bond with Marlowe until Cam made his move. He had never looked so betrayed as he had a few days ago when we had realized what Elias had done.

But when Marlowe had told me she loved me, I knew it had been the right time. I'd rather deal with a pissed off alpha than miss my chance to bond with my omega after something so special and perfect.

"The only thing that matters is how you feel about this," I

responded. "Do you have any regrets?"

She shook her head and smiled. "Not one."

I pulled her into my chest and sighed, running my fingers through her hair and purring, my heart full.

We were woken up by Elias knocking on the door. "Are you two still knotted?"

Marlowe groaned and shifted away from me, my flaccid, well-emptied cock and deflated knot slipping out of her. "No. Does Cam need to see me?" I asked.

I figured he had decided to wait until we were separated before he let me know with his fists how mad he was. My face had finally healed after Archer's attack, and I wasn't exactly looking forward to another beat down.

But looking at the mark left by my bite on Marlowe's neck, I knew it would be worth it.

"Get dressed," he replied quickly. "Both of you. We need to go to the hospital. Archer was in a car accident."

Marlowe whined nervously the whole ride there, picking at the skin around her fingernails and tugging at her hair. "I'm a fucking curse," she said softly to herself. "Everyone I love dies…"

Cam never let anyone drive his truck, but tonight, he had insisted on sitting in the back of the cab and comforting Marlowe, so he had handed me the keys instead.

"Babe, he's fine. His sister's with him right now. She says he has a few broken ribs and a concussion, that's it."

I could feel her pain and stress more acutely now due to the bond. Her brother, her mother, her father… each death was a weight on her soul, and the news of Archer was pushing her past her tipping point.

Elias turned around in the passenger seat. "Did you know shifters heal two to three times faster than humans? He's going to be back to normal in just a couple of weeks, maybe even sooner."

She nodded, but her nervous tics and vacant expression remained. Fuck, I just wanted to hold her. But I needed to get us to the hospital safely, and concentrated on the roads instead.

When we arrived at the ER, the nurse let us straight through. Marlowe bit back a whimper as we entered Archer's room, not wanting to wake him. Aside from a bandage across his forehead and some bruising on his face and arms, he thankfully didn't seem too injured.

Ivy had taken two chairs and pushed them together for a makeshift bed, looking up from a book as we entered.

"Took you fuckers long enough," she sighed. She struggled to lift her legs over the arm of the chair back down to the ground, her large belly in the way. Cam hurried over, pulling the other chair out and helping her slip her wool-lined boots back on.

She stared at Cam, Elias, and me expectantly, clearing her throat and tilting her head towards Marlowe. "Anyone going to introduce me, or…"

Cam rolled his eyes. "Like you don't know."

Ivy rested a hand on top of her baby bump. "Of course, I do. I found out from at least four different people. Do you have any idea how embarrassing it is to discover secondhand that your own brother's pack has bonded the last omega in the world? I'm starting to think he got into an accident on purpose just so I'd feel too bad to hit him."

Marlowe tore her gaze from Archer's face and her cheeks blushed. "I'm sorry. It's really nice to meet you, Ivy. I'm Marlowe."

Ivy gave her a warm smile. "And I'm sorry for the bitchy betas you've run into. Like any of those females had a chance with these guys, anyway. I mean, look at you, you're adorable!"

Cam reached out and touched Ivy's stomach, absentmindedly rubbing it. "So when is Camden Jr. due?"

"Ha, ha," she replied. "Just as funny as the first time you asked." Ivy noticed Marlowe staring at where Cam touched her and she laughed. "You've got nothing to worry about. Alphas are overprotective over any pregnant shifter, especially ones they know well. They don't even realize they're doing it most of the time."

"Doing what?" Cam asked, his hand still touching her.

Ivy swatted him away and started waddling to the door. "It was great to finally meet you, Marlowe. You and Archer should stop by sometime. The pups have already heard about their new auntie and can't wait to meet you."

"Oh! Right, that would be great. I'd love to meet them, too."

She squeezed Marlowe's arm on the way out. "And don't worry about Archer. The doctor on rotation right now is a shifter too and says he'll bounce back in no time at all."

Marlowe nodded, and the relief and comfort she received from

Ivy flowed through the pack bond. "Thank you for everything."

The beeps from the monitor punctuated the silence and Ivy yawned. "Okay, which one of you big alphas is going to help me back to my car?"

Cam sighed. "I suppose I can."

"Oh wow," Ivy replied, "thank you *so* much for your sacrifice. Good night, boys. Good night, Marlowe."

As soon as she was out the door Archer cracked open an eye and whispered, "Is she gone?"

Marlowe gasped, whipping back towards him. "Y-you…"

"Sorry to worry you," he said, his voice scratchy as he gave a cheeky smirk. "But she was sort of right. It was better to fake being asleep than deal with her anger over not telling her about Marlowe."

"You jerk!" Marlowe cried, smiling and wiping tears from her eyes. "Don't you ever scare me like that again!"

He took her hand, holding it tightly. "Never, I promise."

"What happened?" Elias asked. "Ivy said someone found your car in a ditch and called 911 when you didn't respond."

Archer grimaced. "We should wait until Camden gets back. He's going to want to hear this."

A knock sounded at the door and a beta female walked in. "Hi, I'm Dr. Dubois, just coming in to go over your discharge instructions."

She smelled the air and her eyebrows shot up in surprise. "Oliver wasn't kidding. There *is* an omega in town."

Marlowe's face scrunched in anger at the mention of the male name, and my hackles raised in response. "Who is Oliver?" I growled.

"Whoa there, settle down, alpha," the doctor joked. "He's our bereavement counselor. He handled this young female's case last week." She turned towards Marlowe, her expression becoming sincere. "I'm sorry for your loss."

"Thank you," she replied, turning back towards Archer. "He can really go home already?"

The doctor looked over the papers on her clipboard. "Yes. After patching him up, there's nothing more we can really do for him here. He just needs to rest and take it easy for the next couple weeks. No strenuous activity, hm?" she added pointedly. "I'll have the discharge planner process the paperwork, and I'll write you a prescription for some painkillers if you'd like them. With those rib fractures, you're going to find most movement rather unpleasant. Hope you feel better soon."

She left and a nurse came in briefly right after her,

disconnecting Archer from the monitor and removing the IV from his hand.

"Here," Elias offered, taking some clothes out of the duffle bag he brought. "I figured you might need these."

"Yeah, I don't want you sitting in my truck on your bare ass," Cam quipped, returning from helping Ivy. "We getting out of here, then?"

"Waiting on the paperwork," I replied. I turned back to Archer. "We're all here now, can you tell us what happened?"

Marlowe helped him pull the sweatshirt over his head, and he answered quietly. "Which do you want first, the exciting news or the troubling news?"

45
ELIAS

Cam groaned. "Can't you just say 'good news or bad news'?"

"No," Archer replied, carefully pulling up his sweatpants with Marlowe's assistance. "So which is it?"

"Troubling news," she answered. "I want to end on a positive note."

Archer looked towards the door and then lowered his voice. "Elias, what can you tell me about the wolf you saw last night?"

I already didn't like where this was going and hid my unease to clear my mind, closing my eyes while trying to recall whatever detail I could from the encounter. "It was dark, so I couldn't make out much."

"What about fur color? Was it light?"

"No, it might have been black," I replied. "He didn't blend into the snow. He looked more like a shadow."

Archer nodded. "Any other details? Do you remember his scent?"

I closed my eyes again. "Maybe... it reminded me of those cookies Nolan's mom used to make. Cherry and something."

"Almond?"

"Yeah, that sounds right."

Archer swore under his breath as he tried to pull up his socks, and Marlowe growled cutely at him until he laid back down so she could do it for him.

I could already imagine what the next few weeks were going to be like with those two – Archer hated asking for help, but Marlowe would insist on helping, and hilarity would ensue.

"That wolf appeared in the middle of the road, and I lost control trying to avoid hitting it."

My body tensed, and I looked at Cam. "We need to get those security cameras up immediately."

"I'm thinking the same thing," he replied, cracking his knuckles.

"Wait," Nolan said. "How do you know what he smelled like? You could tell from inside the car?"

"No." Archer turned towards Marlowe and grabbed her hands. "What I am about to say will be upsetting. Those three will be angry, and you will be scared. Are you ready?"

Marlowe's face paled. "Um, no, but go ahead."

"The wolf came up to me and shifted back into human form. He said he was coming for Marlowe. That she belonged to someone else. And then he left."

The news ripped through me like a bullet, and my wolf snarled inside me, pacing and demanding to be released so he could chase down this other shifter and rip out his throat.

Not yet, I told him.

When? he snapped.

Soon.

Nolan and Cam weren't taking the news any better, but fueling the fire was our very own omega. She wasn't scared at all; she was furious.

"Who the fuck does this guy think he is?" she seethed.

"I don't know who he thinks he is, but I can tell you what he's *going* to be if he ever shows his furry ass anywhere near you – my new rug." Cam pulled Marlowe into him, tucking her neck gently into the crook of his elbow and kissing the top of her head. "No one is taking you away from us."

The discharge coordinator came so Archer could pay and sign all the paperwork. After grabbing his meds at the pharmacy, we made our way back home in Cam's truck.

"Well?" Marlowe asked, her eyes nervously scanning the road for the dark wolf. "What was the exciting news?"

Archer grunted as he turned towards the back. "I need to preface this news as well and let Marlowe know she's under no obligation to do anything…"

"Oh, for Moon's sake," Cam grumbled, "Just say it – Elias can shift because he bonded with Marlowe already, right?"

Nolan coughed and tugged at the collar of his shirt, and Archer sighed. "Yes, but now I am starting to understand why." He dug around in his bag and pulled out a small vial. Inside were a few drops of a white, pearly liquid that almost seemed to float as he flipped it upside down.

He gave it to Marlowe, who turned on her cell phone's flashlight, inspecting it closely. Tiny rainbows and glimmers of diamond-like brilliance danced inside the car. "What is this?"

"Luminis," Archer replied. "At least that's what I'm calling it for now. It made up about fifteen percent of your blood sample once I ran it through the centrifuge, and perhaps five percent of Elias's, but wasn't present in mine or the other random human and shifter samples I used as a control. When Elias bonded with you, he ingested some of your blood, and you must have passed it onto him that way."

"Fascinating," she whispered. She passed the vial to Nolan next so he could look at it. "But what is it made of, and why do I have it while other shifters don't?"

Archer smiled, clearly excited to talk about this and forgetting his pain or injuries. "I won't get the data from the spectrometer until tomorrow, and it will take me a while to analyze it. As far as why you have Luminis present in your system and others don't, well…"

"Your mom," I interrupted. Cam kept his eyes on the road, already knowing what I was about to say anyway, but everyone else turned to me. "And possibly your dad. With this new full shifter showing up, and the mystery surrounding your parents' origins, I'm guessing they escaped a shifter commune, and they must never have lost their abilities or their omegas. That's why you, well, are what you are."

We knew these communes existed only because of shifters like Marlowe's parents. But we didn't know how many there were or where they were even located.

"But why would they want me back?" Marlowe asked. "If they can all fully shift and they still have omegas, I can't be worth all this trouble."

Nolan clicked his tongue against his teeth in disgust. "A group of shifters like that, stuck in the old ways when females were seen as commodities, would definitely fight like hell to get a missing omega back. We're very possessive."

"Oh really? I hadn't noticed…" she replied dryly. I winked at her, and she stuck her tongue out at me in return.

Little brat.

"It's true," Archer added. "Before omegas disappeared from our communities, you were still rare enough to be highly guarded from the general population. When a shifter presented as one in the early stages of puberty, they were sometimes whisked away until they reached maturity, when they could be used as bartering chips between powerful packs. Do not underestimate the lengths shifters will go to for someone like you."

When Marlowe's unease leaked through the bond, Cam spoke up. "Including us, babe. No one, and I mean *no one*, is going to take you away from us. Even if…" he paused. "Fuck, I didn't want to entertain this idea, but we might…"

He struggled to get the words out, making Marlowe even more nervous. She let out a breathy whine, and Cam cursed again, finally saying, "We might want to consider expanding the pack for Marlowe's protection."

46
MARLOWE

The entire truck was silent. Nolan and Elias seethed, too stunned with anger to speak.

Another alpha? Like there wasn't already enough testosterone in the house. And would I be expected to...

Seemingly reading my thoughts, Cam answered my question. "I would make it clear to whoever we brought in that he is not entitled to anything you're not willing to give. He'd be bonded to me and me only."

"You already have someone in mind, don't you?" Nolan asked, his tone acidic.

Cam didn't move or blink before conceding. "Maybe."

"*Maybe?*" Elias wrapped an arm around me, holding me defensively. "How long have you been thinking about this?"

"Since today," he replied. "It wasn't even a serious idea, just an option if it came down to it. But now that we know for certain this other wolf is serious about taking Marlowe, and with Archer being hurt, we could really use some extra muscle. We have no idea how big this other shifter's pack is, and I'd like to be prepared."

I took a deep breath, trying to center myself. Not a single day since I'd arrived here had been normal. Was this really going to be the rest of my life? Riding one crisis straight into the next?

"I'm loathe to say it," Archer started, "but I think Cam has a point. The dark wolf shifter pulled my car door clean off. He was strong. *Really* strong. And until my ribs are healed, I'm a weak link. I dislike the idea of bringing in a wild card, but not more than the thought of being the reason Marlowe gets taken from us. So I vote yes."

"Oh, this is an election now?" Nolan sneered. "Because I vote hell no. I'm not trusting one of Cam's buddies in our pack or around our omega. I barely trust her with you assholes."

"Same," Elias responded. "I vote no. These commune shifters might be strong, they might have full access to their wolves, but we still have guns. The four of us... or... five? Marlowe, can you shoot?"

"What do you think?" I snapped.

"Okay, so the four of us with Cam's arsenal can easily pick off a pack of shifters. Let's start stocking up on silver ammo, too, while we're at it."

"Silver?" I asked. "Wait, that's a real thing?" So far, the myths about shifters had all been wrong. When we could shift, we didn't rely on the full moon. And we were born, not made from a bite. We also weren't mindless killing machines, either.

Well, at least *most* of us weren't. Who knew about this mysterious shifter who for some reason thought he had some sort of claim over me?

"Yes," Archer replied. "Silver works for shifters and vampyrs."

Vampyrs? A memory made its way to the forefront of my mind – I had gotten Mike a silver ring for his birthday last year, and he'd been super awkward about it, saying he had a silver allergy and apologizing for having to return it.

"Regardless, it's two against two. Marlowe, you're the tie breaker. Vote no now so we can put this stupid idea to bed," Elias said.

I didn't necessarily want to bring another alpha into our group. Even taking sex out of the equation, it was hard enough balancing the oversized emotions of the four of them. Did I really have the bandwidth to add another?

But Cam's sanity was on a razor's edge, and Archer would feel better knowing there was another set of eyes on me.

"I want to meet him first."

It was past midnight by the time we got home, and while everyone else was exhausted, a thought kept me awake, and I was curious to see if it would work.

I hadn't packed anything sexy, because why would I have, but

I did find it interesting that some short, silky nightgowns had been waiting for me in my drawers when Cam first showed me my nest.

I put one on and then wrapped a robe on top to cover myself.

Archer's room was down the hall. I tiptoed my way over, knocked on the door, and he told me to come in.

He was laying in an elevated position, plenty of pillows piled behind him while he iced his chest with one hand, a book in the other. He took off his glasses and looked up. "Everything okay?"

I nodded and sat down next to him. "What are you reading?" I asked. He showed me the spine and I read the title out loud. "*Fur and Fangs: A New History of the Great War.* Wow, don't you ever read anything fun?"

He tilted his head in confusion and smiled. "What do you mean? This is fun."

"Hmm," I replied, taking his book out of his hand and putting it on his nightstand. "You and I have very different definitions of fun, then."

His pupils dilated and he moved slightly towards me, then winced. "The heart is willing, but the flesh is weak. I never thought I'd ever say no to you, but…"

"Shhh…" I placed my finger on his lips. "You're in luck, because I've been doing some reading as well, and I think I know how you might heal faster."

"Not the way I want to do it," he replied longingly. "I'm pretty sure the doctor told me 'no strenuous activity.'"

I crossed my arms and huffed. "Oh my god, will you shut up for a second and let me talk?"

He chuckled and dramatically closed his mouth, gesturing for me to continue.

"Damn, finally. Anyway, do you know why shifters were such feared warriors in the past?"

Archer looked at me expectantly but didn't reply.

"Because their bodies healed when they shifted."

His expression changed from amusement to surprise, and he cocked an eyebrow.

"It only took about a day and a half between when Elias bonded with me and when he shifted. If you bond with me tonight, you could potentially be fully healed by Tuesday morning."

He remained silent, his eyes waiting.

"Yes, you can talk now."

He took a deep breath. "The scientist in me is thrilled with your proposition, but the alpha in me is… not."

"Oh…" I had thought it was the perfect solution, but I should have expected this. Archer had always been the most hesitant to bond with me. It definitely stung a bit to hear, but I couldn't blame him. He was a cautious, thoughtful male. It made sense that he'd prefer to wait.

"Sorry, I'll let you get your rest then. Do you need more water?"

I rose to get up, but he grabbed my hand and pulled me back down. "Not for whatever reason you're thinking. The alpha in me wants to bond you when I'm in peak physical condition, to claim you in the height of passion. This way feels more like a pity bond," he said, shame creeping along his cheeks.

"It's not a pity bond," I replied. How this alpha could ever think that astounded me. "I don't want to wait a few weeks before you can knot me at full strength again. It's been one day and I'm already craving you."

A deep purr resonated in his chest, and I watched as the outline of his cock grew underneath the thin blanket. I reached and slowly traced it with my fingertips, and he swallowed and leaned his head back, closing his eyes.

"Marlowe." My name was a plea on his breath. "I crave you too, but I can't really move right now."

I took two silk scarves out of the pocket on my robe and grinned. "Then don't." I grabbed his hand and pulled it up near his head, tying it to the headboard, and then slowly moved across him to do the same on the other side.

The robe slipped off my shoulders, revealing the silky, short, babydoll dress, and he groaned. "This is torture, you know that?"

I lowered myself down to his ear, careful not to lean on his chest. "Exactly, Mr. Lim. If it starts to hurt too much, let me know, and the interrogation will stop."

With that, I stood up and began pacing by the side of the bed, my hands clasped behind my back. "We know you hid the codes to the safe, and my boss has given me clear instructions that I am to extract their location by any means necessary."

Archer laughed haughtily, quickly getting into character. "Well, your boss is going to be sorely disappointed, because I'm the only person who knows and I'm not talking."

I stopped and placed my hands on the mattress, bringing my lips to hover right over his. "You were trained well. You hold up remarkably to physical pain. But you see, I have a method that you may not have tried before. It's a specialty of mine, and I have broken every male placed in front of me. I guarantee you will tell me within the hour." I brushed his lips with mine, kissing him lightly. My tongue parted through and darted into his mouth, swirling and teasing as he attempted to stay still and give me nothing in return.

"We'll see about that," he replied with a smirk. "Do your worst."

I bit his lip and laughed. "Oh, I plan to."

Archer's breathing remained even, and I pulled down the blanket, revealing the lower half of his body. He wore only a pair of boxer briefs, and I sat down beside him, sliding my hand on top of his erection. "My, my," I said. "Your reputation precedes you, Mr. Lim. But you know what they say – the bigger the cock, the harder they fall."

He thrust up slightly to meet my touch. "You're free to begin whenever you'd like, but the only thing you're leaving here with is a sore pussy and my cum dripping down your gorgeous legs."

I slipped off his underwear, his cock springing free. I wrapped my hand around his generous girth and rubbed him up and down. "But don't you understand? I won't allow you to spill your seed until you've spilled all your secrets." I licked the bead of pre-cum that had accumulated on the tip. "Coming is for good prisoners only."

He sucked air between his teeth as I got up again, grabbing a small bottle out of my robe pocket. "What is that?" he asked. "Poison?"

I squirted the liquid into my hand and went back to the bed, continuing to massage his cock. "Oh, fuck me," he groaned.

"Tsk tsk, not until you give up the location," I teased. I rubbed the lubrication all the way down his shaft and over his knot and balls. My arms then began pumping in earnest, and I watched as his face contorted, getting closer and closer to his release.

Then I stopped, and he opened his mouth in protest. "What did I say?" I asked. "You'll come when you give me what I want."

"The only thing you want is my knot deep inside you." He swallowed, his Adam's apple bobbing in his throat as he pulled tentatively at the restraints.

"We'll see about that." Satisfied he had climbed far enough down the precipice, I placed my mouth over his head and he jerked his hips up.

"Yes, please, swallow my cock and I'll tell you anything," he moaned.

His cock slid further into my mouth, and I swirled my tongue around him, using my hands to rub his knot.

My head moved up and down, my eyes trained on his, loving the way he watched me. His expression gave away every sensation he felt, and he was soon reaching climax again.

"Don't stop, don't stop, don't…"

I pulled away completely and he grunted in frustration. "I can't take it, you win. The codes are in locker 23 at the train station. Just let me come…"

Smiling sweetly, I patted him on the cheek. "Mr. Lim, do you think we didn't check there? Lying will only hurt you." I pulled my nightgown off my body and sat back on my heels. "At least one of us should get off tonight, don't you think?"

I grabbed one of my breasts and slid my hand down towards my clit, rubbing it slowly. The scent of Archer's lust, sea salt and jasmine, had me dripping wet, and I brought my fingers to his mouth, slowly pushing them inside.

He greedily sucked them clean, his eyelids fluttering as he tasted me.

Then I took his cock, throbbing and ready to explode, and rubbed it against my clit, moving it down towards my entrance. "Last chance, Mr. Lim."

"They're under the bench at the north entrance to Springs Park! I swear it!"

I carefully lowered myself over him, my pussy more than ready to take him fully. Stopping at the knot, I rolled my hips, stimulating my clit until I was just about to come, and then dropped down completely. Our orgasms tore through us, and he ripped through the silk scarves and sat up, ignoring his fractured ribs and sinking his teeth into the crook of my neck, opposite the side Elias and Nolan had chosen.

Stars exploded in my vision, and I reached behind me to grab his thigh for support. "Oh, Archer," I whimpered. His release was relentless, and I surrendered myself to the pleasure, letting my own climax hit me again and again until my body shook from the effort.

He licked the bite marks to help seal them, kissed me, and then laid back down, grimacing and reaching for the medicine on the nightstand. "Worth it," he chuckled painfully, popping one in his mouth.

The connection between me and Archer became stronger, and all the love we felt for each other poured through, my heart feeling nearly full.

Just one more to go.

Normally I enjoyed the time it took for my alphas' knots to deflate, taking the opportunity to cuddle. But I couldn't lay on Archer's chest without hurting him, so I gestured for his book. "Why don't I read that to you?"

He shrugged and handed it to me. "How many shifters do you think have knotted while reading non-fiction to each other?"

I gave him a little shrug. "What can I say, I'm a trailblazer. What page?"

"Seventy-two," he said, reaching down to give my ass a gentle squeeze.

Scrolling through the table of contents, I noticed something strange. "Hey, these battles sound familiar."

"What do you mean?"

"It's just..." My bond with Archer deepened with each moment, his curiosity coming through so clearly it felt like my own. And in the far distance, I could feel Cam seething in anger.

Poor guy. I'd never meant for him to be last. "How were the locations chosen?"

He rubbed his chin with his thumb as he thought. "I suppose the same way lots of battle locations are – geographical advantages, logistical considerations, defensive positioning, that sort of thing. Why?"

"In that book you gave me on shifter history, it mentioned that we first appeared in groups sporadically around the world. These battle locations seem to correspond. Like here – the Battle of Sedona, close to where shifters started the skinwalker legends. And here, the Battle of Mt. Fuji. Didn't shifters come from somewhere near there and start the kitsune myth? And here we have the Battle of Skye in Scotland, nearby where stories of wolf-shifting warriors come from. That can't be a coincidence, can it?"

Archer took the book from me and started reading down the list. "You might be onto something. There's one in India as well and a few others in the Middle East." His cock hardened a bit, making me gasp and then laugh.

"This turns you on?"

He put the book down and reached up slightly, his fingers running along his new mark. "*You* turn me on. Being bonded to an intelligent and wickedly sexy omega is more than I ever dreamed of."

I leaned down, bracing myself on my hands to make sure I didn't put any weight on his injuries. "I have so much love for you all, and I already feel like there isn't enough time in the day to give each of you the attention you deserve. Are you sure you're open to bringing in someone new? I don't want to ruin this."

His fingers pushed back the hair that fell in my face, and he studied my features closely. I lost myself in his dark brown eyes, framed by the kind of eyelashes girls paid good money to fake. A straight nose above his soft lips and a day's worth of black stubble making its way across his defined jaw. He was so beautiful it almost hurt to look at him.

"If having to divide my time with you a little more guarantees I still at least *have* time with you, Cam can bond to as many new alphas as it takes to keep you in my life. Even if we were only alone one day a week, a month, a year... Even if you were so tired by the time my turn came around that all you wanted to do was sleep, it would be worth it. You are that precious to me."

Archer wiped away the tear that fell down my cheek. "I love you," I said, my voice shaky.

"*Nado saranghae,*" he replied, his eyes shining.

My heart skipped a beat. "Next time we role-play, can you just speak in Korean the whole time? Because that is really hot."

He laughed, grabbing my hips and adjusting his knot beneath me. "I think I can manage that."

47
MARLOWE

I woke up on Tuesday morning feeling like a kid on Christmas. It had been a little over two days since both Nolan and Archer had bonded with me, so I had taken them outside to explain how I shifted.

They had followed my instructions, but nothing happened.

We had worked all day, and I had tried everything I could think of, but even my own wolf hadn't felt like making an appearance.

By Wednesday, life got in the way, and learning how to shift went to the back burner as my pack went back to work. We had neglected our careers ever since I showed up and couldn't ignore our professional responsibilities any longer.

For my own job, since I wasn't moving back to San Francisco, it was clear that the best thing to do for them and me was to quit, and I regretfully put in my two weeks. They were allowing me to work that time remotely, thankfully, but I could tell my boss had already written me off and wasn't expecting much.

My job had always given me a great sense of fulfillment, and it hurt to not have that anymore. But for now, I needed to concentrate on literally keeping myself unkidnapped, and unfortunately, that took a lot of effort.

And since the guys had unilaterally decided I couldn't stay home alone while they were gone, we had developed a rotating schedule of "Take Your Omega to Work Day," and Cam declared he got to go first. Especially since Wolfcrest Construction was technically also my company.

I knew he was still upset we hadn't bonded yet, and on top of that, he wanted to play it cool in front of his team. But beneath the grumpy exterior, I could tell he was excited to introduce me to everyone.

He waited by the front door impatiently, two travel mugs full of coffee in his hands as he yelled at me to hurry up.

I wore the only nice outfit I had brought with me – an ivory, loose knit turtleneck, a blue and green tartan A-line mini skirt, espresso-colored tights and brown knee-high boots. My hair was pulled back in a high ponytail, and I had even put on a little make-up.

"Coming!" I replied, running down the stairs.

Cam bit his lip and held his breath for a moment, and then exhaled in defeat. "Dammit, you look cute. Come on, let's go."

I grabbed my coffee and reached up on my tiptoes to give him a kiss on the cheek. He had trimmed his beard, and I took a deep whiff of his cardamom and cedar scent as I lowered myself back down. He was dressed similarly to the way he was every day, in jeans, a flannel over a henley shirt, and a Carhartt jacket with work boots.

"Mm, you look pretty good yourself, hot stuff."

A hint of a smile grew on his face, and he took a step closer to me, our chests touching. "This is either going to be the best day I've had at work or the hardest."

My hand grazed along the erection growing in his pants. "My bet's on the hardest."

He groaned and closed his eyes. "The CFO brings donuts every Wednesday," he whispered.

I backed up and slapped him lightly on the arm. "Why didn't you say anything sooner? All the good flavors are going to be gone!"

Cam chuckled and followed after me as I went out the door, getting into his truck.

I was expecting to pull into one of the cookie-cutter office buildings in the business district on the outskirts of town, but considering how nice Cam's house was, I should have known better.

The headquarters were a striking fusion of prairie-style architecture and modern corporate design. Low, horizontal lines stretched into the landscape and blended into the environment, with wide overhanging eaves. Large windows, framed by sleek stone columns, allowed plenty of light to flood the lobby, already bustling with activity.

Cam helped me out of the truck, parked up front in one of two owner's spaces, of course, and beamed at my reaction. "Nice, isn't it? We built this six years ago. It was the last major project our dads worked on with me before they started to step back."

I wondered what working with my dad might have been like, and my chest ached with loss. It felt silly, but I was jealous that Cam knew him better than I did. Had gotten to look up to him as a kind of second father. "It's still so strange to hear you talk about him," I replied quietly. "Sometimes it feels like you're his kid more than I am."

Cam sighed, wrapping an arm around my waist and tugging me into his side. "Nah, if I was James's kid, that would mean I'm fucking my sister."

My grief evaporated into the cold air and I burst out laughing. "How is it that that's the first place your mind went?"

He leaned down and whispered in my ear. "Because I'm always thinking about fucking you, babe."

My breath snagged, and he pulled me inside, trying and failing to hide the grin on his face. "Alright, let me show you around."

It was, unfortunately, like the grocery store with Nolan all over again.

Nearly everyone stopped and greeted Cam, and he attempted to nonchalantly introduce me as his omega and the late business owner's daughter. I was happy I recognized a few people from the temple and even remembered their names.

After grabbing two of the remaining glazed donuts, we headed into Cam's office. A stone accent wall on the far end of the room blended with the earthy tones of the space, and the large window behind his smooth, mahogany desk overlooked a copse of trees.

He sat down and turned on his computer, and I couldn't stop the giggle bubbling through. He seemed so competent and corporate. A regular Don Draper in Danner boots.

He arched an eyebrow and looked at me. "What's so funny?"

"This," I said, pointing at him. "I don't know, I never pictured you behind a desk in a nice office when you said you worked in construction."

He scratched his head. "How did you picture me?"

I shrugged, reading the various awards the company had received that were sitting on his bookshelf. "You know, with a hard hat on and stuff."

That idea conjured up some very sexy images of my rough and tumble alpha.

Cam chuckled, gesturing to the snowy landscape behind him. "Babe, it's winter. Not exactly peak construction time here."

I crossed my arms and sighed. "Yeah, I get that. It's still weird though."

My laptop was heavy in my bag, and I really didn't feel like getting started on my own work yet. I sauntered behind the desk and scooted myself onto his lap. "So, what's on the agenda for today?"

His hand moved up my sweater and under my bra, and he massaged my breast while he looked through some kind of blueprints. "Hm, I have a meeting at 10 with some of the directors," he replied calmly, eyes still glued to his screen. He pinched my nipple and kept working.

I glanced at the clock – it was only 8:45. "I'm feeling far too wound up to concentrate, how about you?"

Cam pinched my nipple again. "As I said earlier, all I think about is fucking you, so I've had to become a master multitasker. Otherwise, I'd never get anything done."

I rubbed my ass along his growing erection. "Well, my pussy definitely needs to get done. Any chance you can prioritize that?"

His other hand left the mouse and slid underneath my skirt. With the tights and underwear, there wasn't much room, but the extra friction set my nerves on fire. "Always," he whispered in my ear.

His fingers were efficient, rubbing my clit and pushing inside me. I ground against him, feeling my climax build quickly. I bit my lip as I came, holding in my moans as best I could. Once my muscles relaxed, he swiped his keyboard out of the way and lifted me off his lap, bending me over the desk.

I grinned to myself and wiggled in anticipation as Cam pulled my skirt up and my underwear and tights down, removing himself from his jeans and filling me completely in one fell swoop.

I think I might have a thing for fucking in offices.

"Babe," Cam said, one hand braced on the desk and the other gripping my hip. "You feel so good, like a fucking dream."

His thrusting was hard and slow, building in tempo as we raced towards our orgasms.

But it was too soon and I needed more. My whine said it for me, and he pulled out, sitting in his chair and turning me around so I could climb on top of him and control the pace.

"That's it," he said. "I'm here for you. Take what you need."

My hips rolled and circled on his cock, his knot stimulating my clit and building my release once more. When I got too close, I'd change my rhythm, prolonging the pleasure.

I took my sweater off, and Cam licked the skin in front of him, his large, calloused hands firmly grasping my ass to keep me from falling.

Next was my bra, and when his lips soon found their way to my nipple, I couldn't slow down my climax any longer.

"Bond with me, Cam," I whimpered. "I can't wait any more."

"Me neither."

I came and slammed down over his knot, feeling him throb and come inside me. His teeth latched onto my breast, and a pained gasp escaped my lips.

My pack.

My whole pack, connected through me, like I was the thread that held us all together. All their thoughts, their feelings, their emotions… it was beautiful.

The orgasms didn't stop, his cock emptying inside me entirely. I fell forward into his chest, panting heavily into his ear. "I love you."

He wrapped his arms and pulled tighter. "I love you, too."

Once his knot deflated and we cleaned up, he grabbed a pen and a pad of paper off his desk. "I have that meeting right now, so go ahead and get settled. It might last 'til lunch. I'll have my secretary pop by in thirty minutes or so to see how you're doing. Let her know if you need anything."

Hearing about a secretary triggered some ugly emotions, especially after what we'd just been doing. "What does your secretary look like?" I asked. "I need to be prepared so I don't accidentally claw the girl's eyes out."

Like poor Megan. I was *not* looking forward to going to City Hall again with Nolan.

Cam snorted. "Her name's Patricia and she's almost sixty. I think you'll be fine. See you in a bit, babe."

After a quick peck on the lips he left, closing the door behind him, leaving behind his intoxicating cardamom and cedar scent.

I sat in his chair and set up my laptop so I could finally start wrapping up my own work. I still felt guilty with how I was leaving things, especially so close to the holidays. They wouldn't be able to hire anyone to replace me for at least another month or so.

Around 240 emails were waiting in my inbox, and I methodically went to task, wondering if maybe giving them a large donation would clear my conscience.

The knock at the door came sooner than I thought, and before

I could answer someone came barreling in. "About time you actually showed your face..." An alpha I didn't know saw me and stopped in his tracks. "Who the hell are you?"

I scoffed. "I could ask you the same question."

The male in front of me looked a little younger than Cam and my pack, closer to my age. But typical of his designation, he was tall, with broad shoulders and a large chest that his thermal crew showed every line of in excruciating detail. His olive-toned skin was tanned, a hint of a beard shadowed along his square jaw. His black hair was cut short, but curled slightly along his forehead, ears, and the back of his neck.

His dark brown eyes were piercing and calculating as he tried to figure me out. The scent of eucalyptus and lemon finally hit me, reminding me of California. It comforted me for a moment and I adjusted in my chair.

My scent must have finally reached him, because suddenly his eyes darkened and his nostrils flared.

Then he threw his head back and laughed.

Okay, this guy was definitely rubbing me the wrong way, despite the way he smelled. "Care to let me know what's so funny?" I asked.

The male smiled and shook his head condescendingly. "You must be that 'personal business' he mentioned. What, did he give you a made-up job with an inflated salary so you guys could fuck here?" He glanced up and down the parts of me he could see. "Not that I blame him."

"Alright," I sighed, standing up and pointing to the door. "Leave."

"Calm down, sweetheart. I need to drop off some cost estimates he asked for. Why don't you make yourself useful and ask Patricia to show you how the copy machine works? I need three of these."

He unceremoniously dropped the thick packet on my laptop and I growled in response. "Sorry, I didn't catch your name."

He pretended to shiver. "Ooh, scary! I'm Julian Ramos. And you are?"

A slow grin spread across my face. "Marlowe."

"Well, Marlowe, I'd like this done before..."

"But you can call me Ms. Linden," I said, interrupting him.

His face paled. "Wait, as in..."

I picked up my coffee and took a long sip, draining what was left. "The late founder and owner, James Linden. You know, my *father*."

We stood in silence, staring each other down, until he finally lowered his eyes. "Fuck."

My wolf seemed a little baffled at the alpha's submission, but the female sick of misogynistic shit was practically howling. "Yeah, 'fuck' indeed. So, Julian, how about instead of asking *me* to make you copies, *you* go downstairs and get *me* another coffee. Lots of cream and sugar, please." I set the empty travel mug on the desk and gestured to it while I went back to work. "That will be all," I said in a dismissive tone, channeling my best Miranda Priestly.

He grabbed the mug and stomped out, slamming the door behind him. Okay, maybe not the best idea to start making enemies, but that dude was a dick and deserved to get knocked down a peg or two, even if my dad was the only reason I had any sort of power here.

At least I'd wield it responsibly.

48
CAMDEN

I was jogging back to my office from the conference room to grab my forgotten phone when I ran into Julian in the hall.

"Hey, Ramos, what's up?" I asked, reaching out my hand but stopping when I saw he was carrying Marlowe's travel mug.

Julian noticed where I was staring and rolled his eyes. "Nice head's up there, telling me James's freaking daughter was here today and that you guys are together. I just made a total ass out of myself."

I took the mug from his hands and breathed in deeply. "Wait, made an ass out of yourself like, you were flustered, said something weird, and she thinks you're a dweeb, or…"

"Or as in she dominated me and hates my guts."

I bit back my disappointment, although a part of me wished I could have seen my little omega in action. Watching her break an alpha would be very hot.

But this potentially ruined my plans. Julian was smart, capable, and had been looking for a pack ever since he moved here a few years ago. He was like me in a lot of ways, and Marlowe and I were great together.

Then I remembered her terrible first impression of me.

I couldn't hold in the growl that reverberated through my chest. "Did you touch her?" I asked. Was it a little hypocritical to have gotten mad at him if he had, even though I hadn't been able to fight the urge myself two weeks ago? Sure, but she had been unbonded then. Now, Marlowe belonged to a pack, which was supposed to mark her as completely off-limits to any kind of courtship.

245

Well, the alpha shifter version of courtship, which, at least for me, was very hands on.

"Of course not. I just assumed she was your new personal assistant you were fucking or something," he responded, shaking his head in disappointment. "How much authority does she have here? Can she fire me?"

I sighed. "Come on, dipshit, let's see if we can't do some damage control."

We walked back into my office, and Marlowe's happy expression dropped when she saw Julian. "Oh, it's you," she said flatly, getting back to her work.

"Hey, babe." I greeted her slowly, and she gave me a suspicious look. "Here's your coffee. I ran into Julian, and he told me he was kind of..."

"An ass?" She sipped her coffee and winced. "Not enough sugar," she muttered.

"Right, that's the exact word he used, ass."

"Well, good. At least I don't have to add 'liar' to the long list of words I'd like to call him."

Julian rolled his eyes. "I didn't know who you were. I'm sorry."

She stood up, and I could practically see the smoke coming off her skin. "It doesn't matter if I'm an entry level temp or the new owner or anything in between. It's completely unacceptable to treat females that way."

His head turned towards me, confusion spreading across his face. "Wolcott, what is she talking about?"

"Hey!" She snapped her fingers. "Don't talk to him. You're talking to me."

I knew why Julian was agitated. Most females liked being bossed around by alphas, it was almost like a sign of affection.

Not for humans though, and definitely not Marlowe. While there had been a bit of an adjustment period for me in the beginning, I'd really come to love the way she didn't take any shit. She was almost the most wolfish amongst us in that way – aloof and distrusting at first of strangers, but when she did submit for attention and affection, it felt earned. Deserved.

Special.

The corner of Julian's lip curled in a slight snarl. Alphas, on the other hand, did *not* take kindly to being bossed around, and I was sure with Marlowe being the first omega he'd ever met, he thought he was impressing her by being a dick.

This was going down the shitter, fast.

"Look, I have an idea." I moved behind Marlowe, putting my hands on her shoulders. She tensed, but I pulled her back into me and began to purr, the sound calming and relaxing her. I walked her out from behind the desk, a few feet in front of Julian. "Why don't you properly introduce yourselves, from the beginning?"

Marlowe sighed and held out her hand, but Julian went straight in and nuzzled his face in the crook of her neck, trapping her in between us.

Her heartbeat went crazy, and she tried to wriggle away but I held her tightly, continuing my purr. "It's okay," I whispered. "Scent says a lot about a shifter."

She released a breathy whine, finally allowing herself to smell him back.

After a few deep pulls of Marlowe's perfume, Julian took a step away, his pupils fully blown. He looked at me, then back at her, and fell to his knees, grabbing her waist and resting his forehead against her stomach, breathing her in again.

Marlowe stilled, and I couldn't gauge her response. There were too many emotions swimming in the air. Fear, confusion, desire...

I knew exactly what was happening to Julian, though. It was the same thing that had happened to me when I first met Marlowe. Once I scented her, it was like my brain suddenly rewired, and all I could think about was how to protect her, how to care for her, how to make her mine.

That kind of visceral reaction could only happen when someone was a good scent match for you or your pack.

There was a knock at the door and it swung open. Mark, our Director of Business Development, popped his head in. "Hey Cam, are you coming back, or...?" His eyes widened in shock at the sight of Julian on his knees, drowning in the omega female I was currently holding. "Uh, cool. We can just... wait for you then..." He started to close the door and then opened it again a crack. "Should I get HR?"

I said, "No" but Marlowe squeaked, "Yes," the intrusion tearing her out of the moment.

Mark looked at me for confirmation, but I just shook my head, and he left.

Marlowe pushed Julian away and shrugged out of my grip, then turned around and pointed her finger at me. "How *dare* you?" she hissed. "I'm not some kind of drug you can just pass along to all your friends to help them get high. That..." She stopped, rubbing away a few tears that fell from her eyes, smudging her make-up. "…was really messed up."

I reached out and rubbed her arms, lowering my face to hers. "I'm sorry. I know that was intense, but you felt something, right? Like he could belong to you?" I watched her expression carefully, and my heart sank when it turned angrier.

"Wait… *this* is who you want to join our pack?" She pointed at Julian and scoffed. "Uh, no. No way."

I ran a hand down my face in frustration. How had this spiraled out of control so quickly? I had planned on inviting him out to lunch with us, setting him up to deliver some great jokes to make her laugh, and then broach the subject later, maybe tonight with my knot and all that post-sex bliss in her.

At this rate, I'd be lucky if she ever let me knot her again.

Julian, still coming off his omega hit, also looked like he would start crying. But for a very different reason.

"You want me to be in your pack?" he asked softly.

I knew what being in a pack meant to a lone alpha. Julian was a good kid who had narrowly escaped a bad situation back home. He was starting over up here, trying to find his place in a town full of shifters with no connections.

And while I knew this wouldn't impress Marlowe, I had hoped it would be a selling point to the guys – the alpha could fight. He had invited me once to an amateur boxing match at his gym, and Julian had easily cleaned the floor with everyone they threw at him. It was hard to admit, but if push came to shove, he could probably kick my ass, too.

I knew Marlowe was a little freaked out, but Julian was exactly what we needed, and over time, she'd get over their first meeting. Just like she had mine.

I turned to Julian and said, "Yes" but Marlowe growled, "No."

He swallowed, still on his knees when he faced Marlowe again, hands clasped together. "Please, I barely know you, but I feel like I would die for you. I would kill for you."

Marlowe placed her hand on her chest, closing her eyes for a second, and then went back behind the desk to start gathering her things. "One day," she muttered, "Can I just have *one* goddamn normal day?"

She left the room in a huff, and I heard her outside. "Hi, are you Patricia? So nice to meet you, I'm Marlowe Linden… Right, James's daughter. Did he have an office here?… Great, do you have a key?… Even better, can you take me there?"

Julian hadn't gotten up yet, he simply stared into space. "What just happened?" he asked. "It feels like I died, met the Moon Goddess herself, and then she kicked me in the balls."

I sighed. "We got our work cut out for us, Ramos."

My phone started beeping. I grunted, figuring it was the directors wondering if we should reschedule the meeting, but it was a notification from the new security system I'd installed.

ALARM TRIGGERED: SLIDING DOOR BREACH

Adrenaline coursed through my veins. Was that shifter back? Had he brought his pack? I needed to get to Marlowe.

I opened the video as I ran out of my office to find her.

But it wasn't a wolf breaking in.

It was three wolves breaking out. Slamming into the back door, shattering the glass, and heading northwest through the woods.

Straight here.

49
THE GRAY WOLF

Distress.

My pack mate, my omega, was in distress. The human couldn't hold me back, I needed to protect her.

And now, I had two new pack mates, the other humans she had bonded with, to help me.

It took them a moment to get their bearings – they'd been stuck inside their humans for so long, like me – but once they stretched and recognized me and each other, it was time to go.

Protect the pack.

50
MARLOWE

Patricia chatted me up the whole way to my dad's office. She was tall and round in the middle, with short, curly hair, wearing dark pants and what appeared to be a hand-knit sweater.

She exuded a kind, matronly warmth that made me ache for my own mom. Ache for female companionship, period. Ever since I'd arrived in Wisconsin, I'd been drowning in testosterone, and I just wanted to talk to someone who wasn't constantly on the verge of punching a wall.

"James didn't really come into the office much, so he never had a lot in here. The computer might not be hooked up to the new system, but even if it is, I doubt it's been updated. Want me to make an appointment with IT?"

My curiosity piqued. It was a long shot, but if IT could get me onto my dad's account, there might be something, anything, about my mom or my past that would help us figure out who that full shifter was.

"Yes, that would be great. Thank you so much," I replied. She let me in, and tsked at the layer of dust that had settled over the desk and shelves.

"The cleaning crew should still have been coming through here. Let me make sure they put this room back on their rotation. Well, holler if you think of anything else I can do for you."

She closed the door behind her and I walked slowly around the space. The office was similar to Cam's, but lacked the personal touches and warmth. It didn't even smell like anyone, feeling more like a showroom. A blank canvas.

251

I grabbed a couple of tissues and wiped down the desk, making room for my laptop. My hand bumped into the mouse by accident and the screen came to life. Yikes, I didn't even want to think how long this computer had been left on for.

I reached over to turn it off but the screensaver made my heart stop.

It was a picture of us – me, Ezra, my mom, and my dad, from some summer day on Lake Michigan. Ezra and I couldn't have been older than two or three. My parents looked so young, so beautiful, and so in love.

And now, all of them were gone.

Ugly sobs erupted from my chest, and I collapsed my head into my arms on the desk. I had started coming to terms with the fact that my dad wasn't who or what I'd thought he'd been. He wasn't an asshole loser who had abandoned his family. He had left us out of fear or for our protection, trying his best to provide for us behind a curtain of anonymity. Together with my mom, who had specifically recommended my brand of "birth control pills" to dull my scent and heats, he had wanted to keep me hidden in plain sight because he knew someone was looking for us.

But this one small thing, a screen no one would see but him, where he could remember who this was all for, broke me.

It wasn't long before Cam burst through the door. I figured he would have sensed my sadness, but he'd also caused my initial anguish, and I really didn't feel like listening to him explain how I should forgive Julian for acting like an asshole.

"What do you want?" I snapped.

"Marlowe, I'm sorry. I wanted to give you space but this is an emergency." He rushed towards me and grabbed my hand. "We need to go. NOW."

My mind raced with horrible possibilities. I hadn't felt anything through my bonds with the rest of the pack, but I'd been so flooded and busy with my own strong emotions, I hadn't really been paying attention. "Oh my god, are they hurt?"

"No."

We rushed out the door and back outside the building, weaving in and out of the people walking down the halls.

Once we got to the parking lot I slowed down, figuring we'd head towards his truck, but he ran right past it, pulling me along and heading straight to the woods on the southeast corner.

"Cam!" I yelled, already spent. I really hated running. "Where are we going? What's going on?"

He turned around briefly and threw me over his shoulder, ignoring my yelp. "We need to stop the pack. They shifted and they're headed right this way."

Shifted? It was hard to speak from my position and the way I jostled around from Cam trying to run through the snow. "But that's a good thing. Why are you upset?"

He finally stopped once we reached a little further into the trees. "Think about it – you first shifted when you were upset. Elias first shifted when he was upset."

Damn, why hadn't I thought of this yesterday? Cam was so much smarter than we all gave him credit for. "But what are they upset about?"

He sighed, tilting his head and giving me a knowing look. "Oh."

He closed his eyes, nodding as the realization hit me. Then he leaned down and took a deep whiff of my sweater and cursed under his breath. "Yeah, and when they show up and smell a non-pack alpha on you, they're going to hunt Julian down and tear him apart."

I winced. Even if I wasn't Julian's biggest fan at the moment, he certainly didn't deserve that. And as much as Elias and Nolan didn't want a new pack mate, I didn't think they'd feel great if they killed Julian, either.

"You have to shift," Cam said. "Stop them, let them know you're okay."

I looked in the direction they'd be coming from, but so far it was quiet. "It's not that easy. I've only shifted twice – once was completely by surprise, and the other was when my wolf wanted to. I've never summoned her on my own."

Cam's eyes were pleading, his hands gripping my shoulders. "Babe, please try."

I closed my eyes, trying to coax my wolf out. *Hey girl, your boys are coming. Don't you want to say hi?*

Her ears perked up, and her tail began to wag.

"Ugh, fine, but you need to hold my clothes and cover me." There was no way I was destroying this outfit. I took everything off as quickly as I could, mentally leading my wolf into the forefront of my mind so I could shift as soon as I was naked. Once I handed Cam my tights, underwear, and bra, I opened the gate and let her through.

51
MIKE

Grace stood behind Jen in the shower, holding up one of her legs to give me better access to Jen's cunt.

The water was hot, washing away the rivulet of blood from the bite on Jen's neck.

Her breathy moans echoed in the bathroom, driving me closer to my climax. I was about to come, her tight cunt clenched around me, until Grace reached around to run her hand down my chest.

The past couple of days had soured me on her completely. She had been desperate for my attention and praise, yet I could only look at her with contempt. Any sympathy I had attempted to drum up turned to disgust at the thought of her thinking she could replace Marlowe in my bed, my life.

My heart.

The feeling of her touch softened my erection, and I hissed. "Dammit, Grace, what did I tell you?"

Her cheeks heated and she looked down in shame. "Sorry."

I patted Jen on the face and gestured for her to leave with my thumb. She gave Grace a pitying look before retreating to the bedroom, and once the bathroom door closed behind her, I grabbed Grace around the throat. "You do *not* touch me without permission. You are here to please Jen and me on the off chance I want your ass. Otherwise, you keep your hands and thoughts to yourself. Even the sound of your voice grates on me."

She nodded her understanding, and replied in a strained voice. "Just let me go home, then. Why am I even still here if you hate me so much?"

My nails dug into her skin and then I released her, licking the blood from my fingertips. "I still have use for you."

She scrambled out of the shower and through the door, and I looked at my flaccid dick, cursing to myself. Even Jen's best efforts couldn't erase the pent-up frustration building inside me.

Every second I was here felt wasted. Marlowe could be fully bonded to those dirty mutts by now. If she'd gone through a proper heat, they could have even impregnated her, Moon forbid.

I swallowed back the bile that had formed when I followed the path of my own morbid, cruel imagination and finished washing up, now choosing instead to replay one of my favorite memories with Marlowe. Two years ago, we had taken a trip to Monterey for the weekend and had never left the hotel room. The pills she'd been on had suppressed her heats for the most part, but not entirely.

I remembered how insatiable she'd been, not understanding what had caused her usually ravenous libido to sky rocket even higher.

I touched myself, stroking my dick back to life as I remembered the taste of her sweet, sweet cunt.

Once I was ready to go, I joined my servaglio in the bedroom. Jen laid on her back, her legs spread wide and her hands grabbing her tits while Grace devoured her, ass wiggling high in the air and begging me to take it.

I rolled my eyes, seeing right through her ruse. I probably should have taken advantage of her while I could, but Jen's cunt was far more inviting at the moment, and absent the cum I had promised her in the shower.

Walking behind Grace, I placed my hands gently on her cheeks, rubbing them and pulling them apart. Her arousal and anticipation grew. Then I took her by the waist and pulled her to the floor, taking her spot and piercing Jen with my tongue.

Jen was fully aware of my waning feelings for Grace, and while she was also disappointed in my third, I knew she felt bad for the bitch. She beckoned Grace to sit on her face, which she did with some hesitation, waiting to be chastised by me again.

My phone beeped and I stopped to check it while they carried on. If Jen wanted to eat her out, that was her own business.

The warriors have been gathered. Bring your servaglio.

It was time.
In just a day or two, my Lunessa would be back in my arms.

255

I watched as Grace held onto the headboard, riding Jen's face. Jen's nimble fingers pleasured her ass, and my dick throbbed with need. Perhaps one more time, while I could.

I grabbed the bottle of lube from the nightstand, squirting a generous amount on my fingers to prep her. After a few minutes of stretching, I positioned myself behind Grace, adding more lube to my dick and sliding it between her folds. Then I pulled back, pushing apart her cheeks, and entered through the tight ring of muscle.

A sigh escaped my lips when it finally released and let me through, and I grabbed the headboard around Grace as I fucked her ass one last time. Jen's hands now played with mine, and I willed the moment to memory. It was bittersweet to be giving up all the pleasures I enjoyed, but Marlowe was worth it.

52
THE TAWNY WOLF

I stretched my limbs and sniffed the air. My pack was coming.

The human next to me whistled. He juggled the adornments from my human into one arm and reached out with the other. "Come here, you gorgeous girl."

I trotted forward and sniffed his hand. This man would be my pack soon, too. His wolf was waking up. My senses on these things were getting better.

It was only a short matter of time before we'd all finally be together.

He laughed as I pushed my head under his open palm, trying to get him to pet me. Human fingers felt so nice, I loved the way they ran through my fur and scratched my skin.

My pack's scents blew in with the wind and I perked my ears.

"They almost here?" the human asked.

Human noses and ears were so weak. I chuffed my response.

"Alright, no need to get all sassy with me, I was just checking. Do you remember what you have to do?"

That's right, my human side needed me to do something. Her memories came to me in flashes. It was hard to catch. I needed to stop my pack... Stop them from what?

"Let them know you're okay," the human reminded me. "They're here because they think you're in trouble."

I remembered now. My human was upset about something. Ugh, when wasn't she? Humans made everything so complicated.

Yipping in excitement, I bound towards them.

Pack! I'm here! No danger!

They came running up to me, sniffing and nuzzling. My gray alpha came first, followed by my two new pack mates, a silver alpha and a red alpha. I had never seen them before, but I recognized their scents immediately. My tail would not stop wagging. I was so happy to meet them.

No danger? my red alpha confirmed.

I lowered myself on my front paws and yipped again. *No! Let's play!*

The other human had caught up by now. "You fuckers, this isn't fair. Now I gotta go back to work and get my door fixed while you all get to do this. You better pay my Venmo request this time. And don't tear my kitchen up again. Which one of you mutts is Archer?"

We looked at each other. What was he talking about?

The silver alpha tilted his head. *Archer? Maybe me?*

The human pointed at him. "I'm expecting you to keep everyone in line. And let me know when you shift back if your ribs are better."

My silver alpha huffed. *Enough human talk.*

We turned around and followed him through the woods, leaving the human behind. I turned around and gave him one last look as I whined.

"Don't worry, girl. I'll join you soon. Go on, have fun. See you at home."

53
MIKE

Jen and Grace had braided their hair and woven it into crowns on top of their heads. They stood on either side of me in front of the doors to the Council room, nervously shifting on their bare feet.

"You will do whatever they say without question," I warned them. "It is an honor to serve a vampyr elder in any capacity. Do not look at me for confirmation, do not hesitate, and do not talk back. Are we clear?"

They both nodded, their apprehension coming off them in waves. I had told them they needed to come as a formality so their fear wouldn't cause them to do something stupid and ruin this for me.

My fingers ran down Jen's back, enjoying the way her skin pebbled from the sensation. I was going to miss her.

"Enter"

They slipped off their robes and handed them to the guards, revealing their nude bodies as we stepped inside. Along the perimeter of the wall stood thirty massive vampyrs, dressed head to toe in black tactical gear, silver weapons glinting in the candlelight. I could hardly contain my excitement.

This was real. This was happening. My Lunessa would be back in my arms by the weekend, and my mouth salivated at the thought of her sweet taste on my tongue once more. Now that she knew what I was, I wouldn't have to hide my nips and sips. I could drink from her fully.

I adjusted the growing erection in my pants.

The High Elder stood, his arms spread wide. "As originally

promised, and further negotiated with Elder Sable, we offer you a unit of thirty vampyr warriors so you may retrieve your stolen Lunessa. In return, you will cede her bed to us for one night and give to us your remaining servaglio."

Jen and Grace whipped their heads to me in a confused panic, but I didn't move my eyes from the Council. I bowed low, averting my gaze. "I honor the agreement. I present to you my servaglio."

"Mike, what's going on?" whispered Jen.

I rose and took her face in my hands, kissing her one last time. "My sweet second, you deserve more than I can give you. Elder Sable has offered you a place with him. He will provide for you in every way a vampyr can."

She opened her mouth to argue but I hardened my features, silently warning her not to speak. Taking a deep breath, she nodded, holding back the tears forming in the corners of her eyes.

Two guards walked in, carrying a narrow table with built-in straps for the wrists and ankles.

Grace's voice was quiet, full of dread and trepidation. "Mike? What's going to happen to me? Are you giving me away too?"

I shrugged coldly. "In a sense." I took her shoulders and turned her towards me. "*Lie down.*"

Her expression blanked and she climbed on top of the table obediently. The guards strapped her down and placed six chairs around her.

I took one of the seats by her thighs, and the Council filled in the rest. Jen stood behind Elder Sable, her body trembling as he took a firm hold of her ass.

"What a feast!" one of the elders said, licking his lips and sitting down. We joined hands, and the High Elder cleared his throat.

"We thank thee, Goddess of the Moon and of the Creatures of the Night. Grant us life in this blood, and feed our eternal thirst. While you may fade from sight, we will wait."

"For you always return," the rest of us answered in unison.

The power of my compulsion began to fade, and Grace whimpered as she realized what was happening, pulling weakly at the restraints.

The High Elder ran a bony finger down her cheek. "Shhh, my child. Your body serves another purpose tonight. Do not fear, it won't be unpleasant." And then he sank his teeth into her neck. I clocked the moment the initial shock and pain gave way to her pleasure. Her body relaxed and her eyes glazed over, her hips slowly bucking in search of something that could help relieve the building heat in her core.

The rest of the elders each took their bites, in order of rank, and I waited patiently for my turn at the end. The first pulls would be small, and then we'd continue to slowly sip as her life faded, prolonging the feed as long as possible before her heart stopped.

Then we needed to drink as much as possible before the blood turned. Dead blood wasn't fatal to vampyrs, but it was unpleasant.

After she passed, we'd probably have another twenty minutes or so before she became completely useless.

My bleeding heart took pity on my third as my turn finally arrived. Her crime had been wanting to be my Lunessa, to please me better than Marlowe could. If only she had been smart enough to realize that was impossible.

I decided to offer her some reprieve in the end and fucked her with my fingers while I drank. She came quickly, and thanks to the blood loss combined with the vampyr venom now running through her veins, she began to blissfully drift off.

Jen sniffed, holding herself in her arms while she watched Grace fade. I tried to catch her eye and give her an apologetic look, but she turned away from me in disgust.

It was a shame that her affection for me was another casualty in this whole mess, but I supposed it couldn't be helped.

Elder Sable chuckled, pulling her down onto his lap. "Don't worry, chérie. I have a feeling we're going to have a great time together."

The High Elder clapped his hands. "Ah, yes, speaking of great times – guards, let them in!"

The doors opened and eleven women sauntered inside, one more for Elder Sable and then two each for the remainder of us. Two curvy, dark-haired women approached me – one from behind, kissing my neck and rubbing her hands down my chest, while the other sat down on my lap, grinding her naked cunt against my erection.

Draining a human, even shared between the six of us, had filled us with so much blood we'd be hard for hours, if not days. I grabbed them both by the hair, pulling them down towards my mouth. "You're going to take turns choking on my cock until I tell you to stop. Do you understand?"

They giggled their response and went to work, my dick so engorged it was almost painful. I came only a few seconds after the first woman wrapped her lips around my head, and the second took her place once I finished coming.

It was too bad I couldn't have saved this moment for when my Lunessa was back with me. I wouldn't have even needed a second woman. I could probably just fuck Marlowe for two days straight, not pulling out once, and she'd take it all.

I reached over and took another sip of Grace, patting her on the leg. Her sacrifice had secured my future happiness.

Thank you, I mouthed silently.

Her dimming eyes found mine, and she smiled as they went out for good.

54
NOLAN

I woke up in Cam's basement, naked and confused. My skin was cold and tingly, and my hands and feet ached. I'd had the strangest dream, running through the woods...

"My wounds..."

I sat up, now seeing that I wasn't the only one down here. Elias and Marlowe were spooning, asleep in a makeshift nest of couch cushions, while Archer sat against the wall, pushing his fingers into his chest.

"She was right, I'm completely healed," Archer whispered to himself.

"Of course I was right," Marlowe chimed in, starting to rouse. But Elias had other plans, his hands now hungrily running up and down her body while he licked and nibbled along her neck. With a quick jerk he was inside her, and she began moaning.

I wanted to watch, feeling my own cock begin to stir, but Archer jumped up, stretching and laughing as he twisted his chest without any pain. He walked over and offered me his hand. "Come on, let's go survey the damage."

I glanced back longingly at Elias and Marlowe, watching in admiration and envy as he thrust relentlessly into our omega, and she enjoyed every second of it.

Were all omegas so ravenous, or was that just Marlowe?

I let Archer help me up and followed him upstairs. "Hey, wait. Why do they get out of cleaning up again?"

Archer shrugged. "I'm just being pragmatic. They'll be

occupied for the next thirty minutes or so, and I have no idea when Cam's coming home. It couldn't have been easy for him, watching his whole pack shifted and running off without him. The least we can do is make sure his house isn't a disaster."

"Yeah, I suppose," I grumbled under my breath. "But Elias and Marlowe are definitely on the hook the next time this happens."

Aside from some muddy paw prints and the broken door, the house remained intact. Archer found painter's tarp in the garage while I swept the glass, and we sealed the open door as best we could from the cold.

"I think we're going to need to take a page from old shifter architecture and install a wolf-friendly entrance," Archer said.

"You mean a giant doggy door?" I smirked.

Archer rolled his eyes. "If you want to call it that, sure. Of course, we are still learning how this works, and in the future, we'll have more control about when and where we shift. But it wouldn't hurt to make it easier for our wolf forms to get in and out of the house."

I wouldn't put it past Cam to already be thinking about all of this.

Marlowe's beautiful voice, keening in pleasure, echoed up the stairs, and I realized I really needed some pants. Archer and I had shared our omega before, but it still felt weird to just be hanging out naked and hard in front of my pack.

"I want to find out what made her so upset today," I said quietly. I had felt her so acutely down the bond. She had been upset and scared about something, and then had collapsed into unbelievable sadness. "Do you think she ran into another one of Cam's exes? He has a horrible habit of shitting where he eats."

Archer ran his hand over the edges of the tarp, feeling for gaps of cold air. He added another layer of tape and kept going. "*Had*," he corrected. "And no, Marlowe was fine when we saw her, remember? Camden didn't seem particularly rattled either. I bet it had something to do with her father."

Right, that made more sense. My own phone began to ring and I found it in the kitchen, biting back a groan when I saw who was calling. I had totally forgotten about my meeting with Seth, the City Manager.

"Hey Seth, I know, I'm so sorry…"

"I don't want to hear it, Nolan," he snapped. "This is getting ridiculous. I've been covering for your ass since you disappeared two weeks ago, and now you can't even bother to show up to a meeting *you* scheduled? Are you even coming to the Town Council meeting tomorrow night?"

Shit, tomorrow was already the first Thursday of the month. "Yes, of course. Let's go over the agenda in the morning. I'll be in at nine, I swear it."

Seth scoffed. "You better be."

I cursed under my breath when he abruptly hung up. By now, nearly the whole town knew about Marlowe, thanks to gossip and Cam's eulogy at her dad's funeral. But two weeks for an omega honeymoon was pushing it. Especially since I'd likely need to take more time off again in the near future once she started another heat.

My cock twitched at even the fleeting thought of it.

"Everything okay?"

Archer broke me out of my thoughts and I sighed. "Not really. I've been a crappy mayor recently and it's finally catching up with me. Thank the Moon the next election isn't for two more years."

He nodded knowingly. "Yeah, my dean isn't too happy with me, either. Once things calm down, we'll find a better balance."

Once things calm down... He said it like we just had a few extra things on our plates and not like our lives had turned completely upside down since Marlowe had arrived. Of course, if I had to choose my job or her, she'd win in a heartbeat. But I still hoped we could quickly figure out who the creep that had threatened to take her was so we could neutralize him and maybe start living in a mentally and emotionally sustainable way, instead of just rushing from one emergency to the next with no breathing room in between.

All I wanted was to go to work, help make meaningful, positive changes, and then come home, cook dinner, hang out with my pack, and fall asleep with my omega in my arms.

The American Shifter Dream.

Cam came home a couple of hours later, carrying Marlowe's clothes in a bag. He looked defeated as he set them down and walked around, making sure we'd cleaned up. The sight of the door made him furrow his brow.

Marlowe slinked out of her nest from upstairs, coming down wrapped in a blanket. She sunk into Cam's chest and he held her tight, kissing her on the head.

"So does everyone at the company think I'm a total weirdo

now?"

He chuckled. "No, word spread that you made Julian get you coffee and I overheard one of the beta females call you a 'girl boss,' which I think is a good thing."

She rubbed her face into his chest and laughed. "Well, it depends if she was being sarcastic or not."

"I don't mean to interrupt your quarterly review," Elias said, entering the room from the basement. "But what the hell happened today to make our omega so upset?"

Archer and I closed our laptops from where we were working at the kitchen island, giving the conversation our full attention.

Marlowe looked up at Cam and then over to us. "I went to work in my dad's old office, and the screensaver on his computer was a picture of my family. It just... really affected me."

Elias stepped forward to rub her back and comfort her, but I clocked Cam's confused expression. Marlowe was hiding something from the rest of us. I could feel her hesitation through the bond. She didn't seem scared, though, so I wasn't going to push it. People were entitled to privacy, even from their bonded pack mates who could detect deception.

"I'm going to take a shower," Cam announced. He was clearly not going to expand on Marlowe's story.

Marlowe smiled shyly. "Do you want some company?" she asked in a sweet voice.

"Fuck yeah." Cam smacked her ass and she ran ahead of him, laughing as he chased her.

As soon as the door closed and the water ran, Elias turned towards us. "That was bullshit, right?"

Archer opened his laptop back up, returning to work. "If that's her official story, and Camden's fine with it, we should be, too. It won't do us any favors if we call her a liar."

I wasn't going to call her a liar, but she wasn't telling us the full story. I spoke through clenched teeth. "How can we protect her from threats if we don't know what threatened her?" If she had felt something so deeply today that it triggered my wolf to finally be released, it wasn't something we should just sweep under the rug.

"Do you really think Camden would take her safety lightly? After everything he's done so far? I'm sure whatever happened, he's got it under control, and I don't particularly feel like upsetting Marlowe further," Archer said.

Elias's eyes widened. "I wonder..." He walked over to the bag of Marlowe's clothes and stuck his nose inside, inhaling deeply. A menacing growl reverberated through his chest. "That motherfucker let a new alpha rub all over her today. I bet he was trying to scent match a new pack mate."

I jumped out of my seat and snatched her sweater out of the bag, sniffing it carefully. "For Moon's sake, she was drenched in him. Cam allowed this?"

"Is it a good match?" Archer asked.

A good match? A good *fucking* match?

I threw the sweater towards him. "How the hell should I know? Right now, I'm just pissed! Elias and I said we didn't want a new pack mate!"

Elias chimed in. "We can defend Marlowe just fine on our own from those commune freaks. You're fixed now."

Archer walked over to where the sweater had fallen and picked it up, smelling it along the neck. "It's not bad. We should meet him."

I knew Archer was a logical male, and he was usually very good at talking me off a ledge.

But right now, I wanted to dive off headfirst into an angry abyss. "We are not bringing some random alpha into our pack and giving him access to Marlowe! The only way I can even tolerate sharing her with you guys is because we trust each other, and we've had years to build and test that. This is just a knee-jerk reaction, and if we pull that trigger, we could be stuck with a male we don't like. Someone who might hurt our omega. What's the bigger risk?" I yelled.

Archer closed his eyes and took a deep breath, trying to keep himself calm. "I don't want to let jealousy get in the way of what's best for Marlowe. You didn't see that shifter, Nolan. He ripped my car door off with his *bare hands*. I thought he might kill me. And when he told me he was coming to take Marlowe away from us, and there was nothing we could do to stop it... I almost believed him. But now I know he was wrong, because there *is* something we can do, and I'm willing to at least meet the male before I let *my* knee-jerk reaction leave her vulnerable."

I snarled. "I refuse to let your insecurities endanger our omega."

Archer snarled back. "I am not insecure, I'm realistic. But if we want to talk insecurities, how about we address yours? Tell us the truth about why you two don't want another alpha in the group – you both just don't want more competition for Marlowe's time."

I was about to leap over and grab him when Marlowe barked

from above us.

"That's enough!"

We looked up to where she stood by the railing upstairs, both her and Cam wrapped up in towels. "I agreed to meet with any potential new pack mates, and I meant it. I didn't get the best impression of Julian today, but then again, I didn't like half of you when I first met you all, either. Cam invited him for dinner tomorrow night, and I expect you all to give him a fair chance, myself included. Got it?"

Her orders weren't dominating like an alpha's would be, but I bristled all the same. Elias mumbled his agreement to her terms as I shored myself up and smiled through my fury. "But you liked *me* at first, right, sugar?"

She held her hand horizontally above her head. "First impression ratings – Archer." Her hand lowered slightly. "Nolan." Her hand dipped about twice as far down. "Elias." And then she brought her hand down to her knees. "And all the way down here is…"

Cam snapped at her playfully and grabbed her around the waist, dragging her to her nest while she cackled and screamed in delight.

First Elias had her today, and now Cam. I hated to admit it, but Archer was right. I didn't know how I could handle sharing her with another pack mate. These three assholes were already more than enough, and dividing up Marlowe's attentions even further seemed unbearable.

Elias went to the fridge and grabbed a few beers, handing them to Archer and me. "How much do you want to bet this Julian guy is just like Cam?"

Archer rubbed his hand down his face and sighed. "Exactly. I'm kinda hoping they'll have so much in common with each other they'll just hang out by themselves and leave the rest of us alone."

I raised my eyebrows in surprise, now considering that possibility. If the new alpha was actually dividing Cam's attention rather than Marlowe's, maybe he wouldn't be so bad.

"Okay, I'll give him a chance. But I have my Town Council meeting tomorrow night, so I'll be a little late, and someone else will have to cook."

55

ELIAS

"Mmm, that smells amazing. I thought Nolan was at his meeting?"

Marlowe came into the kitchen just as I was putting the pork chops into the oven. She looked so cute in her baggy jeans and sweater, I wanted to rip them off and lock us up in her nest, pleasuring her with my tongue until she forgot all about the possible new pack mate.

I knew where Cam and Archer were coming from, but I was probably the least "alpha shifter" out of the pack. I'd moved the farthest away. I hardly visited. And while I could live with sharing Marlowe, if given the option to have her just to myself, I would take it in a heartbeat.

But I couldn't do that to her. Now that we were all fully bonded, I felt the depth of her love for everyone. I just needed to learn how to adjust my expectations for her time.

"He is. *I'm* cooking." She gave me a blank look, and I rolled my eyes. "Just because he likes to cook doesn't mean he's the only one who can."

Marlowe continued to look at me.

"I lived alone for years, you know. I can follow a recipe," I huffed.

She blinked slowly, and I scrunched my face while reaching over and pinching her cheeks.

"Brat."

She laughed, wrenching out of my light grip and tying up her hair. "Okay, Chef, do you need any help?"

Something stirred in my gut, and I suppressed the purr

building in my chest.

Just because I had chosen to live the farthest away didn't mean I hadn't been lonely.

Betas could easily slip in and out of human society, but with male alphas' "unique" anatomy, we couldn't really date anyone who wasn't a shifter. And I'd never met another alpha or beta female who really excited me the way Marlowe did.

For years, the prospect of returning to a cold, empty home every night had driven me to work harder and later than everyone else in my firm. Sure, it had made me successful, but all I had really wanted was this – someone to come home to, someone to cook meals with, someone I didn't have to lie to or hide from.

I'd started making plans to move back to Maiingan Hollow and to work more permanently from my Eau Claire office, but I'd still need to go to Chicago every couple of months or so. Taking Marlowe with me on one of my trips would help me quell some of these lingering instincts to hoard her time, even for just a few days.

And I had a feeling she would enjoy it as well. Like me, Marlowe preferred big cities, and would likely relish the chance to get out of this small town for a breather every once in a while.

Clearing my throat, I handed her the vegetable peeler. "Sure, if you can take care of the potatoes that would be great."

She connected her phone to Nolan's speaker and turned on some reggaeton, then washed her hands as she got started, slightly swaying and twirling her hips while she worked.

I ignored the broccoli and came up behind her, putting my hands around her waist and kissing her neck.

She giggled and tried to scoot me back with her ass, which had the opposite effect and only made me want to grab onto her tighter. "Stop," she laughed, "I'm going to cut myself."

"Fine," I groaned, relenting.

All of a sudden, the lights went out.

Cam yelled from the basement where he was watching the Thursday night game. "What the hell, guys? Did one of you trip a circuit?"

My eyes adjusted to the darkness quickly, and a blur of movement outside the window raised my hackles.

"They're here!"

The window closest to us broke and a canister came flying through. It landed on the ground next to us with a hiss and began spewing a noxious smoke, dulling my senses.

More canisters were thrown through other windows around the room. I grabbed Marlowe and tried to run upstairs, but large males dressed head-to-toe in black came pouring in through the front and back doors. Two males were barreling straight for me when Cam came snarling up from the basement, shifting into a wolf and grabbing the first male he could see around the neck, dragging him down to the ground and ripping him apart.

Archer shifted next, leaping down from the upstairs balcony and grabbing onto a man who had reached out for Marlowe.

They were covered in kevlar and armed to the teeth with various weapons, swiping expertly at us with large, silver blades.

These males were far too advanced for commune shifters.

With the smoke filling my nose, I couldn't smell anything, but the light of the moon flashed across a knife, illuminating one of the intruders' faces, and his violet eyes narrowed at me.

Vamps.

Nolan was right, her bloodsucking ex had managed to recruit a small army to get Marlowe back.

I kept Marlowe above me on the stairs, creating a bottleneck so I wouldn't be overrun. A vamp swiped at my stomach with his blade and I backed out of the way, countering with a kick to his gut that sent him straight into Archer's waiting jaws.

My wolf was practically kicking down the door to come out, but I resisted. One of us still needed a human mind and opposable thumbs.

"Marlowe, get to your nest and call for help!"

She stumbled up the stairs, tripping in the dark and the smoke, but I heard her footsteps make it to her room, her door slamming shut and locking tight.

Knowing she was out of harm's way for now, I grabbed the arm of the next vamp who tried to thrust their knife into my heart, twisting it behind his back, then pushed him into the outstretched blade of the next attacker.

More kept pouring in, and I didn't know how long we could hold them.

I screamed down the pack bond – *Nolan, you asshole, get here now!*

56
NOLAN

"Moving on to the approval of the minutes from our last meeting. Do I have a motion?"

"I motion to approve the minutes."

"I second."

"All in favor?" I looked around to the council members with their hands raised in the air. "The minutes are approved."

Normally I loved these meetings. There was something so inspiring about watching people engage with their local government. People who felt passionate enough about a topic that they took the time to research and write down their thoughts, overcoming any fears over public speaking to address us and their neighbors.

Even if those topics were stupid or petty, it was still a privilege to be a part of it.

But tonight, I just wanted them all to shut up so I could leave.

I kept glancing at the clock on the wall, and I swore the seconds were moving at half speed.

When Mrs. Silvano, my retired high school English teacher, stepped up to the podium, I bit back my growl.

"Good evening, Nolan. Good evening, Council. I'll make this quick."

It was never quick.

"I know you all have 'real issues' to discuss, but this town is facing a serious problem that no one has done anything about and I'm fed up."

Oh Moon, not this again…

"The cats here are out of control. Just yesterday, I saw one snatch a goldfinch right out of the air in my yard. They're a menace, and if you don't start getting those beasts under control, I will."

A middle-aged female jumped up from the back. "If you ever lay a finger on Milo, I will gut you myself."

"Order!" I yelled, waiting for the crowd to quiet down. Thankfully most of the shifters in attendance were regulars, and were as sick of this shit as I was. We probably went over the "cat" problem at least three or four times a year. "Michelle, no one is killing Milo."

"I just might!" cried Mrs. Silvano. "Why do we even tolerate cats here? We're wolves!"

Michelle laughed. "Oh, I'm sorry. When's the last time *you* shifted, Janice?"

I lowered my head to the table and banged it slowly. *Moon, take me now.*

Terror pierced me straight through the heart, and I gasped, sitting straight back. Arthur, the Council Chair, put his hand over his mic and leaned over. "Nolan, you feeling alright?"

Sweat poured down my face, and my tie felt too tight as I began to pant. No, I wasn't feeling alright. Marlowe was in danger, and my pack was calling for me. They needed help *now*.

My wolf howled to escape, and I knew that was the quickest way back to them. I couldn't hold him back anymore, and he exploded out of me.

57
MARLOWE

I locked the door to my nest and rushed towards the landline on my nightstand. I had laughed at Cam insisting I have one, but with my cell phone downstairs, I made a mental note to thank him for his foresight.

I dialed 911 but nothing happened. The line was dead.

Well, never mind, Cam, my thanks has been rescinded. Of course, if they cut power they would have cut the phone lines, too.

My wolf was ramming herself into the gate in my mind, demanding to be released so she could join the battle raging downstairs, but I denied her. I was just as likely to get myself killed or distract my pack as I was to make any difference. I couldn't trust myself or her instincts.

Dammit! I was more than useless up here.

Every snarl, every scream, every thump of bodies caused me to flinch, and I held back the tears and my own whimpers from giving away my location. If Elias had sent me up here to be safe and away from the fray, I was going to listen.

I ran into the walk-in closet and closed the door, backing up into the corner and curling up into a ball on the floor. The only way I could help was to bring back Nolan. I channeled all of my thoughts towards him, begging him to come back quickly.

We're under attack! Nolan, please…

Heavy, familiar footsteps came down the hall and stopped in front of my nest.

"Marlowe…"

His voice ran its nails down my spine, and my blood froze in

274

my veins. The sound of my name from his lips had once brought me joy and comfort, but now it was simply terrifying. The door knob jiggled for a moment until the whole thing came crashing down.

His footsteps came closer to where I hid, my heart beating so loudly there was no way he couldn't hear it.

"Marlowe, why are you hiding from me? After everything we've been through, do you really doubt my love for you? Do you have any idea what I've sacrificed to get you back?"

The closet door opened and I moved as far back in the corner as I could go. Mike's large frame, dressed completely in black, blocked my only way out. He took a deep breath. "Lunessa, I missed you so much."

"Get the hell away from me!" I screamed. "I don't want anything to do with you. Call your men back and leave!"

He stepped forward, crouching down in front of me. He tilted his head, and his violet eyes, shining in the dark, were filled with hurt as he inspected my neck. "You bonded with them?" he asked quietly, his rage building slowly. "But you barely know them."

I covered my bond marks to protect them. "I was with you for years and barely knew you."

He sighed. "You just didn't know what I was. Now that it's all in the open, we can live as our true selves. And whatever those mutts may have told you, I promise – vampyrs are *not* your enemy, and you being a shifter doesn't matter to me. I love you for you."

"This has nothing to do with you being a vampyr or them being shifters. You lied to me! You cheated on me!" I yelled.

His hand circled my throat, his thumb running along my skin as he closed his eyes. "And I will spend our whole lives trying to make up for that. I won't betray you again, I promise. Just please, come with me. Let's go home."

I shook my head in defiance. "I *am* home. This is my pack, and this is where I belong."

"No!" he hissed. I flinched as he continued, his hand now grabbing the collar of my sweater to bring me closer to his face. "You belong with *me*. I considered letting them live, as a thank you for taking care of you in my absence, but now they'll have to die. It's the only way to sever a shifter bond."

He grabbed my arm and snapped a silver cuff over it, then dragged me out of my room. I kicked and screamed, clawing at every purchase my hands could make, but it had little effect against his armor and bulk. He picked me up and jumped off the walkway into the middle of the living room.

"Finish them!" he commanded the other vampyrs as he ran with me outside into a waiting car.

My pack howled in anguish, trying to fight back against the onslaught of vampyrs and get to me.

Now was the time to shift. Against a group I couldn't do much, but just Mike? My wolf could at least escape him. I opened the gate in my mind, but nothing happened. My wolf was just... gone. I reached back deeper, and the cuff on my wrist began to burn.

"What did you do to me?" I wailed, grasping at the metal as he shoved me into the back seat. I reached over for the other door but it was locked, and the driver sped away as soon as Mike was inside next to me.

"I can't have you shifting, Lunessa. Not until you're under my control again."

The car raced through the dark streets of Maiingan Hollow, making its way back to the interstate.

"I don't love you anymore, Mike, and I never will. I swear, if you kill my pack, I will devote my life to making you regret this day until I kill you. I will tear your throat out, I will..."

Mike grabbed my face and kissed me, crushing his lips into mine. I cried out, trying to push him off but I was pinned down, and even beating my fists against his back didn't stop him. His lips moved down my neck and his hands grabbed my wrists with such force I yelped in pain.

"You will submit," he hissed. "You are my Lunessa, and I am your master!"

The orange glow from a streetlight illuminated his growing fangs, and I screamed as he sank them into my neck. A burn spread under my skin when he latched his mouth over the wound and drank deeply. My vision glazed over and he pulled back, licking drops of my blood off his lips. "Lunessa," he sighed. "I've missed you so much. You taste... divine."

Something dark slithered into my bloodstream – a call to obey, to acquiesce to Mike's demands. My body listened, but in my mind I resisted, planning all the ways I would destroy this male for what he'd done to me, what he was doing to my pack. I watched in vain as he lowered himself to bite me again.

A pair of headlights approached from behind much too quickly, and I braced myself when they swerved at the last second, clipping the corner of the car and forcing us to spin off the road.

58
THE RED WOLF

I was in a building full of humans, their surprise and fear coating the air with a heavy stink. I didn't have time to deal with them, though. My pack was under attack, and my omega was in danger.

Protect. Fight. Rip out their throats.

The crowd parted as I raced out of the room.

"Well at least the mayor is taking the cat problem seriously..."

I hurled myself through the doors – why did humans even have those? – and towards my den. They were there. They needed help. My omega was calling for me through our bond.

I ignored the lights, large machines, and loud horns, taking the most direct way back that I could. Humans could shout all they wanted; I didn't care about them right now. Their wolves were still sleeping. They couldn't understand.

Another shape made its way towards me, turning to run by my side as I got closer.

A dark wolf.

I leapt in front of his path and snarled. *Intruder! Attacker!*

The dark wolf snapped at me. *Not me. Blood takers.*

The blood takers... They were here to take back our omega.

Tonight, we fight together, he said.

Alone? No pack? One wolf could help, but more would be better.

He chuffed. *Alone, but enough.*

59
THE WHITE WOLF

Three blood takers surrounded me, circling closer and closer, swiping at me with their weapons. One made shallow contact along my back, the wound stinging fiercely.

My pack mates were in similar predicaments. We had felled many of our enemies, but we were outnumbered. Our omega had been taken. We had failed.

But we would not go down without a fight.

I lunged for the thigh of the blood taker in front of me, aiming to rip apart his veins and arteries. The weapon of the one next to him found my shoulder, but I wouldn't let go to yelp in pain. I would take down as many as I could while I still breathed.

Another weapon aimed for my side, but the attacker turned towards the door as my red pack mate's howl pierced the night.

Two silhouettes appeared in the entrance, snarling and snapping.

The dark wolf had joined the fight.

He was the enemy of our pack, but tonight, we fought the enemy of our kind as one.

The red wolf jumped over the furniture and crushed his jaws around the head of a blood taker attacking my silver pack mate.

I fought with renewed vigor, taking down another enemy and moving on to the next, but stopped as the dark wolf shifted back to its human form.

Why? I barked. *Humans weaker!* Especially without weapons. Humans couldn't fight without fake claws.

But then the human clasped his hands in front of him, and a ball of light grew as he spread them apart. The blood takers stopped and gasped, then moved to retreat when the ball split and shot straight towards their chests. The lights entered them, glowing from the inside.

Then the screaming started.

60
JULIAN

I pulled out of the grocery store parking lot, glancing down at the bouquet of flowers and bottle of wine on the front seat.

Females liked flowers. At least, I thought they did.

My mom had always seemed happy when my dad had given her flowers, at least. Before they died.

But Marlowe wasn't a typical shifter female, and so far every move I'd made felt like the wrong one.

She was an omega – the first one I'd ever met. And she'd been raised as a human. Cam had talked to me yesterday after she had left the office, and had explained that she didn't like a lot of typical alpha behavior. She didn't like being told what to do. She also didn't like aggression or violence, especially towards other females, and wasn't afraid to argue or fight back.

I hadn't even been trying to court her when I first saw her at Cam's desk. Despite having never met one before, I clocked her as an omega immediately from her sweet perfume. I had also sensed the bonds and could smell the sex in the air. All I had been able to think was that Cam was a lucky bastard, and I had just wanted to flirt a little bit. Who didn't want to flirt with a cute female?

But then she rebuffed me. Got angry, even, flipping the power between us. The fact that she had been able to order *me*, the alpha, to get *her*, the omega, a coffee, confused the hell outta me. The worst of it was, I hadn't been able to tell if I was ashamed or turned on.

And when Cam let us check each other's scents, the way packs made matches, it was like something had clicked in my brain. Some override system that took over and redirected all my thoughts, my hopes, my dreams, and my goals towards her.

I didn't think there'd be any going back now. I needed tonight to go well.

Cam had also given me the lowdown on the rest of the pack – the alphas had been bonded for fifteen years, and half of them were dead set against me. That was a hard group to join, even without the extra complication of an omega. But apparently, Marlowe was the swing vote. If I could convince her, I was in.

So... flowers.

To be honest, it wasn't just the prospect of Marlowe that made me nervous. I also really did want a pack. I felt untethered most of the time without one, craving the support of bonded alphas.

I'd grown up in a small shifter town like Maiingan Hollow up in Montana. Only unlike here, we weren't a thriving community. The only things we had in abundance were poverty and free time – the perfect ingredients for nothing good.

Packs there operated more like gangs. I'd almost been bonded into one against my will before my mom had given me all her savings and told me to run.

I had found my way here and started working for Cam as a general laborer. He had taken a liking to me and started giving me more and more responsibilities.

Now I had people working under me. I was making six-figures with bonuses. I had friends. Hobbies. A life.

Last year, I bought a three-bedroom house, and was going to move my mom in but...

The doctors called it Shifter Repression Syndrome.

In any case, I was alone now. I didn't think I could take it if this pack rejected me.

I pulled up to a red light and stopped, drumming my fingers on the steering wheel nervously, ignoring the little voice inside my head telling me I was going to screw this up.

It felt like I couldn't trust any of my instincts on this one, not with a headstrong omega and half a pack against my bonding in the mix, and that scared the crap out of me.

Biting back my fear, I looked ahead, concentrating on the traffic. A car to my right pulled into the intersection, waiting to turn left, and my adrenaline spiked.

That looks like Marlowe...

There was a female in the back seat - small, with strawberry blonde hair. A dark-haired male was on top of her, holding her down, and she was fighting him back.

A vicious growl ripped through me as I watched the male grab her wrists to keep her from defending herself. Even if that wasn't Marlowe, that female was being attacked and taken somewhere against her will.

I reacted on instinct, making a quick U-turn to follow them. I might be late to the dinner, but I wouldn't be able to concentrate or even sleep at night if I let this go. Whoever she was, she needed help, and that was more important.

I held my anger in check and made sure to keep a safe distance. I didn't want to alert the driver that I was following them.

I watched helplessly through the car's back window as the female attempted to fight the attacker off, but she was so small against him. Every fiber of my being was screaming to help. To protect.

I clenched my teeth, my knuckles turning white on the wheel. I didn't know how much longer I could watch this go on.

Oncoming headlights highlighted his figure, and I saw the fangs clearly in his mouth as he plunged himself into her neck, her limbs flailing in response.

Vampyrs? In *my* city? Oh, hell no.

I turned on my high beams and floored it, quickly making up the distance between our cars. I'd never tried it before, but I watched enough cop shows to try a PIT maneuver. By the time they noticed, it was too late.

I pulled alongside and hit the back corner of the car, then slowed down as it spun out of control and off the road, skidding to a stop on the snowy ground.

After I slammed on my brakes, I dashed out of my truck to confront them. The driver came out first while the male in the back tried to subdue the female. He swore at me under his breath, touching a gash on his forehead. His eyes narrowed at the blood on his fingers and he brandished a silver blade.

"You're going to pay for that, you fucking mutt," he hissed, his voice dripping with venom.

I couldn't stop the chuckle that escaped me as I looked at his miserable excuse for a weapon. Rolling my shoulders and squaring up, I took a deep breath and pointed my chin at him. "Let's go then, Sparkles."

He rushed towards me without hesitation, and I easily dodged his attack, rolling out of his reach and clocking him on the side of his head with a satisfying *thud*. He dropped like a rock, out cold.

"Pathetic," I muttered. I made quick work of his neck, snapping it with brutal efficiency. There was no time for guilt.

I stood back up and turned my head to the real target.

The back door of the car creaked open, and a large figure shot out like a coiled spring, his fanged mouth wide in a vicious snarl. He slammed into me, another knife in his grip. The force pushed me back a few steps, but I dug in my heels, holding my ground as I grunted from the effort.

A high pitched whine from the female inside made my stomach churn.

"Marlowe?" I asked, leaning down and looking around the vamp that was struggling against me.

"Julian?" she whimpered back, her face pale. She clutched at the wound at her neck, crimson drops trickling down her skin.

Her sweet perfume was laced with fear, and combined with the sound of her shaky voice saying my name, I filled with rage and purpose. I refocused on the bloodsucker in front of me. That was *her* blood on his unworthy lips.

"She's mine!" he screamed, his violet eyes blazing. "You won't touch my Lunessa!"

Lunessa... This vamp really thought he could have an omega shifter? Really thought he could take her away from her own pack?

Where *was* her pack? How had he managed to get her away from Cam? There was no way two vamps could subdue four alpha males protecting their omega.

But I had no time to consider what had happened at Cam's house. The vamp swung wildly with his weapon, and I sidestepped before the blade could slice through my coat. He snarled and lunged at me again, but I pushed his elbow up and got him with an uppercut to the jaw. His fangs pierced through his lips and he screamed, blood spraying across the snow.

"You'll pay for that," he lisped, wiping his chin. His eyes turned red in the moonlight, and he took a running jump ten feet in the air, floating impossibly and defying all laws of gravity as he pointed at me. "You're dead!"

"You've got to be fucking kidding me," I growled, trying to brace myself. We definitely never went over how to defend against flying opponents in my boxing classes.

The vamp grabbed the hilt of his knife with two hands and plummeted towards me. I managed to grab hold of his wrists when he landed, but the force sent me backwards and I landed hard on the ground, my lungs straining for air.

He jabbed a knee into my stomach and lowered himself towards me, the knife inching closer and closer to my chest as I struggled to push him back. The blood from his mouth dripped on my face and he smiled. "It seems the Moon favors me tonight, mutt."

I braced for death, cursing myself for not being strong enough to defend my people. To save Marlowe.

But before he could plunge the blade into my heart, he gasped in pain.

"Think again."

Marlowe stood behind him in triumph, the moonlight outlining her glorious halo of wavy hair, her hazel eyes focused and strong. The driver's silver knife was sticking straight out of the vamp's back.

He hissed in pain as he tried to reach around and grab it, and in his distraction I saw my victory. I wrenched the weapon from his hands and then shoved it through his ribcage.

He fell back, clutching his chest and gasping for air. When he turned towards Marlowe, the fury faded to violet in his eyes and he whispered hoarsely, "Lunessa?"

Marlowe trembled with anger, her small hands balled into fists at her sides. "I'm not your Lunessa," she spat.

He closed his eyes in defeat, dropping onto the ground. Warm blood stained and melted the snow around him, forming dark, demented wings.

I exhaled steaming clouds from the exertion of the battle, and I focused my gaze on Marlowe. All at once, her resolve shattered and she gasped, about to crumble when I leapt up and caught her before she hit the ground.

"I've got you, it's okay," I said, hushing her burgeoning sobs. "You're safe now."

"My pack... my pack..." she cried.

I led her back to my truck. "We're going there right now. I'll get you back to your alphas."

"No," she screamed, grabbing me by the shoulders. "They're under attack, he said he'd kill them!"

Shit. Were we too late? How many bloodsuckers were in town, and how many did it take to subdue Cam and the others?

I took a deep breath, trying to be calm for her. "Close your eyes and reach through your bonds. Do you feel them?"

She did as I instructed, her eyelids fluttering and lips quivering. "Yes," she whispered. "Yes, they're alive!" Her eyes shot open and she scrambled towards my truck, pulling me along. "Come on, we've got to hurry. They need your help!"

We got back in the cab and raced to Cam's house. I ignored the stop signs and honks, flashing my hazards as I wove in and out of traffic. We weren't far, but every second counted.

Especially if those fuckers could fly.

"Thank you, Julian."

She held her trembling hands in front of the heating vents. Dried blood streaked down her neck, bruises covered her wrists. My heart ached as she smiled at me.

"You have my vote."

61

ELIAS

I watched in awe and horror, as the light from the shifter's hands entered each of the vampyrs' bodies, quickly burning them from the inside out. Within a matter of seconds, they had all been reduced to smoldering piles of ash on the floor.

My mind could scarcely comprehend what my eyes were seeing.

Magic. I had just witnessed magic that could easily kill a dozen males without the caster breaking a sweat. How was any of that possible?

Shifters had abilities that humans would likely refer to as magic – we transformed into wolves, for one. Designations and bonds were also greater than what human science could understand or explain.

But this? Nowhere had it been written that shifters – or even vamps, for that matter – could perform something like *that*.

I also couldn't shake the feeling I had seen this shifter somewhere before. It was hard to get a good look at him in the dark with the smoke, but he was big. Bigger than we were, with tattoos that resembled Celtic knots winding along his chest. A bushy beard covered his face, and his long, light-colored hair was half-tied up.

He looked like a fucking viking.

He turned towards the rest of my pack, still in their wolf forms. "*Find her*," he commanded. Even I winced at the dominance in his tone.

Archer and Nolan bolted out of the door immediately, but Cam stalked towards him, growling and snarling.

The shifter smirked. "This changes nothing. When Marlowe is ready, I will bring her to him. Enjoy her while you can."

Cam snapped his jaws and the shifter rolled his eyes, turning back towards the night. "You're welcome, by the way." He leapt into the air, landing on the snowy lawn as his wolf, and bounded off into the forest.

I wanted nothing more than to follow him, but Marlowe came first. Fuck, his *order* came first.

I ran to grab my keys – even if I didn't know where her ex had taken her, I certainly wasn't going to sit around and do nothing. But as I unlocked my car, two howls pierced the air, and an unfamiliar truck pulled up Cam's driveway. Before it even came to a stop, Marlowe tore out of the cab and jumped straight into my chest, nearly knocking me over.

Safe. She was safe.

I hugged her tightly, tears pricking the corners of my eyes while she sobbed. "You're alive!" she cried. "Oh thank god, I was so afraid…"

"You were afraid for us? Marlowe, you have no idea…"

Cam shifted back into his human form and hugged her from the other side, burying his face into her neck as his breathing shuddered.

How had she managed to escape him?

A throat cleared from the truck. "Hey, boss, is this like a nudist pack? Because I don't mean to kink shame, but…"

I finally looked up, and an alpha covered in vamp blood stood before us. The breeze brought his scent, and I nodded my acknowledgement. "You must be Julian. How… how did you find her?"

He rubbed the back of his neck, shrugging humbly. The shame that a non-pack alpha had saved our omega hung between us, but Julian was smart enough not to rub it in our faces. He had *some* social skills, I had to give him that. "I was heading over here for dinner when I saw a female struggling in the back of a car. She looked like Marlowe. I mean, I would have gone after them even if it had been someone else, but…"

Cam let go of Marlowe and made his way to Julian, embracing him tightly. Julian looked a little like he didn't know where to put his hands, and Marlowe laughed. "For god's sake, Cam, put some clothes on. You're going to scare our new pack mate."

I turned back towards Marlowe and raised an eyebrow. "Are

you sure?"

Marlowe grinned, wiping blood off my cheek. "He knocked out a vampyr with one punch. I want him on our side."

I glanced over at Julian. He was a little young, but I supposed his scent wasn't too bad. And if Marlowe was fine with it...

"Well, can't argue with my omega," I replied.

Archer and Nolan came running back up the driveway, and Marlowe let me go to lean down and pet them. They pushed her over in their excitement, licking her and wagging their tails while she giggled.

"You all keep wolves?" Julian asked in amazement. "They're beautiful."

Nolan shifted back into his human form, giving Marlowe a kiss on the cheek below him and then standing to his full height. "Beautiful, huh?"

The color drained from Julian's face. "Wait... you all can..."

Archer shifted back next, picking a leaf out of his hair before walking towards Julian, a wide grin on his face and his hand outstretched.

"I suppose this means welcome to Pack Wolcott?"

62
MARLOWE

Cam's house was a disaster.

Even if we could somehow ignore the fact that the first floor was littered with vampyr bodies and piles of ashes, the smoke that still clung in the air and all of the broken windows made it completely unlivable.

Nolan and Elias stayed back with Cam to talk to the police, while Archer, Julian and I packed a few bags and headed to my dad's house, as it was the next biggest property in our pack and could accommodate us the best.

There were five bedrooms for us to choose from, but that night, I just wanted to sleep with my pack. After we all showered, I went to work turning the living room into a giant nest, dragging all the blankets and pillows I could find downstairs and arranging them so I could sleep in the middle and cuddle with everyone.

Archer simply sat back and watched in delight. "Such an omega," he teased.

I stopped, scrunching my face. "I don't know if that's supposed to be an insult or not."

"It's not," Julian said. He had distanced himself slightly, observing from the chair farthest away. "I never thought I'd see this in person. It's... adorable."

I threw a pillow at his face.

Archer's phone chimed, and he looked down, sighing. "It

looks like they're going to be a while, so Nolan says we should eat without them. I'll go pick up some fast food – you two stay here."

He grabbed his coat, giving Julian a nod on his way out.

I snuggled into my makeshift nest and turned on the TV. My dad had cable, which in an era of streaming entertainment was fascinating yet frustrating to navigate. I scrolled through the channels and pumped my fist in victory when I finally found something to watch on the Hallmark Channel. "Score…"

Julian still sat quietly on the other side of the room, and I patted the space next to me. "Come over here, I don't bite."

The corner of his mouth lifted in a smirk, and he leaned forward in his chair. "Maybe not, but your ex does."

I gave him a horrified look and he laughed. "Sorry, too soon?"

My fingers brushed against the marks on my neck where Mike had bitten me. Compared to the beautiful crescent moons left by my pack, the pinpricks had seemed vulgar when I'd inspected them in the mirror.

I shivered slightly, remembering the way Mike's fangs had felt piercing my skin, but Julian's scent and handsome face calmed me. "Entirely, but I will forgive you if you cuddle with me."

He cautiously climbed into the mess of blankets and pillows, still leaving about six inches of space between us. "Is this good?" he asked.

I muted the TV and turned to face him. "If you're not okay touching me right now, or touching in general, just let me know. I don't want to make you uncomfortable."

"Oh, no, it's not that, it's just…" He scratched his cheek nervously. "You just didn't seem too happy at the office when I…"

"Ah," I replied, remembering how I had pushed him off me. "I just don't like strangers touching me without permission. But you're not a stranger, and I am giving you permission."

He lifted his eyebrows. "Are you sure?"

I scooted closer to him. "May I?"

"Uh, yes?"

I lifted his arm and put it over my shoulder, nestling into his side. His eucalyptus and lemon scent enveloped me, and I must have released a wave of my own perfume because I heard him breathe in deeply. The tension left his muscles, and he began to purr.

"Oh wow, that's the first time I've ever done that," he chuckled.

I put my hand on his chest to feel the vibrations. "Yes, it's adorable."

He pinched my side and I yelped, turning the TV back on and settling into his nook. I'd already seen this movie before, but it was fun to listen to Julian's commentary. He was surprisingly into it.

"Wait, she's gonna lose the bakery unless she sells how many cookies by Christmas?"

"Five thousand."

"Dang, and there's only like, thirteen people in that town. She's so screwed."

His fingers ran along my skin absentmindedly, and his warmth, combined with the dark, quiet peace of my dad's house, lulled me into a deep sleep.

I was gloriously entangled with Julian on one side, Archer on the other, and Elias at my feet, when the smell of food finally roused me from my slumber. It was still dark outside, but Nolan was making something that smelled amazing.

Cam was also awake, drinking a beer at the dining table.

Once I extracted all my limbs from the pile of alphas, I headed over to Cam, sliding onto his lap and resting my head on his shoulder. "How's the house?"

He growled. "A fucking crime scene until Moon knows when." Then he took a sip of his drink and kissed me on the top of my head. "How are you?"

"Compartmentalizing hard, as usual. You sure the cops don't need to talk to me and Julian, too?"

He shook his head. "Nah, we'll take care of it. But speaking of..." he threw his head back towards the rest of the pack and grinned. "I knew he'd be a good fit."

Nolan set a plate with several grilled cheeses on the table in front of us. "Yeah, he's great at punching out vampyrs. But let's not forget our other enemy can burn people alive with magic."

Archer had told me what happened, and I still couldn't believe it. This unknown shifter, the one who wanted to take me, was more powerful than we had even imagined.

"*Magic.*" Nolan reiterated, leaning on the table. "Magic, Cam. Cam, he has..."

"If you say magic one more time..."

Nolan stopped and looked him dead in the eye. "How are we

291

supposed to defend against that? How is that even real?"

My momentary happiness over our victory rose with the steam of the hot sandwiches, evaporating into the night's cold air.

Cam grabbed one and dropped it unceremoniously on his plate. "One thing at a time. Let's just deal with my house and bonding Julian first."

He took one of the cut halves and was about to eat it when I let out a small whine, giving him my biggest puppy dog eyes. He chuckled and lowered it to my mouth so I could have it instead. I took a large bite, smiling as I chewed.

Then he grabbed my chin, inspecting a crumb of bread on the corner of my lips. He licked it off, his cock quickly hardening beneath me.

I felt slick begin to drip into my underwear, and Cam's nostrils flared as he scented my arousal.

He picked me up and carried me back into my nest. The others woke, watching expectantly as Cam laid me on my back, pulling down my sweatpants and underwear in one smooth motion, then tossing them to the side. He grabbed my legs and threw them over his shoulder, diving his face straight into me.

My back arched and I moaned, overwhelmed by the sudden pleasure of Cam's tongue in my pussy and the presence of the whole pack. So far, I'd only been with Nolan and Archer at the same time, and having everyone, including Julian, watching while Cam devoured me was unexpectedly hot.

I'd never thought about having threesomes or group sex before – mostly because it was always assumed the other people would be women, and that just wasn't something I was interested in.

But with all men? No, not men, but alpha males? Alpha males who loved and adored me, who I loved and adored right back? Who had literally fought to the death to protect me?

Yes, this felt right. It felt exciting, and I needed more.

Elias seemingly read my mind and crawled over, slipping my shirt off. His hand massaged my breast as he lowered his lips to mine. His tongue plundered my mouth, staking claim, and I welcomed it, reaching up to run my fingers through his dark blonde hair.

Archer joined next, his mouth on my other breast, sucking and biting gently on my nipple.

Having so many mouths and tongues on me was an assault on my senses, and I couldn't concentrate on the feelings individually. They converged into one overwhelming sensation, and my climax hurtled towards me like a freight train – hard and fast.

When it hit, my mouth left Elias's and I cried out, electric pleasure running through my veins and alighting every single one of my nerves. I collapsed as I crashed, my body boneless yet primed and ready for more.

Cam pulled me down next to him, spooning me against his chest, kissing and licking my neck. His hands moved down my curves, and then he lifted my thigh, positioning his cock right at my entrance. With a low growl he pushed himself inside and I whimpered at the sudden fullness.

The rest of the pack watched, their eyes adoring and hungry, as Cam slid in and out of me with brutal proficiency.

"Look at you, babe. Our perfect omega. You're going to take all our cocks tonight, aren't you? And at the end, if you're ready, you're going to give Julian his first knotting."

He thrust inside harder. "Is that okay with you?"

I was more than okay with that, but it wasn't just up to me. I locked eyes with Julian, his pupils blown as he stroked his cock through his pants. "Julian," I said, my voice breathy. "Do you want to knot me?"

He swallowed, nodding silently.

Meanwhile Nolan had abandoned the kitchen and joined us in the nest, lying down with his head in front of my pussy, watching as Cam slid his cock in and out of me. He grabbed my hip and then began licking my clit, the sensation stealing my breath. While I panted, Archer kneeled by my face, rubbing the head of his cock against my lips. "*Open up,*" he gently barked.

I met Archer's eyes and licked my lips. The command forced my mouth open, and he pushed himself inside. His sheer dominance furthered my pleasure and my arousal as I submitted to his strength, and Nolan eagerly lapped up the slick that leaked out of me.

"Holy shit," Julian whispered, his cock now fully out. He and Elias watched, waiting to join while they also touched themselves.

I had never been so full, so completely engulfed in feeling, both physical and emotional. The trust and love I had for my pack tore through the bonds, their own love mirroring my own. It was sex, but so much more than that. A manifestation of every unsaid word between us all.

Archer held my head steady. He continued thrusting into my mouth, my tongue circling his tip and then sliding against his long shaft as it pushed in further. He bit his lip and his eyes rolled back slightly when he moaned. "Marlowe, you're glorious."

Nolan reached a hand up towards my breasts, pinching my nipple and I snapped, my orgasm tearing through me as every erogenous zone was attended to. I whimpered around Archer's cock, the vibrations bringing him closer to the edge. He grunted loudly, and thick ropes of salty cum burst into my mouth and down my throat. He withdrew slowly while I swallowed, watching his face. He grabbed my cheeks and kissed me with fervor, his tongue sweeping my mouth and tasting the traces of himself left inside.

My pussy clenched around Cam, and he fought the urge to insert his knot, instead holding himself steady while he delivered his own release. When he finally pulled his cock out, Nolan flipped me over onto my stomach. "*Hands and knees,*" he barked.

My body was so sensitive, just his words and the power brought me to climax again, slick dripping down my legs. Nolan pushed himself inside with no resistance, pausing to ride out my orgasm before beginning to find his own. "Marlowe," he sighed. "You feel so good."

Elias kneeled in front of me next, grabbing my chin and lifting my face as Nolan rutted me from behind, his hands running up and down my back

"Can you handle another one?" he asked.

I nodded, reaching towards his tip and licking the bead of pre-cum off with my tongue.

"Fuck," he sighed. "You're so perfect, Marlowe." He ran his fingers through my hair as he stayed still, using Nolan's momentum and pace to propel me forward over his cock.

Cam rested on his side next to us, fingers grazing my skin wherever he could reach. "Beautiful," he whispered.

Gone was Nolan's careful, deliberate lovemaking from the other night. He thrust into me relentlessly, now gripping my hips as he slammed his cock into my pussy over and over, the sound of our wet skin slapping against each other echoing in the room.

I could feel his desire, his need to reclaim me for himself and his pack after almost losing me with every hard push. "You're ours. No one's going to take you from us," he growled.

Elias moaned in response, lost in a euphoric cloud. "Ours… all ours."

Cam reached underneath us and began to play with my clit, and my nipples tightened in anticipation of another orgasm. "At least one per alpha, babe. You can do it."

My eyes rolled back in my head, my overstimulated body caving to Cam's request. Nolan paused, letting my muscles milk his cock to completion, followed by Elias finally taking control, thrusting himself deeply into my mouth to come down my throat as he reached his climax.

Once he was satisfied he had emptied himself, Elias sighed, rubbing my head as his cock throbbed, finally pulling out when I swallowed his release.

Nolan wrapped his arms around my stomach and pulled me up, bringing my back to his chest. My legs shaking around him, I reached up and grabbed Nolan's hair, pulling him down into a kiss. He moaned, running his hands up and down my body while his cock finally stopped pulsing inside me.

Archer kneeled in front of us, ripping me from Nolan to steal my mouth, kissing me deeply. Our tongues met in a furious dance, his hand cupping and tilting my cheek to allow him even deeper access.

Then he pulled back, resting his forehead on mine. "I love you so much, Marlowe. We all do."

I nodded, fighting back the tears in my eyes. "I love you all, too."

Cam came to my side and I fell into him, resting my head on his shoulder while he manipulated my body, spreading my legs and facing Julian.

"Alright, Ramos, you ready for your omega?"

Julian had taken off all his clothes, his sizable cock rock hard and his knot inflated, ready to go. He walked over and crouched down in front of me. "Are you okay? If you're too tired, I can wait. Or we don't ever have to. It's your decision."

Yes, I was exhausted, but Julian's caution and worry about me filled my heart and gave me a renewed burst of energy. I wrapped my arms around his neck, kissing him deeply. The shock caused him to lose his balance and he fell backwards, bringing me down with him.

We laughed, and I kissed the tip of his nose. "I want this, Julian. I want you."

His Adam's apple bobbed and his cheeks blushed. His cock was flat against his stomach, and I sat back, rubbing myself along him and spreading my slick. His hands rubbed my thighs as he moaned, eyes glued to my breasts as they swayed with each thrust of my hips.

Then I rose up on my knees, grabbing his cock underneath me and positioning it at my entrance. "Are you ready?"

"Moon, yes!" he said.

I lowered myself onto him, watching his face as each inch that slid inside elicited greater and greater pleasure. He fit me perfectly, hitting every right spot and I sighed at the fullness of him, riding his knot like I hadn't already come four times. My body begged for more, begged to take this alpha's knot.

Julian's hips rose to meet mine, rolling and bucking in perfect harmony. I leaned forward, resting my hands on his large, strong chest for balance, my fingers pushing into his tanned skin. "Julian," I whispered. "You feel amazing."

I didn't even notice the rest of my pack. They were remaining silent, letting this moment be between just me and Julian.

My savior. My warrior.

Suddenly Julian reached up and pulled my chest down on top of his. His arms wrapped around my back and he pulled his feet up slightly for leverage and began thrusting into me from below.

"I'm coming," he warned on a hot breath, right before pushing his knot fully inside me and roaring as he climaxed. He squeezed me tightly as my pussy wrenched every last drop of cum from his cock. With his knot locked inside me, waves of orgasms passed between us, and his lips attached themselves to my neck in a suctioning kiss.

Cam came over and took one of Julian's arms off my back. He held his wrist in his hands, and then bit deeply into his skin, quickly licking away the blood he drew.

Julian flinched for a moment, his face soon relaxing when Cam licked the bite closed.

And there he was. It wasn't as strong as my bonds with the rest of my alphas, but an invisible thread now connected me to our new pack mate.

"You're one of us now, Ramos. How does it feel?"

He rubbed his hand through his hair, grinning wildly, his eyes wet with joy.

"So much more than I ever hoped or dreamed."

I nuzzled into his neck, settling down on his chest as he purred. "I know exactly what you mean."

63
ARCHER

I was floating.

It was as though gravity had left me, and I was now untethered to everything in this world except Marlowe.

Was this how it used to be, before omegas and our ability to shift disappeared? How could I ever call what I had before we met Marlowe "living?" I'd been spending my days in Plato's cave, mistaking it for reality this whole time.

News of Nolan's shift, as well as the vampyr attack, had likely spread throughout the town by now, and even in my bliss, I worried about the repercussions. Would they blame Marlowe for the danger that had followed her? Or would they realize she held the power to unlocking our abilities and demand she bleed for them?

Perhaps it would be a good idea to leave town for a bit and wait for things to calm down.

Marlowe's discovery of the connection between the shifters' origins and the battles of the Great War were worth investigating, and might be a good place to start. I'd already sent requests to colleagues at the University of Chicago for access to their libraries – they had the most in-depth collection of original documents from both shifters and vampyrs. Cleverly hidden from the human faculty and student body, of course. Elias had even offered to let me stay at his place over the winter break while I did more research.

I'd also put in a very last-minute application for a one-semester sabbatical leave with my dean. I was due one anyway, and since he was a shifter too, I believed once I showed him what I was working on, he'd approve it without further questioning.

Whether or not my research took that long, I needed time off to figure this out.

I looked down at the makeshift nest Marlowe had built the previous evening, and to where she now slept peacefully in the middle. Julian's knot had deflated hours ago, but he still held onto her tightly, like a child with a security blanket.

Nolan and Cam slept draped around her as well, while Elias sat at the table, drinking coffee and observing the scene, his expression pensive.

He finally noticed me also staring at our omega and spoke quietly. "You and Cam were right; we needed another pack mate. I think Julian is a good fit."

I wasn't going to rub it in, especially with how raw we were all feeling over Marlowe almost being taken from us. If Julian hadn't seen her in that car...

No. "What ifs" weren't going to ruin this moment. Instead I smiled at the look of contentment on Marlowe's face. "Well, he's locked in now, so he better be."

I got up and started to quietly look around the house, not wanting to accidentally wake my exhausted omega.

It was sparse, the home of a man missing his heart. Items picked for utility over design or interest filled every shelf, reminding me of my own home in Eau Claire.

The absence of love and purpose in every corner.

But after watching the inexplicable power of the dark wolf shifter, I was beginning to understand what had driven James to such lengths, knowing that someday his family might be pursued by shifters that wielded powers we'd never seen before.

Nolan was right to be scared. How could we defend Marlowe against someone who could kill all of us with the flick of a wrist?

Was she also capable of this destructive magic?

Were we?

The answers were within reach. I could feel it.

I poked my head into his old office, taking a look at the few books he owned. The subjects were all very predictable – business, economics, architecture, and a few biographies of presidents and other world leaders.

One smaller, older, plain-covered book caught my attention. It looked out of place compared to the untouched books purchased for show.

Twilight Tales of Blood and Bond.

Fairy tales? I wondered if perhaps this was another hidden memento of James's children, a book he had liked to read to them when they were little.

I opened it and a photograph floated down to the floor. The back was covered in small handwriting:

In the age of twilight, when the veil between realms grows thin,
Two stars shall fall, borne in a single womb—
A son of flame, fierce as the rising dawn,
And a daughter of silver, soft as the moon's glow.

Born of light and pain, he is the sword that protects all
The male shall rise, the Alpha of Alphas,
A warrior unmatched, his strength unrivaled,
None before or after shall wield such might.

The female, an Omega of unparalleled grace,
Her perfume shall tame the fiercest storms,
Her bond, the key to the balance of worlds,
For she is the arrow that will pierce the hearts of men and fae alike.

Whosoever claims both shall be crowned,
Ruler of man, lord of the fae,
For their unity binds the realms in peace,
Or sunders them into eternal war.

Male and female twins, an alpha and an omega? Marlowe had a twin brother, but he was dead, and there was no way to know if he was an alpha or not.

Besides, this seemed like another silly story. Maybe it was one Marlowe and her brother liked, and they had pretended it was about them when they were kids.

I turned the photograph over, and my heart stopped.

Marlowe, her cheeks still chubby with baby fat, stood next to a much taller and broader male. They were both dressed in high school graduation caps and gowns, matching wide grins on their young faces.

I rushed back to the living room, shaking Marlowe awake.

She groaned in protest, trying to shoo me away. "I'll eat later, I'm so tired…"

"No, Marlowe," I replied sternly. "It's important, I need you to look at this."

The desperation in my voice brought her out of her sleep, and I could hear her heart begin to race. "Archer, you're kind of freaking me out, what is it?"

"Go take a nap," mumbled Camden. "Whatever this is, it can wait."

I growled deep and low, a warning sound not to take me lightly. That finally got the other alphas' attentions and they sat up.

"Damn, Professor, we're awake, what is it?" Nolan yawned, rubbing his eyes.

I gave Marlowe the photograph. "Who is this?" I demanded.

Her hands trembled as I gave it to her, and then she relaxed, eyeing me suspiciously and smiling. "Archer, did you really just get jealous over a picture of Ezra?"

The blood drained from my face and her expression fell. "Wait, what is it? Why are you so upset about my brother?"

I handed the photo to Camden. He took a minute, staring. Unblinking.

"Fuck."

Marlowe whined. "What's going on? What aren't you telling me?"

Nolan took the photo next, Elias coming up behind him to look.

"Holy shit," whispered Elias. "That's him."

64
EZRA

The guards pounded their staffs on the ground in unison and the heavy doors swung open, their gilded edges shimmering. The air inside the throne room was thick with magic, blurring the edges of your vision in a way that made it feel like you were in a dream. I had never fully gotten used to it, no matter how much time I spent in his court.

Courtiers lounged along the peripheries on ornate, overstuffed couches and chaises. Their bodies were made in every shape and color imaginable, each more feral and yet more beautiful than the last.

A male with chartreuse skin and a square jaw, great tusks like a boar jutting up from his mandible, fucked another male from behind, his gaze following me as his thrusts increased in power. The male beneath him had papery wings that fluttered with pleasure against his aqua blue skin, stroking his cock while a female sitting beside him had her tails lazily wrap around his antennae, rubbing them in sync with his hand.

Across the room, a gray-skinned fae female, with hair and eyes as dark as obsidian, sucked the cock of a satyr-like creature, his horns curled and legs covered in thick hair. He watched me as I passed, drinking me in.

Three fae females sat on another couch, hair as white as snow and skin in various shades of pink, their sharp fangs exposed as they laughed and beckoned me. "When are you going to knot us, alpha? Give us a taste!"

I ignored them, used to their flagrant desire, and continued my long walk towards the throne, my bare feet padding along the floor.

I couldn't remember the last time I had worn clothes, but it didn't bother me. Nudity no longer brought me shame, and my shifter body rarely felt cold.

The fae king lounged on his golden throne with languid grace, his own gaze sharp and appraising as I approached. His long silver hair flowed like a river of moonlight, his aqua eyes sparkling against his marble skin.

His features were delicate, but I'd made the mistake only once in thinking it meant weakness. His lack of scars was a testament to his ability to destroy without effort.

A crown of twisted golden vines glowed softly on his head, its partner waiting on the empty seat beside him.

I sank to my knees and bowed.

"What news do you bring me of my beloved?" he asked, his voice low and smooth.

I rose to my feet, clasping my hands behind my back. The king's eyes flickered briefly down towards my cock, and then back to my face.

"The blockage of magic has impeded her growth, but my sister's powers have reawakened. I believe it's only a short matter of time before she can cross," I answered.

The king clapped his hands. "Excellent news, Ezra. And the vampyr threat?"

"Neutralized."

"Good," he replied. "Should they make another move against her, please take care of them. Those abominations have no sense of self-control and should be eliminated on sight. It will mean less work for us in the future."

He stopped speaking, and I waited for my dismissal. But the king simply stared at me.

Unease, suffocating and slick like oil, filled my veins. The room seemed to darken under the strain of his full attention. Finally, I cleared my throat. "Is there anything else, Your Majesty?"

He sighed, the weight on my chest lifting. "I've just been thinking of my beloved. It really isn't fair that your parents sought to keep you and her away from me. Tell me, did they suffer?"

I closed my eyes, recalling their final moments. The stink of their fear had clung in my nostrils for weeks, and the echoes of their cries, begging for forgiveness in their final moments still rang in my mind.

I'd resented them like hell for what they'd done to Marlowe and me, but killing them had still been painful.

I couldn't let the king know that, however. "Yes, Your Majesty."

He nodded, looking at the rings that adorned his pale hands. "And her pack – a necessary evil for the moment, I'm afraid. When the time comes, will you make sure they suffer too?"

I bit my cheek, hesitating for a moment. Their deaths were even less deserving. As far as I knew, they hadn't wronged me in any way, and my sister cared for them deeply. They reminded me of the types of males I would have been friends with if our parents hadn't kept our true identities a secret.

Would Marlowe ever forgive me for what was to come?

"Yes, I guarantee it."

ABOUT THE AUTHOR

Clara Bracco has always been a storyteller at heart. As a child, she spent countless hours lost in elaborate games of make-believe with her friends. Now, as an adult, she channels that same imaginative spirit into writing and exploring the boundless worlds of fantasy.

She lives in the San Francisco Bay Area in California with her husband, two kids, and their fluffy cat. When she's not crafting stories or getting lost in a good book, Clara enjoys experimenting in the kitchen, learning new languages, going to classical music concerts, listening to comedy podcasts, and seeking out new adventures through travel.

Want to be notified about new releases, including the exciting conclusion to Marlowe and her pack's story?

Sign up for my newsletter at www.clarabracco.com! You'll also receive a special bonus chapter.